GUARDIAN

OF SOULS

MICHELLE ROSSA

3

For those who would go to the ends of the earth for the people they love.

CONTENT WARNING

The material in this novel is for mature audiences only, and is not suitable for minors. Themes in this novel may be triggering, and should be read at your discretion. Themes of which include dissociation, depression, self-harm (Chapters 17 & 26), PTSD/trauma responses due to PTSD, mention of rape, and explicit sexual content such as snowballing.

Themes in this book include hearing voices that are outside of your own. This is a work of fiction, and should be treated as such.

6

Michelle Rossa

PART I

CHAPTER 1

I wander off into that hidden space I've traveled to my whole life, greeted with the same hollowness I've grown familiar with. A space where I'm met with all of the reminders of what I am, or moreover what I am not. A space that obstructs my vision and demands my undivided attention.

It haunts me, coaxing me to relive the very moments that shaped me. Moments that started the descent down, down, down into myself until there was nowhere further to descend to. I watch as she curls in on herself at the very depths of my essence, where she's built herself a protective fortress made out of steel and tears. It wasn't until recent months that I allowed myself to hear those muffled cries, to feel the weight of her agony.

To listen to her pleas, rather than run from them.

Even in my absence to feel the weight of our burdens, she has never shamed me for creating the distance. Instead of her facing our darkness alone, now we face it together. And once more does that once-tamed darkness churn again, though this time it does not seek to enact retribution on our account.

I feel the weight of a calloused hand rest on my shoulder, pulling me back to the surface as the fog of rumination clears. Blinking back into awareness, I feel the tips of my nails embedded into my palms. I look down at my clenched fists, my gaze trailing a sliver of blood as it beads through broken skin. I watch as a cashmere cloth covers my palm as a crimson hue begins to stain through the cream colored fabric. I watch as those familiar calloused hands gently press the fabric into my palm, before my gaze lifts to meet those blue and silver eyes I've grown to admire.

Those lush, midnight-black strands fall loosely above his dark brow as he blots my palms. I watch the worry deepen in his eyes, even through his act to remain calm in the face of everything that has happened in the past few days. His gaze meets mine, a penetrable look that could bring me back from the murkiest of trenches.

He sets the cloth into his jean pocket and interlocks his fingers with mine. No words are shared between us, but it is the silence in his gaze that shares what needs not to be said.

That he is here for me, and I will not face any of this alone.

The intensity from his gaze zaps me back into full awareness as I remember we are not alone, and there is a conversation we were all in the midst of. I let the warmth of his hands guide me back from that faraway place in my mind.

"So how do we free my sister?" The revulsion around that sentence pricks me momentarily, but I continue to let Reimus' warmth be the anchor that keeps me steady.

My mother's identical emerald eyes softly gaze into mine. "I have thought through countless strategies, and only one seems to be our best option."

My mother, who until today I was brainwashed to believe, was massacred. So many truths and lies have unfurled in the past few hours, persuading me to rethink our entire family history. My mother—who is also Queen of The Underworld, wife to King Hades.

How Sebastian was Zeus this entire time, a god himself. A man who is capable of emitting vile acts of desperation for power with no remorse for his actions. A man who put a compulsion spell on a loving, sweet child who has been made to believe her whole life that her father actually cherishes her. The thought of it all makes me sick—

"We must find her through the astral realm."

My gaze shifts to Hecate, the woman—a goddess of witchcraft and sorcery, I've come to find out—and friend, who I've grown to become closely acquainted with. A woman who has sat with me through the ugliness of my trauma purging and shadow healing, and has never faltered from the toll of mentoring me.

My eyes find hers, the golden ethers churning brightly before taming once more. "How do we know she'll listen to you? She doesn't even know what the astral realm is.

She'll just think she's dreaming and won't heed to your message."

A slow, faint nod. "You're right. That is why you are going to astral travel to her."

My eyes widen as my gaze shifts to my mother, searching for any indication that she's as shocked at Hecate's plan as I am. Her face is calm, yet unmoving. Through her eyes, I can see what words don't need to convey. That my mother has been waiting a very long time to see her children again, and she will not be at rest until she has both Makaria and I in her vicinity.

The pain of forgoing any careless acts of desperation just to see us, so that Zeus would not retaliate. The harboring years of hollowness that filled her, and would only vanquish when her children were with her once more. Shame of being utterly powerless in this situation until the perfect opening for us three to unite once more. Even through her eyes of grief and guilt, I realize this was part of the plan all along, and that Hecate's strategy does not catch her by surprise.

I look back at Hecate. "I don't know how to."

At my plea I feel the brief squeeze of Reimus' hand against mine. Our eyes lock and I see the subtle reminder that I am not alone in this. I inhale deeply before releasing slowly through my nose.

Hecate advances towards me until she's in front of me, her hands resting on my shoulders briefly until dropping down to her sides again. She smiles softly. "I will teach you. It will be similar to what we've already been doing."

"It is the only way, Melinoë." My mother says as she steps forward. "Since I cannot reveal myself to Makaria yet, she will only trust you. She will most likely deny what you say, and will most likely refuse to listen to your instructions at first. But through persistence, she will come. She—" My mother chokes as the words leave her momentarily, the pain of her daughter under a form of compulsion evident. She blinks back the tears in her eyes. "She has to come home."

I step out of Reimus' reach, and step towards my mother. I grasp her hands into mine, tears beginning to prick my eyes as shame floods me.

Shame for the anger I once had with Makaria for telling Zeus about what I wanted so desperately to stay between us seems so fleeting now. Because not only did she not know she was under compulsion to tell Zeus of any developments with my gifts, she doesn't know that the father she's grown so close to since she was a child is not even who she thinks he is.

All my life, I've wanted nothing more than to keep her safe from the cruelty of Zeus. To keep her shielded against the side of him he dealt so freely to me, but hid so slyly from Makaria. Though my efforts in the long run didn't even matter because I still couldn't even keep her safe from the one man she's supposed to blindly give her trust to.

I used to wonder what it felt like to have a father who visibly loved and adored you. Only now my heart breaks deeply for Makaria and how she will process the truth of our father.

How she will handle the cold truth that our mother is alive, and we've been fed a lie our whole lives that she was other than. That in order for the deception to be convincing, Zeus was the one who orchestrated the massacre against the witches in our village. My mind still finds itself reeling with all of these truths, so I can't imagine how my sweet, innocent sister will handle it all.

A tear slips down my face, meeting with my mother's finger as she gently wipes it away. My eyes lift from the floor and lock onto hers. She gives me a mournful smile as if she can read every detailed thought that is racing through my mind. I can't change what or who Zeus is, or the terrible things he's done. Just as much as I can't help the wrath I feel in my bones for what I would give to free my sister.

I inhale deeply, releasing roughly. "Okay. We start right away. I don't want her there longer than necessary." My words ending on a rasp.

"We'll start tonight. I will meet back here at midnight, and we will begin." Hecate says as she goes to walk out of the dining room. Before she makes it halfway across the room, she halts in her steps. Turning back towards me, she slightly tilts her head. Her features in her face softening. "For what it is worth, I'm glad you now know the truth. I hope you understand I never meant to lead you on, Melinoë. I didn't enjoy lying to you. I wanted to tell you much sooner about your mother, about everything. But I was under orders to wait until the right moment." She nods towards my mother. "It wasn't my story to share."

The thought of Hecate knowing Persephone was alive this entire time doesn't sit well with me, but I can understand her reasoning to wait. Now that I know my mother is Queen of The Underworld, I know Hecate is only following orders.

I can understand that it wouldn't have been right for Hecate to reveal all of the personal details that should have only belonged to my mother to share with me.

I smile tightly as I nod. "I understand. I will see you tonight."

Hecate nods in response, and makes her departure from the dining room to the main entrance of The Guardians Palace.

My mother brings me into her embrace, as her face burrows into my shoulder. Tears stream from my eyes once more as a scent that only a child could know wafts towards me. Nostalgia overwhelms me as familiar notes of lavender remind me of being cradled in her arms when I was sick, or when she'd sneak me a piece of chocolate before dinner. I inhale her scent and let it wash over me as the tears slip violently free.

I bury myself in the fact that my mother is *alive* once more.

My mother pulls away from me, her swollen eyes matching my glossy ones. "I have missed you so terribly. I will never be able to apologize enough for missed time, for everything that you went through—" Persephone shudders as her lips tremble. She clenches her jaw for a moment before continuing. "But what's important is that you know the truth now. That I did not willingly evade you and Makaria—"

"This was not your fault. *He* did this to us. He *will* pay for what he has done." I seethe through my teeth.

My mother's lips form a wicked grin, her previous fallen tears vanishing from her porcelain cheeks. "Yes, in time he will." She promises, the will of retribution in her gaze potent. The kind of retribution that only a mother who has been wrongfully kept from her children could enact.

Footsteps approach the dining room followed by an audible gasp. I look over to find Aven wide eyed and gaping at us. He immediately kneels down as he bows his head. "Y–your Majesty, I—I had no idea you would bless us with your presence this evening."

My gaze swivels back to my mothers. "Wait, he knows who you are?"

"She is Queen of The Underworld. Everyone in Vulir knows who she is." Reimus explains after an eternity of remaining silent.

My gaze moves to his. "You knew who my mother was?"

Reimus tentatively takes a step towards me. "I knew who The Queen of The Underworld was, but I had never met her. I had no idea she was your mother."

"What about Hades?" I ask, my mind stalling on the truth that my mother is married to King Hades, who she rules beside in The Underworld. That thought alone jars me, and also fills me with pride knowing my mother has that kind of title. I wonder what Hades is like, and I wonder how much he knows about my mothers' history.

I wonder what he knows about Makaria and I, and what type of man he is both on and off the throne.

"Hades is a god that doesn't travel to the land of the living often, if at all. He remains in The Underworld, so I've never met him either."

My mother nods. "He's correct. No one living today has seen Hades in person. It will probably always remain that way."

"Why?" I ask, brows furrowing.

"Because Hades doesn't see a need to venture to the land of the living. He loves his realm, and his people, and has many obligations he seeks to uphold in The Underworld. The one time he thought making an appearance was vital was a few years ago, but knew the risks were too high. So, he sent someone else instead."

"Alastor." I whisper.

My mother nods. "Hades and I have watched you all these years, though we knew we couldn't retrieve you for fear of Zeus retaliating. But we knew the time would come when your soul would seek to venture here. To Vulir. So until then, he sent Alastor to you. To protect you, to be a companion in those dark times."

My lips tremble as I fight back the clog on my throat. When I first saw that adoption poster in the market, I knew I was drawn to Alastor in a way that was beyond normal.

Maybe that was a part of my soul guiding me to Alastor, knowing who the beautiful steed belonged to.

My mothers voice gently rings out and disrupts my thoughts. "You may rise."

At my mothers orders, Aven rises as cheerfully as he always is. I realize the poor man has been kneeling for the past few minutes, but the joy on his face tells me he holds no animosity of our forgetfulness.

"Shall I make you a plate, Your Majesty? Oh, it would be an honor to serve you!" Aven chimes gleefully.

"Yes, that would be wonderful. Thank you—"

"Aven, Your Majesty. You may call me Aven." He says before he bows at the waist, raising once more to skip to the kitchen. After the doors close behind him, the faint echoes of excitement trail into the dining room.

I giggle to myself as Reimus chuckles. "He will never let anyone forget this moment." He turns fully towards my mother, bowing at the waist. "I am Reimus, Your Majesty."

"Oh, please. None of that." My mother says waving her hand at Reimus to stand up straight. She smiles as he does. "It is nice to meet you, Reimus."

He nods and smiles softly. "The pleasure is mine."

The three of us move ourselves over to the long cherry-oak table, my mother on my left, and Reimus on my right. A bottle of sweet red wine is brought out to us courtesy of an extra cheerful Aven.

And for the first time in eighteen years, I have dinner with my mother.

CHAPTER 2

"Tell me about The Underworld."

My mother sips her wine as Aven clears away our dishes. I watch him every now and then glance at my mother, though she makes no effort to tell him to stop. Through her demanding yet calm demeanor, I witness a version of my mother that I've never seen before.

A Queen.

Persephone smiles genuinely, her gaze narrowing slightly. "The Underworld is beautiful. Far more vast than most believe." She chuckles, her eyes softening as if in her mind she's somewhere else then in this room. "The souls rest comfortably, and still share a lot of that same enthusiasm as they did when living. Even if their memories are stripped from most of them."

"They lose their memories?" My seat turned towards my mother, as Reimus had done the same. We've sat like this even through dinner, as I haven't been able to take my eyes off my mother. As I haven't been able to fully wrap my head around the fact that my mother is alive.

Hopefully soon, that fact will fully settle in.

"When one dies, in order to enter the gates of The Underworld, one must drink from the Lethe River. The water once drunk numbs and clears away the memories of the newly deceased."

My eyes widened slightly. "So they forget who they are? Wouldn't that cause more unrest?"

Persephone smiles softly. "It actually does the opposite. When souls are newly crossed over, they must first be judged. During which, every accomplishment, every heartache, *everything* floods back to view. On top of being newly deceased, this usually overwhelms the souls. Both positively and sometimes negatively. So when it is time to drink from the Lethe River, most souls are ready to finally be at rest. Sure, they think of those still on the living plane, and how their lives will function without them, but at this point they're usually ready to let go."

"So, where do they go after they drink from the Lethe River?" Reimus stirs calmly behind me.

"Majority of the souls end up in the Asphodel Meadows. A place where souls go who aren't wholly good nor bad. They just…*were* in their days of living."

"And they just…wander around? For the rest of eternity?" I ask, feeling the weight of Reimus' presence behind me. I inhale it, drinking it in.

"Once they enter the Asphodel Meadows they essentially foster new lives for themselves. Some socialize easily with the other souls, some are much more introverted. Some grow gardens, some hold gatherings for celebrations. It is not much different from the land of the living, except being that the souls cannot remember their previous lives."

My mind begins to conjure up scenarios of how the people live in The Underworld. How dark, and depriving others who wouldn't understand must make it, yet how ordinary and blissful it must be for those who have experienced it.

I reach for my wine, feeling the cool surface beneath my fingertips. "So, where would one go if they were bad?" My mind instantly thinks of the man who killed Eiran, the same man who tried to take advantage of me in the astral realm. How I can feel the wrongness of his fingers against my skin, and how badly I want to sever those areas of my skin clean off. After going back to the Sephyra Forest, and Reimus burning his body to ash, I told myself that I would be able to move on. I would be able to walk away from this unscathed.

But the feeling of those rough hands is like a brand on my skin that I want desperately to be rid of.

Jarring myself from my thoughts, I swirl my wine and take a generous drink, desperately trying to wash down the unease that is rising to the surface.

My mother's emerald eyes do not falter from mine, cold and unmoving. "Those who have committed the most vilest of acts go to Tartarus. An abyss in the deepest parts of The Underworld."

"Are there a lot of souls who go there?" Wondering if one soul in particular resides there, but not bothering to ask.

"No. Only a few reside there, The Titans being one of them."

My brows furrow at the unfamiliar title. "The Titans?"

My mother inhales quietly, shakily. It's evident that there's something else she's not telling me, but considering she has revealed so much already, I don't pry. Considering that I'm—well, my mother, Makaria and I—are immortal goddesses, we have all the time in the world for more of my mothers past to be revealed.

I wonder to myself; if my sister is a goddess, what exactly is her divinity? Does my mother know?

"The Titans have a special place in Tartarus for the treason they committed. They took something invaluable and will forever pay for it."

"How do they pay for it?" I ask, unsure if I want to hear the answer.

My mother gives a sinful smile unlike any I've ever seen before. She pauses for a few moments, drinking from her wine before answering. "They spend the rest of their eternity forced to be eaten by a flesh-eating disease. I made sure it was a very *slow* process."

My throat works on a swallow as my gaze adverts for a quick moment, before landing on my mothers again.

"Only when they are nothing more than flailing strips of flesh on bone, do they regenerate whole again. Where it begins all over again."

Clearing my throat, I shake off the gruesome image that plants itself into my mind. "And who deems punishment in The Underworld?"

"Both Hades and I do. But The Titans, I saw fit to theirs." She keeps her gaze trained on me.

I nod my head, emptying the rest of my wine. I consider letting Aven pour me another glass but consider that Hecate would be displeased if I showed up to our first session intoxicated. Instead, I let Aven take my glass away.

My mother clasps my hands into hers, the warmth of her familiar and soothing. She watches me for a moment, eyes becoming glossy. "I am so eternally happy, Melinoë. To have you, and soon your sister, with me again. I can't explain to you how lost I have felt in your absences."

My lips flatten into a tight smile. "I've missed you so much. I'm so—" I inhale deeply before starting again. "Angry that he did those things to you. To us." I release my breath on a shaky exhale.

My mother squeezes my hands. "He will never come between us again. You and your sister will be safe with me, in The Underworld."

My brows slam downward as I yank my hands out of hers. "In The Underworld? I can't stay here?"

I turn my head to look back at Reimus, the perplexity on his face evident that he would do anything but be on board with this.

"Melinoë, The Underworld is the only place that Zeus doesn't have access to. In order to portal into The Underworld, you have to reside there, or at the very least be a psychopomp. A god who helps the living cross over into death. And Zeus, though all powerful, is neither of those things."

Memories of the other day in the village with Reimus appear in my mind's eye. Of us spending the day showing me around Vulir, only to be intercepted by the woman screaming for her husband. Her husband, who died in my arms, and then also approached me as a physical, tangible entity. I remember being out for two days afterwards, finding it strange that I would need that much time to rest when I've been in contact with the dead in other ways before.

But that time was different. I actually helped that man crossover, which means I'm not only the Goddess of Ghosts, I'm also a psychopomp.

A true Guardian of souls.

I look over at my mother. "How am I supposed to portal to The Underworld? I don't know how."

"I will teach you." She gives a close-lipped smile, her gaze uneasy. "But Melinoë, when we release and bring your sister home, you both must stay in The Underworld. Zeus will retaliate, and I won't lose you both again."

"No. I'm staying here." I look over at Reimus, seeing the admiration in his eyes for me. I know he understands the reason why I don't want to remain in The Underworld. Because he does not have the capability to venture there.

Also because being forced to reside somewhere is essentially replacing one imposed prison for another.

"Melinoë, you are the Guardian of the dead. It has always been your birthright to remain in The Underworld where you can watch over the souls. It is where you are meant to be."

Clenching my teeth, my breathing ragged. "I can be Guardian of the dead in The Underworld *and* still be here in Vulir. I *won't* reside solely in The Underworld."

"Why, Melinoë—"

"Because that's not what I want!" I roar as I shoot up from my seat. My fists clenched tightly as my breathing staggered, fire flowing through my veins. I don't care if Zeus will be out to get me once I free my sister, I don't care that I'm supposed to be Guardian of the dead. I'm tired of not making choices for myself, and I choose to primarily reside here.

As if my mother understands the words unspoken, she slowly stands up from her seat and nods. "We can discuss this another time." She clasps my elbows gently, and the fire roaring through my blood begins to slowly dissipate at her comforting touch. "Nonetheless, I would like to show you to The Underworld. If you will allow me that much."

Inhaling and releasing the remaining temper away, I nod my head. She smiles softly and brings me in for a hug, in which I embrace her fully. Regardless of my stance on where I will reside, and knowing I will not falter from my choice, she is still my mother that until recently I was believed to be dead. And that rush of gratitude for her being alive will out trump any sudden rage.

She pulls away, gazing at me. "I'm so proud of you, Melinoë." Her hand comes up gently to my cheek, her thumb grazing the soft skin. "I will return tomorrow afternoon."

Suddenly an iridescent gateway appears next to her. I gasp at the otherworldly fluidity of it, trying to peer my gaze beyond it. Through the opening my gaze fixates over the faint hues of obsidian-colored towers against the blossom of a deep coral and magenta sky. I nearly trip as I step forward, trying to get a closer view. But before I can take another step she turns around, forcing my gaze on her.

My mother smiles sweetly. "I love you."

My lips tremble at the three words I haven't heard for eighteen years. Words that were never exchanged between Zeus and I, ones that my ears have hardly been blessed with hearing. They shake me, and comfort me.

My lips cease their trembling as I smile. "I love you too."

My mother walks through the portal as it closes behind her.

CHAPTER 3

In the silence of the portal closing, I turn to Reimus. I finally have a moment alone with him after everything that has unfolded since we first stepped into the dining room together.

He steps towards me, his hands gently coming up to my jaw. His eyes search mine, as if he has no clue where his words begin and end. I see the worry etched into those beautiful blue eyes.

Worry that I will have to reside permanently in The Underworld, and what that will entail for us.

"Don't." I say as his lips part to speak. My hands come up to his. "Vulir is my home. This is where I'm meant to be."

"But Persephone said—"

"I *know* what my mother said." I seethe, pulling myself away from Reimus, turning away. My hands begin to curl inwards, before opening at my sides again. I close my eyes, taking a breath before I face him again. "I know what she said. But staying in Vulir is my choice. I will go to The Underworld. I will fulfill my role as Guardian of The

Dead, and I will do what is needed of me there. But that is not my home. My home is here, with *you*."

Reimus watches me, that uncertainty of whether he should come to me or give me space, visible as he shifts on his feet. After a few moments, he fights his uncertainty and approaches me once more. His hands interlocked with mine at my sides. "Tell me what you need from me, and it is yours."

I study the steadiness in his gaze, the surety of his statement. We could stand here and pick through everything that has unfolded today, strategize what we'll do once Makaria is freed and back here with me, how being a Goddess—one of nightmares, at that—means for me. For the both of us.

But my bones ache with an exhaustion that runs deep throughout me, and I have no words left to share. Not today at least.

"Can you just sit with me? I just need—"

In an instant, Reimus has me lifted into his arms and is carrying us across the dining room, up the stairs, and into his bed chamber. My head rests against his chest as he strides over to the lounge chair next to the fireplace. He seats us with me cradled against his chest, embers crackling next to us.

He holds me close to him, running his fingers through my long black hair. The warmth and solidness of his body comforting me, bringing me fully into his embrace as the churning of my thoughts dissipates.

A few moments later, I close my eyes and drift off to sleep.

⁓

I awake to the gentle nudge of Reimus. "It's almost midnight."

I groggily open my eyes, the fireplace still lit and I still curled against him. I slowly stretch out of his hold, seating myself upright on his lap. "Why couldn't Hecate have picked an earlier time to do this." I say, rolling my eyes.

He chuckles as he brushes my hair back from my face. "I'm sure Hecate has her reasons. She always does."

I turn fully towards him, my legs straddling on either side of him. I lean forward close enough that only an inch separates our lips. "Yeah, I guess so." I bring my lips to his. A gentle kiss, though nothing short of passion. His hands splay underneath my jaw, bringing me deeper into the kiss.

After a moment, he pulls away. "Go. We can always continue this later." A smirk widens on his face.

I crawl out of his lap, standing up from him. "We'll see." I say playfully. I walk towards the door and down the hallway. I walk past window after window, the moonlight greeting me through the glass. When I arrive in the dining room, Hecate is already there.

"I was beginning to wonder if you'd show up or not." She says, sarcasm dancing with her words. A lightheartedness that normally would suggest nothing world-shattering actually occurred in the past twenty-four hours.

Yet, it's because of everything that has unfolded that I do not question it further. And in the face of everything that still has yet to happen, I don't care to sulk over it at the present moment."I'm here now."

"Good. Let's begin."

We exit the dining room and head into an open chamber, the same one where I learned my first protection spell. At the reminder of that day, my fingers come up to the crystal hanging around my neck. Feeling it's cool weight against my skin, easing my surfacing anxiety.

We walk to the center of the chamber, scarcely lit from a few torches along the wall. Painted on the ground in the center lies a five-pointed star, surrounded by a circle. All around outside of the circle are different symbols etched into the ground, some simple, some complex.

I look up at Hecate standing next to me. "This is new."

"I did the honors of drawing it."

"When?" Knowing I just saw her only a few hours ago, I can't imagine she drew this in that short of time. It covers nearly the whole center of the ground.

"Yesterday."

I was still out yesterday, and hadn't woken from my strange slumber yet. Which means Hecate knew exactly what needed to be done when I woke up again.

"This was always the plan, wasn't it? You mentoring me was never just going to end at healing my shadow. It always involved this."

Hecate's golden eyes pierce mine, bright enough to light up any shadow. "Mentoring you goes far beyond accepting your shadow."

"When will I know I've learned everything I've needed to?"

Hecate smiles softly. "You'll know."

After everything that Hecate and I have worked through together so far, and with everything that's been revealed, I'd think I would've been far too exhausted to pick up mentoring with Hecate for a while again. But that determination to free my sister from her own prison gives me the adrenaline I need to keep going.

Nodding, I step to the very center, arms splayed out beside me before falling to my sides again. "So where do we start?"

Hecate steps in front of me, her legendary amethyst robe trailing with her. "We will start by first getting you comfortable with astral traveling."

"How do we do that?"

Hecate gently holds my hands into hers. "Being in the astral realm is different then just your regular dreaming. When you're...*awake* in the astral realm, you have full control over where you are. Where you go. You are able to tap into your astral body."

"Is my astral body the same as *this* body?" I say gesturing to myself.

She chuckles softly. "Not quite. Your astral body is the essence of who you are, your consciousness. It is something that is not of the physical plane, but of the spiritual."

"So I have to separate the two?"

"Essentially. It's called an out-of-body-experience. If you were mortal, you would only be able to achieve it through sleep. But since you are not, we are able to achieve it through the intention of the mind. It takes time to master, but we will get there."

"I have to learn to come out of my body? I—I don't know if I'm capable of that." Nervousness causes me to bite the inside of my cheek.

She squeezes my hands gently, her eyes searching mine. "You are capable, Melinoë."

"But if my sister and I are neither mortal, then why do we have to wait until dusk to practice? Shouldn't I be able to reach her when she's awake?"

"No. Because your sister, as of right now, is unaware that she is not mortal."

Right. As if I could forget that important detail.

How will she react when I am able to reach her in the astral realm? Will she even understand what is going on? Will she think she's just dreaming?

What will happen when I break the compulsion spell, and I tell her that her father isn't who he says he is? How will my sister's heart shatter when I tell her that her own father put a compulsion spell on her—

Hecate squeezes my hands once more, interrupting my jarring thoughts. "We will free your sister. And when we do, she will go through her own grief. As you have, Melinoë. But she will understand. She will make sense of everything."

In which I will be by her side in whatever way she will need for me to. She won't handle her feelings alone.

I inhale deeply and release at once, nodding. "I'm ready."

"Good. Now, I'm going to continue to hold your hands, becoming the anchor for you. It's important that you find your way back to your physical body. People can become lost and lose their way. So feel my energy, and listen to my voice. Understood?"

I look down at our conjoined hands, and match her gaze again. Another deep breath in, and out again as I release my nerves. "Understood."

"Close your eyes. And *relax*. Try not to move, and allow yourself to sink into your body."

Closing my eyes, I focus on my breathing and the feel of Hecate's hands as my guiding anchor. I breathe in and out, over and over until my breathing slows further, and further.

"Good. Now focus on connecting with your astral body. Imagine the pure consciousness of it, separate from your physical body. And *relax* further into it."

I continue my breathing, slow and steady. I relax further down into myself, deep into the abyss. As I travel down further, and further, I begin to feel my body tingling.

It starts from my toes, and radiates to my ears. It traverses from tingling, to full body vibrations.

"Relax, child. Keep going."

Hecate's voice is audible but far off somewhere from where I am. I take comfort in her presence, and let the vibrations travel along my skin. I continue focusing on my breathing. Until suddenly I feel myself jerk forward involuntarily. The movement is so sudden I panic, completely losing my focus and opening my eyes—

The room we stand in is exactly what I remember walking into, except it's not. The dim fluorescent light from the torches above me ceases their smoldering embers. Everything here is bleak, the darkness crawls along the walls and along the floor below my feet.

"Hecate—"

I turn around as air traps itself in my lungs. I behold two women standing, hands intertwined with one another. One being Hecate, and the other—

Holy fuck.

"Focus, child."

Hecate's words echoe overhead, distant yet close all the same. I tremble slightly as I watch myself stand there, my physical body continuing to hold her hands. I gaze at my long, wavy hair. I step to the side as I observe how it travels down along my back, just above my waist. I look down at myself, then my hands. My breath hitches as I examine myself in this form. My eyes widen as I bring one hand up to touch the other, then jerk it away when I can *feel* my energy rippling from my astral form.

A faint glow emanates from my chest. Holding the protective crystal in my hand, I feel the weight of its magic against my fingers. I set it back against my chest as I look at myself once more. I bring my fingers up to my physical body's arm, like magnets drawn to one another. Curiosity claiming me I clamp down on my arm—

My body convulses forward harshly, merging myself back into my physical body. I feel myself fall backwards, but Hecate keeps me standing upright.

Panting, a harsh breath leaves me. "I'm sorry."

Hecate furrows her brows, still holding onto my hands. "Whatever for?"

My gaze narrows slightly. "I wanted to see what would happen if I touched my physical body, and I accidentally brought myself back. I didn't mean to."

"Managing to merge with your astral body on the first attempt is satisfactory enough. But now you know how to come back to yourself when you're in the astral realm." A proud gleam in her eyes shines as she watches me.

"That's how I do it? I just come back to my physical body by…touching it?"

Hecate releases my hands slowly, as if she's waiting to see if I'm able to keep my balance after having my first out-of-body-experience. "Correct."

My hands fall to my sides, looking down at myself. Understanding that I just stepped out of my physical body flooring me. I look down at my protective amulet Hecate made for me, remembering the glow it ensued.

A finger comes up to it, tracing the crystal. My gaze meets her. "When I was in the astral realm, it glowed. I've never seen it do that before."

"That is because in the astral realm it is easier to see, and feel magic. And I spelled that to protect you both physically, and energetically."

I nod my head. "Thank you."

She nods in response, a hand clasping my shoulder. "I think that is enough for tonight. Get some sleep and I will see you again tomorrow night."

She begins to walk out of the chamber doors, her amethyst robe trailing behind her.

"Hecate."

She halts her stride, turning towards me. "Yes, Melinoë?"

"Do you think my sister will be able to recover?"

The unspoken truth that has filtered my mind since learning of my sister being under a compulsion spell has begged me the question. The harrowing possibility of not only learning your mother is alive but also that your father has manipulated you your entire life, completely changing you from the sweet optimistic girl you always were, to being hardened and cold.

Like I once was.

Hecate watches me for a moment, sighing. "I really hope so."

CHAPTER 4

I make my way upstairs into Reimus' bedchamber, my feet dragging every step of the way. I open the door to find him sleeping on the lounge chair, exactly where I left him. Except this time I find his black journal on the table next to him.

I quietly walk over, standing over him. I take in the gray shirt, noticing the way it hugs his shoulders as one arm rests behind his head, and the other at his side. My gaze travels lower from his hand to the waist of his pants, and lower.

I move to sit myself on his lap, the fatigue I felt moments ago suddenly gone.

Reimus stirs beneath me, his hands coming up to my waist. He makes a noise low in his throat that sends heat through my veins. "Well this is a nice way to wake up."

I chuckle softly as I learn down slightly, my hands resting on his chest. "I didn't think you would mind me waking you."

"Spitfire, you can wake me up like this whenever you wish. I will never complain." His voice husky and gruff. He finally opens his eyes, trying to discern where I'm at mentally written visibly on his face. "Do you want to talk about it?"

I shake my head. "Not right now." My hands roam the plains of his chest. Reimus watches me intently, his hands not moving from my hips. As if he's trying to judge how sound my thinking is right now. But as I sit on his lap, my mind wishes to distract itself with other things instead of talking.

I can feel how much he loves it.

"I want to talk about it all. Just—" My eyes lower to his chest for a moment, before gazing at him again. "Just not right now. Okay?"

His hands begin to tighten on my hips as I slowly rock my hips against him. As if submitting to my plea to not talk right about how everything has changed, to not badger me on it, he answers my plea with a grin. "Okay. No talking then."

I grind my hips against him, his hard cock against my aching pussy. All I want is to feel him inside of me.

Reimus makes a noise low in his throat again, wetness pooling from me. "If I didn't know any better, I'd say you're doing this on purpose to me."

"Doing what?" I ask, my voice husky. I continue grinding on him, fully aware he can feel how wet I am. I watch his impatience grow, and I edge it on by lifting my shirt, tossing it to the floor. I watch as his gaze fixates on my breasts, his hands gripping tighter around my waist.

"You know exactly what you're doing." He says through clenched teeth. He begins helping me move along his cock, a ragged breath leaving him.

I bring my fingers up to my nipples, slowly tracing the hardened peaks. "I don't know what you're talking about." I say breathlessly.

His grin widens before he leans up, his tongue flicking a hardened nipple. I arch into him, and he chuckles in satisfaction. His mouth closes over as he wrings a moan from my lips, his tongue trailing my soft skin.

His hand reaches down, a finger sliding down through my wetness. His finger rubs in between my folds, taunting me. Teasing me. I moan and rock my hips now against both his finger and his cock, aching to be touched.

His lips leave my nipple and trail along my neck. He kisses the skin there so featherlightly. "How about I just give you exactly what I know you want."

His finger slips away as he hauls me up with one arm, and removes his pants with the other. He keeps me hauled up as his other hand strips my leggings and my underwear down, and off my legs in one move. He sits me back down on his cock, and groans at my wetness. In the next second, our lips clash with one another.

His tongue clashes with mine as he positions his cock at my entrance. My hands wrap around his neck as I moan softly into his mouth. He chuckles before he inserts himself in one deep thrust. I gasp at the fullness of him.

His hands at my waist as I grind against him. I moan into his mouth where he begins pistoning up into me. I lift my face from his, my moans turning into screams as my orgasm builds. But before it can send me over the edge, he pulls out.

He eases himself out from under me. "Turn around."

I do as he says and turn around, facing the back of the lounge chair. Reimus kneels behind me, grabbing my wrists and positioning my hands into holding the back of the chair. I arch my back as he grips my hips, lifting me to my knees as his thigh splays me wide open.

Before I can turn my head to look back at him, my head yanks back as he bunches my hair into his fist, while the other is holding my waist. I gasp as he thrusts himself slowly into me, pulling out again before thrusting hard inside me.

He pistons in and out of me, keeping me locked into place as he fucks me hard. Cries of pleasure tear from my throat as I hold onto the back of the chair.

He lets go of my hair as it moves to the front of my neck. He holds me steady in place as he lowers his head. "You're so wet for me." He breathes below my ear. His hand on my waist moving lower to my clit. He begins trailing it, eliciting louder cries from my lips.

I breathe harshly. "I love it."

He nips my earlobe, causing me to whimper. "That pretty pussy feels so good around my cock." His lips trail to my neck where he kisses me. "Come for me, little spitfire. Let me feel you grip my cock."

My cries continue as he fucks me and plays with my clit, I feel myself coming close. I can tell he's close too. So I tease him a little before I finish.

"Do you want to come in this pretty pussy, Reimus?" I moan out breathlessly. I feel him tense behind me, and begin ramming into me. "Maybe next time you can fuck my face, and come in this pretty mouth, too."

Reimus loses control and goes feral. He turns my face towards him, and kisses me violently. Our tongues clash together as my climax reaches me. I cry into his mouth as ecstasy roars through me, when Reimus thrusts deep into me as he pulsates inside me. He groans into my mouth, and I rock back on him. His hand on my waist gripping into me as he subtly trembles beneath me.

His lips leave mine as he pulls out of me. I turn myself around, facing him. His finger comes down to my pussy, trailing his come that's seeping out of me. His finger plunges in, eliciting a gasp from me before pulling out again. His finger comes up to my lips as I greedily suck his finger.

He pulls his finger out of my mouth, a thrill coursing once more through my blood. He grins at me. "Next time, it will be those pretty lips I fuck."

He gives me a kiss before standing up to retrieve a towel. After he cleans us off, he moves us over to his bed. Where underneath the silken sheets, do I fall fast asleep. Asleep for the first time not in my bed alone, but in his arms.

CHAPTER 5

My feet pressed against the balmy ground, the concrete's heat matching the late morning air. Summer is currently at its peak, with the days awfully humid. Perched on the edge of the balcony chair, I find my thoughts racing, contemplating as I brush the tangles from my lengthy hair.

Today I'm to meet with my mother, where she will show me around The Underworld.

Though I should expect nothing different, I'm nervous of what is expected of me. Understanding of who I am now, and what my title bores, I know that I am to fulfill a certain purpose within the realm. I just worry that I don't know the extent to what these duties are, and if I'm capable enough to fill them.

I begin to bounce my knee swiftly, the motion a direct reflection of the resistance I feel within. I thought once I came to Vulir, that the decision of putting myself last was over. I finally got to choose myself, choose how I wanted to live my life without feeling guilty for not fulfilling a duty brought upon me. I was able to finally start anew, with instead of myself being placed on the back burner, I was first for once.

Though what if that cannot be with whatever I am to uphold in The Underworld? What if that is part of my path, is that I am to always come last?

My knee bounces erratically, my back bowed stiff. My gaze looks upon the open landscape before me, to the far end where I can see Alastor grazing with Gizelle. I watch him, hoping the sight of him happy can ease my ever-growing nerves. When I feel a hand rest on my knee, I jerk my head up.

I exhale as I meet his gaze. "Way to spook me."

Reimus chuckles. "My apologies." He hands me a mug of coffee with a bowl of cinnamon oatmeal.

"Thanks, but I'm not hungry." I say, taking the mug from his hands and setting the bowl down on the table next to me. I take a sip, and the warmth comforts me. I take another drink, hoping it'll ease my growing anxiety.

"Tell me your thoughts."

I peer up at him, my gaze narrowing as he seats himself next to me. "I have too many."

His gaze softens, a yearning in his eyes pleading to be of any help to me he can be. But his calm demeanor shows none of it on the surface. "When do you ever not have too many thoughts?" He winks.

I laugh at his sly remark, playfully jabbing him in the shoulder. He gently guides my face back to him, catching my smile while it still lingers.

"There she is." He smiles, his perfect teeth glinting in the morning light.

I watch him for a moment, my head nuzzling into the palm of his hand. I inhale deeply before releasing slowly, audibly. "Everything in my life has changed. Everything." I say pulling my face from his hand, meeting his gaze. "I'm furious. With Zeus, with what he's done to my sister. To my mother." My jaw clenches tightly before easing once more.

"And what of you?" Reimus asks, tucking a strand of my hair back behind my shoulder.

My eyes shift from his to the empty space beside us, to an air pocket of nothingness. My mind wanders to that girl, the one down, down in the depths of me. She whispers to me lovingly, yet pained. I breathe her in for a moment, before releasing her once again. "Zeus made it clear a long time ago how he felt about me. He never pretended to like me, he was always upfront about his detest for me."

Twirling my fingers in my lap, I begin to bounce my knee once more when Reimus rests a hand on it, stilling the movement entirely. I keep my gaze lowered, not bringing it to meet his just yet.

"It's different with Makaria. He paid attention to her, visibly adored her, whether it was just to fulfill his facade or not. But when she learns the truth about him, I'm afraid she'll lose that innocence that I've tried so hard to protect in her."

Reimus gently rubs his thumb along my knee, the simple gesture breaking the barrier of my thoughts open wider. "It is not your job to protect her in that way though." He says calmly.

"I know." I finally look up at him. "I know it's not."

His eyes search mine. He tilts his head as a somber smile meets his lips. "But I understand after caring for her most of your life, it could feel that way."

I scoff, the corner of my lip lifting up, a failed attempt at a half smile. I exhale. "I can't believe Zeus is a *god*. The whole being poor thing was just an act then. I wonder where Zeus keeps his riches, where he went off to each day that he said he was going to 'work'."

Reimus shrugs a shoulder. "I'm sure his real residence is someplace in Olympia."

"Where is that?"

"It's said to be the Realm of The Gods."

Olympia…another part of my lineage that I have no knowledge about. Great.

Reimus, as if reading my thoughts, glides his hand onto my cheek. "We take it one day at a time."

Exhaling raggedly, I nod my head. "One day at a time."

He brings me in for a kiss, savoring the feel of his lips against mine. Saving it for later when I portal to The Underworld with my mother, when I may need to remind myself of the one person anchoring me through all of this.

He pulls away, his hand reaching for the bowl of oatmeal. Sliding it into my lap, he grins. "Now for the love of everything, eat. Otherwise I'm going to have to wither your attitude later."

I laugh deeply while taking the bowl. "But you love the attitude."

His grin widens. "Indeed, I do." Heat pools low at his sinful smile. "But I love it more when I know you're taking care of yourself."

His gaze softens from wicked to nearly pleading. Silent in those blue and silver eyes of his is a man who loves to fuel my temper, but even more wants to take care of me. The silent request to be the first man who shows me what it feels like to be prioritized, to be the one taken care of instead of the other way around.

So I take the bowl of oatmeal, shoving a spoonful into my mouth, and I accept his silent plea.

I walk into the dining room, where I presume my mother will meet with me. After eating that oatmeal, I took a shower while Reimus went into the village to do a security check-in with Dimitri. Ever since that night when I first approached Reimus' bedchamber, I haven't seen Dimitri since. Reimus says he prefers to stay in the village, for whatever reason I'm not sure.

As I lean against the cherry-wood dining table, I begin to feel it. An obscure change in the room's energy. Not a moment after I step away from the table, a portal appears a few feet away from me.

My mother steps out, donning a sleeveless royal blue gown. The length of it brushing along her mid-calf, with rose gold lace along the trim. My mother has her long black hair pulled half up in a bun, the other half flowing down her back.

She approaches me, embracing me in a tight embrace, as if she still can't believe that I'm finally here with her. I wrap my arms around her, my feelings the same.

She pulls away from me. "Are you ready?"

I peer around her shoulder, staring at the portal behind her. My gaze tracks over it, the iridescent swirls twirling with one another through the opening. I shift my gaze back to her, exhaling raggedly. "I'm ready."

Persephone smiles. "And you are aware of what part of me showing you The Underworld entails?"

"Yes, I am."

My mother nods. "If this becomes too much, I can bring you right back. I know this is all a lot at once, Melinoë. But," She grabs my hand as we walk towards the portal. "I am excited to show you my realm. I think you will grow to like it there."

We stop in front of the portal, my gaze trained forward. Nerves begin to ricochet throughout my body, my fingers slightly trembling. My mother squeezes my hand, pulling my gaze back to her.

She watches me, giving me the moment I need to pull myself together.

Taking a few deep breaths in, and out again. I lock eyes with my mother, nodding my head. "I'm ready."

Persephone nods her head once, before guiding us through the portal. Where we enter The Underworld.

Where I will meet Hades, The King of The Dead himself.

48

CHAPTER 6

I step through the portal, my mothers hand entwined with mine. The portal closes before I can turn my head around to take an affirming glance back at the dining room I just portaled out of.

Gazing ahead of us, my eyes widen. My mother lets go of my hand as I aimlessly step forward, my mind in awe.

Standing on a hill overlooking miles of lush greenery, lost to the vibrancy of the colors. The horizon above showcasing hues of colors, ranging from violet to dark magenta. Stars glimmer faintly throughout the sky, some behind billowing plumes of clouds. Peaking through the grasslands are white funnel-shaped flowers, scattered along the plains. My gaze travels further down the meadows, fixating on the vast array of small cottages throughout.

I watch as a man kneels upon a bed of fresh soil, a garden trowel in his hands. A patch of red tomatoes bloom next to him. My gaze glances over as many cottages as I'm able to see from here, watching as the people meander around.

"This is the Asphodel Meadows." My mother says, a subtle interruption in our silence as my gaze wanders.

"They really do look at peace." I say breathlessly.

Persephone chuckles. "We try to give them the best afterlife possible. We want our people to feel comfortable."

"And they do this everyday?" My gaze continues to roam.

"They hold celebrations from time to time, but essentially yes. Unless they decide to join The Transmigration."

I turn my gaze to her. "What is that?"

My mother steps forward, her gaze overlooking her people. "Once after the winter solstice, and once during the spring equinox, we hold what is called The Transmigration. When souls who wish to experience a human life again are granted the ability to reincarnate."

My gaze follows hers, watching the people meander about far below us. "But if they're at peace here, why would they want to reincarnate? Why do the human experience all over again?"

"Because sometimes the souls feel it is better to go through the trials of life, that even to be able to feel pain again, is better than to not feel anything at all."

I turn towards my mother then. "They don't have feelings when they're here?"

"They feel contentment, and peace. But there is no sadness, no grief, no pain. They are just." My mother turns towards me. "Though the people take comfort in that, some do wish to *feel* again."

My mind spurs as I remember a detail my mother mentioned yesterday. "So not only do they forget their memories when they drink from the Lethe, they lose all emotions too."

"Essentially." Persephone says.

I begin to gaze around below again, a faint desperation beginning to surface. My gaze jumps over each stretch of land, over each soul that meanders about as it searches for one in particular.

"You will not find him here."

I turn to my mother, our identical emerald eyes meeting. Hers glow brighter than I've never seen them before, as if enhanced by being in her realm.

I sigh as disappointment deafens my mind. "Why not?"

She exhales slowly, quietly beside me. "Because he will not let himself fully crossover yet."

My brows slam together. "Why?"

She nods towards me. "He knows what happens when you drink from the Lethe, and…"

My breath hitches as emotion slams into me. "He doesn't want to forget me."

My mothers voice softens as she slowly shakes her head. "No, he does not."

I should have known that he would be this stubborn. Eiran, who I have known almost my whole life, is as much a stubborn ass as I am.

The man who also nobly fought for me months ago, only to cost him his own life in the end. The man who isn't a stubborn ass at all, and it is only my grief that implores me to think that he is stubborn for not allowing himself to fully crossover.

As long as I live I will never forget that day in The Sephyra Forest. How before our last moments together, I was ready to finally let him in. Finally ready to give us the chance that we deserved to both have. And though I'm happy where I'm headed with Reimus, I will never forget all of the lost time I could've had with Eiran.

My lips tremble as my mother brings my hands to hers. I look up at her. "I don't deserve him. His sacrifice, his unconditional love. He deserves to rest." A tear slips from my burning eyes.

My mother gently wipes it away. "But you *are* deserving, my child." She says as a smile curves her lips. "Forgive yourself dear."

A shaky breath leaves me as I blink back the dampness. "For what?"

She narrows her chin slightly. "For being in survival mode, and therefore not knowing how you felt sooner."

Tears stream down my cheeks as my mother brings me into her embrace. The smell of lavender drifts from her, a scent I will never forget of her. I drink in the familiarity, the memories of being cradled in her arms surfacing.

After a few long moments, she pulls me to face her. "You were a child who was neglected, and abused. You did only what you thought was best. Eiran still loved you and forgave you through it all, and he only wants you to forgive yourself too."

Wiping my red-rimmed eyes, I shake my head. "I don't know if I'll ever be able to."

My mother solemnly smiles. "You will."

I take a few breaths before I step back from her arms. Nodding my head. "Thank you."

Persephone nods, a portal beginning to open behind her. I gasp, not expecting it. "Come. There is someone I'd like you to meet."

I take her hand and step up to the portal, the middle a shimmering tangle of pastels. I look over at her, nodding my head.

She smiles before we step through the portal, and I stand before the King of The Dead.

I stumble onto rich umber floors, the sleek marble glistening from the overhead chandelier. My gaze fixates on the dark walnut executive desk in front of me, intricate small details pleasing to the eye. A leather, high-backed chair to match.

The room is painted seamlessly to match the furniture, giving an ambiance of constant darkness that is only brightened from a window to the left. Pointed cinquefoil arches carve the back wall, hundreds of books filling the shelves within. A leather couch placed next to the window, with an overgrown fern plant to accompany it.

I walk over to the desk, noting all of the scattered paperwork. A few single candelabras scatter the wide desk, lit by off-white tapered candles. The dripping of wax falling over the jet-black holders. "Where are we?"

"We are in my office."

My whole body swivels around at the sound of a man, standing beside my mother. My eyes widen as I step back into the desk, involuntarily. I watch as fading plumes of black shadows dissipate around him, until they clear completely. He's noticeably taller than my mother, a haunting presence to him that I've heard only through fairy tales.

Or what I thought was one.

His black hair is pushed back from his pale face, a dark beard crawling up the plains of his sharp jaw. His deep caramel eyes shine starkly against his features. He dons an all black suit, formal and professional as I expected any God of The Underworld to wear.

Forgetting all of my manners for a few moments, I jerk down into a half kneel, my head bowed down. "Your majesty."

Hades chuckles deeply as his voice rings of one who holds true, limitless power. "That is unnecessary from you."

My gaze finds him as I stand up straight. My eyes shift between him and my mother, and I suddenly see an ease to her that I've never once seen before. Like being in this close proximity to her husband gives her a comfort that no one else can give.

Persephone steps towards me, but it is Hades who speaks. His voice is deep, unruffled. "It is a pleasure to finally meet you, Melinoë."

Even through his sharp features, I watch the ease in his face, in his words. As if knowing who my real father is has no hold on him whatsoever. That the thought of who my mother was impregnated by doesn't hold burdens close to his heart.

Hades tilts his head slightly, as if discerning the thoughts from my head. I internally shake them free, clearing my throat as I force a smile. "The pleasure is mine." Unsure of how to continue the conversation, and well—feeling intimidated by his presence—I say the first thing I can think of. "So, do you spend a lot of time here?" Gesturing to the room around us.

Hades gives a half shrug. "Yes, and no." He gives a faint smile, and I could've sworn my mother tensed up for a moment.

"Are we…is this your palace?"

He nods. "Yes. This is our living quarters."

I nod my head, looking around aimlessly. Before my mother rests a soft hand beneath my shoulder. My gaze turns to her.

"Let me show you around, dear." Her smile is genuine on her face, as if she's been waiting my whole life to show me her real home. I nod back, a grin lifting. I look over to Hades. "It was nice to meet you."

He watches me, nodding his head. "I hope to see you again soon."

My mother and I walk out of the office, down the hallway to a round stone archway leading to the grand staircase below. I step up to the railing, my fingers tracing the iron detailing. The patterns swirling and weaving into each other, similar to that of vines. Looking behind me, next to the archway are floor to ceiling columns of terracotta. I turn back towards the staircase.

An antique rug bleeds down the entirety of the stairs, the rich hues of mahogany and charcoal the only colors in a room of stone. I walk down the staircase with my mother, admiring the vases on each stand at the ends of the staircase. We walk towards the left of the palace, along the sleek stone flooring.

We come to an opening, the windows at the back wall beginning to line my sight.

"This is our kitchen." My mother says as we enter the room. She continues talking, but my awe at the architecture refrains me from hearing a word.

Three large arched windows nearly cover the far wall, a single-basin sink situated under the first. The same dark walnut color paints the numerous cabinets, including the high ceiling walls. Chandeliers hang above an off-white, marble-top kitchen island with small houseplants at the center. I look up at the skylights above, hues of that cotton candy sky illuminating through.

"Are you alright?"

My mother interjects, bringing my gaze to her. "Sorry—yes. I'm just….I can't believe this is where you live."

Persephone chuckles. "We have good taste."

I look over to the french oven range. Gods, they really do have great taste. I couldn't imagine being served dinner in a kitchen like *this*.

My mother steps towards me, her features softening. "Is this too much?"

My mind unraveled from the wander, and now focusing on her. "No. I mean—it's a lot. But everything is just so beautiful. That's all." I say, hopefully easing her concern.

She nods. "Good. Just after everything we've talked through, after everything I've shared with you, I wanted to make sure."

I frown slightly, reminded again not just what I've been through, but my mother as well. I can't imagine the sorrow my mother has gone through.

If it weren't for the love my mother has shown Makaria and I, I would've thought that my mother being impregnated against her will would cause her to resent us. That harrowing thought causes me to wonder if those feelings of resentment ever did arise. A thought that I do not let take residence in my mind.

She said she never regretted us, no matter what. I believe her when she says that. She loves us, and would do anything for us. That I'm certain of.

Shaking off the what ifs, and embracing the presence of being with my mother now, I tilt my head. "So, you spoke yesterday of wanting to teach me how to portal."

A close-lipped grin curves up her lips. "Yes. I'd like to start today. If you don't mind."

I smile at my mother. Feelings of uncertainty tempting to sway me, but I dust them off. "I'd like that."

She guides us to a set of glass doors, leading us past the kitchen as we venture outside to the courtyard.

CHAPTER 7

After over half an hour of my mother explaining to me how to achieve portaling, and what helped her most when she first learned, she brings her index finger up to her temple.

"It starts here." She says as she lowers her hand. "Portaling is a will of your mind. Visualizing the place you're trying to venture to clearly in your mind."

"What if you accidentally portal to the wrong place?"

Persephone shrugs. "It happens. That's why it's important to learn with someone when first starting out, someone to bring you back in case you cannot do it yourself."

The thought of being trapped somewhere with no one to help you get back gives me chills.

"It is far easier to portal to someplace you know, than to somewhere you've never been. So let's start by visualizing The Guardian's Palace."

Standing with my feet firmly planted in the grass, my mother to my right. She suggested bringing us out to the courtyard would be a great practice area. Though the place is more like an English garden, with shrubs of greenery as wide as I can see. Lavender, hyacinth and rose bushes scatter along the landscape, a large stone fountain situated at the center of the garden. Curved brick paths lead one around the landscape, and also to a private area near a tall cypress tree.

Closing my eyes, I begin visualizing The Guardian's Palace. The layout of the dining room, the feel of those black silken sheets against my skin. The porcelain clawfoot tub that sits underneath the window, home to a few hanging fern plants. I breathe in and out deeply, centering into the place I get to now call home.

I imagine myself leaping through The Underworld, like opening a door into The Guardians Palace.

"Good. Keep going." I hear my mother say.

I continue visualizing, picturing it as clearly as I possibly can. My earlier hesitation to learn portaling is now turning into a desired want. After a few moments, I begin to feel something stir before me.

Opening my eyes, I see scattered traces of swirling fog before me. Like broken fragments of glass floating in the air that vanish a moment later.

Huffing, I look towards my mother. "I almost had it."

"It will take practice, Melinoë." She says, turning to stand in front of me. "That was a great first attempt."

Taking my mothers compliment and accepting it, rather than resisting it. I nod as I give her a half smile.

Movement through the bushes startles me, causing me to back up a step. The sound of heavy panting comes closer to us until a large three-headed dog breaks through the shrubbery. I scream in response, shielding behind my mother like a defenseless child.

The three-headed dog runs up to Persephone, each head fighting to get a lick at her face. She bellows a warm, deep laugh at what I realize is the affection the dog is giving.

I step out from behind her, marveling at the large creature. "What is that?"

"This is Cerberus. Don't let his size fool you, he's friendly." She says before bringing her hands up to alternate petting each head. A wide smile lights up her face, so genuine.

Cerberus sniffs towards me, and nearly tackles me as he tries to lick my face. I turn my face, laughing at the irony of it all. A terrifying, three-headed dog who is just the goodest boy right now.

I laugh at the thought, petting his soft black fur before moving on to his numerous heads. It carries on as I realize I'm petting a three-headed dog, in The Underworld. And for the first time in a long time, through all that I have faced and the hardship I've surmounted, I *laugh*.

Unable to remember the last time I truly laughed this genuine.

After my mother and I sat in the courtyard together, with Cerberus laying next to us, his excitement evident in the wag of his tail, she portaled me back to The Guardian's

Palace. Before returning back to The Underworld, she pulled me in for one more embrace.

"I will be back same time tomorrow." She pulls away, a smile lighting up her beautiful face.

I match her smile. "I'll see you then."

She turns away towards the portal, and I watch as it closes behind her.

The day has come and gone, sneaking towards four in the afternoon. I decide to go looking for Reimus, when I find a note on the dining room table. I read the familiar handwriting:

I've gone into the village. I'll be back before dinner.

— Reimus

I smile at the note, deciding to fold it into my pocket. Aven will have dinner prepared in an hour, so for now I decide to walk up to my room and rest until then.

Once I reach my bedchamber, I realize the silliness of this room now. How I stayed in this room when I first arrived here, hating to be around Reimus and using it as a safe getaway room for myself. Though now, as things have changed between us, I can't imagine I'll want to sleep anywhere other than his bed now.

That thought jarring some forgotten romantic within me I didn't think I'd ever see.

Before I decide to turn out of the room, I feel an energy stir towards the window.

I slowly peer around, and gasp.

Running towards the man in the far end of the room, I choke on a cry. I immediately try to wrap my arms around him, forgetting I can't feel him anymore. I nearly bash myself into the wall but catch myself before I do.

Eiran laughs deeply, the glow of his deceased form iridescent. *"I'm sorry, but that is hilarious."*

I try to hit his shoulder out of reaction, but just end up swatting at the air. I laugh as I wipe away the dampness in my eyes. "You're such an ass."

"A good-looking ass, though it be." He winks, the spark of life still there, however dead he truly is. He tilts his head, the wink fading. *"So...you know everything now."*

Being as this is the first time I've seen him since reuniting with my very alive mother, and learning the truth of who Sebastian—Zeus really is, and the truth of Makaria's situation, I sigh at his comforting presence. "Did you know? When you—you know."

He slowly nods. *"Once I crossed over, it was like I was given a magnifying glass, able to see everything for how it truly is."*

"You're also failing to mention that you refuse to *fully* cross over into The Underworld." I say annoyedly.

His gaze is steady, watching. *"That is true."*

"I wouldn't hold it against you. You've been through enough in this life, I want you to be at rest."

His eyes narrow slightly, as if wanting to avoid my gaze but can't bring himself to fully look away. *"I can't be at rest. Not yet."*

"What do you mean *not yet*? What are you waiting for? I know you're refusing because you don't want to forget me."

"It's not just that." He says pointedly.

"Then what is it?" I raise my hands, confusion arising.

He stares at me for a moment. Those features in his golden eyes are stark, but calm all the same. *"It's not my time yet."*

Understanding begins to flood me, that he's just not willing to let go yet.

I frown at the realization of how insensitive I've been. "I'm sorry."

I feel his energy surge as he steps toward me, the same energy coursing through my cheek as his hand rests there. He half-smiles. *"Don't be."*

Wishing I could reach up and hold his hand, my eyes widened slightly as the most obvious statement came to me. "So…I'm assuming you know."

"Know what? About you and Reimus?" He says as he pulls his hand away, a grin pulling on his lips. *"You were always meant to find him, Melinoë. I've come to peace with that. I am only happy for you."*

"I just hope that he understands that you're still a part of my life. How do I be honest with him about that?"

His grin remains the same as he watches me. *"I think you misunderstand how willing he is to understand you."*

Sighing at Eiran's words, I nod my head.

"I must go, for now." He says with a wink. *"I'll see you soon."*

In the next moment, his soul vanishes like incense to the air. I stand there for a few moments, pondering over what Eiran said.

I know Reimus would probably be understanding that I still talk to, and see my dead best friend. Who I've also slept with…and was kind of in love with. It's not like that anymore. I've moved on—well, I'm trying to.

Gods, what a mess of a conversation this will be.

But no matter what, I know what Eiran said is right. Reimus deserves to know.

I walk to settle myself onto my bed, only something stops me from fully laying down. As if a deep inner tug within me causes me to walk from my bedchamber, out into the hallway, and into Reimus' bedroom. I walk over to his bed, without thinking much about it, and curl under the silken sheets.

The smell of patchouli envelopes me, his lingering scent comforting me in a way that I've never felt before.

As I rest in his bed, I realize maybe I have truly moved on. The thought nulls me as I lie awake, waiting for his return home.

CHAPTER 8

A sudden boom jolts me upright in Reimus' bed, silken sheets pooling down to my waist. I listen as the main entrance slams shut, while hushed voices filter the main corridor. I pull back the sheets, jumping out of bed as footsteps hurry up the staircase. I hear Reimus hushing out commands, followed by a feminine voice complying.

Footsteps draw closer to me, accompanied with grunting sounds. Sounds that slither through the hallway as I slip through the open doorway.

I gasp at the sight of Reimus hurrying Dimitri down the hall. His left arm hoisted around his waist to support him up, with Dimitri's right arm around his shoulder.

"What happened?" I glance at Dimitri's head as it slumps forward while Reimus nearly drags him. I step closer to wrap Dimitri's left arm around my shoulder, but halt instantly when I see it.

My hand comes up to my mouth as I watch blood pool from an open wound on his shoulder, down his bicep. Dimitri grunts in pain as Reimus hauls him forward.

Reimus looks at me, his words clipped. "I need towels."

I hurry into Reimus' bedchamber, sprinting into his bathroom. I whip open the linen closet, pulling out a handful of white towels. I run back out into the hallway and follow the blood trail to Dimitri's room.

Reimus sets him down on the bed, and Dimitri grunts in pain. I rush over to Reimus' side, towels in hand.

Reimus grabs them from me, applying pressure to the wound immediately. Dimitri shouts in pain as he does.

"I have to stop the bleeding." Reimus holds his hand in place, turning his head back to me.

"What happened to him?" Terror coloring my tone.

"I don't know. He was doing his normal security check when I got word from Charon that something was wrong." Reimus looks back down at Dimitri, his jaw clenched tight. "He was in his drago form. His wings are shredded."

My hands tremble at my sides, my gaze frantically searching Dimitri. "Why—"

"He had to shift." Reimus looks up at me, agony clouding his eyes. "If his shoulder weren't dislocated and bleeding out, I would've been able to tend to his wings right away."

"But if he had to shift, and his wings are still battered…"

Reimus watches me for a moment, before narrowing his gaze back to his friend. "Which means when he shifts again, it's going to be the worst pain he's ever felt."

I seat myself next to Reimus, guiding a hand to his shoulder. His body tense beneath my fingertips. "Will he be okay?"

Reimus turns towards me, and reaches for my hand. His skin is ice cold, as if to match the rage that I know is brewing within him. "Eventually." He gives a solemn look. "I sent Nora downstairs to grab supplies to stitch his wound closed. He'll need time to heal, but he'll be okay."

My gaze shifts to Dimitri. The golden notes of his brunette hair dull against his pained face. His eyes shut tightly, his breathing sharp and ragged.

The sound of footsteps racing down the hallway trains my gaze to the doorway, not long after a woman hurries through it. "I've got everything I need. We need to do it now."

She pays no heed to me, the entirety of her attention fixated on Dimitri. I stare at her wavy, bright copper hair as it falls just above her shoulder, a hue reminiscent of the most luminous sunset. She opens the tin of supplies; thread, a needle, and saline. She kneels beside the bed while Reimus shifts his weight to facing more towards Dimitri.

Dimitri opens his eyes at the movement, his gaze shifting wildly. Reimus exhales, his voice calm amidst the chaos. "On the count of three."

Dimtri clenches his jaw, nodding his head curtly.

"One…two…."

An audible click sounds as Reimus pops his shoulder back in. Dimitri shouts in pain, his head slamming backwards onto the pillow. He exhales raggedly before going mute once more.

I watch as the woman begins working on his wound as soon as Reimus pulls his hands away. She dabs the saline solution onto a clean towel, cleaning the wound. She glances at Reimus, forcing a close-lipped smile before she lifts her gaze to me.

The woman smiles, her hazel eyes like pools of earthen gems. "Thank you." She glances back up at Reimus. "I've got it from here."

I nod my head as Reimus and I stand up from the bed. I watch her attention fixate back onto Dimitri.

"I will check on him later." Reimus guides his hand behind my back, ushering him and I to leave the room.

We walk towards the door as I take one last look at her, sitting next to Dimitri as she readies herself to stitch his wound up. I face back around, looking up at Reimus as we walk down the hallway.

"Who is that?" Curiosity in my tone.

"That's Nora. She's a healer at The Sanctuary, the best in the village."

"She's beautiful."

Reimus chuckles. "I'll be sure to tell her that. I'm sure it will fuel her ego."

We step inside Reimus' bedchamber. He tosses his blood soiled shirt onto the ground as he makes his way to the bathroom.

I step in front of him, inspecting him. I bring a hand up to his chest, my gaze trailing over his skin. "Are you hurt?"

He pauses, grinning softly at me. "Are you worried for me?"

I roll my eyes at him, examining him with a sense of franticness. His hand gently cups my chin, urging my gaze up towards him.

"I'm okay." A promise, through his eyes and his words.

I nod, my gaze falling on the dried blood on his chest from holding Dimitri up. I instinctively walk over to the closet, pulling out a hand towel and some soap. I walk towards Reimus, waving him over to the clawfoot tub.

His grin deepens as his hand comes up to his chest. "Are you going to bathe me?"

I narrow my chin faintly, my brows raised. "Are you going to stop asking questions?" Unable to resist the faint smirk that crawls up my lips.

He gazes at me, a soft emotion in his eyes even through our teasing bickering. He nods as his hands come to his pants. He unbuttons them as his gaze remains on me, not faltering once even once he's removed them. He straightens as my gaze dips lower for a moment, before lifting. Instead of desire, a different sort of primal need arises within me.

He leans to turn the water on before he steps in, seating himself against the cast iron surface.

I perch myself upon the cherry-wood chair, admiring him for a moment as the balmy water rises. I dip the towel under the running water, pulling it out as I lather it with soap. I scoot myself closer to Reimus, leaning over his chest.

A primal nature within me takes over as I wash the blood away. Beginning with his chest, and working my way down his arms. I stop every now and then to catch Reimus staring at me, his gaze longing and relaxed. A few loose strands of my hair fall over my shoulder, in which he caresses them back behind my ear. A smile pulls up my lips, before falling again.

"Do it again."

I drag the hand towel through his hands, lathering away the blood in between his fingers. I scoff at him. "Do what?"

"Smile at me."

I look up at him, and can't resist the smile that curves upwards once more. A smile that I hadn't seen much of in my life. Until I met him.

"You are magnificent." He says awestruck.

Never having been spoken of like this before, my throat closes up. The warmth in his praise causes my heart to swell as I lean forward, and kiss him. A soft, tentative kiss.

I pull away an inch, before my lips press against his once more, before pulling away altogether. My eyes flutter open to meet him, his brightly colored eyes churning.

He leans forward to pull me in again when I push a hand against his chest, making a tsk noise at him. "Aven will be most displeased if we are late for dinner." I peer sidelong at him, a teasing grin curving my lips. I rinse the towel out under the water, before wiping the soap off his chest.

Reimus chuckles at me, but doesn't argue.

I finish washing the soap off him, enjoying the stillness that I feel when I'm around him. A part of myself has begun to sliver open since I met Reimus, a part I never thought I would be open to again.

We both sit in silence as I perform a selfless act for someone else, this time without feeling an obligation to. I'll never regret taking care of my sister, I would do it all over again if I had to. But in doing so, I realize I lost so much of my childhood youth being obligated to grow up as fast as I did. I never thought that I would be willing to be so selfless like that again, fearful that whoever is on the receiving end would only take advantage of my generosity. Or rather, like Zeus, be ungrateful or *reward* me with violence for my selflessness.

But sitting here, washing away the blood on Reimus, I realize maybe that part of me still exists. Maybe that part of me is still willing to show up.

As I finish wiping off the last of the blood, I look over at Reimus, un-shockingly still staring at me. I grin as I look at the man who is responsible for the widening of my once caged heart.

CHAPTER 9

Before heading downstairs for dinner, Reimus and I walk back over to Dimitri's room. We step through the bedchamber to find Dimitri unconscious.

Nora remains seated beside him on the bed. "I gave him a mild sedative for the pain. He'll most likely be out for a few hours." Nora turns to Reimus before shifting her gaze to me.

"Thank you." Reimus says, shifting her gaze back to him.

She nods curtly, rising from the bed. She makes to exit the room, but not before halting in front of me. "You must be Melinoë. I'm Nora." She smiles.

A smile of my own matches hers. "It's nice to meet you."

"Is it true?" She asks.

I turn my head to the side, glancing at Reimus before shifting back to her again.

"Can you really make people hallucinate?"

My eyes widen slightly, A chuckle from Reimus pulling my attention to him.

He throws his hands up, an innocent grin on his face. "I may have mentioned our first interaction to Dimitri, who may have mentioned it to Nora."

I look back to Nora. Unsure if she's asking because she's mortified to know this, or because she's intrigued. I clear my throat. "It's true."

She gasps, a wicked grin plastering his lips as if I just gave her the juiciest gossip. Her index finger taps along her chin. "Damn, that's badass. Have you done it to anyone other than Reimus?"

Thinking of the man in Hellen Park, I chuckle aloud. "It's possible." I look up at Reimus, who tilts his head. A silent notion as if to insinuate his curiosity.

"Well I need all the details next time. But for now," She goes to bring me in for a hug, shocking me entirely. "I have to get going. It was great to finally meet you." She pulls away, her multi-colored eyes vivid and gorgeous.

I stand there partially immobilized, unfamiliar with the overly-pleasant interaction. I've never met this woman before in my life, and a hug is not what I would expect from a stranger. The niceness of her gesture sparks an emotional pull in me that I've longed for my entire life.

Friendship.

I clear my throat and smile back. "It was nice to meet you as well."

Nora turns towards Reimus. "I'll be back tomorrow to check on his stitches. His arm needs to stay in that sling. So no matter how much he bitches about it, don't let him remove it." She says, turning to walk towards the door.

I watch her leave the room, before turning to Reimus. He watches me intently, longingly. "She's nice."

He nods. "She's very active within the community. She does a lot for the women at The Sanctuary, and for those in the village." Reimus steps towards me, linking my arm into his. We exit Dimitri's room to head downstairs for dinner.

As we make our way down the hallway, I begin to smell whatever it is Aven has prepared for us tonight. My belly growls with anticipation.

"Does she heal with magic?" I ask, trying to ignore my building hunger.

"Tonight with Dimitri's injuries, that wasn't the case. But in other instances, yes."

We both walk down the winding steps, until we reach the bottom. Heading towards the dining room, where Aven has already set the table.

Reimus pulls out a chair for me, pushing my chair in after I've seated myself. He pulls the chair to my right out for himself.

I make a noise similar to a laugh that doesn't leave my lips. "Do you wish to be close to me tonight?"

Aven comes around to fill my glass with deep red wine. I thank him as he cheerfully steps away to fetch Reimus a glass of whiskey.

He sets it on the table, Reimus thanking him. He takes the glass in his hand, his gaze falling onto me. A half grin curving upwards. "I always want to be close to you."

Trying to bury my smile into my wine glass, I lift it to my lips when Reimus gently catches my wrist. I look at him as I lower my glass.

"You never need to hide from me."

I forget the wine entirely in my hand as Reimus' gaze pierces into mine, siphoning the breath from my lungs. The hunger I felt moments ago suddenly mute.

My throat works on a swallow as my tongue feels like a boulder in my mouth. I give him a shy smile. "I know."

The statement being the truth. That he wants to shoulder not only my happiness with him, but my burdens as well.

His thumb caresses my wrist gently, our silent moment interrupted by him releasing my wrist to grab my plate. He begins piling a serving of pork roast, leafy vegetables, and fresh bread. Only when he serves me, does he then serve himself.

Since the day I first met him it's been the same gesture, seemingly effortless to him.

As I jab my fork into the roast, Eiran's words chime through my mind.

Just give him a chance.

As I swallow the piece of roast, I ponder silently to myself what do I have left to lose with unveiling parts of myself to him? He clearly wants to be a part of my life, so why can't I fully let him?

I grab my glass of wine, taking a sip before setting it down again. "There's not one thing that would chase you away?"

Reimus studies me carefully, an understanding in his eyes of what I mean. He chews his piece of roast, taking a cloth napkin to wipe his lips. He sets it down. "Nothing that comes to mind when it comes to you."

I gaze at him for a moment, before taking a drink of my wine. "Okay." I begin, audibly clearing my throat. My gaze finds him once again, no trace of fear visible in his eyes. "Growing up I took care of Makaria, considering Sebastian—Zeus, was not around much." I pause, before continuing. "Eiran was the only person who saw me. He never made me feel invisible. So when I set out to come to Vulir, he came with me."

Reimus watches me, silently coaxing me to continue.

"We ran into poachers, and they killed him." Clenching my jaw, Reimus places his hand on top of mine. A silent and comforting confirmation of his presence. "When he died, I lost a part of myself. But the truth is…he's never really left. He still visits me, especially now that my gifts have grown stronger. And having him around, it's…"

"I understand."

I gaze at him, not realizing it had fallen to our joined hands moments ago. His calm eyes watching, studying. I open my mouth to explain again.

"You do not need to explain yourself, Melinoë. I understand the importance of him in your life, and you being a Guardian of The Dead, it only makes sense for him to still be in your life, even if not physically."

Overwhelming ease floods my body, cooling the nerves I once had to have this conversation. At his acceptance of me, regardless of what I come with, it only strengthens the trust I'm beginning to have for him. I look at our conjoined hands, trailing my thumb along the back of his hand. "It's been a treasure to still see him. Even if it's partly because he refuses to drink from The Lethe." A harsh chuckle at the sadness of the thought.

"What is The Lethe?" He asks, curiosity flickering in his eyes.

I tell him about what I've learned thus far about The Underworld. Where the souls go when they cross over, and about The Lethe River. I tell him all about meeting King Hades, and being shown him and my mothers living quarters.

"So he won't fully crossover because he knows what will happen when he drinks from The Lethe." He says by way of confirming what I explained.

I sigh audibly. "My mother says he doesn't want to forget me. When I saw him earlier today when I got home, he said it wasn't his time yet." Guilt begins to swell in my mind. "I knew I would have a difficult time grieving, but I didn't even think for a moment how he might be grieving his old life. He will always be a big part of my story, and I do appreciate his visits, but I want him to be at rest."

Reimus brings a hand up to caress my cheek. "Maybe enjoy the time you do have now, and let him decide when it's time for him to finally crossover."

I lean into his touch, and an unexpected tear flows from my eye. He gently wipes it away as another slips free. "Thank you."

His brows furrow slightly before straightening again. "For what?"

I close my eyes, blinking the sudden dampness away, when I open them to gaze at him once more. "For listening to me."

I find myself moving from my chair, and curling into his lap. He doesn't hesitate as he nuzzles my head to his chest, and I shamelessly breathe him in.

He kisses my forehead, wrapping his arms around me. "You're welcome." His voice heavy, lips muffled against my head.

After a few moments, Reimus lowers a hand beneath my curled legs. He stands up from the chair, with me still cradled in his arms. He walks us up to his bedchamber and lays me down onto his bed. He walks over to his closet, pulling out a short-sleeved cotton shirt of his.

He walks over to the bed, setting the shirt down as he waves a hand at my shirt. My hands go to my form fitting shirt, lifting it off over my head. He takes his shirt, fitting it over my head before lifting each arm through each opening. The material is both soft and loose against my skin. He lifts my pants off, before lifting his shirt over his head.

He moves to the other side of the bed, lowering himself onto it before bringing those silken sheets over me. He nuzzles himself behind me.

"You should probably check on Dimitri. See if he's awake yet."

Reimus pulls my back against his chest, breathing along the top of my head. "I will later when you go to see Hecate. For now, I'm exactly where I need to be."

Smiling against his arm laid underneath my head, I breathe in deeply before releasing slowly. Against the hardness of his body, I've never been more at ease than I am right now.

And before that thought nulls me comfortably to sleep, a familiar silhouette coaxes me to peer my gaze down to the foot of the bed. I watch for a split moment as Eiran stands there with a content smile on his face before vanishing entirely.

CHAPTER 10

I awake a few hours later, to the moon illuminated high in the sky through the open balcony. The cool, balmy summer air filtering through the open doors, caressing my skin. I listen to the sound of Reimus breathing steadily behind me, and turn myself over to face him.

At some point he shifted to laying on his back, one arm now resting under his head. His black hair falling forward, just above his brow. The hard plains of his jaw set against his full lips. My gaze narrows, staring at his muscle-bound chest. My eyes dance over the hard plains of his beautiful body, trailing lower and lower.

Gods, it's disgusting how good he looks even when he's sleeping.

My gaze turns heated as it lands on his waist. I study the twist of the strings of his dark navy sweatpants, unsure when he changed into those too. Even soft, his cock still bulges through his sweats, causing wicked ideas to surface my mind.

I grin devilishly, looking up at Reimus' peaceful face. I watch him as I reach a hand over, untying the strings.

I begin lowering my hand underneath the waistband, my fingers trailing along the velvet soft skin. As my hand wraps around him, he instantly hardens at my touch. Reimus moans softly as he stirs awake.

I watch his breathing begin to quicken, eyes lazily opening. I smirk as I pump him slowly once, and Reimus sighs heavily as his gaze shoots to me.

"Little spitfire, what are you——*oh, fuck*." He sighs into my touch as I begin working him, slowly to start.

He widens his legs, shifting himself as he jerks into my hand. I watch the way his body reacts to my touch, fuelling a primal need within me that wants to satisfy.

I watch the rise and fall of his chest, as cum beads at the tip of his cock. I brush my thumb over it before pumping him again.

He moans before chuckling. "Gods, I love the way you touch me."

I smirk as I begin to lower myself onto the bed, in between his legs. I lock eyes with Reimus, his chest rising at the sight of me between his legs. "Do you love it as much as the sight of me kneeling between your legs?" My voice husky as I lower my tongue to the tip. I trail it along that sensitive spot.

He grunts through clenched teeth. "I love absolutely anything you do to me. But especially—"

His words are cut off as I fit him into my mouth, slowly sheathing him deeper and deeper down my throat. He blows out a ragged curse, wetness pooling low.

I work him with my mouth, gliding my tongue along his cock. I look up, our eyes locking once more. "Gods, you're so fucking beautiful with my cock in your mouth."

I moan at his praise, the vibrations causing him to jerk upwards. His hand reaches to bundle my hair into his fist, cursing as I suck him faster.

"*Fuck*, baby please—don't you fucking stop."

His body begins to pull taught, knowing he's close. I pull away, a moan leaving his lips as I do. "Stand up."

Without hesitation, he stands up next to the bed. I lower myself to the floor, kneeling before him as his cock jolts forward. I kiss the tip, running my hand along him. My sultry gaze finds him. "I believe I remember saying how I wanted your cock the next time."

His gaze pierces into mine like steel, a trembling breath leaving him. He doesn't deny me, and his hands grab my face. He smirks as the tip of his cock pressed against my lips. "As you wish."

He sheathes himself into my mouth, in one slow thrust. I can tell he's holding back, and before I have time to protest, he does exactly what I asked.

He holds my face steady as he pumps into my mouth over and over, cum beginning to drip down my lips. He notices and curses loudly as he whimpers with need. I bring my hand up to his balls, gently caressing them.

His entire body goes taught as he thrusts into me harder, his cock filling my throat as I take him entirely. My eyes tear up from the force of him, but damn does it send a heated thrill through me.

"You look so good while my cum drips from those pretty fucking lips." He stills as he jerks forward, whimpering as he ejaculates in my mouth. I let some of it drip out for his satisfaction, but I greedily swallow the rest.

His body trembles as I swallow him dry, grunting as he pulls his cock from my mouth. He lifts me in one fell swoop onto the bed, before laying himself next to me.

He grabs me by my waist, picking me up and setting me on his chest. I gasp as the wetness from my pussy meets the rough plains of his chest. He looks up at me, stricken with need. "Your turn."

He pushes me up until my pussy reaches his lips, my legs straddling the sides of his face. I moan as his tongue flicks at my clit, wasting no time to please me. I jerk forward as I bring my hands to the headboard, gripping onto the dark wood.

I writhe against him, his tongue exploring as cries wring from my lips. His hand comes around and smacks my ass, causing a whimper from me.

I ride against that perfectly, silken tongue, my fingers digging into the headboard. "*Gods,* that feels so fucking good."

Reimus chuckles, the vibrations racking my clit. I grind harder against him, feeling myself getting close to finishing. But he halts his exploration, pulling me lower just enough so he can speak. "You know what I would love more than watching you squirm as my tongue flicks your clit?" He says huskily.

My impatience forces me to bring myself back to his lips, but he holds me still. I huff out a breath. "What?" I nearly whimper.

He grins wickedly at me. "This."

He pushes me back up, and his tongue digs deep into my pussy. He holds me up, and brings me down again on his tongue. I cry at the way it feels.

His tongue burrows deep inside me as I begin to take over and fuck his tongue. He curves his tongue inside me, hitting that one delicious spot.

I grind him, pleasure cries tearing from my lips as the pressure builds inside of me. I watch as cum drips down his tongue, straight into his throat.

He removes his tongue and sucks my click as I grind my release against him. Screaming as ecstasy clouds my vision before I begin to fall limp against him. Panting, I lower myself to lie next to him. He turns over, grabbing my face to his as he kisses me. My tongue laps against him, my cum soaked against it. I drink him in, as well as myself. I fall into him down, down, down until I'm so full of ecstasy I can't even feel the bed around us.

Finally, our lips pull apart. His hand resting against my cheek as release dances in his eyes. His thumb caresses my sated skin. "You are the greatest gift I never knew I could be blessed with." He kisses me softly, before getting up. He shoves his sweatpants to the ground, and heads into the bathroom. I turn over as I watch him turn the shower on, heat already rising from the stream.

He turns around, grinning. "You coming?"

Looking over at the clock, I realize I have thirty minutes until I'm to meet with Hecate downstairs. Grinning myself, I hurry out of bed. Padding over to the shower before Reimus scoops me up, my legs wrapping around his waist. I laugh against his embrace as he pushes me up against the tiled wall. Like we're two lust-sick fools who can't get enough of each other.

And before we both wash up from pleasuring one another, he takes me against the balmy tiled wall. Where burrowed so deep inside of me, the thought of being in lust doesn't seem all that true anymore.

CHAPTER 11

I enter the dining room, Hecate appearing before me.

"How was your first time in The Underworld?" She asks by way of greeting.

I tuck my still damp hair behind my ear, shoving the heavy strands behind my shoulder. "It was good."

Her golden eyes alight on mine as she nods. "I presume you met Hades."

My eyes narrow for a moment on her robe, chuckling internally to myself that she is never without it. I fix my gaze back to hers. "I did. He seems…nice."

She tilts her head. "Nice?"

I shrug. "Why? Is he not usually?"

Hecate laughs as she steps forward. "No, just that he's known more commonly for how *intimidating* he is, not normally for his niceness."

I frown slightly at her words, wondering how misunderstood he must feel from those who paint him as just one way. If he even cares at all. "I guess I could understand why that is." I move towards the center where Hecate stands.

She holds her hands out, and I rest mine into hers promptly. Momentarily closing my eyes as I take a few deep breaths in and out. The anticipation within me settles to some degree before I open my eyes to look at her again.

"Ready?" She asks. Her gaze briefly flickering over my face before straightening.

Once I nod my approval, we both close our eyes and begin.

⁓

I make my way up the stairs, my hand caressing the railing the whole way up. I pay attention to the dull sensations of it along my fingertips, a reminder of where I am.

Walking along the hallway, I begin to hear faint talking. Close, yet far away all the same. I step closer to the room the sound is traveling from.

"He came at me out of nowhere." Dimitri says to Reimus, his tone full of frustration.

Reimus sits next to him on his bed, a sharp look on his face. He curses, narrowing his gaze away from Dimitri. "What did he look like?"

Dimitri clenches his jaw, shame evident in his features and billowing around him. Like a palpitating cloud of energy, pulsating his emotions around him. Energy that I can visibly *see*.

Standing in the doorway, I take two steps closer to them, and listen.

Dimitri loosens his jaw. "It happened too fast. I got word from Charon that there was a woman screaming in the Sephyra Forest. I shifted, flew over, and found her already dead." He works on a swallow, pausing. "Charon met me there, and said he'd take care of her body. I remember soaring up in the sky, when out of nowhere I got hit." He brings his hand over to his left arm, hung in a sling. He winces at the discomfort, clearing his throat. "I look down to see him staring up at me. As if he was *waiting* for me. Before I could bank down again, he was gone. Vanished like thin fucking air." He shakes his head, anger rising. "He had dark hair. Young, couldn't have been much older than us."

Reimus brushes his hair back with a hand, stilling completely. He lowers his hand before darting up from the bed. Looking in my vicinity, I freeze. I didn't realize this may be an invasion of privacy, but Hecate said it was important that I tried it on someone other than Makaria for the first time.

Reimus stares in my direction, his body tensing like a bow strung back. He turns his head back slightly, though still not looking at Dimitri. "Do you feel that?"

Dimitri sits up from the bed, sniffing. His facial expression smoothes out as concern blankets it. "I can smell it."

Reimus shakes his head. "I can't see anything though." He begins to step forward, defensiveness radiating from him like smoke from a brand. He goes to take another step forward, when he stops. That smoke dissipates as a different feeling takes over: pride.

"Impossible." The shock in his voice battling with the grin of pride stamped on his face.

Dimitri stands up from the bed, joining Reimus at his side. He faces him. "What?"

Reimus' grin deepens as his body completely relaxes as he figures it out. "She's in her astral form."

"Melinoë?" Dimitri asks, turning his head to look in my vicinity.

Reimus nods slowly.

"How? We'd still be able to still see her."

I look down at my necklace, bringing my index finger and thumb to the glowing talisman. My attention lifts up to Reimus again as a grin of my own forms. I start to exit the room, when I notice the plate of finished food Reimus must've brought up for Dimitri. My smile widens at what lays on top of the ceramic dish.

Testing my limits in this form, I pick up the stainless steel steak knife. I watch Dimitri's mouth gape open as I twirl it in my hand before throwing it hard and fast in his direction.

Except I don't aim for him.

Reimus' hand shoots up, catching it by the handle as the blade hovers only a few inches away from his eye. His face remains calm and amused, his grin deepening. He stares toward my direction and laughs before tossing the knife in the air, catching it by the handle once more. "A good effort, little spitfire."

I smile at him though he can't see me in my astral form. I wink at him, turning away from the room as I head out into the hallway.

I make my way downstairs, back to where Hecate and I stand, our hands joined together. I glide over to my body, reaching my hand out. The moment it makes contact with my physical body, I feel that same bodily urge forward as I merge with myself again.

Jerking forward, my wide-eyed gaze rushes to meet Hecates. I smile at her. "It worked."

A wicked grin widens on her face, her gaze narrowing briefly to the talisman hanging from my neck. "I knew it would. I spelled the damn thing."

We share a laugh together as I pull away from her, my eyes narrowing as I trace the obsidian crystal. When Hecate first made this for me, I knew its purpose was to protect me. But little did I know that in the astral realm it would also produce an invisibility around me from those immortal or capable of profound sight—for instance, a drago. "But when I make contact with my sister, she'll still see me?"

"Yes. Because we'll be making contact with her astral form."

I nod. "And the compulsion spell, how do we free her from that?"

Hecate's eyes remain steady on mine. "She will become overwhelmed if I approach her in the astral realm. So when the time is right, and you're strong enough in astral traveling, you will break it yourself."

My brows furrow as I shake my head. "I've only been taught protection magic."

Hecate narrows her chin. "Child, I'm not short of memory. I remember what I've taught you so far." She smiles faintly before loosening a breath. "I will teach you. It is a few simple words that you'll chant aloud. It'll break the binds that Zeus has over her."

I scoff as a laugh escapes me. "I don't know about easy."

Hecate raises her head as she reaches a hand out, resting it on my shoulder. Warmth evaporating from her gaze. "Have more faith in your abilities, Melinoë."

Her words strike a deep chord within myself, taunting me to pay attention instead of brushing her compliment off.

"Have as much faith in yourself, as I always have." She brings me in for a hug.

I wrap my arms around her, loosening a breath as I drink in her words. A friend that I've grown to admire and trust.

She pulls away, her golden eyes alight on mine. "Tomorrow we'll try traveling outside of the palace." She wiggles her eyebrows. "Don't mess with him too much now."

I snort as a chuckle leaves my lips. I tilt my head, smirking. "I suppose he should be wary of pissing me off then. For his sake."

Hecate chuckles as she turns on her heels, and leaves the room.

I make my way up the stairs, heading back for Dimitri's room. I figured now is as good as any time for me to explain.

I make my way to the opened door, Reimus waiting for me. I smirk at him, my head held high as I approach him. "Did you like my party trick?"

He laughs as he stands up, meeting me halfway. "It was intriguing." He presses a kiss to my forehead, his breath warm against my skin. "Am I allowed to know how you did it?"

His lips pull away as I look up at him. "Remaining invisible to you, or throwing the knife?"

His eyes glitter like pools of wicked amusement as he smirks. "Both."

I look over at Dimitri, watching the two of us. I nod as a greeting to him. "Glad to see you're doing better."

He half-smiles at me. "Could be worse."

I turn back to Reimus, and lift my hand up to my necklace. His gaze follows my fingers, huffing to himself as a chuckle slips free. "I should've known."

"Hey, so it would be cool to not be left in the dark. You know, in case you guys wanted to share at all." Dimitri interjects, standing up and approaching us. Annoyance faint in his tone as he waves a hand.

"Hecate spelled it. I was told it was for protection, but I didn't know to what extent that protection lied." I say, lowering my hand as my gaze lifts to Dimitri. "Hecate also spelled it specifically for when I astral travel, to remain invisible from others." I glance at Reimus.

He watches me, as if he understands the subtle yet unspoken words that haven't been conveyed.

She knew all along that this was part of the plan.

"Well that's…fucking terrifying. How do I know you won't plug my nose when I sleep now?" Dimitri says by way of joking. I glare at him, then look back to Reimus. I furrow my brows in confusion at the sudden change in his demeanor. Until understanding surfaces within me.

At a distant memory of what happened to me in the astral realm—or, what almost happened. I watch as his jaw clenches, his eyes now like rivers of rage. Trying desperately to keep it bottled up.

I rest my hand on his chest, bringing his attention back from far away in his mind. I whisper to him softly, reassuringly. "His soul is trapped. He cannot hurt me anymore."

Reassurance for the both of us.

Reimus loosens a breath, nodding curtly. He leans down to press a kiss to my cheek. Pulling away, the rage once simmering begins to drastically vanish. Either that, or he's hiding it from being plainly broadcasted on his face.

I lower my hand as I step over to Dimitri. "So you have no idea who did this to you?"

He shakes his head. "I only saw him for a split moment, staring up at me from the ground. Everything went dark after that."

Reimus stands next to me, his hand brushing my hair back. A gesture of him reminding his presence, and also his way of calming himself. "We will find who did this."

Dimitri works on a swallow, turning his head away. "And when we do—" Dimitri makes a noise low in his throat, anger pooling just beneath his skin. Demanding to be utilized against whoever attacked him.

Demanding retribution.

He looks up at me, then Reimus. "I won't be caught off guard this time."

Reimus tense beside me, not in fear for Dimitri but for the punishment that Dimitri will inflict upon whoever is responsible for his wrath.

I step forward. "What happened to the woman?"

Dimitri hesitates, something other than anger plaguing him now. "She was already gone when I got there." He shakes his head slowly, his gaze narrowed. "I had Charon take her body to the cemetery to be buried, before ushering her soul over to The Underworld."

I reach for Dimitri's hand, squeezing it gently as his gaze lifts to mine. "It wasn't your fault." I say softly.

He watches me for a moment, before nodding.

"Did we know who she was?" I lower my hand.

He shakes his head. "She wasn't from here."

"Something doesn't make sense about this." Reimus says as I stand next to him again.

"My question is how did he get through the shield?"

"He wasn't through the shield."

I gaze at Dimitri.

"Her body was right outside of it, along the border. Same with him when I managed to see him for that split second before he vanished."

My eyes widen as I look up at Reimus. "That can't be a coincidence."

Reimus stares straight ahead at Dimitri. "It's not. Whoever he is, knew about the shield."

"Which means..." I trail off, a chill running down my back at the sudden understanding.

"Which means the woman was a ruse." Reimus stares at Dimitri. "That Dimitri and myself were the actual targets."

CHAPTER 12

"Are you sure he was young?" I ask Dimitri, my skepticism of who did this racking my mind.

He nods. "I only say him for a second, but I'm positive."

I exhale raggedly, nodding curtly as I try to clamp down on the building anxiety.

Dimitri tilts his head at my reaction. "Why?"

I look up at him, before gazing at Reimus. A silent exchange between us before I speak. "Because I thought for a moment it might've been Zeus. But if he was young, it can't be him. Unless he shapeshifted himself to appear that way."

"Who's Zeus?" Dimitri asks.

Reimus watches me before turning to Dimitri. "Zeus is Melinoë's father." His jaw ticks as he clenches it tightly. "But I think a more appropriate term would be a manipulative and vile prick."

I glance at Reimus, reaching for his hand. When he looks at me, I give him a knowing look.

Both a look of reassurance that I'm safe now here with him, and also a look of gratitude for his presence that anchors me to my sanity.

Dimitri narrows his chin slightly. "Well, if it was him, I'll be sure to torch his ass not only for me but for you as well."

I look up at him, grinning faintly. "I appreciate that." My grin fading as I sigh heavily, fidgeting with my fingers in my lap. "But he's King of Gods, so I can't imagine he'll be so impervious to attacks."

"We'll just keep a more watchful eye on things." Reimus says as he gently places his hand on mine, stilling the nervous energy. "For now, we stay on our guard." He looks over to Dimitri.

Dimitri nods at both of us.

I force a smile on my lips, even though the thought of Zeus being potentially who attacked Dimitri feeling unsettled within me.

And as Reimus and I later lay down for sleep, I find my eyes wired open. Unable to calm myself to sleep until much later on.

⌒

The next morning I made it an effort to come out to the pasture, knowing I haven't been out here in a few days.

The late morning sun beats down on me as I come up to the fenced-in paddock. I watch as Alastor's ears twitch backwards, his head following suit. A nicker sounds from him as he lightly gallops towards me.

My heart warms as a wide smile greets my face. "There's my boy."

He nudges his head gently into my chest, and I answer his call for attention with lots of neck rubs.

"So…when were you going to tell me you actually belong to King Hades?" I ask.

Alastor huffs at me, shaking his head as I go to grab his bucket of grooming supplies.

"I'm assuming that's your way of saying you weren't." I giggle to myself, as I grab his curry comb and begin making circular strokes on his fur. I watch as specs of dirt flake off. "You've been rolling around in the mud I see."

He gives me another nicker, and I continue grooming my horse. Well—turns out he's not really mine after all. A beat of sadness courses through me for when the day comes I have to give him back. Maybe Hades will let me still see him whenever I want.

A large part of me holds onto that wishful thinking, as I've grown attached to Alastor.

After finishing with the curry comb, I switch to a hard brush, brushing with the pattern of his hair. I talk to him about visiting The Underworld, and how wrong my impression of it was. How I never expected it to be so beautiful, to visibly see the souls so at rest.

Once I grab his soft brush, I feel the subtle approach of someone behind me. Only when I'm greeted with the familiar whiff of lavender do my shoulders loosen in tension.

"He looks really happy." Persephone says behind me. I hear the rustle of chains before the click of the gate opening. I turn my head towards her as she closes the gate behind her.

I smile. "I'd like to think so."

In response to my mothers presence, Alastor whinnies, nodding his head at her. But he does not walk to her. He stays right where he is as I finish brushing him.

I nod my head towards Alastor. "Does Hades miss him?"

Persephone chuckles softly, the perfect laugh between soft and sultry. "He would probably be upset by me telling you this, but yes. He does very much."

I work on a swallow, my abandonment issues surfacing into my thoughts. "Will I still be able to see him?" The unspoken truth of *because I've grown really attached to him* hovering between us.

My mother smiles as she stands on the other side of Alastor, her hand coming up to his neck. "Whenever you wish to. But I think for now, Alastor is fine to stay here a while longer."

"Really?" I ask, glee dancing in my voice.

She chuckles. "You seem to not be the only one who has grown attached. I can sense his protectiveness of you."

My gaze shifts to Alastor, and he glances at me for a moment. I drop his soft brush in the bucket, grabbing for the hoof pick. I give him a pat on the side, before standing with my back towards his front.

Kneeling down, I run my hand down his leg, a gesture that I need him to lift his hoof off the ground. Leaning slightly into him, I hold his hoof with one hand, using the pick with the other. "So someone managed to get near Vulir yesterday." I say to my mother as I pick at the mud and debris.

My mother speaks calmly, but the hint of concern is there. "Do we know who?"

"No. Dimitri couldn't get a good look at him. He was in his drago form." I say, lowering Alastor's foot down while I step back to do his front. "His wings are battered pretty badly. Reimus says it'll be very unpleasant when he has to mend them."

"Because when he shifts back, his wings won't unfurl like they're supposed to." She sighs. "It's extremely painful."

As I finish, I lower that hoof to move onto his other side. I look at my mother. "Do you know how long it'll take? For him to recover?"

"It's not necessarily how long it'll take. The Draghi heal fairly quickly, so once his wings are mended he will be completely healed. But the process of mending them itself is what harbors the physical toll." Her vibrant eyes bore into mine. As I move to lean down, my mother grabs my arm. I look down at her wrist, then up again. "If he knows you're here, Melinoë—"

"We don't know if it's truly him or not." I narrow my gaze off to the side, staring at the barn entrance.

Her brows scrunch forward as she lets go of my arm. "How can you be so sure?"

I sigh. "Because Dimitri said it was a young man who attacked him. So I'd like to think it wasn't Zeus." I bring my gaze back to my mother. "I hope it wasn't at least."

Tension brackets around her jaw. "He can shapeshift to appear as anyone, Melinoë."

"I know." I seethe. I roll back my shoulders, trying to ease the unsteady energy within me. "If it was him, then I know why he attacked Dimitri."

Persephone's gaze hardens onto mine, her emerald eyes churning brightly. "This is exactly why I suggested staying in The Underworld with me—"

"I'm not leaving Vulir." I seethe, my gaze boring onto my mothers. I begin to feel a rise of energy swell within me, before I shake it off and exhale to release the building inferno within. In a calmer tone, I start again. "I'm staying here."

My mother watches me for a few long moments, until she slowly nods. "Vulir is supposed to be a safe zone. Untouchable. Though everyone in Olympia knows this, it doesn't mean that gods don't get bored and rebel against the rules."

"The Realm of The Gods, right?" I lower my gaze to Alastor's hoof, leaning down to grab it.

"It's where all the gods and goddesses reside. Well, most. Some choose to live astray, away from the civilization of immortality."

I begin using my pick to chip away at the debris. "Why would someone not want to live there?"

She chuckles behind me. "Who knows. All I know is that when you've been alive for hundreds of years, there are some gods who become bored. And partake in drastic things to fuel that boredom."

I chuckle, my smile fading as realization hits. A jarring realization that I cannot die either, being that I'm immortal. The thought pulls me under before my mother rests her hand on my back.

"I'll wait for you inside. This heat is unbearable out here."

I turn to see her portal form. Before she steps through it, she looks back at me. Shrugging her shoulders, a grin appears on her porcelain face. "Why walk when I can just portal?"

The portal closes behind her, and I scoff to myself as I finish cleaning Alastor's hooves.

I stand firmly upon the soil of The Underworld, in the same spot we practiced in yesterday. I breathe deeply and slowly, centering myself. Visualizing an accessible gateway to lead me to The Guardian's Palace.

The image of the dining room clearly in my head, growing to frustrate me as nothing appears before me.

I huff my frustration, opening my eyes. "I can't do it."

"Yes, you can. You just have to keep practicing." My mother encourages, though sternness is evident in her eyes.

"I'm *trying*." I shake my head, closing my eyes once more.

"But do you truly *believe* that you will?"

I open my eyes to find Hades standing before us. My eyes widen as I watch pitch black shadows slithering around his body, dissipating in the air around him.

He approaches us, his hands held behind his back. "Portaling, like any other magic, is both as a result of your will, and your belief." He steps up to my mother, giving her a kiss on the cheek. My mother's smile at his affection warms my heart for a moment, grateful that my mother has someone who truly cares for her.

That she did indeed receive a fate far kinder than the one Zeus imposed onto her.

His eyes bore into mine like darkened voids. "Anyone can perform magic, but if they do not truly believe in their capability, then the results will never materialize."

Without even a flinch, a portal opens up next to him. Comparably different in appearance to my mothers, with shadows curling around the opening. I stare in wonder, the effortlessness of his will. His portal begins to then move across the landscape. I gasp as he stands tall and still, while moving the portal all around us, before landing next to him again.

The portal finally closes, Hades gesturing a hand out. "If you wouldn't mind, I'd like to help you. Try another tactic."

I look over to my mother, her answer written all over her face. *It's your call, he won't be upset if you decline his offer.* I look back at Hades, feeling suddenly so small around The King of The Dead. But instead of fighting his offer, I decided to give him a chance.

I nod. "That would be fine."

He nods as my mother gives him a parting kiss. He watches her like she's the very essence of his life, the entire center of his world.

She turns to me, giving me a hug. "I will come back in a little while." She walks away as I hear her shout at Cerberus, who I'd imagine snuck up on her. I giggle internally, before looking at The God of The Dead.

He looks down at the talisman that hangs around my neck. His smile curves upward. "When you've known Hecate for as long as I have, it makes it easy to pick up on her magic."

Looking down, then up again. My mouth curves up one side. "She spelled it for protection. Especially since we've been learning astral travel lately."

"And how is that going?" His voice is so eerily calm.

I shrug. "It's going well. I'm hoping tonight I can accomplish traveling somewhere outside of The Guardian's Palace."

He watches me. "And what do you think about that?"

Confused, I slowly shake my head. "What do you mean?"

He steps next to me, the very energy of him reverberating like an ocean wave lapping against a brick wall. "Do you think it will happen?"

"Well, yeah. It has to."

He chuckles. "I didn't ask if you *had* to, I asked if you believed it would."

Suddenly I stammer for words as I truly ponder his question. It forces me to dig deep to find a semblance of myself that truly believes that I'm capable of performing the act, but the truth is, I'm more petrified that I will let everyone down when I can't.

I meet his gaze. "I hope to." I say quietly.

He watches me for a moment, studying. "When you think of your gifts, what do you feel first?"

Calculating, admitting the first thing that comes to mind. "I feel different."

"Define different."

I fidget with my fingers before pulling myself to answer. "I feel like I have all of this darkness inside me. Like it *waits* for me. And I'm sometimes afraid of what I could do with it. Like I'm not meant to be a carrier for what's inside of me."

Hades nods slowly. "Ashamed of what brews within."

I narrow my gaze, suddenly finding a pebble on the grass to be interesting.

Hades rests a hand along my shoulder, pulling my gaze back to him. "That darkness is not your enemy, Melinoë. It is as much a part of your essence, as the light is."

"That's the problem. I don't *want* it to be. I want to be the bright, cheery girl that I'm probably meant to be. Not this…dark cloud of misery."

He tilts his head. "Do you feel miserable?"

"No. I just…" I trail off, sighing. "Sometimes I just think I hold a lot of it within me." I confess quietly.

He nods. "Your darkness is the furthest thing from misery. Just because you are not one certain way, does not mean there is something wrong with you."

A long exhale leaves my lungs. Before I can say anything, Hades lets his hand fall back to his side. "For just a moment, I want you to imagine what it would be like to welcome the darkness. Accept it."

When I furrow my brows, he puts his hands behind his back, nodding his head for me to close my eyes. As I do, I breathe in and out slowly.

"Imagine the darkness as your ally, rather than your enemy."

I focus on my breathing, each exhale bringing me closer to that pocket of darkness deep within me. I follow that void of unnatural silence, the deafening air surrounding me. I feel her where she always is, curled up in the corner. Her eyes are red-rimmed and full of tears as she jolts her head up at my approach.

I study her, a well of discomfort taunting to frighten me. Always looking at her as the other, I study her as one and the same. Never having been the worst parts of myself, but the parts who cried for acceptance.

I reach my hand out, her face slackening before bursting into tears. She grabs my hand, gripping hard. An unfeigned smile widens her dirt-flecked face as we finally begin to bridge that gap from one another.

"Good. Now, visualize The Guardian's Palace."

Dark cherry-wood appears in my mind, a table long enough to seat a party of twelve. Occupied with those tall-backed vintage chairs, ones that I have dined with Reimus in every night now for months. Those gorgeous canvas paintings hung around the walls, with hanging candle sconces mounted intricately throughout the room. I frame every detail to my mind. I let the images saturate my mind, finding solace in the place I get to call home.

"Open your eyes."

I open my eyes, gasping as my hands come up to my lips. I gaze wide-eyed at Hades, who is grinning from ear to ear. I look back in front of me, shock coursing through my body. Wetness dampens my eyes as an overwhelming sense of pride takes over.

I fall to my knees, unable to stop the tears that flow down my cheeks. My throat clogs up as I stare at the portal in front of me. I study the dark swirls of shadows as they merge together in the center, the clearness of the dining room apparent through them. My gaze lifts up, staring at the obsidian black fog that connects around the portal opening.

I stand up shakily from the ground, stepping towards the creation of my will, of my own magic. My fingers trace the thick tendrils of smoke that weave around the portal opening. I choke on a cry as I stand before a portal I weaved to fruition. Not only through the power of my mind, but by the power of my darkness. I allow myself to fall back down, deep into that well within. I find her watching me, a sense of ease beginning to brighten her once bleak eyes.

Hades stands next to me, pulling me back as he pats his hand on my back. I lift my gaze, finding my mother had returned at some point. She watches me a few feet away, a grin of pride stretching along her full lips.

Hades grins softly. "The darkness wielded as an ally, not an enemy."

CHAPTER 13

My mother and I moved our way back inside into their living room for pastries and tea. Their living room is just as exquisitely appealing as the rest of their palace.

A Victorian chandelier hangs above a set of two black tufted leather couches. A lit fireplace flickers against the wall, an identical tufted chair nearest to it. A maroon vintage rug rests in the middle, beneath a chestnut cocktail table. On the mantel above the fireplace is an open case, an assortment of different amber colored liquors.

Tall, round-topped windows with diamond leaded glass line the walls behind us. Filtering in the magenta hues of The Underworld sky into the dimly lit room.

I gently swirl my scoop of sugar into my ceramic teacup, setting my spoon down onto its matching saucer. "Where do I inherit it from?"

Persephone sets her teacup down, staring at me. Her shoulders sink slightly as she exhales, the question of what I mean unnecessary. "I'm not sure."

I sink back into the leather sofa, the crackling sound of the fire next to me. "Did I ever accidentally project it onto you? When I was younger?"

Persephone half smiles as she chuckles. "Only when you were in my womb. I used to call them fear spells. Every now and then, you'd kick like crazy, and I knew that it was only a matter of minutes before I began to feel it."

"What would you feel?"

Her gaze wanders for a moment as memories flash before her eyes. "Just undeniable feelings of fear. They were mild, though I knew at those moments your gifts would one day surmount to something far greater."

I nod as I set the chamomile and honey tea down.

"Have you used that gift on anyone?" She asks.

I ponder over the few times I have, one of which on Reimus, even if it didn't work. A slow stretch of a smile appears on my lips as I bring my gaze up to her. "Maybe."

She huffs softly. "Hades and I always wondered to what extent that gift lied."

"And what about him? Being The King of The Underworld and all. Can he invoke fear into people?" I ask timidly.

"If he truly wanted to, I guess. But he's more of a god who prefers to highlight the truths in others."

I tilt my head slightly. "Why?"

She blinks, a lazy shrug following. "Because most people when met with their true selves, the dark aspects of themselves that they cannot hide from, is a much more powerful strategy than any other fear-inducing gift."

I nod my head as understanding ensues. I loosen my breath. "He helped me with that today."

She takes a sip from her tea before setting it down again. "In what way?"

I narrow my gaze. "For a long time I've looked at my shadow as something that controls me, something that only wants to bring me reminders of painful memories. But today, I realized that it wasn't trying to torment me." My eyes look up at my mother, her gazing unmoving. "It wanted to help me *understand* it. And in doing so, become a part of *me* to wield, instead of my fear wielding it against me. And that's when I finally made it. The portal."

She nods slowly at me, pride swimming in her face. "Your darkness was never your enemy, Melinoë. Your fear was."

I allow her words to fill me, sink into my bones. I hold onto that truth, and store deep within me.

"When I free Makaria, what will happen?" I ask quietly.

My mother's gaze softens. "The plan was to bring her here, where she would reside and be safe from Zeus' retaliation. What the plan was for the both of you."

I whip my gaze to her, as she holds a lithe hand up before I can say anything.

"That *was* the plan, before I realized that I would be no better than Zeus in forcing you into something. Forcing you both to reside here against your free will." Her eyes flicker, the emerald color churning vividly. "So it will be her choice, as I am leaving it yours. She may stay here if she wishes, or stay with you in Vulir. All I care about is you both are safe."

I stand from my seat, and plop myself next to her. I take her hands, holding them. I watch the worry float through her gaze for a moment, before it vanishes. I gently squeeze her hands. "Thank you." I say before I wrap my arms around her.

A choice, something I have not known fondly of growing up.

I pull away from her, her eyes glazed. "But you are *nothing* like Zeus. You never were."

Persephone's lips tremble, as she nods her head curtly. "But I still failed you both. Regardless of the circumstance, you both will *never* be kept from me. Not again." Her mouth tightens, anger tensing her shoulders. A tear rolls down her cheek as she brings me into her embrace.

We hold each other for a long while, sharing our tears and muffled words. The only thing missing now is Makaria.

I'll bring my sister back.

I will not fail her in that regard.

⁓

After I portaled myself back to The Guardian's Palace—with my mother beside me, in case I accidentally got myself lost—I watched as the portal closed behind her, grinning at my accomplishment the whole time until it did.

As I turn around I jump back, startling myself.

"Woah." Nora says, leaning against the dining room table. Dimitri stands in front of her, shock written on his face.

Reimus stands next to him, grinning at me as pride swims in his eyes. "Welcome back." He walks over to me, kissing me as if nobody else is in the room. He pulls away, a wicked grin on his face. "Does this mean we can just portal into the bedroom instead of walking for now on?" He winks.

I shove my hand into his shoulder, rolling my eyes. "I think I much prefer you doing the work of carrying me up."

He laughs deeply, his teeth glinting in the candlelight. "I think you know I have no qualms with doing all of the work."

A breath gets trapped in my chest, my cheeks blushing slightly. I try to resist my grin, and fail in the process.

"I like her. She's zesty, like me." Nora says, grinning like a cat.

"Zesty?" Dimitri asks, an eyebrows raised.

"Yes, *zesty*. As in sassy? Badass?" She says, rolling her eyes at Dimitri before she approaches me.

Reimus chuckles, his fingers lightly touching my wrist at my side. "She is certainly those things."

Rolling my eyes at him, he gives me a look, his words shown plainly on his face.

Remember what I told you about rolling those pretty little eyes at me?

I swallow the sudden lump in my throat, ignoring the heat threatening to pool low. I fix my gaze on Nora. "It's good to see you again." I look over at Dimitri, nodding towards his slung arm. "How's the arm?"

He exhales audibly. "It could be worse. Nothing compared to what it'll feel like when I shift."

Dread pools low within my belly, almost forgetting about them needing to tend to his wings. I grimace. "I'm sorry."

His face is stone cold, the dread of shifting visible on his face. He nods curtly. "Thank you. I'm just ready to get the day over with."

I jerk my head over to Reimus, my eyes widening. "You're doing it today?" I nod to Dimitri's arm. "Doesn't his arm need to be fully healed first?"

"His arm is already mostly healed. Draghi heal wounds quickly, the arm sling is more of a precaution for now. But yes, we need to tend to his wings sooner rather than later." Reimus looks towards his friend.

"Why?"

"Because if we don't work on healing them soon, the cartilage could form the wing permanently. How it is right now." Dimitri interrupts. I watch him nearly shiver.

I look over at Reimus, then to Nora. "You'll be helping?"

The healer nods her head before grinning. "I'm the best in Vulir."

I look them all over as I stand a little taller, a little more fearless in the face of everything that has happened. I land my gaze once more on Reimus, determination and something akin to care surfacing within. "Tell me what you need from me."

CHAPTER 14

My bare feet are firmly planted in the large terrain as sweat begins to bead above my brow. A result of the bolstering heat upon us, and also from my own nerves racking my body.

Reimus approaches me from my left, a calloused hand gently cupping the underside of my jaw. He lifts my gaze to him. "You ready?"

I nod. "It's very likely it won't work though."

His thumb gently caresses my balmy cheek. A shy grin curves up his face. "It will. You just need to trust yourself, like I always have."

He lowers his hand before walking over to Nora's side. She stands off to my right, about twenty feet in front of Dimitri. I watch him give Nora a nod. "We're ready."

She nods back, then faces me. A ghost of a grin appears, just for a moment before being replaced again with stern focus. "Get ready, girl."

"Does anyone want to tell me what exactly she needs to get ready for?" Dimitri asks, skepticism in his tone.

Nora faces him. "Just remember what I told you. Under no circumstances can you shift back until I tell you to."

She steps a few feet towards him, her gaze boring into his. "No matter how painful."

He exhales raggedly, clenching his jaw as he nods. And for the first time, I watch as true fear illuminates in his eyes. He opens and closes his hands at his sides. "Let's get this over with."

Reimus gives me one final glance, before looking towards Dimitri. My gaze shifts towards Nora, who brings her hands up to her chest, palms facing up. I watch as she closes her eyes, her expression softening. "On my signal."

Dimitri grows visibly tense, stepping from one foot to the other. I fight the urge to share his same unease, and instead center into myself. Breathing in, and out again. Calling to that darkness within, the source of my power.

My gaze fixates on Nora, waiting. I watch as bright luminescent light begins to glow in her palms, my eyes widening as it grows brighter.

I shift my gaze forward, centering myself deeper and deeper with every breath. I sense Reimus walking towards his friend, but I don't take my eyes off of Dimitri.

Reimus begins running towards him, and that's when I feel it. The deafening buzz of Nora's magic.

"Now!"

On Nora's command, Dimitri shifts into his drago form and the whole world rumbles from the roar of his agony. I fall to my knees, my mouth gaping open as my hands come up to cover my ears. I shut my eyes against the gods-awful sound, but I promised myself I would be able to do this.

Releasing my hands I stand on shaky legs. I watch as Dimitri flails around, gasping at the sight of his wings.

The dark scales of his skin are identical to Reimus. His wings resemble shredded fragments of silk, torn from the seams and hanging loosely. His head jerks towards me, his eyes shining like lustrous embers of gold. He roars again, thrashing his head to look back at the damage. He whips his head around, his back bowing as his mouth goes taught.

My gaze shifts towards Reimus as he shifts into his drago form, before falling next to Dimitri. My breath catches at the sight of them, side by side.

"Keep him down, Reimus!" Nora shouts as she begins jogging towards them. I follow her but keep at a safe distance.

Reimus lowers his head to Dimitri, a low shrill erupting from his throat. He lays a ginormous claw along Dimitri's neck, pinning him down. Dimitri tries to thrash against him, but Reimus is almost twice his size.

Nora approaches them, her palms faced out towards Dimitri. Immediately her hands project a blinding silver glaze onto his shattered wings, and that's when his roars intensify.

I watch as Dimitri flails his tail, the camouflaged barbed spikes coming dangerously close to hitting Nora out of reaction to the pain. Reimus loops his tail around his, stretching it over next to him, restraining it down.

Reimus glances at me, a subtle nod. I give him an affirming nod as I fall down, down, down into that reservoir.

Calling up that power that nestles deeply within. I let it wash over me, claiming it.

I open my eyes, setting them upon Dimitri. I focus on him, slowly infiltrating his mind. I begin walking closer to him, no longer afraid. His head snaps towards me, his eyes locking onto mine.

I submerge myself into his mind, crawling through the protective barriers. And once I've made my way in, I take control over it.

Only ever having known how to visualize terror, I focus on something slightly less. I manipulate the feeling of numbness coursing throughout his body, infiltrating him to believe that his wings are perfectly intact, and that not an ounce of pain is flowing though his body. I steady myself into his mind, sinking my fingers into the swells of his thoughts.

His eyes begin to soften as he stares at me, his thrashing minimizing severely under Reimus' hold. I breathe life into my magic, and therefore into his mind.

"Keep him just like that!" Nora shouts, the sight of silver light glowing brighter next to me.

I breathe deeply, manipulating Dimitri to do the same. I watch as his gaze softens, the belief that he's under no discomfort beginning to take over his mind. I watch as his lips slacken, no longer held tightly together. I watch from the corner of my eye as Reimus loosens his hold, but not entirely just yet. As if under a spell, Dimitri doesn't even notice.

After a few minutes, Nora's shout breaks the silence. "I'm almost done."

I begin to feel my control slipping, exhaustion threatening to plague my energy. I watch Dimitri closely, not noticing any shift in his demeanor. But I begin to feel myself tremble, knowing I won't be able to hold on much longer. I finally slide my gaze to Reimus, giving him a knowing look, and also a warning.

Help.

Someone help.

He watches me closely as my fingers begin to slip from his mind—

"Don't let go."

I freeze at the sound of a feminine voice stirring beside me. Before I can look over my shoulder, I watch Dimitri's face go completely still. His eyes no longer on me, but on the woman next to me. I watch Reimus show a similar shock to his features.

I finally look over, and the spitting resemblance tells me exactly who she is. My knees begin to tremble as I exhale a shaky breath. "I can't hold on much longer."

"Yes, you can." The deceased woman says before she makes her slow approach to her son.

A choked cry threatens to leave my lips, but I shove it down as I maintain the control on my magic. I look over at Nora, then at the once battered wings. His wings now like magnificent silver threads of cartilage, woven anew. I watch as sweat trickles down Nora's forehead, her knees beginning to buckle. But she doesn't falter, she remains standing tall as the tethers of her magic heal the remaining section of his wings.

I turn back towards Dimitri, his mother kneeling before him. A cry sounds from deep in his throat, a tear falling from his eye. She rests a hand on his snout as he nuzzles into her palm.

"I am so very proud of you, my son." She says, the outline of her spirit similar to the silver glow pooling into his wings. She smiles deeply. *"Never forget how much I love you."*

Nora's silver light refracts as she falls to her knees. "It's done." She says raggedly.

My control on my magic slips completely and I stumble onto the grass. I hold myself up by one arm, breathing heavily as I watch Dimitri's mother make her way towards me.

"How did you know?" Is all I can manage to say as the air evades my lungs.

She shrugs her shoulders nonchalantly. *"You called."* A soft grin curves her lips. *"I came."*

My breathing begins to even itself out as I stare up at the woman until a moment later she disappears. My gaze flickers over where she just stood, as if she'll reappear before me.

Reimus is at my side in an instant, having shifted back. He gently pulls me up. "Are you alright?"

I nod my head, standing up on my two feet again. I look over to Dimitri.

His gaze targets mine, his stance still and unmoving. My gaze shifts to his wings, like glowing moonlight against the sun high in the sky. After a few moments, he finally shifts back. His mouth trembles slightly, slowly shaking his head. "How…"

"I don't know." I admit. "I felt my control on you slipping, and I called out for help." My throat works on a swallow as my mind numbs. "She just came."

He makes his way towards me, no longer wearing the sling around his arm. His eyes find mine, disbelief clouding them. He shakily falls to his knees, his head bowing towards my feet. "I—never thought I would see her again. Thank you." He begins to cry.

I kneel down with him, bringing his gaze back up to mine. I grab his hands, holding them. I nod my head. "You're welcome."

He squeezes my hands tightly before releasing them. He stands up, holding his hand out for me. As I grab it he pulls me up onto my feet. I turn my gaze over towards Nora, astonishment written on her sweat-lined face when Reimus pulls my gaze to him.

He tucks a damp strand behind my ear, a grin painting his handsome face. His gaze narrows slightly, his nostrils flare as he huffs. "Guardian of The Dead."

Dimitri wide eyed, loosens a breath. "Indeed."

CHAPTER 15

After we made our way back inside, Nora and I found ourselves in Reimus' bedchamber. Both of us having taken to our own chaise lounge, a cool damp towel on both of our heads.

"That's never happened before, has it?" She asks, finally stirring in her chair after laying there for a long moment.

I lift the towel from my head, my body having cooled down tremendously from the sweltering heat outside. I shift myself to sit upright, my gaze meeting hers. "No. Not on command at least."

Her bright copper hair sticks to her forehead, assuming identical to how I must look. A grin does not pull at her lips this time. Only the widening of her eyes to show any indication she heard me. "I've never heard of anyone being able to summon spirits like that."

I exhale. "Neither have I."

We share a long moment of silence together, before she clears her throat. "I felt your magic slipping."

My eyes narrow. "It was for a moment. I didn't think I'd be able to keep my hold on his mind. That's when she showed up."

Nora turns to face me fully, a half smile curving up her lips. "But you managed to hold on."

I chuckle, a lazy smile appearing. "So did you."

Her half smile turns into a full on grin. "Some baddasses we are."

We share a laugh as Reimus and Dimitri step into the room. My gaze first notices Reimus before it lands on Dimitri. I watch him gaze at Nora as gratitude accompanies his gaze.

"Thank you." He shifts his gaze to me then. "Both of you."

I nod. "Feeling better?"

He exhales audibly, a soft smile appearing. "Much better."

Reimus kneels next to me, grabbing the damp towel. He gently swipes it across my forehead, the silver in his eyes contrasting brightly against the blue. "You did wonderful today." He looks over to Nora. "You both did."

"Yeah, yeah, we're the best. We know." Nora says sarcastically, standing up from the chair. She begins to walk out of the room, before her eyes meet mine again. "See you soon, girl." She winks before leaving altogether.

Reimus tilts his head, half-looking back towards Dimitri when he turns on his heels and exits the room as well.

"Where are they going?" I ask.

"Anywhere but here."

My brows slam together, a laugh escapes me. "Why?"

He lowers the towel to my neck, the coolness a relief against my warm skin. He slowly lowers it to my collarbone, causing my skin to pimple and raise. "Because I'm going to spend the next several hours showing you exactly how appreciative I am of you."

He lowers the towel to my chest, as I inhale sharply.

"What you did today was extraordinary." He lowers the towel beneath my shirt, the straps falling off my shoulder. My breath hitches as he lightly traces the towel against my breast, then along my nipple.

"Pride doesn't seem to properly convey what I feel." He moves a corner of the soft fabric along my nipple, moving in circular motions. My back arches, a low moan escaping my lips.

He removes the towel, and sets it on the chair next to me. He lowers my strappy shirt as my breasts heave out. He lowers his head to my neck, soft kisses caressing my skin. "And I think your hard work should be rewarded appropriately."

A breathy moan escapes me. "There's nothing appropriate about this."

He chuckles against my skin, his lips traveling lower to my breast. He looks up at me as his mouth hovers over a hardened nipple. He grins wickedly. "Did I say appropriately? I meant indecently."

His mouth closes over, his tongue lapping against my hardened skin. I moan at the feel of his soft tongue against me. My hands come up to his hair, my fingers tangling into their wavy strands.

He pulls away and lifts me up from the chair, carrying me to the bathroom. He sets me on the counter before walking over to the shower. He turns the water on, steam already rising from the stream of water.

He pushes my legs open, fitting himself in between them. He tilts his head at my shirt. "This is in my way." He says, before lifting it off of me.

My breath hitches as the cool air kisses my skin. He moves his hands to my waist, his head lowering. "These too." He unbuttons my khaki colored shorts, pulling them and my underwear off me until I'm on the counter, bare before him.

His eyes track over my body slowly, the heat in his eyes branding my skin. He grins as he lifts his shirt off, then removes his pants. He presses himself into me, his cock hard at my entrance. I whimper as I squirm myself closer to him, before his hand wraps around my throat, forcing my gaze onto him. He lowers his lips to only an inch apart from mine. "So beautiful."

He lifts me from the counter, his cock pressing hard against my silken skin. He grunts as he carries me to the shower, towards the far wall where a three tiered ledge is built into the wall.

He sets me on the middle ledge, walking back out to grab two towels. I watch as the water glistens down his muscular body, my gaze lowering as it trickles off his hard cock. He sets one towel behind me, the other on the ledge above me. He grabs my chin, pulling my gaze back to him as he teases my entrance with his cock.

"You're going to get on your fucking knees, and spread those pretty legs wide open for me."

I gasp as Reimus lifts me, turning me around so my knees rest on the towel behind me. I spread my legs for him, my rear completely exposed for him. I put my arms on the ledge above me, where he slides the second towel towards me.

"For your elbows." He says, before sliding it under them.

My back arches as Reimus slips a finger down my pussy, in between my silken folds. I moan as wetness pools there.

He lowers his head to my spine, trailing kisses down it before he lowers himself to the floor. I feel his hands come to my thighs, gripping them. I gasp as I feel his warm breath dance at my entrance.

"Now allow me to show you my appreciation."

His tongue laps in between my folds, causing me to writhe against his tongue. Cries of pleasure flow from my lips as he tastes and sucks and twirls that delicious tongue of his.

His mouth closes over my clit, my back arching even deeper as he sucks that sweet little nub.

My cries intensify as my orgasm reaches me, sending me over the top as he continues to suck my clit. I bow against him, and I feel his mouth grin against me.

My body begins to relax again as he pulls away, his hand coming to slap my ass. It wrings a breathy gasp from me as he stands himself up again.

I feel him tease my entrance with his cock, and I whimper at my eagerness to feel him fill me entirely. He chuckles as his hands come up to my waist, drilling me down on him in one thrust.

He grunts his satisfaction before he lowers his head to my ear. He nibbles on my ear before twirling my hair in one of his fists. I let out a low moan. "I'm going to fuck you, little spitfire. Until nothing but my pride is dripping from you." He tugs my head back slightly, pulling my face to be more level with his.

He pulls out slowly, before burying himself to the hilt. "What it's like to worship a goddess like you."

The ridges of his cock like a taunting delight as he pulls out once more. "To be able to fuck you." The last of his words before he thrusts in deeply.

He rams into me, pleasure coursing through my body as he plummets into me over and over. His fullness stealing the breath in my lungs, my mind a lustrous daze at the feel of him buried deep inside me.

His hand holds my hair tightly as he grinds into my rear. My pussy gushes with wetness, Reimus grunting his approval.

"Please—don't stop." I plead through my cries.

Reimus chuckles as a moan escapes his lips. "Abso-fucking-lutely *anything* you want." His other hand moves to my shoulder, gripping me in place as his hand in my hair tightens. "It's yours."

He rams into me, his words heating my blood as he tenses up behind me. His grip on my hair loosens completely as he twirls me around, hooking an arm around me to keep my back from pressing against the edge.

His hand grabs my neck, bringing my gaze up. "I want to see those magnificent eyes when I cum inside you."

I moan against his hold, my eyes not straying from his as he bucks into me. He whimpers as he thrusts deep, wringing a cry from my lips. I feel him unload himself into me as I wrap my legs around him to deepen him further. His body trembles as he whimpers his release. Our eyes never leaving one another.

Only when he brings his lips to mine does the gazing cease. His tongue parts my entrance, my lips parting for his eagerly. I feel him slowly pull out of me, cum dripping from me. He pulls his lips from mine, gazing at me once more as our breathing staggers.

The sound of the water hitting the tile floor is the only reminder I get that we're in the shower right now. I begin laughing at the reminder as Reimus smiles at me.

His hand comes up to my cheek, worship and something else swimming in his eyes as he stares longingly at me. He caresses my damp skin softly, his voice hard and gruff. "A fucking gift, from The Fates themselves."

CHAPTER 16

Silken sheets rest loosely along my hips as I rest my head on my elbow. After Reimus and I finally got around to washing up, we made our way to his bed where he took to brushing my hair. The delicacy in his effort in brushing through the tangles, the feel of his hands weaving carefully through my hair.

Afterwards he threw a towel around his waist and ventured downstairs. Coming back sometime later with a bottle of wine, and a platter of food.

I laughed as my gaze fell to the tray. "This cannot be our dinner."

He looks at me quizzically. "Sure it is."

I laughed again. "And how does Aven feel about our choice for dinner tonight?"

He'd grinned at me, that gods-damn beautiful smile of his. "I told him this morning to take the night off. He insisted on at least prepping us something, but I told him it was unnecessary."

The once-filled tray of prosciutto, sicilian herbed olives, grapes, mandarin orange slices, sourdough bread, vegetable soup, and an array of cheeses are nearly gone now. As I sip from my wine, I watch Reimus as he lays at the foot of the bed, propped up on an elbow as I am. He trails a rough index finger along an exposed calf. The touch of his finger causes goosebumps to raise along my skin.

"What was she like?"

Reimus unaffected, his gaze still sharpened upon my leg gives a smirk. "She was kind. Very brave." He chuckles, his voice gently caressing my skin. "When we were coming into our drago forms, Dimitri went through temper tantrums trying to adjust. She was always there to set his ass straight."

"How old were you both when you learned how to shift?"

"Twelve. It takes time to learn to shift properly, but after that it's effortless." His gaze meets mine, his finger still moving along my bare skin.

I drink from my wine before setting it down on the bedside table. "And what of your mother?"

He pauses for a moment, a smile curving up one side of his face. "She was a fierce woman. She never backed down from defending those she loved." He raises his gaze to mine again. "No matter what it cost her."

I lower myself down the bed until I'm sitting in front of him, my legs folded beneath me. "She sounds like a brave woman."

His gaze falls to my belly, before leaning in to kiss the soft skin. He looks up at me, his lips hovering over my skin. "Brave like you."

I scoff at his words.

"Do you not think you are brave?" He asks, his lashes lowering as he sits upright with me. I watch as the sheets pool low to his waist, distracted by the nakedness that I know hides beneath.

I bring my gaze to him. "I think I have endured a lot, and therefore have learned how to survive."

His hand reaches for mine, his thumb tracing my wrist. "And if not brave, then what do you call that?"

I pause, my gaze hardening slightly. "I call it being resourceful."

He brings my hand up, tugging me closer to him until my breasts rest against his hard chest. A shaky exhale leaves me as a featherlight kiss grazes my shoulder. "I fear you do not give yourself enough credit, my goddess." His lips graze my neck, my back arching into his kiss.

I chuckle. "I think you give me far too much credit."

He suddenly pulls away, his vivid blue eyes earnest and steady. "No." He rests a hand along my cheek. "I give you the correct amount of credit, and I will keep showering you with it until you believe it to be as much as I do."

I bring my hand to his, his skin warm beneath mine. I lean into his palm as I search for the truth in his eyes, desperate to obtain even a fraction of the admiration he feels for me. His devotion is a remedy I've craved my entire life, and it now sits right in front of me.

I lean in, a soft kiss to his full lips. His hand lowers to the back of my head, his lips savoring mine as he brings me in closer.

I fall deep into him, uncaring of any limits I once told myself I wouldn't cross. I fall, fall, fall, the fear of how far I'll allow myself to sink into what this is seeming so foolish now. This man cares deeply for me, as I do for him.

He pulls his lips away, my heart blossoming at the sight of his grin. His hand comes up to flick my nose, drawing a laugh from me.

I watch his body tense for a moment, before he loosens a shaky breath. His loose dark strands fall above eyes that pierce into mine. "That laugh…" He trails off. "I never want to be parted from it."

He kisses me long and deeply, his hands coming up to my waist as he pulls me on top of him. I moan into his mouth at the feel of his already hard cock, pressing against me.

I straddle him, his hands skimming my thighs as I bring my hands to his chest. I pull away from his lips, a grin on my face as I narrow my gaze. I grind my hips into him, pulling my heated gaze back to him. "And is there anything else you wish to not be parted from?"

A wicked grin curves his lips as his hands tighten around my waist, before one lowers to grip his cock. He grunts as I grind against him once more. A chuckle drips from his lips as he positions himself at my entrance, wetness dripping from me already. An eager cry leaves me as he teases me with the tip. "I could think of one thing." He says through a heated gaze

He inserts himself, burying himself deep inside me. His hand skims up my side until it cups my breast. A moan escapes me as his thumb trails around my nipple, my gaze heating even more. And as my hips grind against him, I let everything but my words show him that I wish to never be parted from him either.

I stand from the bed, looking over to watch the rise and fall of his chest before stepping into the bathroom. I handle my personal needs, before coming out to slip on a pair of clean underwear, black leggings, and a rose-colored short sleeve shirt.

I twist the doorknob slowly, peering over my shoulder to make sure I don't wake Reimus. As I hear the faint click of the knob, I pull the door open enough to slip through. I pull the door closed behind me before walking down to what I now call the work room.

I enter the chamber, dimly lit from the torches on the walls above. I meet Hecate in the middle of the room. "You know, they might as well call this Hecate's room. You're the only one who uses it."

She chuckles, her dark wavy hair swaying faintly from the movement. "I think that's precisely what I'll tell Reimus and Dimitri to call it."

I approach her, chuckling. "I'll back you up on it."

She exhales as her smile begins to lessen. "I heard you helped repair his wings."

I shrug my shoulders. "It was Nora who actually repaired them. I just helped keep him calm long enough for her to work."

Her gaze, steady and strong, doesn't falter from mine. "By calling up his mother."

"Yes." I admit.

She studies me. "That's no small feat, Melinoë."

I shift from foot to foot. "I know."

"And how do you feel having been able to do that?" She steps closer to me.

"I feel…" I trail off, trying to formulate the right words. "Shocked. I wasn't intentionally calling *her*, it just happened. But I am The Goddess of Ghosts, Guardian of The Dead. So…I'm learning to be more comfortable with everything that title comes with."

She nods as a smile grows. "Good. I'm glad you're feeling more comfortable."

I give her a half smile, before I begin to pull out my hands, in which she lays a hand on my inner arm to halt me.

"I think you're ready, Melinoë."

Nerves begin to crowd me as I comprehend what she means. I work on a swallow. "I could get lost finding her."

She grabs my arm softly, tilting her head. "You won't get lost, I'll still be here to anchor you."

I straighten my back and stand a little taller, as she places my hands into hers. Having practiced several times now, the thought of astral traveling to my sister terrifies me. But if this was always part of the plan, then I can no longer hide from it.

I have to be ready. For her.

I nod, releasing any fears of my capability of astral traveling to vanquish my body. "Okay."

"She will be confused, so don't explain more than what is necessary. Not until we bring her home."

I nod.

"This is important." She begins, seriousness etched into her glowing skin. "When you find her, you will need to focus on identifying the magic around your sister. You need to be able to see it, *feel* it, in order for the chants to break it."

Inhaling deeply I nod my head curtly. She squeezes my hands, pulling my gaze back to her.

"You must believe in yourself, Melinoë. Magic only works when you *believe*, do you understand?"

Biting my inner cheek, I nod. There is no time for me to doubt myself right now. I have to believe I can bring my sister home, that I can wield the kind of magic to break the compulsion that's around her. "I understand."

Her golden eyes churn brightly. "Good. Now repeat after me."

Hecate begins chanting four sets of words, urging me to repeat them once she's said them. She asks me to repeat them again, and again. After a few times, she smiles. "It's time."

I inhale deeply before releasing again. I close my eyes, as I center into myself. Down further and further into the part of me that is neither tangible nor physical. As my breathing slows down and I feel my surroundings begin to feel hazy, I hear Hecate far away. As if she isn't standing right in front of me.

"You can do this." She says.

I let her words be my guidance as I step out of my physical body, and merge into my astral one.

As I channel into that darkness within myself, I remember what Hades told me. I let his words guide me as I try to bring my portal alive again.

"The darkness is not your enemy, Melinoë."

Channeling deep within, reaching my hand out for it, I breathe her in. I begin to visualize the one place I think to find my sister. The feeling of the night air seeping through the bedroom window, the soft violet sheets on top of her bed. And quicker than I imagined, I open my eyes to a portal take form. The shadows tracing around the opening becoming more of a welcomed embrace, than a fearful one.

I smile as I look back at my physical body, hands conjoined with Hecate's before I turn back around. I step through the portal, my astral body merging through.

I step through the portal into my sister's bedroom. My eyes look up at the woman sitting on her bed, hands slackened at her sides as her mouth gapes open at me.

I watch as her lips tremble, my gaze shifting to her physical body sleeping beside her. She stands up shakily as I choke on a strangled cry.

"Melinoë?" She gasps as she heaves a breath.

She rushes towards me as I meet her halfway before we both fall to our knees, embracing one another. I sob uncontrollably into her arms as she does mine.

Through my near hyperventilating, I whisper into her shoulder. The sweet familiar scent of her wafting through my nose, even in her astral form. It lulls me into her presence as a shaky smile spreads across my lips. "Hello, sister."

CHAPTER 17

I cradle my sister's head into my shoulder, the feel of her soft platinum blonde hair against my trembling fingers. I can't recall how long we've been weeping with one another. I can only focus on the fact that my sister is in my arms once more.

She frantically pulls me away, her gaze tracking over me before her gaze lifts again. "I—I don't understand. I've been here before, but I thought this was just me dreaming. But I—" She stammers as she grips my arm, squeezing it once, then twice. "I can feel your arm. How—"

"Makaria, I don't have much time to explain right now. But I need you to listen to me carefully."

Her gaze grows wild as I pull her hands into mine. She ceases some of her trembling as I squeeze her hands. "This is real." I gesture to her body. "You are sleeping, but we're in the astral realm."

"Astral realm? Like a dreamscape?" She pleads.

I tilt my head, wiping away the wetness from my eyes. "Kind of. I—"

"*Where* did you go?" She demands as she yanks my hands. "I was worried for you. But oddly enough, I don't remember feeling much else other than that when I'm awake." She gestures around us. "But when I'm sleeping—when I'm here, I feel separate from myself. Like something doesn't belong." Her eyes flicker wildly before landing on me again. "What's wrong with this place?"

I exhale slowly, not wanting to go into the specifics of everything right now, but knowing that if I were in her shoes I would want to be told the truth. Regardless of how much it would destroy me.

I begin to brace myself as I unveil a fraction of the truth to her. "The reason why you feel so out of place here, and not entirely connected to yourself, is because you're under a compulsion spell."

Her body stiffens as confusion clouds her sweet face. She pulls her hands out from mine, stumbling to stand upright. "What do you mean?"

I slowly stand up with her, a frown pulling at my lips. I struggle for a moment on how to explain this as briefly as I can, knowing I don't have the time currently to divulge into everything. I open my mouth, closing it again, struggling to find the words. I look over towards her physical body sleeping, knowing she will not remember this when she awakes.

I turn to her once more. "Sebastian is different from what he's made us believe our whole lives." I purposefully omit the fact our mother is alive, deciding to divulge that when the time comes. When Makaria is back with me in

Vulir. "His real name is Zeus. He is immortal, and has the means to use his powers to his advantage."

She slams her brows forward, shaking her head as she backs up. "No."

I remain where I'm standing so as to not further overwhelm my sister. The sight of her thoughts rummaging through her head for answers, as if she could've spotted this before, breaks my heart as I remember how it felt to hear the truth for the first time.

For my sister it's different. He used his manipulation against her, and I can't imagine how she will process that vile truth.

I calm my shaky voice. "He has known that I'm different for a long time, and he compelled you to let him know of my advancements."

Her gaze jerks up towards mine. "Advancements? What do you mean you're different?"

"I mean that I too, am immortal."

She gasps, her hands coming up to her chest. "You're lying."

I advance a step towards her. "I'm not. I can—"

"Prove it." She seethes.

I halt, but give into my sister's plea. As I gaze upon her, I decide to go easy on her as I climb through her mind. I watch as her eyes widen as I manipulate her to imagine the room around us swaying. She gasps as she looks around, trembling at the snakes that slither up the walls. She swirls her gaze back to me as I retract fully from her mind.

She steps towards me, her hands closing into fists at her chest. "My gods." She breathes. She looks over at herself sleeping on the bed, as her fingers come up to her lips. She turns back around to face me. "He…compelled me?" Tears begin to line her golden set eyes.

I tentatively step towards her, slowly reaching my hands out to gently grip her elbows. She flinches, and I remove my hands entirely. "I'm so sorry Makaria. This was exactly what I tried to protect you from. I had no idea until I came to—"

"But he loves me? He…" Her words trail off as she begins breathing raggedly. "He's my father. Why would he do that?" She shouts.

"Makaria…"

"Why! *Why* would he do that!" She begins screaming, her head shaking quickly. I watch as her breathing ramps up, her eyes widening as her hands come up to her face. A harsh cry erupts from her as her nails begin digging into her cheeks. Streaks of blood running down her cheeks.

Bile rises in my throat at the sight as I panic, quickly shifting my gaze to her physical body as I try to identify the magic around her. I hover over her, desperate to feel for it as my sister grows more distressed.

"You're wrong! He wouldn't do that to me!" She begins crying hysterically, and as she falls to the ground, her shoulder bumps into her bed. It causes the energy to stir around her physical body just enough for me to find the faint flicker of the compulsion spell.

Akin to a clear film around her, I study how the compulsion magick hugs tightly to her physical body. I begin to reach my hands out to it, to better feel it when my sister begins hyperventilating.

I retract my hands, scurrying onto the floor next to her. I bring my hands up to pull her nails away from her face. My voice trembles as I speak. "Makaria."

My sister pulls back from my hold, clawing at herself once more. As if the pain were a physical entity that had latched itself onto her, and she desperately were trying to tear it off. The breath in her lungs goes nowhere as she falls into full blown hysteria.

I did this to her. I said too much, too soon.

I cradle her against my chest, rocking her, trying to soothe her into my arms. "Makaria, I'm right here. Do you hear me?"

She sobs as her body trembles violently against me, her tears branding themselves onto my arms as her hands still against her cheeks.

My own tears slip out for her, trying my hardest to hold my composure for her as she completely and utterly falls apart in my arms.

"But he loves me! He's my *dad*." A choked scream muffles from her lips as they press themselves against my shoulder.

I choke on my own words as my mouth trembles from the feel of her pain. Like having your head forced down into a pit of oil, suffocating and without light. Pain that I can feel potently here in the astral realm.

I said too much.

"Melinoë, come back."

At Hecate's words, I glance up to see her standing above us. I keep Makaria cradled in my arms as Hecate kneels down to us.

"Melinoë, we must return. Now." She says sternly.

"No. My sister—she needs me right now." I cry as Makaria lifts her head. She locks eyes with Hecate, too drowned out into her own heartache to even question who she is.

Hecate lays a steady hand on Makaria's shoulder as she closes her eyes and mumbles a few chants out loud. A few moments later, she releases her hold and stands up.

I watch as Makaria completely ceases her bodily trembling, her crying, all of it. She merely looks up at me, gives me a hug, and stands up to lay next to her physical body.

I stand up, watching her in disbelief before I swerve my gaze to Hecate. "What did you do?" I demand.

Before I can say another word, she grabs my hand and opens a portal. I look back at my sister laying in complete calmness, the far opposite of just a few moments ago.

Before I have time to say goodbye, I'm yanked through the portal with Hecate. She pulls me forward and takes my hand as she rests it on my physical body's shoulder.

Where I merge with myself once more.

CHAPTER 18

I stumble forward, catching myself before falling to the chamber ground. I whip my head towards Hecate, my gaze hardening on hers. "Why did you bring me back?" I seethe through my anger.

Hecate watches me, sorrow evident in her eyes.

"She needed me, and you brought me back. I needed more time!" I bellow as I step towards her.

"Melinoë." She says calmly.

I begin pacing the room, anger crowding my logic. I pinch the bridge of my nose, the quick sting of my fingernails drawing me back to the image of my sister clawing at her face. I lower my hand as it trembles at my side.

"Melinoë." Hecate advances a step towards me.

"What did you do to her?" I lift my gaze, staring straight ahead.

She remains quiet for a moment. "I used magic to sedate her."

My gaze flings to hers. "Will she forget?"

"No. She will remember the next time she is in the astral realm, but she will be…more calm."

I pace again, my mind a mess of thoughts and what ifs and emotions I don't have the stomach to ponder over. My breathing begins to quicken as I pace more hurriedly.

I feel Hecate advance another step. She quietly pleads once more. "Melinoë…"

Unable to distract the surge of emotion rising any further, I lose myself to it.

I fall to the floor as a cry tears from my throat. I weep as my knees burrow into the hardwood floor, my heart splintering in my chest.

Hecate comes to my side and I immediately pull her into me. She wraps her arms around me as I sob for my sister.

Burdening my sister with a truth that no one should ever have to be on the receiving end of.

A truth that will very likely break her from the inside out, threatening to harden her altogether.

"Thank you." I weep on her shoulder.

I feel Hecate still against me. "For what, my dear?"

My body trembles as she embraces me. "For easing her pain. Even if just for one more day."

Hecate exhales, her hold on me lightening no less. A moment later, I feel the sudden rush of footsteps down the hallway.

"What happened—" Reimus halts abruptly, going silent. I listen to him enter the room slowly, his footsteps like faint echoes. I feel him kneel next to me.

I pull myself from Hecate, and she wipes the wetness from my eyes. She gives me a kiss on the cheek before she gazes at me again. "I'm so sorry the weight of this fell onto your shoulders." She gives a mournful smile before nodding to Reimus.

His hands wrap under my jaw as he examines me. Then, without saying another word, he scoops me up into his arms and carries us out of the room.

My mind numb to my surroundings, with only the sound of my sister breaking apart to fill the silence.

After he laid me on the bed, he went back downstairs. What I assumed was just to talk with Hecate more about what happened, he showed up sometime after with a cup of hot tea.

The smell of chamomile wafts towards my nose, slowly steadying me back into the present. I take a few sips from it, letting the warmth of the ceramic cup soothe me. After minutes of aimlessly staring into space, I bring my gaze to Reimus.

His pained eyes watch me as he seats himself next to me. He rests a hand on my cheek, his thumb grazing the damp skin gently. "Tell me what happened."

I meet his gaze and loosen a breath. "I told her what our father had done, about the compulsion. She—" My words strangle on a harsh cry as Reimus takes the ceramic mug from my hands, setting it on the nearby table. He pulls me into his arms, cradling me against his chest.

I cry deeply, my lips trembling at the reminder of the distress in my sister's screams that I will never forget. The crimson that stained beneath her fingernails at the force of them scraping back her skin.

"I told her too much too soon. I should've lied for the time being."

"You did what you thought was best." He kisses the top of my head, his words vibrating against my hair.

"In the process I told her the worst news she could possibly receive." I pull my red-rimmed eyes to look up at him. I shake my head at him, my gaze flickering over him. "I've never seen her like that before in my entire life."

I rest my head back against his chest, the feel of his skin beginning to soothe me. I notice the quickening of my breathing slow down as I nuzzle my head into his shoulder. "I hate this for her."

He rubs my hair back from my face, stroking the wavy strands. "I know." He says, his voice low. "I know."

For a long time, Reimus continues to hold me like this. He doesn't move from where he's seated, with me curled into his lap. He simply continues to stroke my hair back, as he occasionally presses his lips to the top of my head.

I begin to tell him about finding my sister in the astral realm, and how it felt to hold her in my arms again. I tell him of the conversation we had, and how she reacted to what Zeus had done to her. How she handled it.

As I unload everything onto him, I feel myself begin to sink deeper into the connection that is between us. It doesn't override the pain I still feel for my sister, but it helps to know that this man is there for me through it all.

To shoulder both my joy, and my pain with. Never again alone with it.

Sometime later he brings us up the bed, curling us underneath the silky sheets. The press of his body behind me stills me completely, bringing comfort to my nervous system far deeper than ever before.

"We will figure it all out. Together." He says as he kisses my cheek, wrapping his arms snuggly around me. I breathe him in deeply, patchouli enveloping me as my eyes begin to droop closed.

Before I fall victim to my body's sudden exhaustion, I whisper against his hold.

"Together."

CHAPTER 19

My fists burrow into the palms of my hands, curled at my sides. My body grows more rigid each passing second, my patience wearing thin. After a long moment, my emerald eyes peel open as I stomp my foot on the polished hardwood floor.

"Fuck."

I take two steps back to where I've been sitting for the majority of the morning. Plopping myself on the dark caramel sofa, frustration plaguing me as I sink into the leather cushions.

Reimus left with Dimitri early this morning to take care of some things in the village. He asked how I'd been feeling, to which I lied and said I was fine. But I know I didn't fool him, his eyes told me he knew that wasn't the truth.

The chandeliers hanging above being the only light to penetrate my dreary mood. My mind is like a never-ending carousel of the memories of last night. They spin round and round in my head, painfully reminding me of how my sister took to the truth. I can still hear her screaming, the sound deafening and hollow.

What will happen the next time I see her? Will she react the same way?

For the past twenty minutes I've been trying to summon a portal to find my mother in The Underworld. Feeling initially confident since I have had the success of doing so before, but for some reason I'm unable to now.

Which means I have to sit here and wait for her to appear. Which, considering I've been down here mindlessly staring into the abyss for two hours now, I'd say that should be fairly soon.

I prop an elbow on the arm of the couch, resting my forehead onto my fingertips, and I wait. Alone with only the turbulence of my thoughts to accompany me.

A short while later, I feel the buzz of her portal and lift my head off the tips of my fingers. I watch as her portal materializes before she walks through it. It disintegrates, vanishing behind her.

She steps forward, halting as she finds my gaze. Her shoulders tense, her body unnaturally still as she narrows her head slightly. "She knows."

I stand up, stepping towards her. I want to lift my chin in an attempt to display some kind of strength, but right now I cannot.

I frown, nodding slowly. "Yes, she does."

Persephone approaches me. I watch as her worried gaze flickers across my face, noticing the bleakness in my features. Her eyes lower as she studies the slump of my shoulders, the evidence of how it went visible in my posture.

She reaches for my hand, squeezing it gently to urge my gaze up. When my gaze meets hers once more, that's when I see it.

A mother who feels shame for her children having to divulge these disheartening truths. Her eyes turn glossy but tears do not escape them. I can see the resistance she holds against them, as if she won't let herself fall apart in front of me. Because to fall apart, would mean she could no longer maintain the strong composure that she has for so long.

I can see the unspoken thought rummaging through her mind. That she must remain strong. Not for herself, but for Makaria and I.

I inhale, my lips beginning to tremble as I tell her everything.

There's a moment when I witness that strong exterior begin to sliver, just one moment, before she mends that barrier once more. She takes me into her arms, and the contact of her warm embrace persuades the tears in my eyes to escape.

"It was horrible." I weep, my face brushing against her shoulder. She only holds me tighter.

After I've pulled myself together, I pull away from her. She wipes the tears from my eyes, a grave smile appearing. "I'm sorry this could not be easier for you." She says softly. "If I could go, if I could do it—"

"I know." I tuck my hair behind my ears, nodding my head. "I know you would if you could."

She tilts her head. "Why don't we take a day off? From mentoring with me and Hecate."

The thought of taking a break floats through my head, understanding beckoning me. But I didn't go through all of this work just to take a day off. I didn't unload the biggest betrayal to my sister just for me to take a day from her, when she may possibly need me the most.

I promised myself that I would bring my sister home, and another day unaccomplished in that sets me on edge.

"No." I step back from Persephone, watching her intently. "She needs me now more than ever. We keep going until she's freed."

She slowly nods her head, understanding that by the sternness in my tone, that I won't be persuaded otherwise. "We keep going then." A moment later, a portal opens up behind her. She reaches her hand out for me, and I eagerly take it. "To bringing Makaria home."

I stand next to her, the portal an energetic magnet that lures me into it. I stare out into the opening, The Underworld churning within it. We begin to step through it when I force a grin to curve up one side of my face. "To bringing Makaria home."

"Again."

After an hour of willing myself to form a portal, and dismantle it over and over again, the command to will it again would probably infuriate me.

But all I feel is determination, so I will form and dismantle my portal as many times as I need to. In order to ensure I can efficiently bring my sister home.

I will my portal to appear, taking me only ten seconds to do it this time around. Coming from initially taking sixty seconds to materialize one, I'd say we're making progress.

My portal forms before me, those familiar shadows like a welcome reward as they weave around the center.

"Hold it." Persephone orders.

My concentration akin to a brand on my mind as I maintain the hold on my portal. I follow her command and maintain that hold.

One minute passes.

Two, then three minutes pass.

My grip on my magic begins to slip, but I find it in myself to retain that hold. My back straightens a little taller when I do.

"Very good. Now walk through it, then bring yourself back again."

My gaze looks over at my mother. "I can't. I tried portaling here this morning. I couldn't get it to materialize."

She smiles at me. "You will this time."

My heart begins thrashing in my chest, the thought of portaling back here stilling me. "I *can't*. It won't—"

"It will work." Hades says, his shadows dissipating against the magenta sky as he materializes next to my mother. A grin greets his face before he steps towards me.

I study him, the planes in his face solid yet calm. He watches me, the intensity of his stare making me want to shrink into myself. But I remain standing tall.

I take a few deep breaths in and out again, before nodding my head curtly. I turn back around, facing my portal. I close my eyes as I chant internally to myself.

I am worthy.

I am capable.

I open my eyes, watching the The Guardians Palace living room churn within the center. The glow of the hanging chandelier reflecting off the roar of the fireplace. I breathe in, releasing as I walk through.

My foot steps onto the hardwood floor, as my other still stands on the grassy terrain of the courtyard. I lift that foot, bringing it with the other into the living room, and close the portal behind me.

I turn around, an antique coffee table in place of where my portal just was. I relax, centering myself as I begin to will my portal back.

I close my eyes as I stand there, remaining calm. I begin to visualize The Underworld, my mother and Hades standing in the midst of the lush landscape. I imagine the shadows that form around my portal, like thick tendrils that blend into the air itself. I evoke them from the depths of my darkness, an ally to be wielded rather than an enemy to be feared.

I breathe in, holding it for just a second when the buzzing feeling causes me to exhale sharply.

My eyes dart open, and I nearly cry at the sight of my shadows as they swirl around the center.

I slowly walk towards it, holding the portal open through my concentration. I step up to the opening, bringing my hand up to the perimeter. My fingers lightly graze it, the shadows slithering along my hand before they glide up my arm. Their cool embrace caresses my skin as they reach up to my cheek. The dark threads poke my cheek, wringing a giggle from my lips. I laugh as the shadows lightly wrap themselves around my arm before extending to the other. I breathe life into the darkness, feeling its power coil around me. I lean my head back, closing my eyes. I meet with that little girl deep within me, watching her as she stands tall for the first time. No longer cowering in the corner.

She brings her gaze to mine, color painting her once-dull skin. She gazes at me, a wide grin on her face. "Welcome home."

I pull myself back, my gaze again on the portal. I walk through it, my head held high as the shadows slither not only around my portal, but also around me.

I step out onto the grass, my gaze pulling up to meet my mother and Hades. Both of their expressions are identical to one another's.

Both wearing a proud smile.

I look down, watching the dark tendrils lap around my legs before dissipating entirely. And as I meet their gazes once more, I share a similar reaction.

CHAPTER 20

Slowly wiggling my fingers as I twirl my hand around. Shadows slither along the tips of my fingers as they emerge from my skin. A result of my will to show themselves once more.

"You will get used to it."

My head turns to find Hades strolling towards me, two glasses of amber liquid in his hands. He reaches one towards me.

My gaze lowers as I take it from his hand, nodding my thanks. The smooth whiskey slides down my throat as I take a sip. The rich notes of spice lingering on my tongue. "Perhaps."

After I emerged from my portal, my mother congratulated me on my accomplishment. Her grin was wide and sincere, and it melted my heart at the sight of it.

She then had to venture to The Asphodel Meadows to tend to something, but told me not to wait up as she would be awhile. While I could've portaled back home, I decided to portal to their living room. Needing a moment to myself to let it all sink in before carrying on with the rest of my day.

Pulling my back from the cool leather couch, I shift to the edge of the seat. I lift my gaze to Hades as I lean forward, my elbows propped against my knees. "Somehow I have a keen feeling this is only the beginning."

His dark eyes stare into mine, like solid steel voids. He shrugs a shoulder. "Perhaps it is." He moves to seat himself in the chair across from me.

I bring the glass to my lips, taking another sip. I lower the glass over my knee, the tips of my fingers holding it by the rim. I shift my gaze to the fireplace, fueling my inner contemplation.

We sit in silence for a few moments, until I hear him cross a long leg over his knee. His black pants contrasted against the glow of the fire. "I heard what happened with Makaria."

My gaze does not lift to his, it remains trained on the fire. I exhale, draining the rest of my whiskey before setting the empty glass on the coffee table. "I didn't realize how badly it would affect her, to share so much at once."

"It will take time."

My gaze lifts to him. "She shouldn't *need* time. None of this should even be a reality for her."

His stare is calm, unmoving. "Neither of you deserve what you have been dealt."

My gaze flickers over him before lowering to the fire again. "Can I ask you something?"

"Of course."

I hesitate for a moment before forcing my gaze back onto him. "How can you even look at me?"

He drains the rest of his whiskey before setting the glass on the mantel next to him. He turns his gaze back to me. "What do you mean?"

I loosen my breath. "How can you look at me knowing I am a child of my mother and a man who…" My voice trails off.

Understanding flashes in his eyes, his face remaining unmoved. He's silent for a few moments before narrowing his head slightly. "Because you do not deserve to be blamed or looked at differently for a choice Zeus himself undertook."

"But I am a constant reminder of that choice. I wouldn't be here if it weren't for him—" I clench my jaw, loosening a breath as I lower my gaze.

His stare hardens as he watches me for several long moments. "I cannot begin to imagine the shame that surrounds how you were conceived, Melinoë."

My throat threatens to clog up, tears fighting to strain my eyes as one slips down my cheek. I realize at this moment that I haven't really processed this part of our family history, and how much of an impact it has on me.

"But that shame does not deserve to fall onto your shoulders."

I lift my gaze up to him.

"I love your mother fiercely, Melinoë. Without her, there is no reason, no driving force for why I do anything at all. My life would simply cease its purpose entirely." He pauses as his gaze softens, becoming distant for a moment before bringing himself back. "I accept Persephone for everything she is, including the things that she has fallen victim to. Things that were not her fault." His jaw ticks subtly before smoothing out again. "And part of accepting Persephone wholly, is also accepting her children as if they were my own. An oath that I'll never regret making."

I stare at him for a few moments as his words register within me. The tension that begins to coil within my heart and my belly tightens, threatening to suffocate me with his admission. The will to form a response escapes me as a sudden need to vacate the room overwhelms me.

He's no different from Zeus. We cannot trust him.

The voice inside my head badgers me to lift those protective barriers, a former false security blanket that promises to soothe me once more.

I quickly rise from the couch. I meet his gaze as I nod towards my empty glass on the table. "Thanks for the whiskey." I say tersely, before willing a portal to open.

As The Guardian's Palace comes into view in the center, I remain faced forward as I stride towards it.

"Melinoë, I apologize if I said anything—"

Before he can finish his sentence, I hurriedly walk through the portal until my feet hit my living room floor.

Once the portal closes behind me, my knees tremble as they threaten to sink me to the hard floor. A moment before I give in, I hear someone walk towards the entryway.

Bright copper hair bounces into the room, her hazel eyes gleaming against the brightness of the late afternoon sky as it peeks through the windows.

"If you're looking for Dimitri, he's not here." I say, immediately hating myself for how sharp my retort sounded.

She slows her approach, presumably at the sight of how rigid my posture is. She tilts her head slightly. "Actually…I was looking for you."

My eyebrows scrunch together briefly. "Why?"

She shrugs a shoulder, her stare unmoving. "I heard what happened when you tried to retrieve your sister, and I thought maybe you needed a friend."

The breath from my lungs, though suddenly hardened in unnecessary defense, escapes me entirely. My stiffened back relaxes as it subtly bows forward, my jaw unclenching as it loosens. Like a tidal wave that washes over me, crashing my defense mechanisms at the sound of one simple word.

Friend.

My lips tremble as tears rush from my eyes. A strangled laugh leaves me as I brush the dampness from my cheeks away.

Nora rushes to me with no hesitation. I wrap my arms around her instantly as we embrace one another. As the sincerity from Hades voice rings in my head, confusion for how he may have overstepped.

And as the guilt for pushing him away expands, so do Nora's arms as she embraces me just a little tighter.

At some point Nora and I took to raiding the liquor cabinet. Shoving away bottles of whiskey, bourbon, and rum. We both laugh at the insane amount of booze that this palace has for just two people.

Having settled on a bottle of sweet red wine, I lean over to top off Nora's glass. I set the bottle on the ground next to us as I swirl the dark red liquid in my glass.

Our backs lean against the couch, legs sprawled out in front of us on the floor. She crosses a leg over her other before a drunken laugh tears from her lips. "Do you think he still thinks about that day?"

A laugh creeps from my throat, a nice change from the crying that was earlier. I have the wine to thank for the change in my mood, and also the company of Nora, too. "I sure hope so."

She snorts. "Maybe now he will think twice about being a creep to women in parks."

We both share a deep bellied laugh, the reminder of that man in Hellen Park I made hallucinate still fresh in my mind. As if that day was just yesterday.

At the sound of footsteps coming from the hallway, Nora and I look up to find Reimus and Dimitri walking into the living room.

Reimus chuckles, his gaze immediately on me. "Drunk before dinner has even been served? Looks like we missed out." He nudges Dimitri.

Nora laughs. "Melinoë was just telling me about her wondrous gift of mind manipulation."

"Did she tell you she used it on me the first time we met?" Reimus says, grabbing two glasses before pouring two earfuls of whiskey in them. He hands Dimitri one before he leans against the mantle.

Nora gasps, nudging me. "You did not."

I chuckle. "It wouldn't have mattered. It didn't work anyway."

"I would have loved to hear it nonetheless." She sips from her wine. "For Fates sake, I would give anything to see that."

Dimitri rolls his eyes at her, his voice low as he grins at her. "You would love that wouldn't you?"

I watch Nora still at his words, fighting the smile curving on her lips.

"The question is why was I able to get into Dimitri's mind, but not yours?" I look up at Reimus.

"Because Dimitri was in a weakened state. His protective barriers weren't strong enough in place, which allowed you to sneak in."

I tilt my head. "As in a shield—but for your mind?"

Dimitri nods. "The Draghi learn at a very young age to shield. Because one who knows how to enter our minds, knows how to see what's within. Who can later use it against us."

"Interesting." I say before bringing the wine glass to my lips.

Nora leans into me, whispering into my ear. "If you ever get the chance again, promise you'll let me know what's lurking in that big head of his."

"I heard that." Dimtiri sighs.

Nora and I giggle to one another, an energy coursing between us. A bond that's beginning to strengthen and blossom.

Aven comes into the living room, his hands tied behind his back. He nods to Reimus and Dimitri. "Good evening lads! Shall I prepare dinner for the living room tonight?"

I look over at Reimus, admiration glistening in his eyes. He gives me a wink before turning towards Aven. "Yes, please. Thank you."

As Aven ushers in trays of grilled chicken sections, tangy potato salad, and crispy baked potato skins, conversation fills the air around us as the four of us spontaneously decide to eat dinner tonight on the living room floor.

Reimus seated to my right wipes his index finger along the crease of my lips, a hint of potato salad on his finger. He dabs it onto my nose, wringing a laugh from me. I wipe it away with a cloth napkin when he kisses me softly. He pulls away, that handsome smile lighting his face.

"Gods, get a room." Nora scoffs.

I grab the last chicken wing from her plate, taking a bite.

Her gaze shoots to mine. "Rude. I was going to eat that." A smile curves up the side of her lips as she reaches over to Dimitri's plate, swiping one of his. When he swivels to look at us, we both burst out laughing.

As the four of us eat, drink, and laugh together, I feel myself shamelessly soaking up this moment.

Understanding sprouting within, shedding light on that abandoned part that nestles deep inside of me. That demands to protect itself from everyone around me, but simultaneously wants nothing more than to be loved and included.

I look up at Reimus, my gaze softening on him as gratitude fills me. For his patience in giving me the space to actively work towards fighting my fears.

The space to actively work and heal those parts of myself that forget my worthiness to be happy.

CHAPTER 21

The warmth of the setting sun gleams against Alastor's mane, those fiery orange hues like welcomed brands along my back. I watch as sheddings of his coat fall to the ground, dark strands that extinguish the green terrain beside my black boots.

Nora left shortly after dinner, so I found myself coming out to Alastor's pasture.

I swipe the soft brush along his side, the comforting presence of him soothing my anxious heart. Because in a few hours, I'll be meeting with Hecate, to once again astral travel to my sister.

I exhale audibly as I confide in Alastor. "I never wanted her to suffer."

He whinnies as he lifts his head.

My paranoia the closer I get to midnight unravels deeper and deeper. How will my sister be when I see her again tonight? Hecate said that her spell would keep her feeling calmer, but to what extent?

He turns his head, nudging his nose into my side.

I finish brushing him and set the brush back into his bucket. Stepping in front of him, I bring my hand up to rub his neck.

"She's being revealed the truth of our lineage. Unfortunately, she cannot run from it either. It's the kind of weight that you're forced to bear, whether you want to or not."

I feel the familiar presence of Reimus behind me, like a warm cloak on tired skin. His scent of patchouli and sandalwood wafts toward me before I hear him open the pasture gate. Fully aware he's been silently standing there for a few minutes now, only deciding to break his silence to let me know he's near.

He latches the gate shut before walking towards me. I feel the brush of his calloused hands pull my hair back, gently caressing the strands behind my ears.

Still facing Alastor, I give him one more rub down. "I was just about to come inside."

Reimus begins twirling my hair into a braid, a chuckle catching low in his throat. "I fear I just didn't want to be courteous and wait."

I laugh as the brush of his knuckles slides lower down the middle of my back. "Because of your desire to always be near me?"

Reimus finishes the end of my braid, his hand coming to tap my waist. The weight of his hand causes goosebumps to raise along my skin. He lowers his head to my ear, his voice low. "Always."

I turn to face him, my hands coming up to his chest. I stand on my tip toes and bring my lips to his. My hands sliding up his chest before wrapping around his neck.

He deepens the kiss, his hands roving along my waist for a moment before pulling away. "Come." He interlocks a hand with mine. "I want to show you something."

I say goodnight to Alastor, and we make our way back inside.

When we enter his room, he lets go of my hand. I study him as he steps inside his walk-in closet, heading toward his wall of hung shirts.

I cross my arms, tilting my head. "Are you going to dress me in one of your shirts again?"

He chuckles. "Not this time."

His deft fingers part the rack of shirts directly in the middle, pushing them away to reveal the bare wall. My eyes widen as my arms fall back to my sides when my gaze realizes the tall concealed door.

He places his hand in the center of it, mumbling a few words to himself. I watch as visible light flickers the perimeter around it before vanishing. The faint click of a noise is the only sound I hear before Reimus opens the door.

I take one step toward him when my hands cover the choked noise that escapes my lips. My knees give out on me as a tear slips down my cheek.

He reaches inside to retrieve the items before closing the door. He turns around to approach me, my gaze wholly focused on what he carries with him.

"I thought you might want to have these back."

He kneels down to the floor in front of me, my hands unable to cease their trembling as I grab Eiran's sword. My fingers immediately trace the ruby crystal at the center of the bronzed pommel, as vibrant as the day I first saw it.

My hand lowers to the hilt, the ash-colored lattice like tiny grooves against the beds of my fingertips. My gaze hesitates, the memory of his blood painted along the blade still fresh in my mind. I lower it tentatively, a choked sob creeping out of my lips.

"I cleaned and polished it." He says softly.

I grip the hilt in my hand. So much had happened since I arrived in Vulir, I was completely sidetracked from getting his things back from Reimus. "Why wait until now to give these back to me?" I lift my gaze to him.

His eyes shimmer like calm tides of the sea. "I didn't want to give them back to you until I had them properly cleaned. The blade itself started to rust with—" He pauses, narrowing his gaze before fixing it on me again. "I thought given everything going on, with your sister, that giving them to you now was when you might need them most."

I loosen my breath. I look back down at Eiran's family heirloom before my gaze fixates on the hunting bag in his other hand.

I drop the sword to the ground, a sob bursting from my lips as I reach for it. I bring it close to my chest, and a quick inhale has me turning my gaze back to Reimus.

He tilts his head, a frown pulling at his lips. "I had to wash it, along with his clothing inside. I'm sorry.

Everything was awfully muddy and soiled from the rain—"

"It's perfect." I say setting the hunting bag down. My fingers sliding the zipper down. I peer inside, my shaky hand lowering to grasp onto the dagger laying right on top. I pull it free, marveling at the freshly polished blade. I set it down before my hand sinks into the cotton material.

I pull the gray short-sleeved shirt out of the bag, my lips trembling uncontrollably as I cradle it to my chest. I breathe in deeply, uncaring that the scent of Eiran has been washed from his clothing. All that matters is that I have something physical of his left, something that cannot part from me.

I wipe the dampness from my eyes before setting Eiran's shirt and bag to the side. I look at Reimus, finding no trace of jealousy or uncomfortability within his eyes, but only that of genuine care churning. And in that moment, the tether that's been fortifying itself for months binds itself completely.

I close the distance between us, grabbing his face into the palm of my hands. "Thank you." He lowers himself to a seated position as I straddle him. "This means everything to me." I close the remaining distance, the fullness of his lips against mine deafening the room around us. With nothing to drown into but the feeling of his hands resting on my waist, and something deep within brimming wide open.

I pull my lips away, my eyes lifting to his. Reimus gazes at me admirably, his soft stare causing my belly to flutter. I lean in, brushing my lips against his softly. The taste of whiskey lingering on his lips. I drink him in, my tongue parting his lips open for me. My tongue makes long, slow strokes against his, savoring him.

His hands lower as he lifts us from the ground, moving us to his bed. He lays me down gently, his hard body resting on top of mine. My hand caresses his chest until I reach his waist, but I don't rush to take his pants off yet.

I want to take my time with him.

Our lips softly clash together as his hand skims up my leg, his thumb tracing my inner thigh. I arch my back into his touch as his thumb grazes higher and higher up. He lightly rubs along my leggings, until he's right at my entrance.

I gently push him up, heat radiating from his gaze. I lower my hands to slip off my leggings until I'm bare to my underwear. I go to lift off my shirt, when he grabs my hand. He brings my hand to his lips and kisses the inside of my palm.

He lowers his lips to my navel, slowly beginning his ascent up as his hands lift my sapphire shirt. My breasts become exposed to the cool air as he lifts the shirt over my head. His lips explore my skin longingly, as if he's mapping out every detail to my body.

His gaze meets mine again as he kisses underneath my breast, wringing a soft moan from me. His lips hover over my nipple, his soft breaths causing heat to pool low. His tongue laps around the hardened peak as I arch into him.

The weight of his hands spreading my legs apart like brands of ecstasy against my skin.

His finger lowers along my folds, my breathing growing ragged. Wetness pools through my underwear as his finger taunts me, wringing soft moans from my lips.

His lips close over my nipple, my back bowing off the bed. My fingers tangle themselves into his soft hair as I open my legs further for him. He grins against me as he sucks on that sensitive skin.

His finger slips through my underwear, slipping inside me slowly. "Please." I breathe.

He lifts his lips as he kisses up my neck. "Let me just listen to you for a minute." He says gruffly. I grind my hips forward, desperate to bring his finger further inside of me. Instead, his other hand holds my waist down, still making his slow departure in. "Let me drown myself in those beautiful sounds."

His finger slips halfway through, a cry of eagerness slipping from my lips. I push my head against the sheets, anticipation overriding me. I need to feel more of him.

I moan at the feel of him resuming his movement until his finger descends fully. He halts for a moment before slowly bringing it out again. I can feel myself dripping along his finger, ready to beg him for more.

He kisses my neck as his finger buries deep into me. A cry escapes me as he begins plunging in and out a fraction faster. I try to buck my hips into him, but his other hand holds me firmly down. I reach my hand to his pants, his hard cock swollen against them. He grunts at my touch before his finger slips out of me. His hands go to his pants, unbuttoning them before lifting his hips to slide them off. His cock heaves out as he lowers himself back down.

He slowly buries himself in me, his cock filling me wholly. His body trembles as he buries himself to the hilt, a moan escaping me. His hand comes up to my jaw, forcing my gaze on him. "You are everything." He slowly pulls out before burying into me again. His gaze piercing mine. "Everything."

And in that moment, I feel that tether stretch and expand as it interlocks itself with him.

He grinds against me, but not like how we normally fuck where it's hard and fast. No, this time it's different.

I tighten around him as his cock plunges into me, slowly as if he's in no hurry. As if this moment is all that we have, and he plans to savor it as much as I am.

I bring my hands to his jaw, forcing his lips onto mine. His tongue laps along mine, savoring and tasting me. I moan into his lips as his body grinds against mine, my hips moving with his. His hips press against mine, and I crave his touch more than I've ever thought possible.

His hand moves to my thigh as he hikes it up, allowing him to get deeper. He pulls his lips away as a cry tears from my lips. The feeling of him moving inside of me is not enough, and too much at the same time. My gaze fixates on his once more, his eyes slightly wide as he studies me.

He leans down to kiss the underneath of my jaw as he begins bucking into me. His pace grows feral as he fucks me harder, cries wringing from my lips. My orgasm chasing me, overriding my every sense. I scream as it takes over every nerve.

His body grows taught as he buries himself deep as he whimpers through his release inside me. I kiss his neck as he whimpers against my shoulder, his cock pulsating inside me. He stays buried inside for a few long moments before pulling out entirely.

He brushes the hair back from my face, kissing my swollen lips before walking to the bathroom. He returns with a towel, using it to clean us both off before laying himself behind me.

His arm wraps underneath me as he tugs me close to his chest, cradling me snuggly to him. The scent of him lulls me deeply as my eyes grow heavy with sleep. I burrow myself against his warmth, the pace of his heart like a familiar drum against my skin.

My breathing deepens as he begins running his fingers through my hair. Unable to stay awake any longer, I fall deep asleep.

CHAPTER 22

My still damp hair falls down the middle of my back as I pull on a clean black shirt. I bring the sleeves up to my elbows, flipping my hair over my shoulder when Reimus reaches for the brush in my hand.

"How are you feeling?" He says as he trails my hair back, gently beginning to work through my tangles.

"Fine."

He rests his other hand on my shoulder, the weight of it causing my shoulders to relieve their stiffness. I lower my shoulders, and unclench my jaw.

I meet his gaze in the vanity mirror, loosening a breath as he gives me a gentle gaze. "I feel afraid."

He continues brushing my damp long hair, moving up towards my scalp. The gesture comforting me.

His voice is calm when he speaks, his gaze lifting to mine. "Do you think she will come with you willingly?"

I bite my inner cheek, gaze narrowing. "I don't know. I think tonight I will just…sit with her."

He finishes brushing back my hair, setting the hairbrush on the vanity before gently turning me around. His hand raises as his thumb gently caresses my chin. I lift my gaze up to him. "Then for tonight just sit with her." He kisses my cheek, warming my skin.

I force a half grin. "I know I'm to bring her home, but will I know when is the right moment?"

His eyes glazed against the glow of the fireplace, his head narrowed slightly. "You'll know." He forces a grin.

I stare at him for a few moments, before bringing my lips to his. I kiss him once, then twice before pulling away. My lashes flutter open. "Thank you."

He nods as his grin deepens. "I'll see you in a while. You don't want to keep Hecate waiting." He winks.

A faint chuckle leaves my lips before pulling away entirely to head downstairs.

I enter the work room, Hecate standing precisely where she has since the first night we've met in here. As I approach her, I try my best to remain positive and not nervous for what kind of state my sister will be in. "Good to see you again, Hecate."

She nods, a smile on her face. "You as well, dear. Are you ready?"

I close the distance, my hands already raised out in front of me. "Yes. But tonight I just visit. I'll break the spell another night."

Hecate nods. "Of course." She reaches her hands out, interlocking hers with mine.

I close my eyes, beginning to center deep into myself. In a few moments, I find myself in my astral form, looking back at my physical body.

"Wow, that happened much quicker than usual."

I take a step back, willing a portal to open to take me to Makaria's bedroom. Once it materializes, I waste no time walking through it.

I step out the other side, Makaria sitting on the floor next to her bed. I close the portal behind me and slowly walk towards her.

"Makaria?" I whisper.

She keeps her gaze trained forward as if she didn't hear me. I begin to lower myself to the ground next to her, studying her. I take note of the broken fingernails and my heart plummets deep into my chest. I lift my gaze to her face, the underneath of her eyes sunken and gloom.

I tentatively reach my hand for hers. The force of my energy as it rests on top of her hand does not stir her. She merely sits there unfazed. "I'm so sorry." Both at what I had no choice but to reveal, and also for everything else she has yet to find out.

She doesn't stir at my energy. Her face lifeless and drained of any light.

I want to cry at my sister's pain, I want to be able to take it all away.

"I knew how he treated you."

I freeze internally, my chest caving in at her voice, raspy and broken.

"I knew and said nothing. Knew that if I admitted to Sebastian—" She pauses, working on a swallow. "Zeus treating you unfairly, that I'd also have to admit that I was the favorite. And I couldn't do it."

Her gaze lifts to mine. "And now what you said, about him putting a compulsion spell on me…where does that actually leave me? I've been trying to wrap my mind around it when I'm here, since I cannot remember when I'm awake."

My hand goes to squeeze hers, a tear slipping down my cheek. "I'm so sorry, Makaria."

Her blank face gazes at me, all emotions aside from despair wiped from her eyes. "So am I." She faces forward again, her astral body unnaturally still.

I lift my gaze up to her physical body, wrapped underneath the blankets of her bed. I peer up, finding the barrier of the spell snuggly around her. I study it, taking in the structure of it.

"That woman did something to me."

I bring my gaze back to Makaria. "Her intentions were only to help you."

"I know." She slowly pulls her hand from my grasp, raising it up in front of her face. She twirls her fingers slowly, her voice monotone. "I can feel it. The compulsion. It feels like…my energy suffocates against it."

I bite my lip, holding myself together for her. I clear my throat. "It will not suffocate you much longer."

She turns towards me, the semblance of hope in her eyes fleeting before it's wiped from her gaze entirely. "Will you be the one to free me?"

I fight back my tears, nodding my head curtly as I desperately reel in that fleeting spark of hope for the both of us. "Always."

Her eyes glisten as she nods her head faintly. "I will feel it all again, won't I?"

A tear slips from my eyes as I quickly brush it back. "I'm afraid so."

She exhales, a long moment of silence stretching between us. "Tomorrow." She turns her gaze forward again. "Tonight, I'd like to remain numb to it all before I'm forced to feel it all again."

I nod. "Whatever you need."

My sister gently leans her head against my shoulder, the energy stilling around her like a hollow vessel. I feel her energy pulsate for a brief moment before deafening once more. And as I sit with her on the hardwood floor of her bedroom, I'm greeted with nothing but the silence to comfort us.

CHAPTER 23

I find myself unable to move from my seat. The plate of scrambled eggs, bacon and mixed fruit is now empty in front of me. My fingers tap along my mug, only a sip of coffee now remains inside. My nails against the ceramic mug fighting to distract the noise circulating inside my head.

Today is the day my sister comes home to me.

"Melinoë."

Reimus' voice jogs me from my thoughts, pulling my gaze to him.

He watches me, setting down his mug. "I was supposed to do a check in with Dimitri today at The Sanctuary. I think I'll reschedule."

"No, it's fine." I down the last of my coffee, pushing my chair out from the table. "I have to see my mother today anyway."

"I thought she decided you no longer needed to mentor with her on how to portal?" He says gently, scooting his chair out as well.

"Not for that." As I walk away from the table he gently grabs me, urging me to face him. My gaze hardens on him before it softens at the angst in his eyes. I sigh deeply, my curt voice settling to something far more gentler as I relax in his grasp. "I have to prepare her."

His calloused hand comes up to brush my hair behind my ear. He nods. "But if you needed something—"

"I'll let you know." My gaze melts into his. "I promise." I lean up to kiss him, letting the warmth of his body soothe me before I pull away.

I watch his eyes light up as the portal materializes behind me, a grin curving up his lips. "Impressive."

I match his grin before turning around to face the portal to my mother's palace. I walk towards it, turning around before I step through it. "I'm impressive in many other ways, too." I wink before I turn back around, stepping through it. The portal closes behind me as Reimus' laugh stifles with it.

I walk through the hallway of the palace, heading for the kitchen where the faint murmurs of chatter linger. I step through the pristine kitchen, finding my mother seated at the table with Hades. She doesn't turn her head towards me, but waves her hand over. "Come sit with us, dear."

I walk over, Hades grabbing at a grape from my mothers plate. She swats at his hand as his face lights up with a smile. "You bastard, get your own." She scoffs playfully.

"But I want yours." He grins, tossing the grape into his mouth.

She rolls her eyes at him as I take a seat next to her. She turns towards me, her arms wrapping around me. She releases me, gesturing to the platters of food laid out. "Hungry?"

I shake my head. "No thanks. I just ate actually."

She gazes at me as she plops a grape into her mouth. Her previous smile begins to falter as a mothers knowing filters in her face. "Today is the day."

Like a mother's intuition, she sees right through me without me having to say a word. I nod. "Yes."

My mother works on a swallow as something akin to fear flashes across her eyes. Not fear for her daughter coming home, but for the detrimental fact that she will have to burden her with the truth of our upbringing.

Hades rests a hand along her back, as his gaze turns to me. "Are you ready?"

Shame begins to cloud me at our last interaction together when I stormed out on him. I wash that interaction away, saving it for another time to feel guilty about. "I am."

He smiles faintly as he nods. "Good." He leans in to kiss my mother on the cheek, loosening the tension in her body partially. She smiles against his affection as he stands up from his seat.

When he grabs his and my mothers empty plates, he sets them in the sink before exiting the room altogether.

Persephone turns to me as she takes my hands, cradling them into hers. "I was going to check on the souls this morning. Would you like to join me?"

I nod, grateful for the excuse for a momentary distraction. "Sure. I would like that."

As she stands in her blush silk pajama set, she snaps her fingers and instantly changes into a floral summer dress. The ruffles at the ends fall to right below her knees, the violet sleeveless dress hugging her perfectly.

I look down at myself, clad in black leggings, and a white short sleeved shirt. I chuckle. "Well, it looks like I'm dressed down now."

She laughs as she snaps her fingers, a gasp leaving my lips as she changes my outfit.

I look down at the deep, saffron orange dress as it pools down to my knees. My fingers trail the silk material that glides along my body like water. Straps that connect around my neck, plunging my breasts up. I look down at my talisman still hanging around my neck. "You didn't change my necklace."

"Hecate would be most displeased if I did." She chuckles. She stretches her hand out to me. "Come, they're waiting."

I take her hand as she manifests a portal for us to The Asphodel Meadows. We step through it onto the grassy terrain, people meandering about.

Suddenly, a soul sees my mother and gasps with glee. "Queen Persephone!" He starts rushing towards my mother, as a few other souls follow his excitement over.

I stand back, unsure of how to interact with them. I watch as my mother lights up from their presence. She greets many of them with a warmth to her that I've never read of queens having in my childhood stories.

A woman peers over the small crowd that's gathered. She approaches me. "Are you Melinoë?"

I nod. "Yes, I am."

She gasps, bringing her hands up to her grinning lips. "It's her!" She yells before falling to a knee, and bowing her head.

The small crowd gathers now around me, and follows the woman's same gesture. They all, one by one, bow to a knee. "We are so honored to finally meet you."

My breath hitches as I meet my mothers gaze, scrunching my brows at the grand gesture. She nods her head, insinuating that they will stay kneeling until I tell them otherwise.

I clear my throat. "You may rise."

They all rise, the woman clasping her hands. "Would you enjoy a cup of tea? Oh please say yes! I have been *waiting* to meet you."

Persephone chuckles. "She would love one. Thank you, Shyla."

Shyla begins storming into a nearby home as the others talk amongst one another before the crowd disperses. I step next to my mother. "I am not their Queen, so why did they bow for me?"

She tilts her head, smiling. "Because you are their keeper, their Guardian. Aside from myself and Hades, you are the only goddess they will bow to."

I loosen my breath. "Goddess of Ghosts."

Persephone nods, grinning. "Guardian of Souls."

Shyla comes back with a cup of chamomile tea, the heat warming my fingertips. I watch her excited gaze as I take a sip from it, licking my lips. "This is lovely. Thank you."

She smiles widely. "Can I show you around? It would be a great honor."

I look over to my mother as she nods faintly. I look back at Shyla. "I would love that."

She reaches her arm out, interlocking it with mine as she guides me forward. She begins guiding me through The Asphodel Meadows, souls waving at me as she does. Many of them fell to their knees, some of them with shock written on their faces.

She talks to me as if she's known me her entire life, not an ounce of apprehension apparent. She tells me all about how she spends her time, which mainly consists of tending to her garden and knitting. She introduces me to a few of the souls, one of them named Irwin. He begs to show me the sprouting of his tomato patch, pride swimming in his eyes at his little garden.

I laugh as he tells me his garden is better than Shyla's, in which she sticks her tongue out at him. I admire the vibrancy in their smiles, a particular liveliness that even death cannot take away from them.

I watch these souls one by one, talk to me as if I've been a longtime friend to them. A friend that they admire, respect and trust. My heart begins to swell at all of the attention from these kind souls, and it causes something deep within me to spark.

Where suddenly I begin to feel this deep gravitational pull towards these souls, towards ensuring their safety. A strong internal knowing that my home and my heart cannot just belong to Vulir. That my heart in some primal way, now belongs to these people as well. As the title of who I am begins to flourish and mature within me.

CHAPTER 24

After spending the afternoon getting to know some of the souls, and being led around The Asphodel Meadows, I finally bid my mother farewell—for now.

She brings me into her warm embrace, before pulling away again. Her emerald eyes are steady as she narrows her head. "I will wait for your return."

I nod. "How will you know when we've made it back?"

A half smile curves faintly up her lips. "I'll know." She tucks a loose strand back behind my ear.

I step back as I materialize a portal to appear behind me, the effort of it seeming to become little. I force a smile on my lips. "I'll see you soon."

She nods before I turn around to step through the portal, back into the dining room of The Guardians Palace. The portal closes behind me as I halt, staring at what lies on top of the long table.

Clear pedestal vases traverse up the center of the table, filled with baccara roses and lush greenery. I approach the table, my fingers coming up to the first vase placed at the center. A smile crawls up my face as I lean down to brush my nose against the petals. Inhaling deeply, I let the sweet scent fill me as joy beams in my chest. I lift my face when I hear footsteps.

Aven walks into the room, halting in his stride as he sees me. "Melinoë! You're back!" He approaches me, glee evident on his face as he cups his hands up to his chest. "Do you love them?"

I chuckle softly. "Yes, they're wonderful. Did Reimus put you up to this?" I smirk.

He chuckles. "I would be lying if I said he didn't. Did you see the rest of the palace?"

My smirk remains as my brows raise. "There's more?"

"Oh! You must see." He gives me a wink before he interlocks his arm with mine, and strolls us out of the dining room. We step out into the hallway and my eyes widen.

Mounted along the hallway walls are glass planter vases, the detailing in the glass exquisite and pristine. The mounts itself hang on the walls like golden filigree, subtly hidden by the fern-like greenery busting out of the glass vases. Baccara roses fill each vase, painting the hallway in beautiful shades of dark red.

I gasp, my hands coming up to my mouth when we enter the living room, vases of baccara roses everywhere. On the mantel, on the coffee table, on the walls. My head swims at the abundance of my favorite flower as I turn around, gawking at it all.

"There are more upstairs as well." Aven says, reminding me of his presence.

I turn towards him, my mouth still gaping open. "He did all of this?" I say breathlessly.

Aven smiles, nodding enthusiastically. "Indeed he did."

I laugh as my eyes fight to dampen. "Why?"

"Do I need to have a reason?"

I turn around to see Reimus standing in the doorway, clad in tapered black pants and a black button up shirt. His sleeves rolled up to his elbows as his muscles strain against the shirt. His gaze pierces into mine before narrowing down to my dress. His gaze lowers slowly as he takes in every crevice of my body, causing my skin to crawl in a desirable way.

Aven steps around, excusing himself. "Dinner will be ready within the hour." He begins walking toward the doorway as Reimus leans off the wooden frame.

"Thank you, Aven." Reimus says, his voice low and thick. Aven gives him a pat on the shoulder before he makes his way to the kitchen.

I begin to close the distance between us. "You know, I would've been just as happy with *one* vase of roses."

He chuckles deeply, approaching me as he runs his fingers through my long hair. He shrugs. "One vase didn't seem enough."

He rests his hand on my cheek, his thumb grazing my skin as I lean into it. My lashes fan open as I peer up at him.

He gazes at me for a few moments, longingly as if I'm the only person in his entire universe. He sighs, chuckling again. "One vase was definitely not enough."

I gaze up at him, his striking blue eyes like vessels I want to fall deep into. I raise onto my toes, closing my eyes as I brush my lips against his. I wrap my arms around his neck as he wraps my legs around him, picking me up. His hand is like a steady weight underneath me as he sets me on the couch.

Bringing me up to the edge, I gasp as I hold myself up with my elbows. "What are you doing?"

He lowers himself on the ground before me, spreading my legs to each side of his shoulders. He smirks at me. "I'm readying my dinner."

I laugh. "No interest in waiting for what Aven has prepared?" I say huskily.

He lowers his gaze, his eyes like heated brands on my center. "This is the only thing I'm interested in eating at the moment." He lifts his gaze to mine as he brings his hands up to slowly remove my underwear. The feel of the fabric against my skin suddenly bothersome as the cool air kisses my entrance. "If that's alright with you." He says as he kisses a knee.

My breath hitches at the touch of his lips, a taunting teaser of how they'll feel elsewhere in a moment. He slips my underwear completely off, and I instinctively spread my legs a little wider for him. "I suppose that would be fine." I say playfully, though the heat boiling my skin is eager for him to hurry.

He grins up at me as he lowers his lips to my inner thigh. I arch my back, wanting more. He brushes another kiss just an inch higher. "Good. I would've been displeased had you not obliged."

A soft moan leaves my lips as he nears the crease of my thigh. I look down at him, marveling at the view. This submissive side of him that wants to please, to worship me charges that inner goddess within. "Tell me how much you enjoy being on your knees for me."

His lips move to my entrance as he places a gentle kiss, his lips already shining with my wetness. I moan as his tongue slips out, tasting, exploring. I grip the leather couch cushions, my hands holding on to steady me.

His mouth hovers over my pussy as he looks up at me, wicked heat lining those perfect eyes. "Why tell you when I can just show you?" And his eyes remain on mine as he descends his mouth on me.

His tongue alternates between licking between my folds, and flicking my clit. My breathing quickens as I writhe against his mouth, soft cries coming from my lips.

I whisper breathlessly to him, my gaze darting to the open doorway. "I don't want Aven to hear me."

His gaze stays on mine, his tongue still tasting me as cum drips out of me. He lifts his mouth as he lowers his hand, a finger slipping slowly into me. "This is our palace. So I will fuck you," His finger enters me fully, before pulling out again. "And taste you whenever, and wherever I please." He kisses my clit again as his finger buries within me once more. "Is that understood?"

His finger thrusts in and out of me as I moan at the feel of him. "Yes." I hiss.

"Good girl." He lowers his mouth once more as his tongue begins circling my clit, his finger moving in and out of me.

I soon cannot keep myself quiet as the moans become screams of pleasure. I feel myself begin to tighten around his finger, my arms shaking subtly. I throw my head back as my breasts kiss the cool air, hardening the rosy peaks. And I know that his gaze has still not strayed from me.

I scream as my orgasm overtakes me, causing me to writhe ferally against him. He only grins against me.

It lingers, my mind overwhelmed with erotic delirium. I look down at him as he removes his finger, lowering his mouth to drink me in. I writhe against him as I cry out his name until my body falls limp.

He lifts his head, his lips glistening against the glow of the chandelier above. I reach an arm out, grabbing his shirt to urge him closer. His lips crash with mine as our tongues clash together, the sweet taste of me lingering between us. His hands cup underneath my jaw as I fall hard into him, letting him devour me whole as he shares the taste of me with him.

He pulls away, resting his forehead against mine. I feel a smile form against my brow. He opens his mouth to say something when he closes it again. He kisses me on the forehead, before reaching for my underwear. He slips them back on me then stands himself up.

He holds a hand out. "Now for Aven's dinner."

I laugh deeply as I take his hand, and notice his body stiffen slightly before smoothing out again. My smile falters as I peer up at him. "What?"

He shakes his head, a genuine grin reaching his full, now swollen lips. "Absolutely nothing." He says as he interlocks his hand with mine, the force of his touch alone is like a perk to my nerves. Energizing and waking them up after being asleep for a long, long time.

We make our way to the dining room, and for the entire duration of dinner I forget what lies ahead hours from now. I forget that my sister comes home, and forget about my impending worry of how everything will go. As if being in his presence makes everything else disintegrate from existence.

Since I've met Reimus I've found myself laughing more than I ever have, the curve in my lips making far more of an appearance these days. The capability to still find joy after drowning through the darkest waters is a gift that I will never take for granted.

I watch Reimus as he drinks from his whiskey, his gaze for once on something other than me. I gaze at him as he sets his glass down before lifting a fork. A calmness rests in his face, and a primal need within me stirs frantically that never wants to see anything other than that live on his handsome face.

And how I wouldn't hesitate to punish anyone for bringing him any ounce of misery.

CHAPTER 25

I stand at the center of the work room, five minutes prior to midnight. I resist the urge to engage with the energy of fear and worry, to pace anxiously around this room. Instead, I keep my feet planted firmly onto the ground, my chin up and back straight.

I breathe in and out, slowly and deeply. I focus on centering into myself, willing every ounce of courage still left in me to the surface.

Reimus steps closer to me, his hand brushing against mine. His voice is calm when he speaks. "I am with you."

I turn my head towards him, smiling faintly. I lift my pinky to graze his hand, a small unspoken gesture of appreciating the closeness of him right now. I nod before leaning in to kiss him.

After dinner I'd asked him the one thing I struggle to ask of anyone. Knowing by now that he's a safe space for me to lean on, a solid weight to carry me through any obstacle.

I'd asked him to be here with me tonight. In which he cupped my face between his calloused hands, and smiled at me softly.

"I planned on being nowhere else." He'd said. His eyes alight with that loyalty I've never had to question.

I pull away, facing forward again when Hecate portals into the room. She steps towards me, her face calm but stern.

She approaches me, clad in her infamous amethyst robe. She glances at Reimus, nodding before her gaze is on me again. "Are you ready?"

I nod, the fear suddenly clearing away as determination replaces it. "I'm ready."

"Do you remember the words?" She asks as she approaches me, her hands still at her sides.

I nod again. "I do."

She nods slowly. "Focus on that barrier, then chant those words. Don't stop chanting them under any circumstance. You'll know when it's been severed." She reaches her hands out to me, I hold them with my own. "Once it's been severed, she'll need to enter her physical body again. Come back here, and portal back to her in *this* body." She says squeezing my arm. "Then you bring her home."

I exhale deeply. "I'm ready."

Hecate nods. "You can do this."

I squeeze her hands as the surreal reality of finally reuniting with my sister overwhelms me. Not having to meet her just in the astral realm anymore, but being able to have her *here* with me. Out of the cruel binds of that power-hungry man.

The sudden wetness in my eyes fights to escape, but I reel it back. I'll save the crying for later.

I close my eyes, getting right to work. I breathe in and out, steadying my breath as I fall into myself. After a few moments, I'm stepping out of my physical body, and merging into my astral one.

I turn around, looking back at Reimus and Hecate. The gloom of the astral realm reminds me of the difference between being here, and in the realm of the living. A portal for Makaria's room materializes and I inhale deeply before stepping through it.

My feet step out onto her hardwood bedroom floor, my gaze lifting up to find her standing near the bed.

I take a step towards my sister, forcing a smile as I narrow my chin. "It's time."

She blinks at me, the bleakness still apparent in her eyes. She exhales raggedly, as if the reminder of feeling the pain of her fathers betrayal resurfacing is all she can think about.

I step towards her. "You will not face this alone." I look over at her physical body tucked in, sleeping. "I am right by your side through it all." I look up at her.

She loosens a breath as she nods. "Just do it. I don't want to be here any longer." Though she's still decently calm from Hecate's spell, her voice cannot hide the pain it truly feels deep down.

I step up to the bed, pulling back the sheets. My gaze focuses on Makaria's blush pink pajamas for a few moments before locking in with the spell barrier. I watch as the translucent barrier wraps snuggly around her, like cling wrap to a filet of meat. I latch onto it with my mind, and begin chanting the words.

I mumble those words over, and over, and over. It takes far longer than I thought it would, telling me the power in the spell is very strong. But I don't let it daunt me. I keep going.

After a long while, I finally hear it. A faint click as I watch the barrier suddenly snap off. It slithers off my sister in one fell swoop, like dust falling from a shelf. My eyes widen at the difference I can feel in her energy when it does.

I whip my gaze to her as I hear her stumble. She places a hand over her heart, her breathing beginning to smooth out entirely. "I—I feel it. It's gone." She looks up at me, her gaze weary as if she didn't truly believe she had a spell on her.

My gaze hardens onto hers. "Makaria, I need you to connect back to your physical body." I point to the bed. "All you need to do is reach your hand out and merge back."

"Okay." She says shakily as she steps up to the bed. I wait for the very last moment before I portal myself back, making sure she's safely merged with herself. She looks up at me, smiling faintly. "See you on the other side, sister."

I nearly choke on a cry, clenching my jaw to keep it together. I force a smile, knowing that there is still more that has to be revealed to her. But the excitement to have her home with our mother and myself again blazing that ember of hope within. "See you on the other side."

A portal materializes behind me, ready to enter it as soon as she emerges back into her body. I watch her reach her hand out, the tips of her fingers beginning to brush against her arm—

I watch as her astral body flings back into her physical one and I immediately jump through the portal. Racing back to my physical body, I sink back into myself, my eyes flinging open to gaze at Hecate.

She lets go of my hands, her gaze wholly on me. "Now, Melinoë!"

I immediately open another portal, back to her bedroom and rush through it. I keep it open behind me as I behold my sister sitting upright in her bed. Distress written on her face.

I rush over to her, knowing she will not remember our interactions while in the astral realm, but I can't afford to explain everything right now. Not until we've made it back.

She stares at me, her eyes going wide as I hurry over to her. "What are—"

I grab her without hesitation, dragging her out of the bed. She yells at what I can only imagine is my not-so-gentleness, but I do not care.

I only care about getting her out of here, once and for all.

I drag her by the arm to the portal, her eyes stricken with confusion. She gapes at the shadows that slither around the portal, utterly silent.

We approach the portal and my head whips back towards the door. The faint sound of deep laughter raises the hair on my neck, a cold sweat threatening to balm my skin. I turn to her, my grip tightening out of sudden panic. "Hold onto me." Without giving her a moment to ask questions, I wrap her arms around my waist as I guide us through.

As we step out onto the dining room floor, Makaria tumbles to the ground. She begins panting heavily as she gazes frantically around the room. I step towards my sister, kneeling to the ground with her. "Makaria."

I go to reach my hand out to turn her towards me when she swats at me. I retract my hand as her eyes finally lock onto mine. The pure terror shining within them causes my heart to lurch out of my chest. "What's going on?" She screams, her voice trembling.

My body freezes itself to the ground, unable to move from this very spot. Sorrow engulfs me at the thought of having to explain everything to her again. "Makaria, I know that this is all very confusing right now. Let me explain—"

"Who are you?" She shrieks.

My entire body goes ice cold, a numbness stifling the very breath from my lungs. The feeling of my knees sinking into the rug beneath me suddenly akin to pins and needles sinking into my bones.

I shake my head slowly, dread draining the color in my face entirely. Draining the courage in my heart.

My lips tremble as I fail to find words other than one in particular. "W—what?" Disbelief robbing my thoughts entirely.

Hecate kneels down next to me, Makaria scooting away from us entirely. I feel Hecate's presence, her energy leaks into mine and tells me she is just as confused as I am.

I cannot move.

"Why did you take me? Please—don't hurt me." She screams as she begins hysterically crying. Her face crumples up as she hikes her knees up to her chest.

As I kneel there my gaze maps her every frantic breath. The pure terror in her eyes.

Terror for *me*.

The energy stirs behind me as Makaria's face gapes open. I don't have to turn my head to know who it is.

Her eyes gaze at our mother wildly before she shakily stands up onto her two feet. Her knees tremble as she sobs violently. "Mom?"

My gaze tracks her as she sprints to our mother. I watch as they embrace one another, Persephone sobbing just as uncontrollably as Makaria is.

I shake my head slowly, unable to understand. "I don't get it." I mumble out, my lips suddenly feeling heavy against my face.

My mother turns her head back towards me, her sobbing quickly lessening as she takes in my blank face. Her eyes fixate on my posture, and then my energy. She turns her head back to Makaria, taking her face into the palms of her hands. "Makaria, do you know that woman over there?"

She turns around, terror stark on her face. She shakes her head frantically. "No. She grabbed me, brought me here. I—"

And in that moment, I completely drone out to everything around me. As I sink down from my knees to my bottom, the dining room floor feeling weightless below me. As if I might sink right through the floorboard, and into the void that currently surrounds my body and my mind.

As my sister stares at me, with terror instead of relief in her eyes. Having absolutely no clue who I am.

Michelle Rossa

PART II

CHAPTER 26

My narrowed gaze upon the glowing flames ensnares my bones. The heat evading from the fireplace melts itself against my face, the only indication I'm still able to feel anything at all.

My arms rest limply at my sides, mimicking the weakness burrowing inside my chest. I'm not sure how long I've been standing here, but I cannot let myself move. If I do…

The breath in my lungs begins to feel foreign, unable to feel the rise and fall of my own chest. I feel the glide of someone else's skin graze my hand.

"Melinoë." Hecate nearly whispers. Never once in my time of knowing her have I ever heard her sound pained.

I do not look at her.

If I move, I will fall apart.

She speaks quietly again. "I did a clarity spell." I hear her work on a swallow, a sign of nervousness that is wholly unlike Hecate. "It appears that her…forgetfulness is as a result of breaking her compulsion."

I keep my gaze trained forward. Listening to her words, fighting for control on my legs to keep them from buckling. A tear streams out against my resistance, clenching my jaw as the devastation builds within me.

"It is not permanent. She will remember in time, we just do not know how much time it will take. Or what can be done to fix it."

My lips begin to tremble as I clench my fists. I feel the sting of my nails scrape into my palms as I welcome the pain. A brief distraction from the pain rippling inside of my hollow chest.

Hecate's gentle hand comes up to rest on my shoulder. She rests it there for a few moments, unsuccessful with stifling the growing tremor in my body. She pulls away silently before she begins to walk away.

"I heard him."

I hear her footsteps halt, the turn of her body as she looks towards me.

"Before Makaria and I stepped through the portal, I heard Zeus laughing. The faint echoes of it at least." I loosen the grip on my fists, opening and closing my fists at my sides. "I remember thinking to myself 'if he knows I'm taking Makaria, why isn't he stopping me? Why find humor out of this if he hates me so much?'" A broken laugh leaves my lips, full of anything but amusement. "He knew I'd do absolutely anything for Makaria, so he used it against me. I played right into his hand." I lean forward, bringing my hands up to perch onto the mantle. My fingers dig into the wooden detailing.

Hecate steps towards me. "She will regain normalcy. I will—"

"You'll do *what*? Mentor her?" I seethe as my gaze finally whips towards her, cold and hard as ice. "She is *terrified* of me. My own sister thinks I *kidnapped* her. It doesn't matter. Nothing fucking matters anymore!" I roar as I turn away from the fireplace.

I bend down towards the coffee table, snatching the vase of roses and hauling it far across the room. The glass vase shatters against the wall, water dampening the hardwood floor as the dark-red flowers scatter.

Red-hot agony mutes my mind as I stride over to another vase. My hands pry it from its mounted home on the wall, hauling it against the floor. I go to the next one and destroy that one.

Again.

And again.

Until familiar hands wrap around me, clearing my mind from the fog of despair. I turn around and begin slamming my fists into his chest as devastation surfaces fully, demanding for me to feel it.

"He'll never let me free! I'll never be free of him!" I scream as I cease my thrashing in Reimus' hold, before my knees give out completely and I stumble to the ground.

I bang my fists against the ground, agony stinging my skin as my fists meet the broken glass shattered all around me. Uncaring of the pain I'm inflicting in my hands, desperate to feel any kind of pain to distract me from the agony in my heart. I slam my fists against the ground again.

And again.

And again.

Until Reimus catches my wrists, holding them in place firmly. I open my eyes and watch as trails of crimson streaking down my wrists now slithers between his fists.

"Melinoë." A pained roughness to his voice.

I lift my dampened eyes. I watch as a tear slips down his cheek, a show of his deep worry and sadness for me. My lips tremble before I wail on a harsh cry.

He reaches his hands under me, lifting to cradle me against his chest. His lips press against the top of my head repeatedly as he rocks me in his embrace.

I cry in his arms for a long while as his warm hand caresses my arm and back. I finally open my eyes, narrowing my gaze to my hands. I stare at the dried blood now crusted onto my skin before lifting my gaze to the room around us. To the shattered glass scattered around the room, to those beautiful baccara roses submerged in puddles of water.

As if my heart could weigh any heavier in my chest, it sinks a little lower as I realize what I had done.

I shoot up into a seated position, my gaze locking onto his. A choked cry leaves me. "It's—everywhere. I'm so sorry." My lips tremble at the disaster I've created, out of the wonderful gesture that Reimus did for me.

"I don't care about the mess." He says as he pushes my hair back from my face. "I will get you a hundred more of those roses. They can be replaced, your well-being cannot."

He leans back slightly before he lifts the shirt off his back, crumpling it into his hand. He uses his other to inspect my hands, checking for any possible glass protruding out of my skin. I watch a franticness come alive in those eyes, a steady determination as he uses his own shirt to wipe the blood off my hands.

I hear the crunch of glass as I look up to see my mother stepping towards me. Her eyes both swollen and red, similar to mine.

Reimus finishes cleaning what he can, at least until I can wash up. He helps me to stand up as a patch of glass around our feet disappears. My gaze lifts up to my mother, her eyes alight on mine.

She lifts her hand and with a gentle wave of her wrist, the entire room gets put back together again. The vases exactly where they were, all filled with those baccara roses. The existing broken glass and puddles of water on the ground now completely gone.

I swallow, shame coloring my voice. "Thanks."

She steps up to me, her hands cupping my face gently. She exhales raggedly. "I had no idea, Melinoë. I didn't even think for a second that Zeus would have enchanted the spell to have this effect on her."

I peer around her before lifting my gaze back to her. "Does she know everything now?"

Persephone nods her head curtly. "She does." A deep agony floods my mothers eyes.

"Does she…" My words trail off as I can't even finish the sentence. The question of whether my sister wants to see me or not, the moment I've been waiting months for. A bleak fever dream that came and never went.

She steadies her gaze, sorrow painfully evident. She closes her eyes before opening them again. Loosening a shaky breath. "She needs time."

Knowing everything that's probably clustering her mind, I don't blame her for needing space to sort through her thoughts. Though it still hurts greatly that my sister doesn't want to see me.

For I'd envisioned this to go far more differently.

My lips tremble as tears surface again. I nod my head vaguely. "How is she ever going to remember me?" I choke on a cry as my mother wraps me in her arms.

I hear her sniffle into my shoulder. "I will make sure she does." She pulls away, her cheeks dampened. "Whatever it takes, it will be done."

I exhale shakily, narrowing my gaze.

My mother wipes the tears from her eyes, straightening her shoulders. "She's going to stay with me for a while, while she processes everything. In the meantime I need to speak with Hades, figure out if he knows how to help get her memory back."

I nod, defeat slumping my shoulders.

She gently squeezes my arms before turning her head as my sister walks into the room.

She tentatively approaches us, her gaze roaming cautiously over me. I watch as she studies me, akin to someone studying a stranger on the street. The puzzled look on her face threatens to snap my very bones in half.

She stares at me blankly, her own despair coloring her energy.

Persephone looks at me. "I will return tomorrow with any updates. Get some rest, if you can." She materializes a portal behind them, my sister turning around gasping at it.

I simply nod my head, exhaustion plaguing the capability for anything more as of right now.

I stand there as I watch as my mother and my sister walk through the portal to The Underworld. My sister staring at me the entire time warily until it closes.

I look over at Hecate, standing and waiting patiently.

I approach her. "I'm sorry for snapping at you."

She tilts her head. "No need to apologize."

I force a weak smile, a faint nod following.

"Let's reconvene tomorrow." Her hand reaches out for mine, gently squeezing it before pulling away. She makes to exit the living room, her amethyst robe billowing behind her.

Reimus approaches my side as I turn my gaze towards him. I reach my hand out to his, desperate to feel his warmth. He lowers his head to press a soft kiss to my cheek. I lean into his shoulder as he brings our conjoined hands up to his chest. He presses another soft kiss, this time on my crimson stained knuckles. "Let's go wash up."

I nod my head as we walk upstairs, my feet heavy beneath me with each step that I take.

CHAPTER 27

It's not permanent.

Hecate's words echoe within the walls of my head as Reimus washes the blood from my hands. My shoulders slump forward as I perch on the edge of the counter, my gaze trained to my hands. I watch the dampened fabric weave through my fingers, staining the towel a crimson hue.

"How can she know?" The first words I've spoken in the past thirty minutes creep wearily through my lips.

Reimus keeps his gaze trained on my hand. "If Hecate says it's not permanent, then I trust her word." He turns on the faucet, rinsing the rag under the water before turning it off again. He wrings it out before cleaning my hands a third time.

The blood has been removed by now, but I still do not interrupt his concentration. "I can't imagine it will be easy to fix."

His jaw clenches as the towel slows its tender exploration. He remains silent as he finishes another round of washing my hand, setting the towel on the edge of the sink. His gaze lifts to mine. "He deserves no mercy for what he has put you and your family through. And I will gladly show him none when that day comes."

My eyes bore into his. "He is a god, Reimus. It'd be nearly impossible to kill him."

His shoulders loosen as a calm, wicked grin curves his lips. "But not entirely impossible."

He steps in front of me, pushing my hair back behind my ear. He kisses my forehead before taking my hand, helping me off the counter. We walk out of the bathroom towards the bed.

As I strip off my clothes, I pull on a magenta silk sleep set. Running my fingers underneath a thin strap, I turn around towards Reimus who's already changed into a pair of black sweatpants. "There has to be a catch. A way for her memory to come back."

He lifts his shirt, tossing it into a nearby hamper. "What do you suppose it is?"

I lift back the covers, crawling underneath them as Reimus joins me. I lower myself down until my elbow rests on a silky pillow, my head propped on my hand as I face him. A long exhale leaves me as I shake my head. "I don't know."

He mimics the same stance as he lays his free hand on the bed. "Let's wait to see if Hades has an answer."

I lay my hand down on top of his, my gaze following as I graze the top of his hand. "I don't get it. If Zeus was truly trying to punish me, why wouldn't he make her memory loss permanent?"

His thumb lifts up as he trails it along my skin. He tilts his head, his gaze narrowing. "Maybe he thought the hope of her memory coming back was a greater pain, then having the closure of knowing it wouldn't return at all."

My wary gaze searches his before narrowing. "Yeah. Maybe." I say, the strength to even form words seeming to be a great challenge.

"We will figure it out."

I nod vaguely, my face drained of any enthusiasm.

He lifts his hand, gliding his fingertips up my arm. His touch energizing the tired nerves in my body, like a siren's song that lures them to awaken from their slumber. "Talk to me."

I lift my gaze to his, those blue and silver eyes persuading me to fall into his comforting embrace. Each pass of his index finger along my arm further coaxing those vulnerable thoughts out of me. Not because I have to, but because I am safe enough to do so. A safety I never thought I'd find in someone again after Eiran.

Through my exhale, I let go of my hold on taming my emotions down. My lips tremble as I blow out a breath, wetness escapes my eyes. "I have lived my whole life knowing my father didn't love me. I lived it, dealt with it, and it will be a burden I will always carry deep within. But if I must walk this existence with my sister never remembering who I am? Then I do not know how I will survive this."

The anguish in his eyes blazes as he watches me. He remains silent as I pour myself to him.

"Makaria and I were never close, at least not in the way I wish we were. When it became real that I was going to free her, I decided I wanted to strengthen that bond. After Eiran died, I realized how much time I wasted pushing the people I loved away. So I told myself that once Makaria was home here with me, that I would give us a fair chance to become closer." I choke on a cry as Reimus brushes my tears away. "But now I only wonder if I'll ever be able to have that chance. I wonder now if I am too late."

I sob as Reimus pulls me into his embrace, wrapping his arms around me as my tears hit the hard planes of his chest. He kisses the top of my head, his voice low. "I promise you, we will find a way. I will do *anything* it takes for you to have that."

The tender glide of his fingers through my hair soothes me. I let his warm skin against mine slow my breathing, calming me once more.

He lifts my face up to his as the tears subside. "One day at a time." He kisses me softly before pulling me against his chest again.

I curl myself up to him, the warmth of his skin lulling me. As my roaring mind begins to quiet in his embrace, I find my eyelids growing heavy as they fight to remain open.

After a while of fighting with them, telling myself that I have no desire to sit still right now, I find myself losing the battle on that as well. As my eyes shut close and stayed that way, for the rest of the night.

The next morning after breakfast I found myself pacing the living room. Unable to contain my impatience for what Hades said when my mother spoke to him, my nerves began to get the best of me.

Reimus took to going into the village after breakfast, saying he'd be back later this afternoon. I'd kissed him deeply, a momentary reprieve for the anxious thoughts swarming my mind.

Looking over at the clock as it reads ten, I wonder at what time my mother planned to meet me. I begin to wonder if she must've forgotten. Or maybe she has terrible news and doesn't know how to share it with me yet?

As I exhale audibly, I wipe my clammy palms on my leggings. Shaking my hands off as I turn around towards the portal that now stands before me.

"Fuck it." I say as I walk through it, unwilling to wait any longer as I portal to her instead.

I step out onto the courtyard, the grass damp beneath my sandals. I take a step towards the doorway when I catch a glimpse of something from the corner of my eye. I turn towards it, finding what caught my eye to be a stretch of land far off on the other side of The Underworld.

I squint my eyes as I venture towards it, its view enlarging the closer that I get. I watch as roughly pointed shards of mountain tops come into view, dark against the glow of the colorful sky. Like pitch-black oil running down a clear spring of water. I notice the faint plumes of shadows that slither through the mountains, as if they taunt the very air itself around them.

I train my gaze forward, gasping as I realize I've reached the edge of their terrain. I look down at the edge of the cliff that overlooks the entirety of The Underworld. My gaze lifting up again, studying that far away landscape.

My gaze whips around as I feel the shift in energy behind me. I watch as Hades appears, his shadows slithering around him until they dissipate. "Careful. You would not want to fall into the river below."

My eyebrows scrunch together as I look back around, noticing the river at the bottom. "I didn't even notice." I say as I follow the length of the river. My eyes widen as it seems to travel endlessly. "Does it run through the entirety of The Underworld?" I ask as I turn towards him.

Clad in an all black suit, his dark hair loose and unbound. "For the most part, but not entirely. The River Styx is how the souls cross over when they enter The Underworld."

I walk towards him until we're a few feet apart. "So, they…swim across it?"

He chuckles. "Gods, no. That would be excruciating to watch. No, they are ferried across it by Charon."

"The same Charon who also guards the gate to Vulir?" Shock superseding my previous anxiousness.

He nods. "He is a gatekeeper for both the living, as well as the dead."

When I first met Charon I remember thinking there was something otherworldly about him. The way his black cloak merged into the air around him, like cotton candy dissolving onto your tongue.

I gaze back over my shoulder again at that faraway landscape. "What is that place?" nodding towards it.

"That would be Tartarus."

I turn my gaze back to him. "Do any of the souls live there?"

His gaze hardens on mine for a moment, before dissolving once more. "Tartarus is a place reserved for those who have done the vilest, wickedest of crimes. It is not a sanctuary, but rather a prison."

Goosebumps raise along my arms as my mind conjures up what my mother said the first day I reunited with her. "That's where The Titans reside then?"

Hades stills at the title, not out of fear, but of some kind of remembrance. After a few seconds, he nods his head. "Yes."

"What did they take?"

He tilts his head slightly.

"The Titans," I begin. "My mother said that they took something invaluable from her, that they will be punished there for their crime indefinitely. So what was it?"

Hades watches me, contemplating before he answers. "I'm afraid that is something your mother must answer."

Reminding myself to ask her about that another time, I focus on what I originally came here for. "Did she tell you then?" Finishing the sentence seeming unnecessary.

He nods slowly. "She did."

Anticipation causes my breath to become trapped in my lungs. "Do you know how we can reverse it?"

He narrows his head slightly. "I would need to further assess the magic that still lies within her to better understand how we can move forward."

"But I broke the spell? The magic is gone—"

"You did break the spell." He begins as he steps forward. "But the effects of that magic, what is causing her to not remember you, is still lingering within her. An additional maneuver of the spell."

I curse under my breath as my fists open and close at my sides. I exhale slowly, trying to tamper the growing rage. "Is she doing okay?" Unsure if I truly want to know the answer.

He watches me. "She's alright."

"Don't lie to me." I seethe.

Hades does not lash out or scold me. He simply watches me.

I square my shoulders as I stare at him. "You don't owe me anything, but do not lie to me. Tell me the truth."

His eyes soften for a moment as he lets out an exhale. "She's confused. She comprehends your mother when she tells her of the truth, but she's struggling to connect the dots. And—" He pauses, catching my gaze before starting again. "Aside from struggling with the memory loss of you, she grieves deeply for a father who wronged her."

My lips fight to tremble but I force them to steady. I inhale raggedly as I exhale my shakiness. "Will you tell me when she's ready to have company?" My voice cracks on my soft, but firm plea.

He nods. "I promise I will."

A tear slips from my eye as I quickly wipe it away. I nod as I will a portal to open. "Thank you for the update."

"Melinoë."

I lift my gaze towards him, his presence steady and unmoving.

"I'm deeply sorry for everything you have had to face. I am a stranger to you, and I am not owed an ounce of your time, regardless if I am married to your mother."

I wipe underneath my eyes as I watch him.

"But I want nothing more than to see you three happy. Especially for you."

"Why an emphasis on me?"

His stare does not falter from mine. "Because the things you have faced would cause a grown man to weep at his knees. And you deserve to witness the joys of life."

I turn my head to the side, composing myself. His words settle deep within me to a place that swells far beneath the pits of my soul. I find the glimmer of his words touch a wound that's bound itself to me.

For a moment, I feel the urge to resist what he's saying. To yell at him and tell him he doesn't know what he's talking about. But the part of me that desperately wants to be seen forbids me to, clutching onto that sliver of hope that Hades so willingly shells out to me.

A sliver of genuine care from a man who doesn't even know me but is so willing to give.

I nod, forcing a smile "Thank you." I say as I turn around and walk through the portal back to The Guardian's Palace.

CHAPTER 28

My feet step out onto the grass as the portal closes behind me. I make my trek across the lush terrain, heading for the pastures.

The echo of Hades' words slither through my mind as I make my way towards Alastor. The rising sun's warmth already begins to moisten my bare arms.

Thank gods only a few more weeks left until we're blessed with cooler weather.

With the pasture in view, I focus my gaze on Alastor when I feel his familiar energy suddenly behind me. I halt, sighing as I pivot to face him. "If you're here to tell me everything will be okay then I hate to say that about four other people already beat you to it."

Eiran gazes at me, a silhouette against the bright sky as a ghost of a smile appears on his face. "Then I will not be the fifth."

I stare at him as I step closer, feeling his energy pulsate before it dims again. I narrow my gaze as the previous frustration clears a fraction, deciding to change the topic. "I got your sword back."

"I know." He says calmly, his smile deepening.

I lift my gaze up to his. Sighing as my resistance fades away. "What am I supposed to do?" The unspoken words of my sister linger in the air between us.

He steps closer towards me, his shoulders sinking slightly. "All you can do unfortunately is wait."

I watch him get closer and almost reach my hand out to touch his, but reality keeps me reminded that I can't. "Why do I have this awful feeling that time is not on my side?"

He gazes at me for a few moments as his smile fades. He opens his mouth, hesitating before closing it again. "Time is usually not on our side when the end is not in sight. And I fear we are not close to the end. Not yet at least."

I furrow my brows. "What do you mean?"

He blinks. "I cannot explain it."

"You can't, or you won't?"

"If I reveal how things will happen, then I am breaking a law of The Fates."

I tilt my head. "Laws?"

He nods. "I'm surprised your mother or Hades have not filled you in on that yet. Considering who you are."

I shrug. "I've been a little preoccupied with trying to get my sister back. I'm sure The Fates will forgive me." I frown at the reminder of my sister's inability to remember me.

Eiran goes to reach out a hand, the silhouette of his energy brushing mine faintly. A gentle buzz that vibrates against my cheek. "I know you said you wished for me not to tell you everything will be okay, but in time, it will all come together."

I lean into his energy. "I wish you could just tell me how she remembers me. How can I get her memories back?"

He lowers his chin slightly. "You will know. Soon."

I sigh as I nod my head. "Is it lonely over there?" I ask as I bite my lower lip.

His energy sits, waiting calmly as he watches me. He shrugs a shoulder. "I guess that depends on who you ask. Some may say yes, but it is not for me."

"And why is that?"

His gaze, though one of a spirit now, pierces into mine as if he were still alive. "Because I get to watch over you."

My heart feels like it's being swallowed down to the pit of my belly. I frown at his words. "Because you won't fully cross-over."

He shrugs again. "I will enter The Underworld when I'm ready to. I have unfinished work here before I do."

I huff as I throw my hands up. "I don't understand how you have unfinished work here? If you wanted to just be around me and weren't ready to fully cross-over yet then just say that."

"I told you, it's not just that." He says quietly.

"Then what is it! What is so important that you won't let yourself eternally rest—" I shout.

"I *can't!*" He shouts as his energy pulsates for a single second before calming again. He exhales slowly before continuing. "I can't leave you. Not yet. But not for the reasons you think it's for."

My jaw unclenches and loosens its tension, my eyes softening their gaze. I work on a swallow as I exhale my frustration, knowing that I'm unfairly taking it out on him. "I'm sorry. I am grateful that I'm still gifted with this time to still talk to you, before you…" Have to drink from the River Lethe and forget who I am forever left unsaid between us.

He tilts his head. "There's no need to apologize." He reaches his hand again, the zap of energy reverberating against my shoulder. "Everything has its divine timing. Mine to enter The Underworld just isn't right now."

I gaze at him as I nod my head, forcing myself to believe him. Knowing that it can't be easy for him to completely accept that entering The Underworld means that he loses every memory he's ever had, an ironic fate to think about considering my sister has no idea who I am right now.

I hear Alastor whinny a few yards away from me. I turn my head to see him standing by the fence, his sights steadily on me. I chuckle to myself as I begin to turn myself around. "You know if I didn't know any better, I'd say that Alastor can see you right now."

Eiran chuckles as he peers over to look out at Alastor, before training his gaze back onto me. "He can. I visit him sometimes."

"Really?" I drawl, raising an eyebrow. "Well I'm glad you have someone other than me to talk to." I smirk.

He laughs. "Jerk. Be nice, or I'll send The Keres to pay you a visit."

"The Keres?" I ask, scrunching my nose.

"They're female goddesses of violent death." He makes a face akin to fear. "Let's just say they are not benevolent spirits."

My stomach churns at the thought of that. "Remind me to never allow myself to attract them then."

We both share a laugh as Alastor gives me another whinny. I loosen my breath. "I should get going. He may keel over and die if I don't give him attention right this moment." Sarcasm ridden in my words.

Eiran just gives me a smile, and nods his head. "I'll see you soon. *Spitfire*."

I gasp as I instinctively go to swat my hand on him, but I watch as it just glides through the air. My cheeks redden as heat warms them, a giggle creeping up my throat.

I will have to remind him of the decency of privacy the next time I see him.

Realizing for a moment that I truly am blessed to be able to know confidently, that I will see him again soon. And how not many are able to say the same.

I pivot on my heels as I walk towards Alastor. A smile curving up on my face.

After spending some time brushing and consoling in Alastor, I came back inside to utilize the shower. Gliding the brush through my damp hair as I perch myself on the bathroom counter, a restlessness takes over.

A bent knee bounces swiftly as my bare feet push against the ceramic sink. I bite my inner lip to try to relieve the pent up energy, unable to find that relief.

I set the brush down as I begin braiding my hair back. My arms begin to tire halfway through until they tie off the ends that rests along my waist. I pull a few tiny loose strands out, just in front of my ear as I turn my head to examine my handiwork. I lean closer to the mirror as I bring two fingers up to my temple, staring at my eyes. The emerald hue in them has always shone starkly, but I don't remember them being quite this vivid.

I turn my body before stepping off the counter, heading to Reimus—or rather, our bedroom. I can't imagine that I'll ever sleep in my old room again, when I find myself so comfortable sleeping here with him.

I walk over to the closet, peering at my clothing that Reimus moved over at some point. I shuffle through until I pause on an olive green, ankle-length ruffle skirt. I pull it out as I pull out a black strapless shirt. The articles of clothing that Reimus picked up for me the other day. I smile as I pull the clothing on, feeling still like myself but...pretty. Clothing I wouldn't normally wear but would like to start wearing more of. I twirl my waist as the skirt billows around me, my fingertips grazing the linen texture.

I plop myself onto the bed, realizing I have no idea what to do with my day. My knee begins to bounce again as I contemplate how I'll spend my time.

I could portal back to The Underworld to see if my mother has any updates. And probably look like a lunatic in doing so since I was just there not even two hours ago.

I sigh heavily as the thoughts begin to churn. What if I portal back there, and just wait outside of Makaria's door?

No, I can't do that. My sister deserves the privacy to grieve.

Shooting myself up from the bed, I mentally drudge those thoughts out of my head. Sitting here obsessing over them isn't going to help me. So, I decided on a different alternative.

I lean down to grab my black sandals, slipping my feet through them. Fastening the anklet, I exit the bedroom as I make my way down to the front door. Walking out of the palace, I make my trek down the gravel road that leads to the village.

With absolutely no real destination in mind, I decide to just say fuck it and go roaming around.

My feet occasionally kick pebbles out of my path, my gaze following them to see where they scurry off to. The chatter that circulates the village becomes clearer the closer I get.

Sitting on the edge of the large fountain are two young girls, no older than ten. I watch as they giggle amongst themselves, each of them with a closed fist. I smile as I watch one of them close her eyes, and a few seconds later tosses a penny into the water. Her contentment shows through her bright smile, as the other closes her eyes before tossing a penny of her own.

I come up to the familiar floral boutique, the owner noticing me through the casement windows. A smile lights his face as he steps out of the entry door. He shoves a stem-cutter into the pocket of his camel colored apron wrapped around his waist. "Ah. She who is lucky enough to receive my largest order of baccara roses yet." He chimes.

I chuckle as I approach him, my lashes lifting to meet his gaze. "You may call me Melinoë."

He reaches his hand out. "Quinn."

I take his hand as he shakes it. "It's a pleasure to formally meet you." I nudge towards the window. "Your flowers are beautiful. Do you grow them yourself?"

"Thank you." He smiles. "Yes, I do. When I was a young boy I used to follow my mother around in her garden, and well, you know the rest from there." He huffs.

I chuckle. "I believe I can put the pieces together."

Quinn begins to distribute his weight between both feet, a moment of silence stretching between us before he speaks quietly. "May I ask you something, Melinoë?"

I nod slowly. "Of course."

Quinn meets my gaze. "Is it true? That you can speak to the dead? I heard—or saw really, what you did for that woman a few weeks back."

The memory of helping that woman's newly deceased husband cross over fresh in my mind. To remember what it felt like to feel his energy leave his physical body, and how I slept for two days straight afterwards.

I steady my gaze on Quinn, nodding. "It's true."

His eyes widened slightly. "We've always been a home to those who are gifted, to those who can commune with the deceased, but helping one cross-over…everyone has talked about it."

Unsure about how much I should share with this man, and how comfortable he would be to know that I'm not mortal, I kindly keep it brief. "It is something I am still getting used to. But I'm glad I could give her some closure in his final moments." I smile softly.

His eyes soften as he nods. "She has been very grateful for what you did for her. She grieves easier because of it." He turns his head down the long gravel road to the far end of the village. "She still mourns at his grave a few times a week, but she's a little more at ease because of what you did." He turns his head back to me.

"Where might I find the village's cemetery?" I ask.

He points down towards the way I was heading. "Straight down the road, past The Sanctuary." He gives me a smile. "She's visiting his grave now if you'd like to see her."

I nod. "Thank you, Quinn."

He nods before he begins to head back inside. "Come by sometime, I'd love to show you what other types of flowers my boutique offers."

I chuckle. "I will." I begin my walk back in the direction I was heading. This time with a destination in mind.

I walk through the calm hustle and bustle in the village, people occasionally stopping to stare at me as they murmur to one another. Normally this kind of attention would bother me, but knowing who I am, the title that I possess, I realize the attention is something I may need to learn to live with. And maybe as I get to know more of the locals here, that attention won't feel so intimidating.

I continue walking as I hold my shoulders back, carrying myself in a manner of confidence as I head to the cemetery.

CHAPTER 29

I walk past The Sanctuary, following the gravel road down until I approach a large stone arch. My head lifts up, staring at the curved architecture as my gaze narrows lower to the wrought-iron gate. The top of the gate is akin to sharp iron arrows, with trees positioned at each end of the entrance.

My fingers press against the cold iron gate as I pull it open. I step through when a shadowy figure appears before me.

The figure materializes as a tall lanky man. His alabaster skin is like milk against the swirls of shadow that wrap around him. With two parallel slits for a nose, his eyes like two jewels of obsidian crystal.

He narrows his gaze onto me as he folds his arms behind his back. "I have not seen you before. Who are—" He pauses, his eyes widening slightly. He sniffs at me, staring for a moment as his eyes shrink back to normal. He bows slightly at the waist. "Melinoë. A pleasure to finally be graced with your presence."

I tilt my head slightly. "How do you know who I am?"

He chuckles. "We are not so different, you and I." He brings a hand up to his chest. "I am the Gatekeeper of this cemetery."

Understanding fills me. "You guard the souls here." I say breathlessly.

He nods. "Yes."

I force a smile. "It's a pleasure to meet you. Do you not have a name?"

He shakes his head. "My kind, we are born without. But if you'd prefer, you may call me Keeper." He lowers his hand back behind his back, tilting his head. "Are you here to visit?"

"Of sorts." I look beyond to the many headstones layed precisely throughout the cemetery. "I was hoping to see if a woman was here. I do not know her name, but she lost her husband a few weeks ago."

He watches me. "Ah, and I presume that would be the gentleman you helped cross-over. He was most appreciative of your consoling his wife."

I nod my head. "Is she here? Is…he?"

He pivots on his heels. "Allow me to bring you to them."

I watch the shadows billow around him, similar to how the ones billow around Hades when he portals. The uncanny similarity with mine strikes curiosity within me.

I begin to follow Keeper as he guides me down a pathway through the cemetery.

I look up at him, his height hovering over me. "So you know who I am."

"That you are a Goddess of The Dead, the one who invokes nightmares? Yes, I believe I do." He chuckles. He looks towards me. "We've been waiting a long time for you to come into your title."

I narrow my gaze back in front of me. "I'm afraid I'm only just beginning to. I still have much to learn, to understand."

He smiles. "There is nothing you need yet to learn to be a Guardian for the souls. Just being who you are is exactly what they need."

I sigh. "Maybe."

He halts as I notice a woman kneeling over a grave, flowers laid on top of the dry soil. He pivots on his heels, turning his head to me before walking away. "The spirits talk, Melinoë. All you need to do is just listen." He walks a few steps away before vanishing entirely.

I turn back around towards the woman. She looks up as she hears me approaching, her eyes widening when she realizes who I am.

"You." She says breathlessly.

I kneel beside her, keeping an appropriate distance. "How are you?"

She shrugs slightly. "I'm okay." Her gaze tracks over me. "How did you know I'd be here?"

"Quinn told me."

"Ah, that sweet bastard." She laughs as she turns towards the flowers laying on her husband's grave. Her eyes glisten against the sunlight still shining high in the sky. "He's never left. I thought after burying my husband that I would feel the immediate loss of his presence. It's still there, even if it's faint."

I narrow my gaze onto his grave when a surge of energy pulls my attention up again. Not needing to second guess what it is, I watch her husband as he stands above her. A shy smile lights his face as he pats her back.

"It's okay. You can tell her I'm here." He says as he nods to her.

I look at her, narrowing my head. "He wants you to know he's still around."

She looks up at me, shock strickening her ivory face. Her lips tremble slightly before giving a tight close-lipped smile. "Tell him I love him." She begins laughing. "That I have made sure our tulips have stayed alive."

He laughs as I look up at him. *"Tell her I appreciate it, as they were always meant for her more than they were for me."*

I relay the message as a tear slips down her cheek. She nods her head as she stands up, brushing her chestnut hair back from her face. I begin to stand up with her.

"Thank you." She says as she grabs my hands, cradling them into hers. She squeezes them once. "What is your name?"

"Melinoë." I say.

She smiles deeply. "Thank you, Melinoë." She releases my hands as she begins to walk away.

I watch as her husband follows her, walking with her as she walks towards the exit of the cemetery.

I shout after her. "Wait—"

She turns sound.

"I never got your name." I say.

She smiles. "Irene."

I nod, smiling back. "Take care, Irene."

She nods her head and begins her departure again, her husband walking with her the whole way out.

Wiping the dirt from my skirt, I look up to take in the cemetery around me. My head swivels up as a crow flies above me, his loud caw perforating the silence. My gaze lowers onto the headstones around me, many of them accompanied with offerings of flowers or pictures. I notice one in particular and find myself gravitating towards it.

I approach the headstone, kneeling over a vase that's been tipped over. I frown at the white chrysanthemums that splay over the soil. I lift my gaze, tracing my fingers along the crease of the letters as I read the words carved into the headstone.

SHE WHO WILL BE MISSED

Underneath it shares only an end date, marking the day that Dimitri was attacked. My eyes widen as I realize this is the woman who was found in the Sephyra Forest.

"Whoever you are," I mutter softly. My thumb grazes the cement as I bow my head slightly, closing my eyes. "I'm so sorry you were caught in the middle of all of this. May your soul rest."

My hand lowers as I grab the vase to set it upright again. I take the white flowers, arranging them back into the glass vase, fluffing them the best I can. I push the vase up against the headstone when a faint whisper reaches me.

"Thank you." She says, her voice gentle and warm.

I feel the brush of her energy before it dissipates. I lift my head as a faint smile curves my lips. "You're welcome."

I stand from her grave, though instead of making my way back home, I feel this inner pull to stick around for a little while longer.

I walk the entirety of the cemetery, tidying up graves and offerings from their loved ones. I occasionally hear whispers of gratitude, and my heart warms at each and every one of them.

Occasionally I catch a glimpse of Keeper from the corner of my eye. Standing there watching me as I tend to the graves of the deceased.

CHAPTER 30

I look up from my plate, my gaze meeting the center vase of the still-pristine baccara roses. A smile tugs at my lips as I bring my fork to my mouth, the savory bite of Aven's roasted turkey greeting my taste buds.

"How was your day?" Reimus asks before taking a drink from his whiskey.

"Good." I say before savoring another bite. "I visited the cemetery."

He lifts his gaze to me, a grin curving his lips. "Did you find your time to be enjoyable?" He forks a serving of turkey into his mouth.

I smile. "It was." I lower my fork to grab my glass of sweet red wine. "How was your day?"

He gazes at me for a moment. "We had a newcomer at The Sanctuary today. It's been...a difficult transition for her, but we're doing our best."

"What do you mean?" I say, forking more turkey into my mouth before moving onto the roasted potatoes.

"She arrived at the shield saying she needed refuge from an abusive relationship. I met with Charon at the shield, and my stomach churned the moment I saw her."

My gaze lifts up to his, the pain in his eyes vivid and stark. I watch him in silence as he continues.

"Her arms were bruised, and her ankles—" He pauses as he downs the rest of his whiskey. He sets it down, the fire in his gaze heating. Pure anger. "As if she'd been *shackled*."

I reach my hand out, my fingers wrapping around his hand. I squeeze him gently as his attention turns towards me.

He sighs as his thumb lifts to graze my palm. "She won't speak of what happened. She won't leave her room to join the other women for supper either. She just needs time."

I frown. "If she's once been shackled, I can only imagine she's terrified to trust anyone at this time."

"I don't blame her. Hopefully in time she will see the support that surrounds The Sanctuary." He leans back into his chair, lowering his gaze to our hands.

My gaze remains on his face. "Have many of the other women there shared similar reasons for coming to Vulir?"

He nods. "Most of them do, unfortunately." He raises his gaze to meet mine. "At least Vulir is able to give them a safe new beginning."

I softly grin, thinking of everything I've endured prior to coming to Vulir. A warm ease settles in my heart at how safe I have felt since being here, never having been able to say that before. "Yes, that it does."

His gaze narrows slightly. "Are there any new developments with how to fix Makaria's memory?" He lifts his gaze to mine again.

I sigh. "Not as of now."

His eyes churn brightly. "Have you seen her?" He asks calmly.

I shake my head. "She does not wish to see me." I grab my glass and down the remainder of my wine. Setting the empty glass on the table as I stare off aimlessly.

Reimus tucks a loose strand of my long hair behind my ear, coaxing my gaze back to him. "Maybe tomorrow."

I sigh, pain cleaving my heart. "I doubt that." I tap a finger against the table. "I will wait a few days before I try to see her."

Understanding that my sister's grief right now is not about me, but about a father who wasn't what she thought he was. About a mother that is actually alive, and the betrayal that comes with the lies that surrounded her death. I won't interject myself solely because I'm desperate for her to remember me. I will give her the decency of space to grieve first.

Reimus gazes at me. "You are an extraordinary sister."

I turn myself towards him, propping my legs up into the chair. "What would you do? If it were me." My gaze lifts to his dark strands as they brush above his brow.

"I would probably do what you are doing now." He admits, tilting his head as his finger coils a loose strand that lays against my chest. "But then I would spend day in and day out visiting you, even if you wished to not see me.

I would willingly sit outside those closed doors until one day you decided to let me in."

His gaze lifts to meet mine. "I would spend my entire life trying to regain your memory of me, because not having the pleasure of taking up space in your memories is a life not lived."

His hand wraps around mine as he cages it to my chest above my heart. His gaze fixates on our hands before making a soft noise. "Because if I cannot be a reason for why your heart beats, then I want to be nothing at all." His eyes lift to mine under dark lashes. He grins as he opens his hand over my chest, my heartbeat steady beneath his fingers.

My heart widens at the sight of his gaze, the warmth of his skin against mine. To live a life without Reimus in it is to live one that threatens bleakness. Never in a thousand years did I think I would grow so close to someone like this, to crave their presence as soundly as I do. That even through everything that is right now, I can find solace in the small moments like these with him now.

A man who met me when I was nothing more than a dismantled home, who saw the potential in me to rebuild myself up, and encouraged me to do so from day one. Sticking by my side through both the ugly, and the beautiful.

I scoot my chair back as our hands fall away. I crawl into his lap, straddling him as my hands come up around his neck. His hands rest on my sides, beneath my breasts.

I lean in to kiss him softly, before pulling away. My lips hovering over his. "You are not the reason why my heart beats. You *are* my heart." I lean in to kiss him again.

His hands come up to my neck as he deepens the kiss, my lips parting for him as his tongue slips through. My fingers twirl themselves in his hair, the soft strands like liquid silk against my skin.

He scoots his chair back as he lowers a hand underneath me. Lifting me up with him, he pulls away as he begins walking towards the dining room entryway. "A privilege I will never take for granted."

He takes another step as I squeeze his shoulders, signaling him to stop. He looks at me as a feral grin curves my lips. I nod behind him, gesturing to the portal now behind him.

He turns his head, chuckling as he looks back at me. "You took my request to portal instead of walking to the bedroom." He turns us around as he walks through it, stepping through into our bedroom.

He walks us over to the bed before laying me on top of the silken sheets. I prop myself up onto my elbows, heat following my gaze as it lowers to his hands on his pants.

"Which means I get to fuck you in less time." He unbuttons his pants, loosening them before shoving them down his muscular legs. His hands go to his briefs, his cock swollen against them. He pulls them down as my gaze fixates on his him.

He chuckles as he lifts his shirt up over his head. My gaze travels slowly up his body until his hand forces my jaw up. He leans in closer. "Careful, little spitfire. I might just go right to fucking you if you keep looking at me like that."

I grin against his hold, my hand reaching out for him. "You won't."

His body goes rigid as my soft hand glides over his cock, wrapping it around him as I slowly work him. His gaze hardens as it lowers to my hand. "Don't tempt me." He says through clenched teeth as a soft grunt leaves him.

"You won't because," I begin before lowering my hand to my skirt, Reimus getting the idea and stripping it off of me. He goes to lift my shirt up over my head as I pull him onto the bed next to me.

I push him down onto his back as I kneel next to him, my back arched as I lean lower down. "I'm going to suck you first."

He lets out a ragged exhale as I kiss the tip, my gaze lifting to his as he watches me intently. I wrap my hand around his silken hard skin as I lower my mouth onto him, slowly teasing him. His hips jerk up as his arm comes around my rear, smacking my ass.

His cock slides down my tongue as I bury him completely in my mouth. He curses through a clenched jaw as I move my mouth along him. I moan as I taste his cum beading at the tip in my mouth.

"Fuck." He hisses as his hips buck up.

I feel his finger lower over my ass before sliding inside of me. I whimper as his fingers slide through my wetness, the sound of his chuckle lighting fire in my veins.

I moan against his cock as I suck him, feeling his lower abdomen tightening up. I begin moving against his finger, eliciting a thrill inside of me.

He grunts as his hips jerk up again. His free hand comes up to wrap itself into my hair. "*Fuck*—you're doing so fucking good."

I smile against his cock as my orgasm climbs within me. I lap my tongue around his cock as I moan against him. The vibrations cause him to buck again.

He pulls his finger out, grabbing my neck as he pushes my mouth off him. "On your fucking knees." He says gruffly.

In an instant he's flipping me over, my knees spread apart on the bed as he kneels behind me. He presses his hard cock against my entrance, grunting at the wetness as it slides against him.

"So fucking wet for me." His hand lowers to my pussy as he teases me. I moan as anticipation overwhelms me.

His cock presses into me, slowly filling me. A taunting game of his that I willingly subject myself to. "Tell me it's mine." His voice is husky and rough as he grips my hips, guiding himself in.

I arch my back as he fills me deeper, my mind a lustful haze. "It's yours."

He buries himself completely, a cry erupting from my lips. "Tell me again." He slowly pulls out until only the tip is in.

He buries himself in one deep thrust. "My pussy is yours."

He leans down until his chest is against my back, his hand coming up to my throat as he holds me in place. My pussy drips onto him as he thrusts into me.

"Again."

Another hard thrust. "It's yours."

He pants against my ear. "Again."

My orgasm begins chasing me once more, pleading to be released as he buries himself again. I plead with him. "*Please*." I cry as I feel him shiver against me, begging to feel more, more, more.

His lips lower to my neck as I feel him smile against it before nipping my skin. The only warning I get before he drives into me.

I cry as he rams into my rear, the fullness of his cock overwhelming me as my orgasm rises higher to the surface. I hear him whimper against me as his hands grip my waist, his noises causing me to arch my back even more.

He pistons in and out of me until I feel myself clamping around him. I scream as release finds me, chasing me as he plunges into me.

I hear him whimper as he pulsates inside me. We both ride our highs as I rock my hips into him. He stills inside me as he unloads himself, grunting as he does.

His hands loosen their grip around my hips as he pulls out, cum dripping out of me. He lays himself down next to me, both of us trying to catch our breaths.

He leans down to kiss me, his lips soft against mine. I grab his face ushering him in closer until he's hovering above me. I widen my legs for him, trying to pull him down.

He lifts his lips from mine, gazing down at me. He smirks as his gaze narrows to my breasts. "Not yet sated, little spitfire?"

I feel his cock harden against me again, my gaze lowering. I watch as the length of him heaves against me. "Please."

He shivers at my words before lowering his head to kiss between my breasts. "You never have to ask twice." He lowers himself down to my navel, pressing soft kisses until he travels lower.

I gasp as he presses a kiss to my swollen clit, his eyes alight on mine. He gives me a wicked grin before his tongue sends me into euphoric oblivion.

CHAPTER 31

The portal closes behind me as I take two steps forward, my head leaning to the side. "Hecate?"

"Back here, dear." She calls from the back room. I follow her voice to the back of her store.

Parting through the royal blue beads that hang above the door frame I find Hecate standing near her work table—well, one of them anyway.

I approach her, glancing at the loose herbs scattered on top of a steel tray. A white pillar candle positioned at the center as wax drips down its side, trickling over some of the herbs. Sigils drawn in white chalk trace the perimeter of the tray.

"Am I interrupting?" I ask slowly.

She lifts a piece of parchment paper, the lettering ineligible for me to decipher from here. She holds it above the flame, watching as it catches fire. "Not at all." She says as she drops the burning paper into a black cauldron. The flame roars as if influenced by the magic itself.

"What are you doing?" My gaze trained on the flames licking the cauldron.

Her hands palm towards the cauldron, her gaze focused on it. "Scrying."

My eyebrows scrunch together as I open my mouth to ask what that is.

"Just give me a few moments." She interjects.

I take a step back as I allow her to concentrate. I watch as her gaze steadies on the flame, not blinking even once.

After a minute I notice her gaze flicker upon the flame. I watch it shift from side to side as if reading something within the cauldron. She closes her eyes and begins mumbling to herself, far too quiet for me to comprehend. After another minute her eyes open and the flame extinguishes.

Her gaze lifts to the lit candle before she waves a hand over it, extinguishing that too. She faces me at last. "Thanks for your patience, dear."

"Did you find what you were looking for?" I nod to the extinguished cauldron.

She forces a smile that doesn't meet her eyes. "Yes. And no." She walks over to the tray, lifting it to a long shelf above her work table. She mumbles a few words before the tray disappears.

My breath hitches. "Where'd it go?"

"Nowhere." She lifts a hand to where it just was. "It's still there, but now I'm the only one who can see it."

I tilt my head. "Why hide it?"

"Because I'm not finished with it yet. And I don't need someone wandering in here, tampering with my spell." She walks over to me and brings me in for a hug.

I embrace her back. "Well, I guess that's valid."

She pulls away, shrugging her shoulders. "Can never be too careful when it comes to witchcraft." She gives me a wink before she walks towards the circular table. She sits down, waving a hand for me to do the same.

"I'm afraid I don't have good news on how to restore Makaria's memory yet. Whoever did the spell really took their time with it. It's strong." She says.

I take the seat next to her, crossing a leg over the other. "I trust that you'll find a way."

Her golden eyes churn as they fixate onto me. "I won't stop working until I do."

An exhale leaves me. "Can you tell if Zeus was the one who performed the spell?"

Hecate shakes her head. "It's inconclusive as of now."

I nod as my gaze shifts back to the cauldron. "Tell me about scrying."

"It's a form of divination that allows one to receive information, usually through images." She taps her head, the light above us glinting off her golden rings. She lowers her hand as she straightens her back. "I still cannot see how to help your sister, but I did see something."

An unnatural stillness claims me. "What was it?"

She narrows her chin. "I saw an image of you, kneeling on the ground. You were cleaning a headstone. But your sister…she stood behind you."

I uncross my legs, shifting to the edge of my seat. "The cemetery." My eyes widen as I lean forward. "What did she say?"

"I don't know. As soon as I saw her, the vision cleared. But she looked well. She—" Hecate forces a hopeful smile. "She was smiling at you."

My heart swells in my chest at the glimpse of hope, no matter how vague it may be. I try not to clutch on so tightly to that small chance of hope, but I hang onto it nonetheless.

I exhale a shaky breath. "Maybe her memory will just surface back on its own?"

Hecate lifts her hands from her lap. "It's possible. But I'd like to be absolutely sure. So I'll continue to work towards finding a solution."

My eyes strain against the tears swelling up. "Thank you. I appreciate you more than you know." I exhale a ragged breath. "Even when I'm being a bitch."

She chuckles as she shrugs her shoulders. "You're forgiven." She winks.

I share a laugh of my own as ease begins to surface within me once again. I looked over to the cauldron again, my interest piqued. I nod towards it. "Would you teach me?"

She wiggles her eyebrows as she clasps her hands together. "Oh, I was hoping you'd ask." She stands up as she waves me up.

We walk over to her work table, Hecate to my right as she pulls out a match and a lighter. "When scrying, do not resist what comes to the surface. Let it be, even if it does not make sense." She turns to me. "That's rule number one out of two."

"What's the second?" I ask, my gaze lowering to the table.

"Rule number two," She begins as she lights the match. The flame grows as my gaze lifts to hers. "Is to let your fear of the flame go." She drops the match into the cauldron, lighting ablaze.

I step back out of instinct as the flame roars, licking the inside walls of the cauldron. I look over to Hecate.

"Let go of the fear. And focus." She nods to the flame.

I work on a swallow, nodding as my gaze lowers to the flame. I breathe in deeply as I focus in on it. My mind becomes one with the flame as I dive deeper into its embrace.

Through the lick of flames, a shadowed image begins to part through them. I focus on it, letting my fear go and allowing the vision to take shape. An image of a throne room appears, sunlight illuminating the entirety of the alabaster and gold colored walls. Two chairs sit atop the daze, both adorned in the brightest gold. I watch as a tall man walks up towards the dais, a golden crown atop his head. My view obstructed by his back as I look down—

The vision suddenly changes as shadows swirl around me. *My* shadows.

I watch as they warp around my body, encasing me in. They wrap a barrier of protection around me as I curl into their safe embrace. They whisper to me, coaxing me to unfurl them.

"Do it." They chant.

"Do it."

"Do it."

I look ahead and witness the man in front of me—

I gasp as I feel Hecate's steady hands keeping me in place, preventing me from stepping back. "Focus, child."

I focus on the image of Hades before me, kneeling on the ground of his own realm.

I watch as my shadows lash out, wrapping themselves around him as they restrain his arms out at his sides. My lips begin to tremble as I watch pain lance his eyes—

The vision abruptly clears, the flame extinguishing in the cauldron. I jerk away from the table as I clasp my hands up to my lips. My arms begin trembling as confusion erodes me.

"What did you see?" Hecate's stern voice rings out.

My shaky gaze lifts to hers as I tell her what I saw. When I'm finished, she slowly lets go of my shoulders.

"It's just a random image." I convince myself as I shake my head.

Hecate meets my shaken gaze. "I'm afraid the cauldron never lies."

I exhale a ragged breath, clutching at my chest at the image of inflicting pain upon Hades.

She grabs my shoulders gently, steadying me. "We do not know the context for why you were given those visions."

I allow her embrace to calm me as I regain control of my breathing. I nod my head, lifting my gaze up to her. "Please keep this between us. For now. Don't tell my mother."

She forces a close-lipped smile. "I promise."

After asking me numerous times if I were okay, I finally bid my farewell with Hecate before portalling back to The Guardian's Palace.

The shadows slither around my portal reminding me of the ones I had around Hades, restraining him. I work on a swallow as I step through the portal and enter the living room. I walk over to the couch, plopping myself down.

Thoughts circulate in my mind why I would ever retaliate against Hades. The image of wielding my power not with The God of The Dead, but against him unsettling me for some reason deep in my bones.

CHAPTER 32

As I walk through the bedchamber Reimus comes into view. A leg crossed over another as he leans against the chaise lounge, his black journal and a pen in his hands.

I chuckle as I walk towards him. "Have words ever failed you when you write about me in there?"

His gaze lifts up as a smirk curves his lips. He sets the journal on the side table as he huffs. "No, but I'll let you know if they ever do."

I climb into his lap as I lean down to kiss him. His hand comes around my thigh as I face him, my legs curled up on one side. His other hand rests on my back.

My mind churns with possible explanations for what I saw. A power that I saw in myself through that vision that I have never seen before. My stomach clenches as nerves plague me, wanting desperately to understand it.

But as I look at Reimus now, the thought of worrying about something that may or may not happen is suddenly the least of my concerns at the moment. Knowing that I have full control of what I do with my power and that I decide my fate.

His fingertips tap my back, his brows furrowing. "Everything alright?"

His voice snaps me back into liquid relaxation as it pools through me. Those ravaging nerves crawl themselves out of me, replaced instead with a calmness that only Reimus can give me.

I nod as I play with a loose strand of his hair. "Everything's fine." I lean in to kiss him once more, my heart swelling in my chest. As I pull away I nod towards the journal. "Read it to me."

His eyes steady on me, bright and vivid against the roaring fireplace. "All of it?"

I laugh. "Doesn't have to be all of it. Just one page—" I smirk. "Or two."

He laughs, his hand gliding softly up my back as the other one reaches for the journal. "As you wish." His lashes flutter as he looks up at me, pressing a soft kiss to my chin. "Pick a number between one and fifty."

I smile widely into his touch, leaning to rest myself onto his chest. "Hmm…how about thirty."

He wraps his arms around me, flipping to a page in his journal. "Thirty it is." He says as he presses a kiss to the top of my head. He clears his throat as his chin rests above my head. The soft tickle of his breath like honey against my skin. And when he speaks his voice is smooth like velvet.

"My knees meet the hard concrete, with only the whispers of a forlorn life to surround me. They promise me pitiless oaths that speak of everything I was convinced

I deserved, never having questioned them prior. Until suddenly the jute noose that bristles around my neck pulls me forward, only having ever tugged me backwards. A repetition that coaxed me to keep drowning in the shames of my past.

Though now it is her essence that I find myself drowning in, willingly submerging myself into the vastness that she keeps so intricately hidden beneath. That instead of the weight of my past anchoring me to my knees, it is my willing desperation for just a drop of what I know glows beneath her hardened exterior. As I hold my mouth open for her, I wait. Ready to drink in just a glimpse of her smile that's enough to keep me full, or the fierceness in her gaze that brings warmth to my once numbed bones.

Her presence has tilted the very axis on which my world balances on, and I allow myself to free fall as gravity pulls me towards her."

He presses another kiss to the top of my head as he finishes, stilling me wholly. My heart lunges from my chest cavity as it swells inside me, a pressure that only seems to build.

I lift my head up, my gaze meeting his. My chest rises slightly as I lean in to kiss him, my hand spread across his jaw. His lips part as I deepen the kiss and his rough hand cups my jaw.

After a long moment of feeding the need to feel his lips against mine, I pull away. My gaze both heated and doting. "Read me another." I press a kiss to his cheek, my lashes lifting as I stare at him again.

His eyes pierce into mine, unaware of their effect at softening the very rigidness within me. He smiles. "As you wish."

I lean my head back down against his chest as Reimus reads me another page from his journal. I listen to him speak, submerging myself wholly into his words. A shared intimacy between us as he openly expresses his worship and undying admiration for me.

His voice is gentle as he shares his poetic words, only amplifying the love that's begun to blossom deep in my soul for him. Just as I have been for months now, I plunge myself deep into it as I do not fight it.

As I lie awake I stare up at the ceiling. Unable to fall asleep even after Reimus showed his adoration of me in other ways that don't involve words.

I look over at him, the silk sheets pooling low at his waist. The hard ridges of his abdomen like they were perfectly sculpted by The Fates themselves. I watch the steady rise and fall of his chest, my gaze lifting to the ease etched into his face. I smile softly as I watch him sleep.

My restless energy causes me to slowly stir out of the bed, my naked body kissing the cool air wafting in from the open balcony doors. Summer is beginning to come to an end thank the gods.

I quietly walk over to the walk in closet, slipping on a pair of beige linen pants and a black short-sleeved shirt. I slip on my black strapless sandals, running my fingers through my hair before turning towards the balcony.

I step out onto the stone surface, feeling the cool air kiss my cheek. I breathe in the fresh air, stilling my fingers from fidgeting at my sides. I watch as the shadows materialize, slithering around the portal before me. I step through it until I'm standing at that stone archway. The eerie quiet a settling blanket around me.

I close the portal behind me as I walk under the tall archway, my gaze upon the rows of headstones that fill the graveyard. Utterly pitch dark out here save for the glow of the moon high above as my only source of light.

I walk through the middle aisle unsure of why I felt called to come here. Certain it would rile the nervousness within me more. But as I walk through here an unmistakable sureness fills me.

I walk over to a headstone, a fresh bouquet of flowers set out for this deceased soul. I kneel down as my fingers lightly tracing the daisy petals.

"Quite late for a visit."

I jolt up on my feet, turning around to find Keeper standing before me. His cloak of shadows nearly blending into the darkness surrounding us. I shrug my shoulders. "I couldn't sleep."

He watches me, the moonlight above illuminating his pale face. Those depthless voids pinned on me as he tilts his head. "Why not?"

I hesitate for a moment before answering. "I saw something today. It's had me on edge since."

"And what could have possibly frightened you, Goddess of Nightmares?" He says, stepping towards me.

I do not balk at his approach, finding his presence oddly comforting. I step towards him. "I saw a vision of something that I do not wish to happen."

"And do you have no free will?" He questions.

"I do—"

"Then where, Melinoë, does your fear truly lie?" He tilts his head.

I narrow my gaze. "I never want to use my powers for malicious intent."

His gaze lowers slightly before meeting mine again. "Then you are the only one who gets to decide that fate."

I sigh. "I know."

Keeper watches me a moment longer before pivoting on his heels to turn away.

"What did you mean?"

He halts, pivoting back around towards me.

"When you said we are not so different. What exactly did you mean by that?" I ask.

He stares at me for a moment before making a huffing noise as he smiles. "You come to the cemetery to walk amongst the deceased when you are restless and unable to sleep. You find comfort and ease here, because you feel a protectiveness over them. Aside from the power, and the title."

I watch as the slits in his nose close in as he sniffs the air between us.

"We both are cut from the same cloth. Deep down, I think you already knew that." He nods towards my hands before he turns on his heels once more, making his way through the aisle of headstones.

My gaze shoots down as I open and close my fists at my sides. Not due to a ramp up of anger, but to calm the shadows that have suddenly crawled from my fingertips. My breath hitches as the shadows curl themselves around my fingers before dissipating into the air around me.

CHAPTER 33

Swirling my fork in my scrambled eggs, every now and then I look down at my hands. Remembering what it felt like to feel those shadows form at my fingertips, an effort made subconsciously.

I exhale my wandering thoughts away as I fork a serving into my mouth. Hot coffee wafts towards my nose as the sound of Reimus flipping through the morning newspaper wakes me from my running mind. As if he can smell it, he reaches a hand out and rests it on my thigh.

I allow his warmth to coax me fully to the present. "Are you and Dimitri going to The Sanctuary today?"

He sets the newspaper down as he grabs his ceramic mug, sipping his coffee. "Yes. Just to check on how she's doing."

I jab my fork into the cantaloupe on my plate. "Do you know her name?"

He shakes his head. "She won't speak to anyone. She stays locked away in her room."

I frown at his statement, empathizing for how scary this whole transition must be for her. Not only to have gone from being abused but to seeking shelter in an unfamiliar territory.

I can only imagine the battle internally she must be feeling. Wanting to trust the help but unwilling to get close enough to the others to allow it.

"She just needs time. I'm sure she'll talk when she's ready." I say.

Reimus nods as he lifts his hand from my thigh, his fingers coming up to graze my cheek. "Are you nervous?"

Referencing what I have planned for today, I sigh into his touch. The honest answer pouring out of me. "Yes."

His gaze softens as his thumb grazes my cheek. He narrows his chin. "One day at a time."

I sigh, forcing a smile. "One day at a time."

He leans over to kiss me, the taste of coffee on his lips. He pulls away as he grabs our plates, standing up to take them to the kitchen. I watch him as my heart lurches after him like a love sick idiot who pines for another's touch.

I stand up as I walk over to the doorway, my gaze on his back. I watch him as he stands over the sink, washing our dishes. Unfocused for once on the way his muscles in his back come together or the way his hair loosely sits on top of his head.

I watch him as the words sit so close to the tip of my tongue, that if it weren't for the press of my lips they would stream right out.

Today is not the right day for those words to make an appearance though.

I walk towards him, wrapping my arms around him from behind. He sets the clean dishes into the drying rack, bringing my hand up to his lips as he kisses my fingers.

He turns around, pushing the hair out of my face. His gaze soft and yearning. "She will remember. Maybe not today, or tomorrow. But she will."

I blink, nodding as I kiss his palm. "I will hold onto that hope."

I arrive in The Underworld an hour later, just inside the kitchen. I walk over to the table trying to distract my nerves with the bowl of fruit placed at the center. I peer into it, distracting myself as nerves wrack my body. I look up when I hear footsteps approach the room.

I look up to see my mother clad in a light coral dress, the length falling below her knees.

She embraces me, her arms warm and steady as she hugs me. We share a moment of silence together before she pulls away. "You look well today." She says as she pins a strand of hair behind my ear.

I nod. "I'm feeling better than the last time we saw each other." I peer up at her. "How is she doing?"

Persephone sighs. "She's doing okay. She's finally taken to coming out of her room, and spends much of her time outside."

My eyes widened. "That's good news. Is she speaking? Has she explored any of The Underworld yet?"

Persephone shakes her head. "She only sits in the courtyard, not venturing far. She hasn't spoken much either."

"Do you…think she'd be alright with a visit?"

She smiles faintly. "We could certainly try."

She lifts her hand towards the glass windows overlooking the courtyard. I walk towards one as I see my sister sitting in the grass with her legs out in front of her. Her platinum hair is wild and unbound, falling loosely behind her back.

I turn towards my mother, nodding my head as I walk towards the courtyard doors.

Stepping outside, my hands begin to dampen as I halt in my place. My sister is just a few feet away from me and I freeze as if I have no idea what to say. Not wanting to overwhelm her but desperately wanting to at least just hear her voice.

I take a tentative step towards her. "Makaria." My voice is quiet, nearly whispering.

She sits there, unmoving.

I take another step, feeling the grass curving up my sandals.

Still, she does not move nor speak. As if nothing more than a stone cemented to the ground.

I take a final step, deciding to keep a respectable distance between us. I go to lower myself to the ground and seat myself towards her left.

I rub my hands on my thighs, relieving some of the dampness building under my palms. I stare at my sister with a better view of her face here. My stomach churns at the puffiness above her cheeks, the bleakness in her eyes.

Seeing her current state I decide in that moment that instead of trying to push her to remember, I settle for something less harrowing.

As I sit in the grass I talk to my sister.

I tell her about how it felt to see our mother again, both the turmoil that I felt inside as well as the sodden relief. I tell her that I too, am immortal, and how it's been a journey to accept all that comes with it. I begin to talk to her about Eiran when I see her eyes light up.

"Eiran." She says, her voice thick and raspy.

My chest heaves. "Do you remember him?"

She tilts her head, nodding ever so slowly. "I do."

Trying not to bring too much onto her, I bite back the cry that leeches up my throat. "What do you remember of him?"

She hesitates for a long moment, pondering. "He hunted for my family sometimes."

The use of my instead of ours stinging but allowing her to keep going anyway.

"His hair. I remember it complementing his eyes nicely."

I force a smile. "Yes, he had nice golden brown hair."

"Had?" She asks.

I exhale as I steady my voice. "He died."

She finally looks over towards me, her eyes losing a fraction of that bleakness in them. "I'm sorry."

I nod my head. "Me too."

Her gaze flickers over me. "I know you're my sister. I just—can't remember."

"It's okay." I say, loosening a breath. "It's not your fault."

A ghost of a smile appears before it turns into a frown again. "No, it appears it is not."

I go to reach for her hand but stop myself as I pull my hand away. "I will never let him hurt you again."

She trains her gaze forward, a huff sound coming from her. "He can't hurt me more than he already has."

We sit in silence together for a short while until Makaria stands up. Her posture both so rigid and unnaturally still all the same. As if it is both numbing and painful to be in her body at this moment. "Thank you for sitting with me."

I raise from the ground, forcing a smile. "You're welcome. Would you like for me to visit again tomorrow?"

She gives a faint nod. "Sure." She turns on her heels and walks back inside. I watch her through the window as she approaches our mother, giving her an embrace before turning away from her. Thankful that she at least has the memory of our mother intact.

My mother meets me outside as I walk towards her. "That seemed to go okay." She says.

I nod my head. "Have you found anything yet?"

Persephone shakes her head. "Hecate told me she saw a vision of Makaria while scrying."

I still as the fear of my mother finding out about the vision I saw of Hades surfaces. I will myself to remain relaxed anyway. "Yeah, I was there."

My mother pulls me into her embrace. "We'll figure it out."

I sigh into her embrace before she pulls away, her head turning to the side as a tall man portals next to us. I step back at his sudden appearance.

"Persephone, your assistance is needed." His gaze glances over to me. "When you have a moment."

My gaze tracks over his pearl white hair as it brushes along his broad shoulders. His round gray eyes like beams of vivid light against his sandy beige skin. My gaze peers behind him at his jet black feathered wings, raised high over his head. I take another step back at the sheer size of him.

She smiles. "I'll be there in a moment, Thanatos."

In the next moment he tucks his wings in before disappearing behind his portal.

I look at her. "Who's that?"

She chuckles. "That's Thanatos. God of Death. Literally, speaking."

My eyes bulge slightly. "So—"

"So he aids souls in crossing over when it is their time, bringing them to the afterlife. A psychopomp, much like you in some ways." She nudges me as she notices the widening of my gaze. She chuckles. "He doesn't actually aid in the killing of mortals."

"Ah. Good to know." I say.

The way Thanatos stood before us would've given me full-body chills had I not been acquainted with the death aspects of life by now. His power was like a tangible entity I could feel. Like his power could extinguish the very life from someone if deemed necessary.

I half grin at the memory of ushering that man over to the afterlife. "I haven't had any other experiences since that one day."

She smiles. "You happened to be in the right place at the right time that day. I knew it was you."

I stare at her.

"I knew when Thanatos went to collect the soul and came back stating that he had already crossed over, but not by him, I knew then."

I smirk faintly. "Well considering I'm Guardian of The Dead, I can imagine it won't be the first."

She chuckles. "It likely will not be." She reaches a hand out, squeezing my arm. "I have business to attend to. But I will see you tomorrow?"

I nod. "I'll return tomorrow."

She smiles before stepping into the portal behind her.

And when it closes, I portal myself back home.

CHAPTER 34

I glide the hard brush across Alastor's back as I talk to him. I tell him about meeting Keeper, and now Thanatos, and how uncannily similar the three of us are. Maybe not entirely, but…in one particular way.

Guardians of the deceased.

As I run the brush along his fur I hear footsteps approach the gate. Alastor whinnies at him, the only other person he now does that for.

I hear him chuckle. "I think I might be jealous."

I laugh. "Why? Do you want me to brush you too?"

Reimus comes up behind me, his hands at my waist as he gives me a kiss on the cheek. "I certainly wouldn't say no if you played with my hair."

I toss the hard brush into the bucket, leaning down to grab the soft brush. Reimus stands to my right as I look over at him. A smirk pulling at my lips. "That could be arranged."

His teeth shine in the sunlight as he smiles. He steps up to Alastor, giving him a good rub on his forehead. He remains silent for a moment. "How did it go?"

I begin brushing Alastor's back legs, working my way down before I move over to the other side. "It went okay.

She still doesn't remember me, but it was nice to still sit and talk with her for a while."

"That's a start." Alastor huffs at him, flicking his tail.

I smile. "Yes, it is." After I finish brushing his other legs I toss the brush into the bucket. I sigh as I stand up straight again, bucket in my hand. "So how is the new girl?"

Reimus shrugs his shoulders. "She still remains in her room."

I frown as I give Alastor a neck rub before making my way to the gate. "Is she eating and staying hydrated at least?" I lift the gate lock as Reimus holds it open for me.

"The empty dishes that she leaves outside of her door tell me yes." He says as he closes the gate behind us.

We walk inside the barn as I put the grooming bucket onto the shelf next to Gizelle's. I look at Reimus as he interlocks his arm with mine. A half grin curves one side of my lips. "That's a start."

We walk back to the palace entrance, making our way upstairs as I head straight for the bathroom.

I lean over as I'm about to turn on the water for the bathtub when I feel the buzz of energy behind me.

I turn around, finding Nikolai before us. I look over to Reimus knowing he can see him too.

"You both must come."

I widen my eyes. "Is everything okay, Nikolai? Is it Makaria?"

"No. It's her. She needs help." He says, his voice curt and somewhat frantic.

Reimus stares at Nikolai, his shoulders slightly tensing. Understanding who he's referring to. "What happened?"

Nikolai's worry shows through his face. *"The girls—they were only trying to help. But she panicked—"*

I look towards Reimus the moment his gaze finds mine. I nod in a silent agreement as I materialize a portal before us.

I glance once more at Nikolai. "Thank you for alerting us."

He nods before he vanishes entirely.

Reimus grabs my hand as we walk through the portal immediately, stepping onto the hardwood floor of The Sanctuary.

We arrive right at the forefront of the chaos. I watch as two women rush another over to the end of the room, setting her on a couch. Blood drips down her nose as her eyes blink open slowly. They tilt her head back, mumbling to her as my attention is drawn to the screaming coming from one of the rooms.

"That's her room." Reimus points as we hurry down to the open doorway.

I watch as the new girl thrashes things around her room, blood-curdling screams escaping from her throat. She shakes her hand at her side and my gaze falls to her reddened knuckles.

She snaps her head towards us, her gaze irate as she stomps towards me. Reimus goes to step in front of me but I reach a hand out to stop him.

"She stole it! I want it back! I want it back *now*!" She screams as she approaches me, though she doesn't touch me.

Even as I watch her gaze go wild before me, her screams similar to the one that have stormed out of my lips, I stand there unafraid of her. "What did she take?"

She huffs angrily as her hands shoot out. "My clothing. That bitch took my clothing!"

Trying to maintain a poker face though there has to be a deeper meaning for her punching a girl over some clothing, I keep my energy calm as I step out of the room.

I walk over to the three women on the couch, kneeling before the woman with blood running down her nose. "Hi, my name is Melinoë."

Her lips tremble as she stares at me. She holds a towel to her nose. "Euphrosyne."

I nod. "Euphrosyne, do you happen to know where her clothing is?"

She points her finger towards the laundry room. Her arm trembles as she lowers it. "She left her room to utilize the shower. I thought maybe she'd like some clean clothes."

I sigh as the clarity of the misunderstanding unfolds. "Thank you."

She lifts the towel, inspecting the crimson stained fabric before pressing it to her nose again. "I was just trying to be nice."

I force a smile. "I know you were." I walk over to the laundry room, grabbing the only hamper of clean clothing in there. I walk it back to the girl's room, other women staring at me as I do.

I enter her room as Reimus watches me intently, not having left the room for precaution. "Is this your clothing?"

She snaps her head towards me, the initial anger falling away like frozen ice melting against a raging fire. She rushes towards me, snatching the hamper out of my hands before plopping it down on her bed.

She frantically rummages through it, picking at and tossing articles of clothing aside until she gets to a pair of jeans. She reaches her fingers into a pocket, a wave of relief so visibly washing over her I could see it emulate through her energy.

She pulls out a gold vintage locket, her fingers shaking as she opens it. Tears stream down her face as she plops onto the bed.

I tentatively walk over to her, seating myself next to her. I peer down at the picture of a small child inside. My heart lurching as my gaze raises to her. "Is he yours?"

She looks up at me as she nods. Her body trembles as her silent tears turn into muffled cries. "He still has him." She glances down at her ankles, at the indentation marks around them.

My stomach churns. "Where is he?"

She narrows her gaze. "Back in Olympia."

My body chills at the name of the Realm of The Gods. I gaze at her. "I thought mortals didn't live there?"

She looks up at me, glancing over towards the door. Fear striking her eyes momentarily.

I narrow my chin. "You're not mortal."

She shakes her head. "He said he had no use for me. That I was *used up*." Her lips tremble as she closes them tightly. "I began packing our belongings. Next thing I know, I'm waking up in this forest. And my baby—" She cuts off on a choked cry.

My heart sinks for this woman. I cannot imagine being separated unwillingly from your own child. My voice is low and soft when I speak. "I'm so sorry."

She narrows her gaze back down to the necklace, and I realize then and there what happened. She feared that the one thing she had left to hang onto was parted from her for good when Euphrosyne took her clothing to be washed. She retaliated in a moment not out of spite or anger, but out of sheer panic and sadness. The kind of sadness only a mother grieving could feel.

I gently rest my hand on her knee, stilling the bouncing that started some time ago. She looks up at me, her gaze flickering as she studies me. In the next moment she wails on a harsh cry.

She falls into my arms as she heaves everything she's pent up for days out into the open. And having been there myself, I allow myself to be a safe space for her to let it all out.

I look over at Reimus, silently nodding towards the door.

He nods at me as he smiles faintly, exiting the room to check on the other woman.

As I allow her to feel every daunting emotion, much like Hecate had done for me.

After some time, she pulls away from my embrace. Her cheeks damp with wetness, her eyes reddened and puffy from her tears. She wipes her nose on the sleeve of her shirt, clearing her throat. "Thank you." She looks over towards the door, nodding. "Is she alright?"

I smile faintly, shrugging a shoulder. "Her nose may or may not be broken, and she's a bit shaken up. But she'll be okay…" Trailing off as we're still unsure yet of what her name is.

"Semele." She says as she stands up, rubbing her hands on her pants. Her sapphire eyes staring down at me. "I promise it will not happen again." She walks across the room, exiting her bedroom.

I go to stand by the doorway, watching as she approaches Euphrosyne. She stiffens at her approach before Semele kneels before her.

They stare at one another as Semele speaks softly. "I am terribly sorry for what I have done. I—" She chokes on a shaky voice, clearing her throat. "Please forgive me."

Euphrosyne watches her, hesitating for a moment before nodding her head. She huffs out a laugh, not the kind of reaction I had imagined. "Teach me how to punch like that, and we're even."

Semele huffs as she nods her head. "Deal."

Reimus approaches them, looking down at Euphrosyne. "I will get Nora to come heal your nose."

She nods at him as the two women next to her inspect her face.

I approach them, Semele standing up and stepping back as I do. I look down at the three women, noticing the stark similarities in their faces. All three of them with the same freckles around their noses, their light amber eyes beneath dark curved eyebrows. Each of them with long wavy hair that flows like water down their backs. The two on the ends with beautiful champagne blonde hair, the one in the middle a few shades lighter than them.

"You three are sisters?" I ask.

The three of them nod their heads.

I fold my hands in front of my lap. "What are your names?"

Euphrosyne answers as she holds her hand out to her right. "My sister Thalia," She then gestures to the other sister on her left. "And Aglaea."

I narrow my chin, painting a smile on my face. "It's a pleasure to meet you three."

I hear Reimus approach behind me, Nora trailing with him before she pats my shoulder. "I've got it from here." She smiles before taking Euphrosyne's hand, guiding her up from the couch.

I nod my head as I turn to walk towards Reimus.

"It is a pleasure to meet you as well, Guardian of Souls."

I turn around, my gaze falling on Thalia as she and Aglaea stand up with their sister. Their beauty is striking and utterly magnificent.

"We heard what you did for that soul. We all did." Thalia gestures to the room, to no one in particular.

I frown under the assumption that their reactions will be similar to those who have gawked at me on the streets. "I was at the right place at the right time." Before I can turn around, Thalia chimes out.

"Would you like to join us this Saturday?"

I watch her.

"Once a month, sometimes more, we like to host gatherings here at The Sanctuary. We all come together, eat lots of food, dance, and socialize. It's a good time." Thalia smiles.

I work on a swallow, caught off guard by her kind gesture to invite me to their gathering. Having spent so often of my life in my room, never being invited to parties by my classmates in school, a part of me can't deny the glee that I feel to be invited for once.

A smile spreads across my lips. "I would love that."

Thalia smiles wide as she clasps her hands to her chest. "Great. The festivities begin at sunset."

She and her two sisters begin walking with Nora to a healers room down the hallway. I turn towards Reimus as he greets me with a smile. I look over at Semele, smiling as a portal materializes next to me. I watch as Semele's eyes grow wide, her mouth gaping open.

"I guess I'll see you in a few days." I say to her.

Reimus grabs my hand as we walk through the portal. Semele's eyes fixed on me wholly until the portal closes behind me.

CHAPTER 35

Leaning back against the cast iron tub, I sigh deeply as the hot water envelops me. My eyes flutter closed as my leg remains elevated above the water, Reimus' rugged hands kneading the tired skin at the ball of my foot.

"She feels safe around you." He says.

I softly moan to myself as his fingers move their way up my foot. "Possibly."

He chuckles before he falls silent for a moment. "I mean it."

I flutter my heavy eyes open, gazing lazily upon him. The frothy eucalyptus scented water lapping under his chest, his damp hair slicked back. I tilt my head. "I think she just needed someone to see her. To show her she's safe."

He gazes at me, understanding flickering in his eyes.

"She's been through a trauma. Everyone deals differently. She also has to grieve not being with her son. She just needs to see that we aren't here to hurt her. That it may not be where she wants to be, but she can find safety here."

He raises his hands up to my lower calf, kneading the knots under my skin. I sigh as he begins working them out. "When she's ready, I'd like to know more. I'd like to try and bring her son to her."

My lashes lift to him. I nod slowly as a lazy smile appears. "I'd like the same."

I pull my leg slowly from his hands, crawling into his lap as I straddle him. My hands come around his neck, my fingers brushing against his damp hair.

His hands come to rest on my waist, his fingers slowly grazing my wet skin. "So I guess I should expect you to be home late Saturday night?" He grins.

I laugh before kissing him softly. "Possibly."

He chuckles, a brightness churning in his eyes. "Well all that I wish is for you to enjoy yourself."

I twirl my fingers into his damp hair, smirking as I feel him hard against me. "I'm enjoying myself now." I lean in to nip his ear.

His hands tighten around my waist as he brings me further up him. My entrance rubs against his hard cock. "Are you now?" His voice teetering on a sultry and rough tone.

My smirk deepens. "Do you not believe me?" I grind into him, the peaks of my breasts taught against him.

He lowers his head, trailing kisses down my neck. "I'm not so sure I'm convinced yet." He descends lower until his lips lightly press against my nipple.

I moan softly against him as heat pools low. He lowers his mouth again, this time covering my nipple wholly. I grind my hips into him as his tongue laps against my hardened skin, a thrill buzzing through my veins.

He brings his lips over to the other one, his lashes lifting as he stares at me. I grind against him. "Please." I moan softly.

He lifts his mouth, pressing a kiss in between my breasts. "Please what?" He mutters against my skin. I feel his hand lower from my waist to my pussy, a finger slipping through me slowly.

I cry softly, his gaze not straying from me as he sinks deeper into me. "I need more."

"More what?" He plunges his finger deep in me, eliciting a cry from my lips as he works me slowly. "And do be specific, little spitfire."

I writhe against his finger shamelessly as I watch him. I do not shy away from his heated gaze, but instead devour it wholly.

I grab his head in the palms of my damp hands, his gaze hardening onto mine. Feral, possessive even.

"I want you to remove your finger."

His gaze remains on me, a smirk appearing as he slowly slips his finger out.

I lean in closer, just until my lips hover over his ear. I whisper to him. "Now, I'm going to sit on your cock, and revel in your thickness filling me."

I lift my hips, his cock meeting my entrance as I lower myself slowly. I listen to him grunt against me, heating my blood. Once he's buried deep in me I kiss him agonizingly slowly as my tongue laps against his. I pull away just enough to speak. "Now, you're going to—"

"Fuck you hard and deep?" He lifts me until he plunges me down onto him again. I cry against him. A feral grin widens his lips. "Don't worry, I know how that pretty pussy likes it."

His hands grip tight into my hips as he brings me onto him. His hips ramming into me, splashing water all around us. I cry as he fills me deeply.

His hands crawl up my back until they grip my shoulders, moans creeping out of his lips as he plunges me down onto him over and over.

I grab his hands, lifting them above and behind his head. He interlocks them as he grins deeply. I grind into him as my hands rest around his neck, keeping me steady.

He grunts as his head falls back slightly. "Fuck, you're doing so good."

I feel myself tighten around him as my cries of pleasure intensify. I come undone as I ride him, electricity pounding through me everytime I hear a whimper slip from his lips.

He lifts his head, looking down. Watching me ride him now that the frothy suds have cleared. "Even in the water I can still feel how wet you are." His gaze lifts to mine as I lose it.

I ride him as release implodes through me, crying through my orgasm. A moment later I feel Reimus tense beneath me, his hands coming to plunge himself deep into me, stilling himself there as he pulsates inside me. He grunts as I ride him through our orgasms, eliciting moans from both of our lips. It seems to go on for long moments at a time.

As my body grows limp he lifts me off of him as he cradles me to his chest. We both share a long moment of breathing heavy and deeply, trying to steady our breaths.

Until he lifts us up from the tub, carrying us over to the adjacent shower. He sets me down on that built-in shelf in the wall, where he lathers my body and my hair with soap before bathing himself.

As Reimus and I make our way down for dinner we both turn to each other in mild surprise when we find Dimitri and Nora sitting at the dining room table.

"Nice of you to make an appearance for once." Reimus says as he pulls out a chair for me before seating himself in the one to my right.

Dimitri chuckles as Aven begins ushering out silver trays of food. "I like to keep you on your toes, Rei."

Aven sets down the first tray before heading back to the kitchen again.

"Well it's nice to have someone else at the table with us for once." I say, grinning at Nora.

Aven brings out the last tray as he goes to pull out a bottle of dark red wine. Starting with Nora before moving on to me. The boys fix themselves with whiskey, per usual.

Nora thanks Aven as he trots over to me. Her hazel eyes fixated on me as she holds up her glass. "I told him if he didn't bring me, I'd tell everyone about his little incident last winter solstice."

Dimitri rolls his eyes, swigging a drink from his whiskey. "It's not funny anymore." He frowns as Reimus begins laughing deeply.

I glance between him and Nora. "Incident?" I smirk.

Nora belts out a laugh before setting her glass down. "Lets just say he took quite generously to the quiche that was served, having no idea what was actually in it. His lactose intolerance made him pay the price by nearly shitting his pants." She busts out laughing as Dimitri flips her off.

Aven looks over at Dimitri, guilt faintly painting his innocent face. "My apologies again, Dimitri." He hurries off to the kitchen again.

Reimus chuckles as he begins serving my plate. "He ran to the bathroom like his ass was on fire." He forks a few pieces of smoked brisket onto my plate before adding asparagus and a colorful leafy salad. He sets my plate down in front of me before serving himself.

Nora grins sidelong at Dimitri. "It's okay, Dimitri. I promise I won't tell anyone." She looks over at me. "Aside from Melinoë."

I giggle to myself as I begin forking the tender meat into my mouth. "How is Euphrosyne?"

Nora shrugs her shoulders. "Once I healed her nose she was fine."

"Did you heal her with magic?" I ask curiously.

She nods. "It was a friendlier alternative than popping her nose back into place."

I grimace at the thought. "Yeah, I can imagine."

The four of us eat dinner together, a change of scenery from just Reimus and I. Not that I mind any time spent alone with him, but the extra company is nice.

After the four of us finish Aven comes to collect our plates. Noticing that he forgot a salad plate, I pick it up as I scoot back from the table. I make my way to the kitchen while the three of them talk amongst themselves.

I step through the pristine kitchen, Aven at the undermount sink washing the dirty dishes. I come up next to him, his gaze lifting to mine.

I hand him the plate as he scoffs at himself. "My apologies, Melinoë! I fear sometimes I can be a forgetful brute." He chuckles to himself as he lowers the plate into the sink.

I watch him, something settling within me as I realize he spends much of his time here at the palace. I frown at the loneliness that could sometimes accompany that. "Where did you learn to cook like that?"

He looks over at me, his blonde hair combed back and hanging loosely at the top of his head. He smiles. "I learned a long, long time ago." He laughs as he sets the clean dish into a drying rack. "My mother taught me when I was very young. I was a very shy kid growing up, spending most of my weekends with my mother begging her to teach me how to make a new recipe. I guess she saw my passion for cooking and so every Friday night, I learned a new recipe with her."

My heart warms as a smile tugs at my lips. "That sounds lovely."

"Yeah. I told myself that if I could be even half of the cook and baker she was, that I would have done something right in my life." He laughs before his lips tug down into a frown. "She died many years ago. That's when I met Reimus." His smile reappears. "He saved me in a way. I thought after her death I would never step foot in a kitchen again."

I narrow my gaze before lifting it back to him. "Well you are the best cook I have ever had the pleasure of eating from."

His smile grows as he turns the water off, setting the remaining clean dish onto the drying rack. He wipes his hands on his cream-colored apron before moving his hands to the straps around his back. "Thank you, Melinoë. It has been a great delight to serve you." He removes the apron, setting it on a hook next to the walk-in pantry.

He makes a move to step towards the door when he pauses. He lifts his gaze to mine once more. "In all of the years I've known Reimus, I've never seen him as full of life as he is with you." He rests a hand on my shoulder. "He will forever carry the guilt of his family. But after meeting you, I finally saw that spark ignite within him again."

I place my hand on top of his, nodding as emotion clogs my throat. "Thank you."

His smile meets his eyes, nodding. He lowers his hand and exits the kitchen entirely.

I stand there for a moment taking in what Aven said. My heart both splintering at the grief I know Reimus carries for his family being murdered, and how he still could sit with me through my own pain with ease. Knowing that when he's ready to open himself up to me entirely about that part of his life, that I'll be waiting with the same love he's shown me since day one.

I straighten my back as I walk out of the kitchen and back into the dining room. I pull out my seat as I submerge myself back into the conversation.

I smile at Reimus before I grab my wine glass again. He leans over to softly kiss my cheek as Dimitri and Nora's voices fill the silence. I sit proudly next to the man I love, where no bounds or limitations exist on what I would do for him.

CHAPTER 36

I look over at Reimus, making sure I don't stir him awake. Padding silently over to our walk-in closet, I slip on a pair of black leggings and a white sleeveless shirt before slipping my feet into my black sandals.

The portal opens next to me as I quietly step through it, closing it behind me. My feet step on a loose twig, the fracture sound permeating the air around me.

My gaze roams around as I walk through the cemetery, becoming familiar with the eerie silence.

I kneel down to a headstone, fluffing up the flowers that rest in the vase against it. Even in the dark I could identify a bouquet of roses anywhere.

As I spruce the flowers up I feel his energy materialize behind me. I huff. "It's not polite to sneak up on people."

Keeper chuckles behind me. "It can hardly be considered sneaking up when you are aware of my presence."

I stand up, brushing the dirt from my leggings. I turn around to his form nearly blending into the night sky around us. With only the glow of the moon to guide us. I half-roll my eyes. "Good point."

I walk towards another headstone as he follows next to me. "I would think you would rather spend your time in The Asphodel Meadows than here. At least there, you can actually bond with the souls."

I brush a few specs of loose dirt off the top of a headstone before continuing my walk through the cemetery. I lift my gaze to his, hardly able to see those pitch-black voids. "I like the quietness the cemetery brings me. It's familiar." I shift my gaze forward.

He slowly nods. "Understandable."

He walks with me in silence as I scope out for any headstones that need tidying. "I am surprised though."

Keeper tilts his head. "By what?"

I work on a swallow. "That my father has not come to retaliate against me yet."

"For rescuing your sister." He says.

I looked towards him, confused how he would know that.

He gestures around us. "Spirits talk."

I nod in understanding. Sighing, I reach up to pluck a leaf from a hanging branch above us. "It's better this way. That she's in The Underworld."

"And what about you?" He inquires.

I look over to him, smiling faintly. "I'm exactly where I want to be."

Keeper walks with me a few steps. "And what if Zeus retaliates? What will you do?"

A chill creeps along my spine as I remember the vision I had using my shadows against Hades. I shake it off, reminding myself that I have free will. That nothing is ever set in stone. "I will figure it out."

Keeper's energy pulsates for a brief moment before dimming again. "You have not fully tapped into your power yet, have you?"

I clenched my jaw. "I can't."

"And why not?" He nearly demands.

"Because," I seethe, exhaling a breath. "I've seen what my powers can do and—" I cut myself off, resuming again. "I just can't."

I lift my gaze to him as he nods slowly. "What exactly did you see in this vision?"

I shake my head, shutting down the conversation. "It doesn't matter. I won't allow it to happen." I go to seat myself on an iron bench as Keeper remains standing.

"Don't let the what if of one vision stop you from tapping into that reservoir of power within you. The longer you resist it, the larger it builds. Until one day it can't remain contained any longer and you lose control of it entirely."

I look up at him, his own shadows swirling around him. "So essentially I have to learn to wield it, otherwise it will wield me."

He nods. "Yes."

I look down at my hands, shadows suddenly forming at my fingertips. The shadows move with my fingers as I wiggle them, until they disperse back into hibernation.

"Like I said."

I raise my gaze to him again. "And I suppose you can teach me?"

He raises a hand to his chest. "I am flattered, but no. There is only one man who has mastered the art of wielding shadows."

I work on a swallow as his name immediately pops into my mind. "Hades."

Keeper nods. "But you already knew this, didn't you?"

I narrow my gaze off to the side, not responding.

"What are you afraid of with him?" He inquires softly.

I exhale. "I'm afraid to learn how alike we both are."

He tilts his head. "Why is that a concern?"

I bite my inner cheek, lowering my gaze to the ground before lifting it back up again. "It's not." A long sigh escapes me. "I'm just being foolish."

Keeper nods his head. He brings his hands around his back, straightening his back. "Well, at least you're honest."

In the next moment, Keeper disintegrates entirely before I can respond. With now only the headstones around to accompany me.

I make my way over to a headstone as I spruce up another vase of flowers. Realizing how I've been letting inconsequential fears control my ability to truly bond with Hades.

Knowing that he is not my father, but how it might be nice to bond with him nonetheless.

The next morning after Reimus and I have breakfast I make my way up to our bathroom to get ready for the day. Having made a promise to myself that I would give Hades a chance, and bite the bullet and ask for his help in wielding my power better.

Learning to better accept it rather than fear it.

I decide to forget about the vision I had of him, telling myself over and over again that I have free will. And if I don't want that vision to come true that it simply won't.

Reimus having left to make security rounds with Dimitri, I take a moment to myself before opening a portal to The Underworld.

Exhaling a breath, I stand up straight as I will a portal to appear. Stepping through it until I reach the courtyard, the magenta colored sky both bright and vivid against it.

I see my mother through the dining room window seated in a pretty rose pink gown. I walk towards the entryway, finding my sister at the table with her.

I halt in my steps as they both look up at me.

Persephone smiles. "Melinoë, take a seat with us."

My gaze tracks over to my sister who looks neither bothered or over-pleased to see me. She looks down to her bagel, bringing it to her lips as she takes a bite.

I fidget with my fingers in my lap. "Thanks, but actually I was looking for Hades."

My mother watches me, curiosity painting her porcelain face. She smiles. "He should be out in the courtyard with Cerberus."

I glance over to my sister who looks up and gives me a forced smile.

I look back towards my mother. "Thanks." I walk back outside, walking the winding pathway of the courtyard.

I keep walking until I feel the slight vibrations against my feet, knowing Cerberus is nearby. I wind a corner when I see Cerberus running along the grassy terrain, racing to catch a red ball. I watch as the three heads fight for who gets the ball, the sight both laughable and slightly creepy.

As I approach Hades he turns around. The shock on his face causes my heart to sink slightly. The shock quickly vanishes from his face a moment later as he replaces it with a grin. "Goodmorning, Melinoë."

I nod my head in greeting. "Hello."

"If you're looking for your mother or sister, they should still be inside eating—"

"Actually, I came out here looking for you." I say shyly.

He stares at me, his gaze soft yet steady. "Is everything alright?"

"Yes—everything is fine." I say, twirling my fingers in front of my lap. I sigh. "I was hoping you could help me learn how to better wield my power."

Cerberus comes running over, the red ball hanging out of one the heads mouth. He sees me and rushes over to me, nearly toppling me on the ground.

"Easy, Cerberus." Hades commands.

Cerberus responds by dimming his rambunctious energy. He lays himself down on his belly as his ginormous tail wags. All three tongues hang out of each mouth.

"What have you seen of it so far? Other than mind manipulation?" He asks.

I turn my hands over, willing the shadows to form. They dance at my fingertips before dissipating again. I raise my gaze to him. "That's as much as I've been able to wield."

He nods. "Then you have much to witness yet." His shadows begin to unfurl around him.

I watch as they coil around him like a viper ready to strike on command. I watch as they slowly begin to dissipate, submerging themselves back into him.

"I would be happy to teach you." He says, his gaze steady. "But if I'm going to teach you, I only have one request."

I nod.

He takes a step towards me. "I only encourage you to see beyond the limitations you have set upon yourself. Beyond the preconceived implications of what you think your shadows *can* do, and instead what they *actually* do."

I scrunch my eyebrows. "Which is what?"

He lifts his chin. "They protect you."

I bite my inner lip, nodding my head as words fail me. "Okay."

He nods. "Good. Now try to penetrate my mind."

My eyes bulge as I shake my head. "I don't think I can—"

"Just try." He encourages.

I inhale, nodding as my gaze focuses on him. I breathe into that innate ability to wield hallucinations, the ability to control. I reach that mental barrier within him, a black fortress surrounding his mind. I press against it, unable to penetrate it.

"Focus on your objective, not on the barrier itself." He says.

I burrow myself deeper and deeper as I crawl through the crevices of the barrier. Until suddenly I'm being thrown out and I land backwards on my ass.

I raise up onto my elbows, my mouth gaping open as I gaze up at him. "How did you do that?"

He chuckles. "The shadows not only protect me out here, but in here too." He taps the side of his forehead.

"Oh." I say, standing myself up again.

He steps towards me. "Because when you learn to understand your shadows are there to protect you, not to wreak havoc, then you will better defend yourself against attacks. Like this."

In an instant my hands come up to my head as my eyes slam shut. I grunt at the pain of him siphoning through my memories, burrowing himself into my mind. "Stop!" I shout.

"Build that barrier, Melinoë." He says.

I feel the sharp claw of his shadows scrape against my mind, the agony of it causing me to keel over.

"Let them protect you."

Through the pain of his invasion, I desperately clutch onto the small piece of me that is still coherent. I grasp onto it, willing the shadows through that small opening. Panting, I begin forming that barrier within my mind. The shadows within me suddenly snapping that barrier into place and forcing him out.

I open my eyes, gazing wildly at Hades. I stand up on shaky legs. "You could've at least prepared me!" I shout.

His gaze hardens before me. "An opponent will not give you a moment to be prepared. You need to learn to act quickly while also having some protections already in place."

I steady my breathing, gazing frustratedly at him. I watch his pitiless face as he watches me gather myself. And instead of being insulted by it, I am grateful for it.

I brush myself off as I square my shoulders. "Again."

CHAPTER 37

Again and again, I build that barrier.

Sweat starts to bead above my brow as I maintain that protective barrier around my mind as Hades tries penetrating it. After several rounds of practicing, we moved on to extending that barrier around myself. Or rather what one may call a shield.

I begin to feel my control slipping, my shield splintering as his shadows begin to seep within. I exhale raggedly, trying desperately to regain control.

In an instant I feel his shadows retract themselves back into him, gone within a moment.

"I just needed a minute to rebuild." I say through panting breaths, the exertion exhausting my body. I sway on shaky legs as I lean my arm up against a poplar tree.

Hades watches me. "That's enough for today."

I look up at him, steadying my breathing. I swipe the back of my hand across my forehead as I wipe the sweat away.

Hades lifts his hand, waving it to the side as a glass of water appears. He floats it over to me as I greedily take it.

I take long gulps, emptying it entirely. I go to hand it back to him when it vanishes from my hands. I stare at my hand before my gaze lifts to him. "Will I be able to do that someday?"

He tilts his head as he shrugs. "Possibly."

I stand myself up straight, moving away from the tree. "So the shadows are there to protect me, but you've shown me that they are capable of wreaking havoc."

As I practiced keeping my protective barriers in place, Hades continuously used his shadows to break that shield. Over and over again, his shadows suffocated my mind. Until I finally maintained control, forcing them out completely. Then all they could do was brush up against my defensive barriers.

He steps closer to me, folding his hands behind his back. "They are there to protect you, but they are still yours to wield how you see fit in the moment."

"So they *can* be wielded for harm." I reiterate.

He nods. "That is correct."

I look down at my hands, clenching one into a fist before opening it again.

"When did it start?"

I look up at him. "What?"

He nods towards my hands. "Your powers. When did they start making themselves known?"

I shrug. "Just a few days ago."

His gaze flickers. "Show me again."

I breathe deeply as I feel into that reservoir within myself, willing that power to surface. I hold my hands out, palms up as shadows begin to emerge from my fingertips.

They descend downward and out, floating amidst the air in front of me.

I look up, frowning. "What's wrong?"

I begin to snap them back when I see Hades watch in what seems like utter shock. His eyes bulge ever so slightly, though noticeable from his usual stern set stare. I feel the tension in his shoulders as the energy deafens and pulsates before me.

He steps closer, his gaze on my hands entirely. He reaches a hand out as he gently grabs my hand. My power begins to slither along his fingertips, wrapping themselves around the calloused skin.

The next moment he pulls his hand away, the shadows retracting themselves back to me. He takes a step back as I retract them fully, until they are gone once more.

"Hades?"

He lifts his gaze to me as if forgetting I was here at all. Reminder of that fact paints his face as he schools his shock back into his usual motionless gaze. He nods his head, forcing a tight-lipped smile. "Continue to accept that reservoir of power within and they will forever be yours to wield."

A portal opens next to him as he turns towards it.

"Wait—"

He halts, turning to look at me. A moment of silence stretches between us. "Come back tomorrow if you'd like to practice some more." He turns around and walks through the portal.

As I walked the short way back through the courtyard I find Makaria sitting on the edge of the fountain. I watch as her ruffle white dress flows over the edge of the stone structure, her hair gliding down her back like spun moonlight.

One hand lowered into the water, the other cupping the edge to keep her from falling in. She hears me approach and darts to an upright position, turning herself fully to face me.

She sighs, a hand going to her chest. "Sorry. I did not know you were out here."

I take a seat next to her. "I was over there with Hades." I nod to where I just came from.

Her golden eyes pierce mine as her gaze glances over towards the walkway. "What did you need to see him for?"

"I had questions I needed answered." A bland, not completely untruthful response.

She nods her head looking down at the water again. "Is he…nice?"

I tilt my head. "You have yet to speak to him?" I inquire.

She shrugs a shoulder. "I haven't spoken much since I've been here. Since—" She pauses, clenching her jaw.

I narrow my gaze. "We don't need to talk about it."

She lifts her gaze to mine. "Why?"

I scrunch my brows. "Why what?"

"Why aren't you more furious? I don't remember you. And yet, here you are. Seemingly accepting of it." She lowers her gaze once more on the water.

I inhale deeply at the reminder, willing my emotions to calm. "I'm not okay with any of this. But I'm still here because you're my sister and I love you."

"What if I never remember you? Will you still be so willing to visit me? A ghost of a person who is no longer there anymore?"

I lower my head. "Of course I would."

She lifts her gaze, betrayal and anger swimming in her eyes.

"I'm far from okay with the fact that you don't remember me right now. But it wouldn't stop me from making an effort to see you because you are my *sister*. Not Zeus, not anybody will be able to change that."

She watches me as a long moment of silence stretches between us. Her eyes begin to glisten as she pulls her lips against each other. "I feel *so* much, and utterly nothing at the same time." A tear slips down her cheek as her lips tremble. "A large part of who I am is now hollow and...I don't know if I will ever see her again."

A deep frown tugs at my lips for my sister, never having wanted her to experience pain this deep and soul-shattering. I reach a hand out, laying it softly on top of hers. "You will not face any of this alone."

Her lips quiver as she locks her shoulders, visibly holding back the emotional dam that begs to be let out.

I soften my voice. "But the only way through it, is to *feel* it."

Her shoulders ease the tension, trembling with her lips. Her shoulders slump forward as her breathing ramps up.

"You are not alone. I am with you." My voice coaxes the darkness within her to find safety in unleashing itself from being stuck.

Makaria loses her control entirely and chokes on a harsh sob. Her whole body trembles as she clutches at her stomach, the cotton material of her dress trapped between her fingertips as she begins hyperventilating.

I pull her into me, my hands coming around her shoulders. "I am right here."

She sobs through harsh breaths, her body trembling underneath my hold of her. I begin to slowly rock her.

"You are safe here." a tear slips from my eyes as it falls on top of her head.

As her soul purges every daunting feeling, her breathing begins to steady once more. Through her tears, her body eventually begins to calm itself.

"I really do hope that I can remember you." She says, exhaustion evident in her voice after all that purging.

I still against her for a moment, the little bit of hope left in me clinging onto her words. I exhale as I nod, pulling her away from me.

Her dampened eyes stare at me. Her face a blank canvas of any real feeling now, as if it just purged itself from her entirely.

I lower my gaze. "I hope so, too."

CHAPTER 38

After my sister said she wanted to lie down for a while I portaled myself back home.

Hurrying off to the kitchen I walk over to the pantry, pulling some fresh sourdough bread from a shelf. I close the pantry door as I swing open the refrigerator, grabbing some lunch meat and cheese before closing it again.

I walk over to the counter, assembling my smoked turkey and cheddar cheese sandwich. I return the meat, cheese and bread before plopping myself into a chair at the kitchen island.

I let the silence around me drown out the harsh sobs of my sister. How it felt to hold her trembling shoulders.

She doesn't deserve any of this.

I finish my sandwich and walk up the winding staircase upstairs. Trudging to the bathroom, I walk over to the shower as I turn the water on. A steady spray of hot water fills the shower within seconds as I throw my clothes off and stand underneath the showerhead.

My hands rub my face before traveling up and over my head. The water submerges over me as ruminating thoughts threaten to immobilize me. Drops of water slush down my back, dripping off the ends of my hair as the thoughts burrow into my mind.

She's gone. He wins.

"Stop."

The thoughts sneak themselves into the crevices of my mind.

You will lose everything because of him.

He will find her.

He will keep her prisoner when he does.

My fingers burrow themselves into my hair, scratching against my scalp as I shove the thoughts out.

"I said stop!" I roar.

Calloused hands gently grip themselves around my wrists, pulling them down from my hair.

"Melinoë."

Reimus cups his hands around my jaw, raising my gaze from the floor onto him. The sight of him pulls me back entirely from my thoughts.

My gaze tracks over his hair as it dampens against the falling water. I glance down to his white shirt becoming transparent against his chest as the water sloshes down.

"I'm sorry." I say, gathering myself.

Water trickles down his face as the silver in his eyes churns brightly against the blue. "Are you alright?"

I nod my head, sighing. "Sometimes I cannot control them."

He pulls his hands away before lowering them to take his black oxford shoes off. His gaze remains on mine the whole time as understanding etches his face. "What do they say right now?"

He goes to lift his now soaked shirt free from inside his trouser pants, unbuttoning it before pulling it over his head.

"They tell me that I will lose everything because of him. That—"

My gaze remains on him as he lowers his hands to his pants, sliding them down his legs. Uncaring about the nakedness of him that sits below my vision. And I can see in his eyes as they stay trained on my face, that mine is the furthest thing from his mind.

"That she will never be the same again." A tear slips down my cheek, camouflaging itself against the water.

He raises a hand, brushing the damp strands away from my face. "He does not win."

I frown. "How? He already has."

A ghost of a smile appears as he shakes his head slowly. "He does not win. Even when he's battered you down with his neglect, with his violence—" He turns away for a moment, his jaw clenching before smoothing out again. "You brought Makaria back. You broke the compulsion spell placed on her. And you are a damn brave woman for still standing here today after everything you've endured. That you both have."

I watch him as water drips off his nose.

"I've been implementing further security precautions with Charon and Dimitri. For our people, for *you*." He grazes his thumb against my cheek as his fingers splay themselves along my cheek. His gaze hardens onto mine and his voice is gruff when he continues. "I will do everything I can to keep you safe because I love you, Melinoë. And I will burn his entire realm to the ground if he *ever* lays a hand on you again."

I still in his hold, those words fluttering like hummingbirds in my chest. My gaze softens as it bores into him, my tongue suddenly heavy in my mouth.

Those three words swallow me whole, like moths to a flame as I let them drown into me.

He watches me as my hands come up to his, a different kind of tear slipping down my cheek as my lips tremble slightly. "I love you, too."

His entire face slackens as a choked noise crawls up his throat. He pulls my face up as his lips crash into mine. He kisses me deeply as his body melts into mine like liquid.

He pulls his face away from mine, just enough to gaze at me. "Say it again. Please." He pleads.

A smile curves up my lips as a glow like none I've ever seen before lights up his eyes. "I love you." I repeat.

He kisses me again, backing us up into the wall. His voice gruff when he pulls his lips away again. "I love you." He whispers as he picks my leg up, hooking it over him. "In this lifetime, and every other. I am yours."

I feel his hard cock press against me as my heart bursts wide open inside my chest. My hands come up to his neck, burrowing myself in his presence. At the man I love.

He positions himself at my entrance, driving himself slowly in.

"In this lifetime, and every other." I say into the small space between us. "I am yours."

He buries himself to the hilt, wringing a gasp from my lips before he shows me just how much he loves me with everything but his words.

CHAPTER 39

The steady sound of the crackling fireplace mingles with the serene fluidity of his voice as he reads to me.

My head rests above my hand as I lay towards him, the hard planes of his lower abdomen underneath the palm of my hand as my legs lay limp halfway under the silken sheets. His hand rests over my thigh while his fingertips lightly graze my soft skin.

His head rests against the headboard, a pillow propped up behind his head as he holds his journal in his other hand. His black hair hangs loosely over his forehead as he reads from it. And I absorb every single word like a sponge soaking up every drop of water.

"Had I never met her, I would never have known the totality of what it means to love. What it means to yearn for just a glance from her, how those emerald green eyes could shackle me in place and I would thank her for the privilege to be in her presence. What it means to suddenly center my entire existence around the sole safety of another, and how insignificant the bridges I would happily burn in order to protect her are."

I lower my gaze to the slow rise and fall of his chest, observing every detail of his upper body. I nuzzle my head against my hand as I lift my gaze back up to his sated face.

"It is not my sole purpose to be her savior, as she proves her unending strength each and every day that she chooses to stand even after she has fallen. What is my sole purpose, in this lifetime and every other, is to be the one who proves her wrong. That I am not here to mislead with deception, I am not here to drain her of any remaining spark of life she has left. I am here to be the new standard that convinces her how she deserves to be treated, after living in a previous world that taught her it is not safe, nor wise to soften."

A tear slips down my cheek as my heart cleaves at his beautiful words.

His fingers begin grazing my skin again, sending subtle shocks to my bones. "Even when it is both of our times to leave this existence, and cross-over to The Underworld, I will still not cease proving to her that it is not hard to love her. That even when I have drank from The Lethe, and my memories have escaped me entirely, I will still find my way back to her. In this lifetime, and in every other."

He closes the journal, setting it on the side table to his left. He turns towards me, lowering his hand to brush away the tears that stream down my cheeks. He chuckles softly. "I hope these are happy tears, and not because my writing sucks that much."

A full-bellied laugh escapes me as I lean myself up, propping myself up onto an elbow. Loose strands of my hair fall over my shoulder, brushing my cheek.

Reimus gazes at me, a longing so profound in his eyes. He tucks those loose strands back behind my ear, sighing slowly. "I love to hear you laugh." A warm, genuine smile curves up his full lips.

I lower myself to lay down next to him, propping a hand on his jaw as he shifts to face towards me. Stubble subtly pricks my fingertips as I move them in a slow circular motion.

I flutter my eyes slowly. "When I would come home from mentoring with Hecate, laying in bed drowning in the pain of divulging everything up. When you would just sit in silence with me, with no questions. That's when I knew."

He lowers his hand to twirl his finger around a loose strand behind my back. His light eyes unmoving from mine.

I smile softly. "That's when I knew I loved you."

A half grin curves up one side of his lips. "Even when you thought you loathed me."

I laugh. "Even when I thought I loathed you. Even when I hated myself for loving you, because you were so different from anything I've ever experienced. You were—*are* so much more than I've ever known."

He raises his hand slowly to my neck, spreading his fingers along the underside of my jaw. He leans in, pressing his lips against mine. Goosebumps prick my skin as my nipples brush against his chest.

His tongue pries my lips open, my tongue clashing against his. My hands come up to his chest, roving down his warm skin. They lower further down, his body jerking forward as my fingers touch that hard silken skin.

He grunts against my mouth, our tongues and our lips still intertwined as my hand wraps around him. I pump him slowly to start, having no desire to rush this.

He is mine. I am his.

Those words are like a brand in my mind and in my soul as heat courses throughout my whole body. Wetness begins to pool from my pussy.

He lowers a hand as a long finger rubs against my clit, the movement slow and taunting. He keeps it there before descending down to fill me.

I moan into his mouth as he fills me slowly. I pump his hard cock a little faster, mimicking my building need for him.

A grunted chuckle leaves him before pulling his lips from mine. He lowers his gaze to our hands. "Gods, I fucking love it when you touch me." He lifts his gaze to mine.

I feel cum bead at the tip of his dick, smirking as I continue to work him. I graze my thumb along it, wringing another jerk from his body. He thrusts himself into my hand as he grunts.

He removes his finger quickly from me before flipping me around until my back presses against his chest. He grinds against my rear as he bends his knee upright. He exhales raggedly as his deep voice vibrates against my skin. "But I'm afraid I don't want to wait any longer to feel those lips on me."

I gasp as he lifts my leg to hook it back behind his, fully exposing my pussy. He lowers a hand to his cock, rubbing it against my wetness. I moan as he slaps it against my entrance, taunting me.

"I'm a fucking needy fool for you." He says as he positions his cock at my entrance. Slowly he starts to bury himself into me as his finger comes to my clit. "But I'm your needy fool." He thrusts himself completely, burying himself to the hilt. His finger rubs my clit as he lowers himself to the head before driving himself into me completely again. Cries erupt from my lips as he quickens his pace.

I look behind me, up at his handsome face watching us come together. I reach my hand back to grab his jaw, fixing his gaze onto me. His eyes glazed with desire watch me intently.

"I love you." I say breathlessly through pants of breath.

His gaze grows feral as he clashes his lips into mine, siphoning the breath from my lungs. He starts pistoning in and out of me, fucking me harder and deeper than he ever has before. Cries of pleasure slip from my lips as he drives into me and only intensifies as his own whimpering fills the space between us.

He pulls his lips away, sweat beading at his brow as he breathes fast and heavy. "I love you." He says between breaths.

My orgasm climbs quickly as his finger strokes my clit, sending me over the edge completely as that high crashes into me. I scream as my eyes roll to the back of my head, the orgasm too much and not enough at the same time.

I feel his body tense up as he drives himself into me, his cock pulsating as he unleashes himself inside me. A guttural noise comes from deep within his throat as he continues moving inside of me.

The orgasm lasts moments that feel like a glorious eternity. I moan his name as he trembles behind me, a whimper escaping him.

He finally slows down until he stops altogether, leaving himself buried inside me. His heart beats wildly against my back, his hand trembling as he rests it along my belly. I place my hand on top of his as we slow our breathing down together.

After a while of trying to catch our breaths, Reimus slips his cock out of me. I lower my gaze, his cock glistening with the cum of both of us. I lower my fingers, gliding them along that wetness before bringing them to my mouth.

I hear Reimus softly moan behind me as I suck my fingers, before his hand jerks my face towards his. He kisses me deeply and hungrily as our tongues clash together. Eagerly drowning in the taste of one another.

His lips leave mine, his gaze both sleepy and sated. He glides a finger along my cheek, his chest rising and falling steadily as he watches me.

We both lay like this for some time, as if we both have no desire to part from one another anytime soon. How something about this bond between us truly runs far deeper than surface level. How the tether that's been strengthening for some time now has fully snapped into binds with one another. A chord that magnetizes me to him.

Sometime later, I find myself falling fast and deeply asleep in his arms.

⁓

The next morning I head out to the pasture to find Alastor. I talk to him as I groom him—per usual, while the morning sun beams brightly above us. After I put his grooming supplies away and give him a kiss on the cheek goodbye, I portal to The Underworld.

Arriving outside in the courtyard, I walk through the path surrounded by those white funnel-shaped flowers hoping to find Hades out here. I find Hades at the end of the pathway, standing with his back towards me overlooking The Asphodel Meadows below.

"Melinoë." He acknowledges.

I step up next to him, looking upon all the souls as they begin to meander about for the day. "Hades." I glance over at him. "How did you know I'd be here at this time?"

He stares straight ahead. "I didn't." His hands remain folded behind his back as he looks upon his people. "This is where I normally find myself each morning."

I watch as an older woman waves at her neighbor, the casualness of it so pure. "Why?" I ask.

"Because," He begins, pausing before resuming. "It brings me peace to know that they are safe here."

"Has someone ever tried to harm them?"

He chuckles quietly. "No one would be foolish enough to try."

I look over at him, watching as his eyes glow vividly before dissipating again. A cold, calm stare upon his people tells me that he would protect his people at all costs. How unfair of a wage of war it would be for the opponent to battle with The King of The Underworld.

He turns towards me, his cold gaze softening. "Today I want to practice bringing your power further to the surface, if you don't mind."

My belly clenches in nervousness at the thought of seeing my full potential—at the reminder of the vision I saw of what my power can do. I open my mouth to decline the invitation, when he cuts me off.

"Let go of that fear." He says sternly.

I scrunch my eyebrows together, taken aback by his bluntness. I look off to the side, sighing. "I'm not afraid." I lie.

"You are only lying to yourself, Melinoë."

I whip my gaze back to him as he stares at me pitiless.

"Come." He says as he waves at me to follow him, leading us towards the center of the open area. He stands to face me, a healthy amount of distance between us.

I huff out an exhale. "I don't know how to wield it fully."

He raises a hand as shadows flow effortlessly from his fingertips, descending low to the ground to intertwine themselves into the damp grass. "All you need to do is let go of the fear of what it's capable of, and know that you, and you alone, control it." He lowers his hand as the shadows vanish entirely.

I take a deep breath in, slowly releasing as I fan out my fingers at my sides. I allow myself to travel down, down, down within that reservoir. I try to latch onto it, but I am pushed away from it. My mind begins to resurface the images of my powers restraining Hades, fear pushing me back up to the surface.

"Focus." He chimes out sternly. "Do not let that fear control you. Control *it*."

I find myself losing to my thoughts, the fear of what I'm capable of threatening to siphon any other kind of logic. I shuffle through those thoughts as I pick them free from my mind, their effect seeming less and less the more I do.

Your powers are dangerous.

I grasp onto it, crumpling it in the palm of my hand.

You saw the vision. You will be the cause of his death.

I grimace, initially stunted at the vivid memory. But I fight past the fear and remember that I am the wielder of my own fate. That my powers are not inherently good or evil, they just *are*.

I grab that thought and ricochet it out of my mind, no longer able to burden me with its presence.

I once again find that reservoir of power, this time merging myself with it. The coils of darkness slither through me like a charged essence. I breathe in and out as it weaves through me, becoming one with me rather than against it.

"Open your eyes." Hades says.

I open them, gasping when I witness my shadows flowing freely around me. I look down, eyes wide as they wrap around me like a second skin, a protective armor that is willing and at the ready for me to command.

I lift my gaze to my arms as pure darkness slithers from my shoulders down.

"Now practice commanding them."

I go to open my mouth when Hades holds a hand up, stifling my words.

I look up at him as he points to his temple. "In here." He says, a proud grin curving up.

I look back down at my arm, willing the command from my mind to connect with my power. For my silent command to simultaneously tether itself to the shadows.

I watch as the shadows around my arm begin to thicken, slithering until they create a vambrace. I watch it lock into place as I lift my other hand to touch it. I gasp as my finger meets the hardness of it. Unbeknownst to myself

I begin laughing as I wrap my hand around the solid vambrace, bewildered by the sturdiness of it.

"Great work." Hades says. "Now use them against me."

My smile fades completely as my face pales, the vambrace falling loosely as the shadows slide back down to my fingertips. I look up at him, shaking my head. "What?"

He steps forward, his posture calm and unafraid. "Pretend that I am an opponent." He says as he lowers his hands to his sides.

I watch him nervously as he approaches me, now only a few feet separating us. My gaze goes wild at the challenge to use my powers against him—

The vision.

It all begins to make sense, this is where it all happens. "No. I—I can't." I stammer, my shadows beginning to pull back into me.

"You can, Melinoë." He eyes me carefully. "I promise you will not hurt me."

I watch him as my shadows dissipate nearly all the way when a blast of his power shoots out at me. I duck out of the way, whipping my gaze towards him. "What was that for?" I seethe, my gaze hardening on him.

"If you will not practice defending yourself on your own, then I will give you a reason to." He says as another blast aims for me.

It aims true, striking me in the leg as hot agonizing pain ricochets through my skin. I yell in agony as my hand clamps to put pressure on the red slash across my leg. I fall to a knee, panting as the pain of just that one blast consumes me. Petrified of what something at his full power could do.

"Get up." He orders.

"I can't." I seethe, glaring up at him.

"In any other situation, you would have no choice but to fight through that pain and force yourself up. In any other situation, it would be between life and death." He twirls the shadows at his fingertips. "Get up."

My body begins to tremble with rage. "No."

He shoots another blast of power at me, aiming for the hand that holds my thigh. I tumble to the ground until I lean myself up on my other hand. I scream at the red-hot pain that melts through my skin.

"Get up." He orders again.

My breathing becomes rampant at his command, my teeth clenching together at both the pain and the anger coursing through my body. I feel myself beginning to convulse with it as I glare up at him.

"I will only ask once more before I blast another. This time it will be triple what you are feeling now."

My chest heaves as sweat beads at the top of my brow. I feel the rage swell inside of me, oozing itself from every pore and crevice.

"Feel that anger at injustice, Melinoë. Feel that rage." He coaxes.

My body convulses as I try to tamper it down, the anger too much and boiling over.

"Remember how it felt to be invisible. To stifle your powers."

I growl—*growl* at The King of The Dead as if I had no control over that reaction. My heart splinters at the reminder of being isolated in Zeus' presence. "Stop." I seethe.

"Think of how it felt to watch Eiran, the one who has loved you from the very beginning die right in front of you."

A choked sound leaves my lips as that agony begins to boil over, and not that kind that's coming from my wounds.

"Or what of the thought of losing Reimus. How the torture of that pain would—"

The tether on my sanity instantly snaps as I buck up onto my feet. My mouth gapes open as a scream pierces the air around us, and my arms lash out in front of me.

As I unleash myself onto Hades.

CHAPTER 40

My shadows blast him, causing him to fall to his knees. My mind lost to the rage as I will them to restrain him, a wicked smile curving my face.

My shadows—my power, it pours from me as I give it permission to flow from me limitlessly. I whisper commands of retribution to them, and they nuzzle themselves obediently against me in response.

I watch as his head snaps up, glancing at his arm as my shadows wrap themselves around his wrist. They solidify themselves before extending to the ground, acting as a restraint. Once they do his other wrist I command them to wrap themselves around his neck.

I step towards him as the air around us darkens, wind whipping at my face and my hair. A dark promise unfurls itself from my lips. "You touch him and I will kill you." My grin widens as memories surface themselves into the walls of my mind.

Memories of being neglected, of being unfairly dismissed. At the memory of it, I command my shadows to tighten their grip.

I watch as my shadows coil tighter around his neck, his eyes still unafraid even as I begin to siphon the breath from his lungs.

"Melinoë." He chokes out. Not as a plea, but as a reminder that this was all to get me to defend myself. That he is not the true threat, but only used himself as a target for me to unleash my powers onto.

The fog of rage clears itself from me entirely, my binds on his wrist and his throat dissipating at once. I gasp, stepping back as my hands come up to my mouth. Disbelief wracking my body at what just played out.

He stands up from the ground, rushing to me as he puts his hands on my shoulders. "I am okay, Melinoë." He repeats a second time, then a third.

My wild gaze darts to him, my breathing beginning to slow down as he rubs my shoulders. "Why didn't you stop me?"

"Because you wouldn't have unleashed your powers otherwise." He says gently, his stern gaze softening.

I lower my gaze to the ground, shaking my head. "I saw this in a vision."

He remains silent as I continue.

"I saw myself restraining you with my shadows. I thought I was going to kill you in that vision and—" I look up at him. "I felt that same way just now." I admit shamefully.

He lowers his chin. "I am sorry if this was extreme. But I just want you to be prepared."

I scrunch my eyebrows. "For what?" I demand.

He sighs. "Zeus may be laying low now, but he will eventually retaliate."

I pull away from him entirely. Wanting to curse at him for even thinking of such a thing, for bringing that fearful possibility onto me. But the truth is I know he's right.

I look at him as I admit what I've known even before I freed my sister. "I know."

He looks down towards my hand and thigh, waving a hand as the wounds heal immediately. I glance down before looking up again. "Thanks."

He nods his head.

"Can Zeus travel here?" I ask.

He shakes his head. "Only those who are psychopomps, or are death gods or goddesses may come and go as they please. Which is only a few."

I nod. "That's why my mother wanted Makaria and I to stay here permanently, isn't it?"

He nods. "She just wants to keep you both safe."

I walk to the edge of the clearing that overlooks the souls. I sigh, my gaze fixated upon The Asphodel Meadows. "Then we keep Makaria here for now."

Hades steps to my left, overlooking the souls with me. "And what about you?" He inquires.

I remain silent for a moment as I watch a woman playing with a small child. I grin as I watch her twirl her around in her arms, joy painting their soft faces. "I will be fine."

Hades gently grabs my shoulder, urging me to face him. I look at him, and through his motionless stare the faintest shimmer of concern lies. "Listen to me very carefully, Melinoë."

I turn fully towards him.

"Zeus is King of Olympia. He has far more allies than the typical god does, most of them too cowardly to side against him. If he wishes to harm you, he will go to great lengths to do it. So I advise you to care for your life as much as you care for Makaria's."

"Are you saying you would not stand with me should he retaliate?" Stepping back from his grasp.

"That is not what I'm saying. I will protect you, your sister, and your mother at all costs. But Zeus—"

"I don't give a damn who Zeus *is*. He will pay for what he did to us." I seethe, my temper elevating as my fists clench at my sides.

How could he stand there knowing everything that Zeus has put us through—has put his wife through, and not want to seek justice? After every vile thing that Zeus has done I would have thought The God of The Dead would take matters of revenge into his own hands, set fire to the lands of where Zeus resides. But his compliance is…shocking and disheartening.

"That is the anger speaking. I know you want vengeance, but you must be rational about—"

"Tell me the truth." I snap.

Hades watches me, closing his mouth.

My breathing ramps up, keeping the control on my power locked down. "If I were in danger, would you come out from The Underworld to help me?"

Hades watches me for a moment, hesitating.

"Would you or would you not face him if the time ever came?" I seethe.

His gaze remains on me, watching me as he contemplates how to answer. But his silence tells me everything that I need to know.

I huff out a broken sound, turning on my heels as I open a portal for myself.

"Melinoë, it's not that simple. I—"

I whip my head around, charging at him until only a foot of space stands between us. "Yes, it *is* that simple. If you care for my mother as much as you say you do, then that means you care for her children just as much."

Hades' pained face slackens as he watches me, a frown pulling at his lips.

"You are King of The Undeworld, for fucks sake. And you are scared of Zeus?"

Hades' gaze hardens instantly, his voice cold and sharp. "I am not afraid."

Even with the cold set in his eyes it doesn't frighten me in the slightest. I nod slowly. "I wish you would've said that you were. Because all that tells me is that your fear of him is not what holds you back."

His stare softens as guilt swarms his face. Understanding the thread of truth behind that statement. "Melinoë—"

I raise a hand, not interested in hearing anything more from him. "It's fine. I can handle myself." I say as I begin walking towards my portal. When I approach it, I turn around. An image of Reimus coming to my mind as an internal smile calms my fury. A reminder that I'm not alone, not anymore.

I turn around, walking through the portal until it closes behind me. Though this time, instead of The Guardians Palace I arrived at the cemetery.

I huff out a frustrated exhale as I walk through the cemetery, stalking the temper out of me. I walk towards a bench just in front of a weeping willow tree, plopping down onto the cool metal.

"Rough day?"

I swirl my gaze over to the side, rolling my eyes at Keeper when I see him. "I'm fine." I say curtly.

"Of course you are. You're always fine." He says, the hint of dry sarcasm like annoying wind chimes against my ears.

He moves closer to me, remaining standing. "What troubles you, Goddess of Nightmares?" He asks.

I inhale slowly, exhaling the frustration out of me. I shake my head. "Nothing, just—" I pause, looking up at him. He stares at me through depthless voids. "Is Zeus really all that powerful?"

He shrugs a shoulder. "He is King of Olympia, doesn't that tell you enough?"

His bluntness aggravates me for a moment before I simmer that temper once more. "Yeah, I guess it does." I sigh.

He stands there unnaturally still. "I understand that he is your father."

I shake my head. "He's just the man who I share genetics with. Nothing more." I say curtly.

"So if you share genetics with him, doesn't that kind of make you powerful, too?" He asks.

I shrug a shoulder, lifting my gaze to him. "Maybe."

He smiles sharply. "Well, then I guess only time will tell. Now won't it?" He winks before he starts walking away. "You have a visitor." He says over his shoulder.

I look over to my left as he seats himself next to me. A shy smile curves my lips. "Hey."

Eiran smiles back at me, the silhouette of his soul illuminated by the shine of the sun. "Hey yourself."

"Are you here to scold me about my interaction with Hades?" I ask.

He tilts his head as he lays an arm along the back of the bench. "No. I understand where you're coming from."

A fake half-grin curves up one side of my lips as I lower my gaze to the grass beneath us.

"But I can tell you that he's not lying when he says it's complicated." He adds on.

I nudge a loose rock in the grass with my foot. "Sure."

"You have to understand that Hades doesn't ever leave his realm, unless he's called to Olympia which is rare."

I keep my gaze trained below me. "That's still not a good enough excuse."

"You're right. It's not."

I look up at Eiran.

He narrows his head. "I think you just caught him off guard. He never had to leave The Underworld to defend

Persephone before. Even when she was with you and your sister, she forbade Hades to come after her."

"Why?"

"Because she knew there was a reason why Zeus wanted to keep her children under his eye, and she stuck around to try and figure out why. She traveled to The Underworld here and there to see Hades, until Zeus cast her out completely."

"Do you know why?" I ask.

Eiran watches me intently, hesitating before finally admitting. "I cannot say."

I tilt my head to the side. "You cannot say, or you do not know?"

He stares at me. "I cannot say."

I nod faintly, turning my gaze up to a crow flying high above us. A caw that pierces the silence around us.

"I'm happy for you, by the way." Eiran says softly.

I look up at him, my gaze catching on his genuine smile. My cheeks heat as I smile in return, my gaze lowering as I understand what he's talking about. "I'm happy, too."

Eiran's smile doesn't falter. "As you deserve to be."

I lift my gaze back to him, a faint dance of sorrow caressing across my heart. Knowing that I would have never met Reimus if the events that happened between Eiran and I hadn't. "Thank you."

"Well, you better get moving if you want to make it in time." He says.

I furrow my brows, confused at his statement. A moment later my eyes widen as I jolt up from my seat. "Shit—I have to go."

Eiran starts laughing, the sound a familiar warmth to my heart. His eyes light up as he watches me. "Have fun."

I grin at him as a portal opens next to me. "I will try." I wink before turning on my heels and rush through the portal.

Hurrying up the stairs to the bathroom to get ready for the gathering at The Sanctuary tonight.

CHAPTER 41

I don't have a clue what I'm supposed to wear to a *gathering*.

As I rummage through our closet, I settle on a black ruffled skirt and a black strapless top to match with it. I shimmy the skirt up, patting it down as it brushes against my calves.

I walk towards the vanity mirror, running my fingers through my wavy hair. I tuck it back behind my ear then pull it back out to the front, cursing at the absurdity of my nervousness.

What if they think I'm strange? Or that I'm weird? Ugh.

I reach for my obsidian necklace, clasping it around my neck as he comes into view through the mirror. I chuckle. "Here to watch me?"

Reimus chuckles as he steps away from the doorway. He approaches me, pulling my hair back as he runs his fingers through it. "Watching you is my favorite pastime."

I smirk. "I imagine it is." I turn around from the vanity, reaching up to give him a kiss before turning away.

"They will love you." He says, forgetting that with his heightened sense he can probably smell the nervousness from me.

I look up at him, sliding my feet into my black sandals. "Well with my luck, I'd say there's a fifty-fifty chance that you're wrong."

He steps up to me, his eyes alight on mine as he gently lifts my chin up. "They would be absolute fools not to like you."

I watch the surety in his eyes, the tenderness in his face. A shy grin appears on my lips as I shrug a shoulder. "It would be nice to have girl friends."

He smiles. "It'll be fun." He leans in to kiss me, his full lips soft against mine. He pulls away. "But for the love of The Fates, don't drink too much. I don't need you attempting to portal back here and you get yourself lost in another realm."

I laugh deeply at that, light dancing in his eyes when I do. "I promise."

The setting sun begins to illuminate through the balcony, an orange glow casting against the wall beside us. Reimus nods towards it. "Go. I'll be waiting to hear all about it when you return."

I lean up, pressing a kiss to his lips once more. I pull away, smiling as a portal opens up next to me. Excitement bubbles up within me as I remove myself from his grasp and walk through the portal.

Stepping out onto The Garden, I close the portal behind me as I gaze around at all the women present. Some faces are familiar, some are not.

I look over at the tables full of food, pitchers of different colored drinks spread along them. As I walk to approach it I'm interrupted by the sound of music playing.

I look over to find Fae females playing harps, banjos and flutes. Pointed ears with long, sharp claws that protrude from pale-olive toned skin. Each one wearing either a pastel colored dress or a skirt.

I watch as some women socialize with one another, and as some dance to the upbeat music that the Fae play. I glance over all of them—

"Who are you looking for, silly child?"

My skin pricks in remembrance at that voice. I turn around, gasping when I see him. "You."

The Fae male laughs delightfully. "Yes, me. Of course." He waves a hand through his nonexistent hair. "Who else would it be?"

My wide eyes stare at him for some time before words can register. "You're the one that helped me in the Sephyra Forest. I never thought I'd see you again."

He watches me motionless, moving a hand to my hair as he inspects it. I flinch slightly, not expecting it. He laughs. "So skittish are we now? But yes, it was me. Thanks for remembering."

I chuckle as he sets his hand down. "Your information was helpful."

He shrugs nonchalantly.

I look around. "So if this is a gathering for just women, then how come you're allowed in?"

He smirks. "I may be a male, but I am one of the girls." He raises a hand, twirling his fingers. "Plus, my lady friends supply the music." He gestures to the Fae females playing the instruments.

I nod, looking at the Fae females playing their instruments, joy painting their faces. I look back at him. "What might I call you?"

He smirks. "Sage is fine. And what of you, Goddess of Nightmares?"

My smirk rises to match his. "That, or Melinoë is fine too."

He nods. "Pleased to see you finally come into your title."

"Melinoë!"

I turn my head to see Nora making her way through the crowd of women hurrying up to me. She brings me in for a tight hug, jumping up and down as she embraces me.

"I'm so glad you could make it!" She says pulling away.

I chuckle. "So am I." I look over to Sage.

"Enjoy the gathering." He says before skipping away.

"Have you tried any of the food yet?" Nora exclaims.

I shake my head. "I just arrived moments ago."

A mischievous look creeps up onto her face. "Then allow me to show you to the offering tables."

She loops her arm into mine, ushering us over to a long white table. She guides us to three glass pitchers, each filled with a different liquid.

Nora points to the first one. "This one is huckleberry," She then points to the middle. "Dragonberry."

The name makes me chuckle. Reimus will get a laugh out of that later.

She points to the last one. "And this one is a fireball punch. It's exactly how it sounds—spicy as fuck."

I laugh as a grimace curls up my face. "Who would want a spicy drink?"

She shrugs her shoulders. "Your guess is as good as mine. Oh—they're all decently spiked by the way. So drink them *slowly*, otherwise your head will be spinning for hours."

Looking at the options, I point to the middle one. "I'll just take a glass of dragonberry."

She grabs two glasses, a wicked grin on her face as she squeals. "Twinning."

I furrow my brows. "Twinning?"

She rolls her eyes, filling the first one. "As in samesies? Because we're having the same kind? Try to keep up, girl." She hands me the glass before filling up her glass with the same punch.

I take a sip of it, the fruity flavor cascading on my tongue. I grimace as the potency of the liquor hits me. "You weren't kidding."

She laughs, playfully rolling her eyes. "I'm never wrong." She guides us down to the food laid out. Platters of fruit, fresh baked bread, jams, strips of cooked meat, pies, and pasta salads line the entire table. Lifting my gaze to the table across from us, realizing that table is just as full.

"Wow. This is…"

"Paradise?" She asks.

I look at Nora and we both burst out laughing before we both fill ourselves with plate after plate of food.

After two heaping plates of food I down the rest of my dragonberry drink. Uncrossing my legs, I stretch them out in front of me as I prop myself up by my hands. Nora mimicking the same stance.

I watch as Euphrosyne, Thalia, and Aglaea walk towards us. Each of them with cheerful smiles on their pristine faces.

"Melinoë! You must come dance with us!" Thalia exclaims as she leans down to hold out her hand.

"Yes! Please come dance!" Euphrosyne chimes.

Nerves begin to coil in my belly, not ever having been one to dance. I don't even know if I know how to. "Oh, I don't know. I appreciate the offer but—"

Nora gets up onto her feet quicker than I can blink. She grabs at my hand, yanking me up. "Oh, don't be a tight ass. Let's go."

I get onto my feet as Nora pulls me to the dancefloor as the three sisters guide the way. I look around at the crowd of women around us, each of them dancing and looking like they're having a great time.

I work on a swallow as I yank my hand back from Nora.

She stops and turns towards me. Curiosity on her face as it softens. "What is it?"

Shame colors my cheeks unwillingly as I whisper to her. "I don't know how to dance." I lower my gaze to my fingers as I fidget with them.

I raise my gaze as Nora stares at me for a moment before smiling softly as she leans in to whisper. "Do you want to know a secret?"

I watch her, waiting.

She shrugs her shoulders. "I don't either."

I stare at her for a moment until she reaches her hand out again. This time waiting for me to take it. "But how fun would it be to dance terribly together?"

Something blooms within me at her proposal. That stone wall that has kept people at a distance for my whole life splinters through the foundation. I feel the warmth trickle in as I smile, grabbing her hand.

As we make our way to the dance area the music speeds up as women around us start dancing away. I look around, noticing the fluidity of how they dance. While noticing some of them seem to have no idea what they're doing, but having fun anyway.

I stand awkwardly staring at Nora as she begins to move her hips. She starts waving her hands in the air before skipping in a circle around me. I turn around watching her, watching the carelessness of it. I look down at myself, beginning to swish my hips, trying to feel comfortable with it. A woman howls, jerking my gaze to her. She smiles deeply as she prances around, similar to how Nora is.

I instantly try to fight the smile that threatens to curve my lips, but I force myself to let it flourish as I begin prancing around.

I throw my arms in the arm, swirling my body around as Euprhosyne joins me with her two sisters. We dance in a circle together as Nora takes Thalia's hand, the five of us forming a dance line. Nora skips as she weaves us through other women when I feel someone grab for my hand.

I look to find Semele pulling me from the dance line, taking my other hand. She smiles as she lets herself go to the music, shimmying our arms up over our heads. I let myself go as I move my hips, letting the music take me to a place far beyond the fears of my mind.

I find myself laughing as I dance my heart away, a youth-like energy flowing through my body as I just let it all go and *dance*.

CHAPTER 42

The sound of Nora's drunken laugh fills the space between us. I lazily stare up at the night sky as our heads lay flat against the cool grass.

"So you really threw a knife at him?" A snort that turns into a giggle escapes her.

I laugh as I shrug. "We have a very…spontaneous kind of relationship." I look over at her and wink.

She laughs again, her eyes squinting.

I look back up at the glowing stars above us, the music and women dancing still going strong around us. I lift my gaze higher, noting a chain of stars clustered together.

"We should name it."

I look over at Nora. "What?"

She nudges up towards the sky, lifting a hand to point at the cluster of stars. "That cluster right there shines nowhere else other than right above Vulir."

I look back up at it, awe softening my face at that fact.

"No one's ever named it. We all say it's the constellation that points to home. To Vulir." She lowers her hand back to her side. "It deserves to have a name."

I stare up at it, contemplating as I take in the formation of it. I notice on each side the stars curve upwards as thin lines of them protrude downwards, fanning themselves out like a wing. The brightest star of them sits right at the center, right in between the two curves.

"It looks like a bird." I say quietly.

Nora chuckles. "It kind of does."

We stare at it a little longer, sharing a moment of silence before we both say in unison.

"Phoenix."

We both look at each other as our lips curve upwards in silent agreement on its new name.

The sound of someone approaching has me lifting my head up for the first time in thirty minutes. Immediately feeling the woosh of dizziness as I move. "Shit, you weren't kidding about those drinks."

Nora laughs as she sits herself up too. I look over at her as she shrugs. "I warned ya."

I chuckle as Semele approaches us, lowering herself down to sit next to me. "If I don't take a break from dancing I fear I might break my knees."

I chuckle, gesturing to Nora. "Why do you think we sat out when we did?"

"I figured it was because you two were just too drunk to dance anymore." Semele says playfully.

"No amount of drunkenness will ever keep me from shaking my ass, girl." Nora chimes in, a giggle trailing her words. She stands herself up, wobbling at first like a newborn fawn before steadying her stance. She yawns, bringing a hand up to her mouth. "But I fear it's past my bedtime."

"Awe, can't hang?" I say teasingly.

"Oh, I can hang." She holds her hand up. "But I need my beauty rest." She flips her copper hair over her shoulder, hardly making a difference as her hair brushes right along her collarbone. She looks down at me, smiling. "Thanks for coming out tonight."

I smile back, nodding. "I'm glad I came. Goodnight."

Nora walks towards the entrance back into The Sanctuary while Semele and I remain seated.

I look over at her. "How are you doing?"

She looks at me, her features softer than when I first met her. She shrugs a shoulder faintly. "I'm managing."

My heart sinks a little in my chest as I glance down at her ankles. The skin there not as red and bruised as it was before. "They look better."

She looks down, working on a swallow as her gaze lifts back to mine. "I suppose they do."

I hesitate before I continue. "Do you want to talk about it?"

She shakes her head as she stares ahead. "There's no point."

I narrow my gaze, leaning in ever so slightly. "Well, if you ever change your mind, I'm a good listener."

She turns to me as her sapphire eyes pierce into mine. Half of her cinnamon brown hair tonight is swept up into a bun while the rest flows down in loose waves to her mid-chest. She forces a smile as she nods curtly. "I'll keep that in mind."

I glance over to the three sisters as they laugh amongst one another. "So you're from Olympia?"

Semele follows my gaze. "Yes. But I'm originally from Lothario, a small village right on the border."

I turn back towards her. "And that's where your son still is?"

She looks at me, clenching her jaw subtly. "Yes."

I frown. "Is there any chance he could be freed?"

She shakes her head. "Not without him noticing."

"Who is he?"

She pauses momentarily, sorrow swimming in her eyes. "Dio."

I gaze at her, watching the uncomfortability rise in her face, not wanting to pry any further. But also wanting to understand her story more. "So you walked all the way here? How far is Lothario?"

"Gods, no. I didn't walk. I portaled."

My eyes raise, but smooth out again. "Right. Because you're immortal."

She nods. "Vulir has always been known to be a safe haven for women, so I portaled here. I thought if I waited out here for a while I could come up with a game plan to free my son. Maybe for us to start over here." She lowers her gaze to the ground, the hope in that success drained from her face visibly.

I clamp down the anger that rises within me for this woman, only wanting to be with her son and can't because of some abusive bastard. "Why not just free your son and live in Olympia together?"

She looks at me, shaking her head. "Because he would find us. And if I free my son, we must be somewhere far from Olympia."

I watch as Euphrosyne and Thalia begin carrying their sister Aglaea up and away from the gathering. I chuckle at the sight of Aglaea drunkenly hanging onto both of her sisters, her eyes nearly closed completely. I overhear Thalia as she tells her the consequences of drinking too much.

I look at Semele, watching the same interaction as well. "Well whatever your plan is, I want in."

She whips her head towards me. "Are you mad?"

I smile. "No. I just hate to see strong women being taken advantage of."

Semele sheds a tear, watching it trickle down her cheek before she wipes it away. She exhales raggedly, taking a minute before answering. "I'll let you know when I'm ready."

Turning my gaze back to the remaining few women standing around I realize mostly everyone has gone inside or left. I stand myself up, reaching my hand out for Semele.

She takes it as I pull her up.

My stomach suddenly churns as nausea roils through me, it hits me hard and fast like a wave crashing against my feet. I flinch my hand away as I jerk it up to my stomach.

Semele's gaze follows. "Are you alright?"

The nausea quickly vanishes as if I'd imagined the whole thing. I rub at my stomach, confusion clouding me for a moment as I nod vaguely. "Yes, I'm fine." I lift my gaze to hers before bringing my hand down again. "I guess that's my sign that the spiked drinks have affected me far greater than just being intoxicated."

Semele chuckles as relief dances in her eyes, her shoulders sagging ever so slightly. "Yeah they're pretty fucking potent. Are you sure you're fine to get home by yourself?"

"Yeah, I'll be fine." I smirk as a portal materializes behind me, Semeles eyes not widening in the slightest. "I'm only a second away from home anyway."

Semele snorts a stifled laugh. "Get some rest."

The remaining women outside with us gasp in shock and I chuckle at their reactions. I turn around, walking through the portal until I'm stepping out onto that familiar bedroom floor.

As the portal closes behind me I see Reimus laying in bed. His hand propped up behind his head with his other resting on top of his chest. The drunkenness—and the nausea, no longer seems apparent anymore as the hard planes of his chest come into view.

I slip off my skirt, letting it pool to the ground before lifting off my top. My bare skin kisses the warm air complimented from the fireplace roaring beside me.

I approach the bed, watching the rise and fall of his chest as he peacefully sleeps. I smirk as I climb on top of him, the sheets the only thing between us now.

I lean down, giving him a soft kiss on his lips before moving lower to his neck. A noise catches low in his throat as he stirs awake.

He chuckles, his voice deep and gruff from sleep as the hand on his chest comes to graze my shoulder. "You're home." He smiles sleepily.

The sight of him so perfect. The old me would've strangled myself for even admitting that.

I kiss him on the neck again. "Yes." I say sweetly.

I feel his hand lower down my arm as it brushes against my breast. He makes a humming noise. "And you're naked."

"Yes." I say softly, trailing kisses lower to his collarbone.

His hand lowers to my hip, gripping me gently. "How convenient."

He hardens beneath me through the silk sheets as my gaze lifts to his. His bright eyes gaze at me as I smile wickedly. "Indeed."

He removes his hand from behind his head as he lowers it to my hip, caressing my soft skin. "How was the gathering?"

"It was a great time actually." I smile genuinely.

"I'm glad to hear it." He raises a hand slowly up my side, his slow movement causing goosebumps to prick my bare skin. His fingers trace circles underneath my breast. "Did you try some of the spiked drinks they offer?"

I chuckle, both at his question and the featherlight feel of his fingers. "Nora warned me it was potent so I was smart to drink it slowly. But it still got me pretty drunk even as an immortal."

He chuckles, his voice deep and husky. "Yeah, it's strong stuff." His index finger raises up, slowly gliding over the hardened peak. A faint gasp escapes me.

I arch my back into his exploration. "Want to know which flavor I had?"

His gaze lowers to my nipple before lifting back up to me. "Which one?"

I giggle. "Dragonberry."

He laughs, the vibration thrilling me to my core. "Interesting." He goes back to circling his finger around that sensitive skin.

I moan against him. "Do you find amusement in torturing me?" Frustration in my voice building, wanting more.

A wicked grin paints his handsome face. "It can't really be torture if you're enjoying it, can it?"

My breath hitches, heat pooling low.

He lifts himself closer to me, his lips hovering over that sensitive skin. "But if you wish to know if I love seeing you aroused—" He pauses as he flicks his tongue out, gliding it around my nipple as another moan escapes me. "Then you should already know the answer to that."

He closes his mouth over it completely, a soft cry escaping me as he tastes me. He pulls away, lifting me until he flips us over. My back pressed against the soft bedding while he hovers over me.

His midnight black strands fall messily above his brow as he spreads my legs wide open. He glances down, a heated smirk on his face. "I think I might show you what my favorite flavor is."

He lowers himself and presses kisses from my belly down to the inside of my thigh. I moan as he presses a kiss right at my entrance, causing me to grind against him.

He chuckles. "I love it when you're impatient for me."

Before I can beg him to hurry he descends his mouth on me entirely as he devours me.

I writhe against him, wetness pooling from me as his tongue maps the entirety of me like he's framing me to memory. I look down as his lips glisten against me, crying as he moves to suck my clit. I grind against him wanting more, more, more.

My orgasm is already building like an inferno as I feel myself suddenly climb over the edge, Reimus not lifting his mouth as I do.

I scream his name as he devours everything that pools out of me.

Once my body falls limp, he lifts his head as I glisten from his lips and down his chin.

He hovers over me as his lips meet mine. I greedily kiss him, the taste of me on both of our lips. As I try to urge him up he breaks away from the kiss.

Lowering himself back down again, he meets my gaze. "I think you can cum again for me, little spitfire." He lowers his mouth on me once again, a moan escaping my lips as I writhe against him.

Until I cum twice more for him before falling deeply asleep.

347

CHAPTER 43

The next morning I awake to the sound of our bedroom door clicking shut. The quiet footsteps draw closer as I hear Reimus set something on the bedside table.

I sniff once, twice. "Is that bacon I smell?" I mumble, my lips pressed against the sheets.

Reimus chuckles, crawling himself back into bed. I feel him slide the covers over himself before he leans over to kiss my cheek. "Possibly." He kisses me sweetly as his calloused hand brushes my disheveled hair back.

I stretch my arms out before turning towards him. I lean up onto an elbow, bringing my free hand up to wipe the tiredness from my eyes. I open them and stare at the tray of scrambled eggs, bacon, buttered toast, and strawberries.

I look at him, grinning. "You know me so well."

He reaches over to grab a mug filled with hot coffee, handing it over to me. My heart sings as the hazelnut aroma wafts towards my nose. He shrugs. "That could be debatable."

I greedily take my first sip, sighing into the mug before I set it on the bedside table.

We both eat our breakfast in bed before he takes the tray of empty dishes back downstairs. I rise from the bed to utilize the bathroom before making my way to the closet.

I pull over a maroon shirt before settling on a pair of black leggings. Slipping my feet into my sandals, I step out of the closet when Reimus makes his return.

"Going to see Makaria?" He asks as he shuffles through his hanging shirts.

Peering my gaze up to him, I nod curtly. "I left kind of…abruptly yesterday."

He picks out a white short-sleeved shirt. Pulling it over his head before he smooths it out. He gazes at me. "How come?"

Not wanting to have this discussion right now, but knowing if I don't have it now, I'll probably just brush it off and let it fester inside of me. I exhale slowly. "I asked Hades if he would stand with me if Zeus retaliated. And at his silence of an answer, I told him he was a coward."

Reimus halts pulling his jeans on, frozen as he watches me for a moment before resuming calmly. He buttons them, his gaze on me wholly. "And what did he say?"

"He said it was complicated." I scoff, the sting of betrayal evident once more.

Reimus tucks in his shirt. "And what do you believe?"

I look up at him.

He stares at me. "Do you think Zeus will retaliate?"

After a few moments of contemplating if I should lie to spare the worry from him, I realize he has done nothing to deserve that from me. So I sigh as I tell the truth. "Yes. I do."

He calmly walks over to me, his eyes alight on mine. "Then we will just have to make sure we're ready for when he does."

He leans down to kiss me, his lips soft but demanding before he pulls away entirely. He walks out of the closet as I stand there remembering another vital part of yesterday I haven't shared with him yet.

"There's something else."

Reimus turns around.

I lift my gaze to his. "Prior to that, I was working with Hades to better harness my power. To get a glimpse of what I'm capable of."

He tilts his head slightly, curiosity in his gaze. "And did you get clarity on what you're capable of?"

My gaze latches onto his. "Yes."

He nods, a deep grin curving his lips. "Good."

My brows furrow, expecting a different response. "You don't want to see?"

He smiles faintly. "I don't need to see proof of your capabilities. I know your strength. I can only imagine the reservoir of power that lurks beneath you."

I grin at his response. "Maybe if you're a good boy, I'll show you my tricks."

He watches me delightedly, a fire now brewing beneath his stare. A wide grin curves his full lips. "And if I misbehave instead?"

My grin deepens as wicked heat ignites my veins. I lazily shrug my shoulders. "Then maybe I need to restrain you until you get it right."

His eyes sparkle at the challenge as he approaches me, his hand coming up to my chest. He brushes the back of his knuckles against my skin. So featherlight, so agonizingly slow. He lowers his lips until they hover above mine. "I fear you are only tempting me with a good time, little spitfire."

My skin heats at his words as he presses a soft kiss to my lips. His hand lowers, the backs of his knuckles brushing lightly over my breast. I gasp at the touch as he pulls away, the absence of him like a cold shock to my nerves.

Before he leaves the room entirely, he turns to lock eyes with me as a smile curves his lips. "I love you."

I smile at him as my heart warms inside of my chest. "I love you."

As he leaves the room I will a portal open beside me, walking towards it. I close it behind me as I step out into The Underworld.

As I start walking through the garden I come to the open terrain just before the edge of the cliff. Her back turned towards me as she looks out upon The Asphodel Meadows, slightly leaning forward.

When she hears me approach she turns around abruptly. Standing in a defensive stance she sighs as her arms fall back to her sides, forcing a smile when she sees it's me. "Hey."

I smile back, approaching her side. "Sorry, I didn't mean to frighten you."

She sighs, turning around as she shakes her head. "You didn't. I just seem to find myself always on guard lately."

I nod solemnly, turning my gaze towards the souls below us. I nod my head towards them. "Have you been?"

"Not yet." She says quietly.

I chuckle as I watch Shyla tending to her tomato garden, the image of her gloating to Irwin filtering through my mind a moment before disappearing.

Makaria glances at me. "What are they like?"

I look at her, seeing the curiosity in her gaze as well as the timidness to fully open herself up to this world yet. Though I don't blame her one bit for being hesitant after everything she's gone through. "The souls are kind. They will try to throw themselves at your feet." I laugh. "But they are happy. They seem to rest easily here."

Makaria studies me, nodding her head. We share a few moments of silence together when her voice quietly breaks the stillness. "My memories still aren't back yet."

I continue my gaze forward, my chest heaving at her statement. I smile faintly anyway. "It will come back soon."

"How can you be so sure?" She asks.

I look towards her, her golden eyes brighter than the last time I saw her. Yet still a dullness wreaks a bleakness within them. "I don't."

She watches me, waiting.

I sigh. "But I have to believe it will come back. Otherwise…I don't know."

Makaria reaches for my hand, her touch stilling me wholly. I look at her as she gazes at me. "I never want to see him again."

I watch as tears fight against her eyes. The starkness in her gaze, as well as the deep hurt. An internal frown pulls at my heart.

She squeezes my hand quickly before lessening her grip again. "Promise me that I will never have to see him again." Her voice ends on a rough catch.

I nod my head curtly. "I promise he will never hurt you again."

"Us." She corrects.

A tear escapes from my eye as it streams down my cheek. I nod again. "Us. He will never hurt us again."

A faint charge of energy pulsates behind me. I turn my head around to lock eyes with our mother.

The portal closes behind her as she walks towards us, a ghost of a smile on her face. Donning a pale blue gown that brushes along the tips of the grass as she walks.

"Goodmorning," She says to both of us, her smile deepening. She wraps her arms around me as she hums in my embrace.

"Morning." I say into her embrace.

She pulls away, turning to give Makaria a hug before glancing over towards the souls. "They miss you already, Melinoë. But don't tell Shyla I mentioned it. She'll never let me hear the end of it."

I look at her, huffing as a grin pulls up my lips. "I'll be sure to visit them tomorrow."

Persephone nods her head, gazing at me for a moment before turning to my sister. "Makaria, would you mind giving us a moment?"

Makaria nods, forcing a smile. "Of course." She glances at me. "See you tomorrow then?"

I smile. "I'll be here."

Makaria pivots on her heels, walking through the courtyard before heading back inside the palace.

My mother steps to my side as she keeps her gaze trained forward upon the souls as we stand in silence for a few moments. "I must apologize for the other day."

Knowing exactly what she's talking about, I keep my gaze trained forward. "You have nothing to apologize for. What I said was directed to Hades, not you." My gaze turns to her.

Her gaze flickers amongst her people before turning to me. Her emerald green eyes glow vibrantly against the magenta painted sky. "Regardless, there is something I feel I must clarify pertaining to the complexity of the pact."

"Pact?" I ask.

Persephone nods faintly. "Long, long ago when Hades took to rule The Underworld, Zeus took to the land and the sky, and Poseidon took to the sea, a pact was made with The Fates. Each one would have complete rule over their lot, and each would reside over their domain."

My gaze strains on my mother, waiting.

"The Underworld is different though, only Hades and very few can enter, not including Zeus or Poseidon. Because of this, a pact was made. Hades is to reside solely in The Underworld unless called to council with The Fates in Olympia. For a long time, this never bothered Hades because he loves his people, everything he needs is here in The Underworld. He has never been one too interested in visiting the land of the living. So he agreed on the terms. But it wasn't until everything occurred with Zeus and I that he regrets nothing more in his life than making that pact."

My gaze narrows slightly, shame clouding me for accusing him of being a coward when in reality it appears he has no choice but to stay here. A frown pulls at my lips as regret surfaces. "I'm sorry. I had no idea."

"You have nothing to feel sorry for. You were right to assert yourself in the way you did."

I look up at her. "So he can't roam the upper world? At all?"

She stares at me, her gaze boring into mine. "Not unless he wants to stir trouble with The Fates. An agreement goes a long way with them. They hold them to a high degree."

"Does this pact apply to you as well?"

She shakes her head. "Though I am Queen of my realm I can roam freely. It paid to be a great advantage when you and Makaria were still under Zeus' control."

"That's what I still don't understand." I begin, as I turn to face her. "If Zeus wanted Makaria and I under his control, why would he have let you see us at all? I remember vividly of you tucking us into bed, having breakfast with us. But you said he had us under a cloaking spell, hidden away from you?"

She nods her head. "He placed the spell on you both after I threatened to turn Olympia into ruin if he didn't allow me to bring you both home. But before that, I thought playing into his game would grant me the access to know *why* he was so insistent on keeping my children under his watchful eye, never budging from letting you come home with me to The Underworld. So for a long while I stayed with you in that cabin. But it was only so long that I could stay away from my realm, from my people and my duty as their Queen. After you turned one, I finally made my return back to The Underworld. I returned to you every single day, staying until you went to sleep, then portaling back to my realm."

I watch as even though my mother stands tall, her head held high, there's a pain deep in her bones that I will never be able to understand. The anxious energy of it shows now as she works on a swallow, fighting it down.

"For a while this didn't bother Zeus, as long as you were under his watchful eye. Until a little over two years passed, and I began to become more persistent in bringing you home. He denied me over and over again, so one day I tried taking you with me."

Her eyes flicker, going someplace far from here for a moment before settling again.

"I was in the cabin gathering your things while he portaled himself to handle business at Olympia—or so I thought. You were in your room taking a nap when he appeared behind me, though he shape-shifted himself to appear as Hades. I swung around, surprised to find my husband in the upper world, not able to tell them apart as Zeus masqueraded his scent and energy to match Hades. I immediately wrapped my arms into him, and—"

She ends on an abrupt choke, her face paling to a significant degree. My stomach begins to churn as understanding of where she's getting at settles vilely within me.

She clears her throat. "His false appearance slipped away after, and said if I ever tried to take you away again, that he would take you to Olympia with him, and I would never see you again." She pauses as she fidgets with her fingers in front of her lap. A quiet, shaky exhale escapes her. "Nine months later, Makaria was born."

The words hit me like a train as tears well in my eyes.

"I was devastated that I could not bring you both home, so for four years I visited. For four years I allowed myself to be in the same household with Zeus just so I could see my daughters. And for those four years, I felt hopeless in ever seeing the day that you'd both come home with me. Until something cracked within me when I saw, as you grew older, the way he began to treat you."

Her eyes harden as she stares ahead, right through me. Her fingers no longer fidgeted and clasped firmly into her palms. "I said fuck The Fates and began to prepare for war with Hades. But I thought I'd offer Zeus a deal first. Give me my children, or see your precious domain burn to the ground. That's when I realized I made my biggest mistake by not going straight into war with him. Because Zeus retaliated with the massacre of those women, those witches, and placed a shield upon you three as he *moved* the location of the cabin, rendering you three hidden from me entirely."

My brows scrunch together. "But I don't remember anything outside of the cabin looking differently though?"

"You wouldn't have. He would've manipulated you to remember the new location, and that only."

My blood boils, my anger rising with it. I clench my fists. "I hate him." I seethe.

Persephone only stands there, unmoving. "That is why this time around, I won't give him a chance to reconsider."

I look up at her.

"I will damn The Fates, damn any pact that has been made, and Hades and I will bring war to Zeus' territory if he even lays a finger on you both again."

I watch as my mothers eyes glow brightly, a buzz of charged energy lighting between us as the grass beneath our feet begins to wilt and die, turning an ashen gray color. My skin pricks as a cold dread fills the air between us as it shifts the clouds above us to separate.

"This time around, I won't let anyone keep me from my children. And I will gladly show him what being Queen of The Underworld entails." She commands, power and authority dripping from her tone. An authority that only a Queen could present with.

A Queen that I'm proud to be a daughter of.

I grin at her as I will my power to the surface, my shadows licking at my fingertips and along my body. I watch as she smiles, pride swimming in her gaze.

She grabs my hands and our powers dance together. They coil around one another, nuzzling into the familiarity of each other. I grin as I gaze at my mother, a silent understanding stretching between us. "Together once more."

She grins back. "Never to be parted again."

CHAPTER 44

After leaving The Underworld I decided to visit the cemetery. Doing my usual walk through of picking up litter, making sure flowers are fluffed up and offerings are not disturbed.

My knees burrow into the soil below me as I wipe dust off of the thick stone. The sun high in the sky above me, heating my back and the top of my head as I tend to this grave.

"Melinoë."

I turn my head around to see Keeper standing there. I nod my head at him, smiling before I turn to face the grave again. "Good to see—"

"Melinoë." He repeats himself.

I turn back around, seeing the worry etched into his face. My body tenses up as I stand up from the grave. "What is it?"

He begins to open his mouth when I hear a shrill off in the distance above me.

My head swivels up, waiting, until I see two large drago's flying above me. Knowing one is Reimus, and the other is Dimitri.

I train my gaze to follow them, noticing them swooping down to land in the Sephyra Forest. I lower my gaze back to Keeper, understanding now that he was trying to warn me.

I waste no time opening up a portal, stepping through it until I land in the Sephyra Forest. The sound of wailing immediately pervades a few yards ahead of me, causing me to jolt into a sprint towards it.

I immediately bring my power to the surface, uncertain of what exactly I'm walking into. The shadows begin to form a barrier around me, waiting and at the ready.

I run through towering trees until I abruptly halt in my steps. I gasp when I find Fae bodies scattered around me, stepping towards them to find a dark red liquid—*blood* running from every orifice. Their eyes wide and mouths gaping open. I command the shadows to slip away as I gaze at the Fae females scattered about.

The same ones who were at the gathering the night before.

I look up to find Sage wailing on his hands and knees with Dimitri and Reimus both now shifted back into their human forms.

I rush to his side, falling to my knees before him. "Sage."

He looks up at me, taking him a few moments to register my presence. His gaze hardens. "My sisters." He seethes, his lips trembling.

"What happened?" Terror in my voice.

He exhales a shaky breath, his wings splayed out behind him as they tremble with him. "We walked home last night after the gathering and went to sleep as soon as we got home." He waves a lazy hand behind us. "Our home lies a few yards back that way."

I look behind him before gazing at him again.

"I woke up this morning, noticing my sisters were gone. I figured they just went scavenging in the woods like we normally do." He pauses for a long moment as he narrows his gaze. "I waited until a half hour ago when I went looking for them. And found them here—" He ends abruptly as his nostrils flare, anger pulsating around him. He glares up at me, a cold chill sliding down my spine. "When I find who did this." His wings suddenly flap up sharply behind him, causing my breath to hitch. "I'm going to take my time with them."

"It's not blood."

Sage and I whip our heads around to find Dimitri kneeling before one of the Fae females.

I stand up and approach Dimitri's side. I lower myself to the ground as I kneel beside him.

He points to a stream coming out of her nose. "It's wine, not blood." He sniffs the air before us. "I can smell it."

He slowly lowers his finger as he swipes through it. As he lifts his finger I watch as the liquid trickles quickly down his hand, the consistency watery and thin, nothing like blood at all.

My brows furrow. "That doesn't make any sense."

Sage kneels next to me, his hands shaking as he inspects Dimitri's finger. He sniffs the air, his eyes widening. "He's correct."

Reimus walks over to us, lowering to a kneeling position. "Sage, do you have any idea who would've done this to them?"

He shakes his head, sorrow draining the exuberant nature of him completely dry. "No. The forest is our home. Those who are smart know not to hurt a Fae."

"It was him." Dimitri seethes.

I look up at him. "Who?"

He turns his gaze to me. His shoulders tense up and his nostrils flare as his gaze hardens on me. "The one who attacked me."

Dread courses through me as I manage to raise a hand, settling it gently on his arm. His gaze softens ever so slightly as I will the dread in my belly to ease itself. A long sigh escapes me. "Or it was Zeus." My gaze travels to the innocent Fae females scattered about.

Sage looks at me sharply. "Why would *he* do this? He has never bothered the Fae before."

"That was before I freed Makaria. He has a reason to retaliate now." I look up at Reimus. "If this was him, this is only just the beginning."

Reimus watches me, studying me as a silent understanding exchanges between us. His eyes churn for a moment before curtly nodding. "Then we stay out of the Sephyra Forest for the time being, and stay within the borders of Vulir. I'll send word to Charon."

I nod my head as Reimus stands up on his feet again. I turn my gaze to Sage when I see them from the peripheral of my vision. Like silhouettes of light flickering behind him, I train my gaze on them as I stand up on my feet.

One of the Fae females walks towards me and I hear Sage gasp behind me. She curtsies as she bows slightly at the waist. "Good day, Goddess of Ghosts."

I step towards her. "Do you remember who did this to you?" I look behind her as the other four Fae females stand behind her. "And of you?"

They all shake their heads. "We can't say that we do." The one before me says. She looks to Sage, a solemn smile on her lips. "Sister. Take care of our people."

Sage's lips tremble as he shoves back a choked cry. He nods. "I will."

She gives Sage a final smile before turning to join the other females. I watch as the five of them join hands as they all walk deeper into the forest. The pearlescent light that billows around them grows brighter and brighter, before snuffing out entirely as they disappear altogether.

I turn to Sage, a deep frown pulling at my lips. I take a tentative step towards him, reaching a hand out before lowering it to my side again. "What can I do for you?"

He stares straight ahead, his gaze unmoving for a few long moments. The reality of these unfortunate circumstances settling in. The only family he's ever had, the friends he's grown to love and spend every waking day with, now suddenly gone.

He takes a sharp breath in. "I just lost the only family I've ever known."

This time I reach out for his hand, gently holding it in mine. "I will find out who did this."

He finally turns his gaze to me, tears streaming down his pale cheeks. He nods his head, lowering his gaze to the ground. His gaze roams from friend to friend, sister to sister. "Bury them."

I watch him as his gaze finds mine again.

"Help me bury them."

I give him a grave smile, nodding before looking back to Dimitri and Reimus. "Go warn our people. Tell them the forest is off limits for now and to remain within the borders. I'll be home later to discuss further."

Reimus and Dimitri both nod before shifting into their drago forms. They immediately take to the skies as I begin digging grave after grave with Sage.

It takes us hours until we have five graves dug, and I respect his wanting for the process to be one of a silent exchange. Every now and then I glance at him to find him pausing, and I watch the reality hit him all over again.

I help Sage gently move each body into their own dugout slot, doing everything that he tells me without hesitation. He generously shares with me how part of the Fae custom is that when you die, you are to be buried within nature, rather than a cemetery. That you are not to be cremated, as it is thought as an insult to the land and to those before them. That as one comes from the soil of the earth, one must also die buried there, too.

I watch as he mumbles words of appreciation to each grave before bidding each one farewell. I stand in silence as I give him the space and privacy to say goodbye to his family, his sisters. Still choosing to be here for him throughout it nonetheless.

When he finally meets my gaze, he nods his head. "Thank you. I will never forget your kindness for this."

I smile faintly, taken aback by his words knowing it is very rare the Fae will thank you. Knowing that it is considered an insult to the Fae as it binds them to watch over the recipient's life. Unwilling to decline his thanks and possibly insult him, I simply nod. "They should be safe here. I'll make sure of it."

He lowers his gaze to the soil as five graves sit next to one another. He lifts his gaze to mine. "Just help me find out who did this."

I nod. "I will. First, let's get you set up at The Sanctuary—"

"No." He says starkly.

My mouth gapes open, closing again as I tilt my head. "It's not safe for you out here." I gesture my hand to the forest around us.

"I don't care." He says sternly. "This is my home. And I will let *no one* drive me out of it."

As understanding fills me, I only nod my head. "Okay. Then I will find you once I know any further developments."

"I'll be just over that way." He nods behind him. He lifts his gaze to mine. "Good day." He turns on his heels and walks back to his home. This time without his companions by his side.

I watch him for a few moments, my heart lurching for the Fae male before I portal to The Guardian's Palace.

CHAPTER 45

As I arrive in the dining room I find Reimus and Dimitri standing against the table. They both watch me as I portal into the room, each with a glass of whiskey in their hands.

Reimus steps away from the table, meeting me halfway. "How is he?"

I sigh. "He's adamant on finding out who did this." I shake my head, huffing. "I don't blame him."

He tilts his head as his hand comes up to caress my cheek. "We will find who is responsible."

I lean into his touch before slowly pulling away altogether. I walk over to the credenza cart, lifting the decanter of that amber liquid. I pour myself a shot, downing it.

"Do you really think Zeus is the culprit?" Dimitri asks.

I pour another shot, my hand trembling vaguely as I try to calm my nerves. I shake my head before turning around. "I don't know. I mean—who else do you know that can make *wine* explode from the inside out?"

Dimitri takes a sip from his whiskey before setting the glass down on the table. "Is that something Zeus is known for?"

I stare at him, the truth of being completely unaware of what exactly Zeus is capable of at the tips of my lips. I look towards Reimus, noticing his narrowed gaze. I follow it, realizing he's staring at my trembling hand. I cease the subtle quiver, willing my hand steady before looking at Dimitri again. "He is King of Gods, so I fear there is much he is capable of." I look at Reimus, his gaze determined and pinned on me. "I think he's warning us."

The unspoken words of *warning me* hanging between us.

Reimus' jaw clenches for a moment. "We've already spoken to the village. Everyone knows to stay within the borders. For now, we've decided no one in or out. Charon is aware of this as well."

I nod, swirling the whiskey before downing it. I set the glass down on the cart, exhaling as the spiced flavor lingers on my tongue. "How did you both know?"

Reimus tilts his head, waiting for me to explain.

"How did you know what happened? I saw you both fly to the site."

"Charon told us." Dimitri states.

I scrunch my brows. "So he was here, at the palace?"

Reimus huffs out a noise. "He told us through here." He taps his index finger against his temple. "When you take your vows and become Guardian of Vulir, you interlink yourself with other Guardians. It's a mental channel that binds you together, making it easier to communicate with one another. Charon gets access to that channel because well—he is a gatekeeper of both Vulir and The Underworld. A Guardian in his own right."

I nod slowly. "Interesting. I had no idea."

"It's better that most people don't. It's meant only to be known amongst those that have direct access to the channel. But there is nothing that I will hide from you." He tucks my hair behind my ear, a half smile curving up. "So now you know."

"It's also fun to bother him when you're bored sometimes."

I look over to Dimitri as a shy smirk crawls up my lips. "Oh, I bet it is."

Dimitri chuckles as he steps away from the table. "I'll be back tonight. I'm going to do a security check around the perimeter."

Reimus furrows his brows in shock. "Wow, you're blessing us with your presence instead of sleeping at The Sanctuary tonight?"

"I do not sleep there." He hisses.

"Fine. Then you just happen to spend a lot of time checking in with the women there. Well, with one in particular." Reimus waggles his eyebrows.

Dimitri shoves him in the shoulder, cursing him under his breath.

A grin curves up my lips. "Wait...please tell me we are talking about Nora—"

"For fucks sake it's not like that. She's a good friend, that's it." Dimitri huffs out, crossing his arms.

I nod slowly. "Mmhmm."

Dimitri shoves his arms to his sides, making for the doorway. "Whatever. I'll be back tonight."

I giggle to myself as I wrap my arms around Reimus, pulling myself into his embrace. He wraps his arms around me, kissing the top of my head before pulling away to look at me.

He leans down, kissing me softly. His lips never fail to be the anchor that keeps me grounded amidst the uncertainty.

He watches me, studying and observing. "What do you need?"

I exhale in his hold, inhaling as I breathe in that familiar patchouli and sandalwood scent of his. I bring my hands to his, cradling them. "I only need you to be by my side. That is all I need."

He smiles faintly, nodding once before kissing me. I give completely in to the kiss, unraveling myself into his lips. I feel him hardly relax into the kiss, his body wound tight as I can practically feel his own internal monologue suffocating him.

But as he pulls away with his lips hovering over mine, I watch him mask all of that away so as to not worry me. "I would spend my days nowhere else." His gaze lifts from my lips, the silver and blue churning together in his eyes. "I love you."

"I love you." I say as I lift my gaze to his. I raise my hands up to his cheeks, the stubble of his jaw poking the tips of my fingers. "There is nowhere else I'd rather be."

The tension in his body only releases a fraction as he gazes at me. "What if your mother is right? What if it's safer for you to—"

My grip on his cheeks tightens slightly, locking my gaze onto his. I shake my head. "I'm not going anywhere."

His hand comes up to brush my hair back from my face. He notices the insistence in my stare and only nods in response.

"Speaking of my mother," I lower my hands to my sides. "I should go tell her about this."

He nods. "I expected nothing else." His thumb caresses my cheek before stepping back. "Take your time. I'll have a hot bath ready for you when you return."

I smirk as I pull out of his embrace. "I hope you mean for the two of us." I say as I walk towards the portal materialized to the right of me.

Reimus chuckles, a mischievous grin appearing. "Your wish is my command."

I turn around, giving him a wink before I step through the portal and into The Underworld.

As I step out into their living room, I find not my mother but Hades standing above the fireplace.

He turns towards me, a glass of whiskey in his hand. He looks at me for only a moment before he asks. "Are you alright, Melinoë?"

"I need to speak with both of you."

He nods curtly, setting his glass down onto the mantel. "I'll go retrieve her. Wait here."

I watch him portal out of the room for only a few moments before portaling back with my mother in tow.

She looks at me. "What's wrong?"

I take a step towards them. "Something happened today in the Sephyra Forest." I exhale a shallow breath. "Fae females were murdered."

Hades and my mother both watch me, waiting.

"When I looked upon their bodies, I thought it was blood that was exiting from every orifice. But instead, it was wine."

"Wine?" My mother's brows scrunch together before approaching me, shock ridden in her tone.

"Does that sound like something Zeus would do?" I ask.

Persephone shakes her head slowly. "I've never heard of him changing someone's blood to wine as a form of punishment." Her gaze flickers over me, confusion in her stare.

I look to Hades, seeing if he knows anything different.

He only shakes his head as well, slowly reaching for his glass again. "Zeus isn't known for that."

It doesn't make any sense. I thought for sure that this was Zeus' doing—something in my gut tells me that it is. But if my mother and Hades are saying otherwise, then that leaves us back to square one.

"But *could* he do that? If he wanted to?"

Hades contemplates for a moment. "I mean, possibly. But that's never been known to be a power of his—" He steps towards me, concern flickering in his gaze. "Is that who did this?"

"I don't know. Nobody saw who did it, I just thought that—" I hesitate, looking up at my mother. "I just thought it might be him finally retaliating."

Persephone's eyes flicker, worry etched into them before smoothing out again. She looks to Hades. "It could be a ruse, an unusual form of punishment that wouldn't normally be suspected of him."

Hades watches my mother intently before bringing a hand to hers. I watch him squeeze it gently, as if bringing her back from her very thoughts. He turns towards me. "Does Charon know what happened?"

"Yes, and he's on high alert at the gate. We're keeping everyone within Vulir, and out of the forest for now."

"Good." He says, lowering my mothers hand slowly. "I will add another level of protection to the shield. Zeus will not be able to penetrate it."

I nod. "Okay."

My mother rests her hands on my shoulders, her fingers faintly digging into my skin. Reading the worry in her face I lift a hand to hers.

"I will be fine. I won't leave Vulir unless I come here."

She nods her head curtly before bringing me into her embrace. She pulls away, smiling as I will a portal behind me.

"Melinoë." Hades begins.

I look towards him.

"I would like a word with you. If you don't mind." He says gently.

I glance at my mother before my gaze falls on him again. I nod, dissipating the portal I created behind me.

My mother rests a soft hand against my cheek. "I'll see you tomorrow." She says before she makes her way to exit the room.

I bring my gaze back to Hades as he folds his hands behind his back.

"I wanted to apologize for the other day. I did not give you the answer you deserved—the truth. And for that I am sorry."

I give him a faint nod. "My mother explained everything."

"It still is unacceptable on my part. You were right to light fire under my ass, because for a long, long time I have been keeping to my realm out of an agreement. But sometimes, circumstances call for damning those said agreements. Like Zeus." He clenches his jaw, working on a swallow. "Not a day goes by that I don't want to see him hung by his own entrails for what he did to my wife. To her children."

I narrow my gaze onto the rug briefly before raising it again. "What would happen? What would The Fates do?"

He huffs roughly. "To be honest, I haven't a clue. I'm positive it wouldn't be good though. But after all that he has done, I'm beginning to care less and less about what risks it would impose upon me. I only care that you, your mother, and my people are safe."

He approaches me, guiding a tentative hand to rest on top of my shoulder. The weight of it is akin to a steady brand. "I failed your mother by not taking matters into my own hands before. She will say none of it was my fault, but I will still blame myself."

For the first time, I watch as guilt swims in the eyes of The King of The Underworld.

"I will not disappoint her again." His gaze bores into mine. "I won't let him hurt either of you again. Pact or not."

I inhale deeply as I nod. My lip trembles slightly as I finally admit outloud what I've been desperately trying to wave off. Not in an attempt to avoid the very real possibility of it, but to avoid revealing it to the people I love. Knowing that it's a byproduct of my deep-rooted, conditioned need to do everything on my own. Proud of how far I've come with even allowing Reimus into my world, as well as the friends I've begun to make, but still having my moments of difficulty with it nonetheless. "I'm scared."

He squeezes my shoulder as he tilts his head. "I know. But know this Melinoë. He cannot break you. He cannot take what is yours, what you've been building."

"What's that?"

"Your power."

I watch the fire light in his eyes, the truth behind his words.

"Remember what I told you." He says. "Your shadows are there to protect you. Use them."

I nod my head, moving to pull away when I stop myself. Instead, I go to wrap my arms around him.

His body goes utterly still against me, keeping his arms still until he slowly wraps them around my shoulders.

"I haven't always been kind to you. But thank you for still not giving up on me anyway." I say into his chest.

I feel the tension in his body begin to slip away as he embraces me fully. "I will never give up on you." He exhales into my embrace.

A tear slips down my cheek as I hug The King of The Underworld. The resistance to pull away does not sneak its way up into my bones, instead remaining idle in the depths of my soul. I close my eyes and for a split second I see her. Traveling that mental pathway down to her as I see her smiling up at me, wearing not her normal ragged garments, but a pastel-colored floor length dress.

I watch as she whispers to me, her words an echo that glide across my chest.

"This is good." She smiles.

I watch her approach a bed, crawling herself under the covers. As she brings the covers up to her chin, I watch as she, for the first time, lies down to rest.

I bring myself back, feeling the grip of my arms around Hades' shoulders. Noticing the tightening of my embrace that I've done unconsciously.

A smile faintly curves my lips, unknowing what it's like to feel a fathers genuine care. But feeling like this moment right here might be the closest I've ever been to it.

CHAPTER 46

Everything else dissolves away the moment my skin meets the hot water.

The tips of his fingers graze featherlight along my arms as he lowers his head to my ear. "Better?"

A lazy chuckle escapes me, my eyes remaining closed as I lean against him. "Much."

Reimus chuckles, his fingers continuing their soft exploration along my arms. "How did your mother take it?"

I sigh. "She seemed…surprised. She said that Zeus isn't known for making people's blood turn to wine, but said that there is probably much he's capable of that we don't know about."

He kisses the top of my head. "And Hades?"

I shrug lazily. "He basically said the same."

Reimus nods his head vaguely. "Well, we still take precaution for now then."

I lean forward, grabbing the lavender soap. Before I can begin to lather it into my hair Reimus grabs it from me. I chuckle. "So eager to cater to me?"

His voice is low and smooth when he speaks. "Always." He gently pulls my hair back, running his fingers through it before lathering the soap into my hair.

I sit there grateful that I am lucky enough to finally experience what real love looks like. To be cared for, and to be treated so gently.

I narrow my gaze to my knees hiked up to my chest. I exhale softly. "He apologized."

Reimus reaches for a container, lowering it to the water before lifting it to my head. "Did he now?" He pours the water slowly over my head, rinsing the soap away.

I lean my head back an inch, gaze trained towards the ceiling. "He said he feels like he failed my mother." I pause for a moment. "He said pact or not he should've taken matters into his own hands."

Reimus finishes rinsing the soap from my hair, setting the container on the side table. "What is the pact?"

I repeat what my mother explained to me. As I do, Reimus brings my hair over my shoulder and lathers the soap into a washcloth. As I finish he begins washing my back. "I guess that explains why he never went after Zeus then."

I sit there for a moment, letting him care for me. My mind conjures up thoughts that press against the walls of my mind. "What would you have done?"

He doesn't slow his movement against my back, he doesn't even hesitate at my question. In a voice that is both calm and calculating, he answers me. "I would've killed him."

My skin pricks with goosebumps at the surety in his tone.

He rinses off my back before turning me around. As I straddle him, he gently guides all of my hair behind my back again. My gaze lifts to his.

He grins as he kisses the bridge of my nose. "In this lifetime, and every other."

My hands come up to his jaw, bringing his lips to mine. I kiss him deeply, slowly before fixing his gaze back onto me. "In this lifetime, and every other."

He smiles before starting on the rest of my body.

⁓

Sometime later Reimus and I make it downstairs to raid the kitchen to find something to eat. Even though Reimus gave Aven the night off, he insisted that he at least make a pizza for us. With Aven's innocent charm and persistence, how could we say no?

As we enter the kitchen, we find both Dimitri and Nora at the kitchen island talking.

Nora turns towards me, raising a glass of wine in the air. "Come drink, girl."

I look over at Dimitri, a look of desperation painted on his face. I grin at him, understanding tickling me as he silently begs me to not mention a word to Nora about what was said earlier. Even though he says they're just friends, I can tell that's bullshit. Well—at least for him anyway.

I nod to Nora. "You're speaking my language." I walk over to the cabinet, opening it to pull out a wine glass. I walk over to the marbled island, setting it down as Nora pours the dark-red sweet liquor into it.

"Where's Aven?" Dimitri asks.

"I gave him the night off." Reimus says as he turns the oven on. He moves to open up the refrigerator, a large pizza wrapped in saran wrap on the middle shelf. Reimus pulls it out, setting it on the counter.

"Pizza!" Nora chimes as she hops off the chair. She walks over, leaning her head over it. "And he even put black olives on it too. Oh, what a great man."

I laugh as I stand next to Nora, noticing all of the wonderful toppings Aven added to it. Fresh slices of pepperoni, pork sausage, tons of mozzarella cheese, black olives, and diced onion. On top of a homemade, seasoned crust.

Reimus removes the saran wrap, holding a hand up to Nora. "And who said I was going to be nice enough to share? I just might hog this between my queen and I."

I look up at Reimus, a smirk fighting to make an appearance on my lips at the title. Heat creeps through my blood as I think of all of the ways I'm going to thank him for effortlessly putting me on a damn pedestal. He smirks at me as if he can hear my thoughts.

Nora pouts as she glares up at Reimus. "Oh, don't be a greedy prick. There's plenty to go around! If someone has to suffer not getting a slice of this masterpiece, let it be Dimitri."

I laugh as I look at Dimitri as he rolls his eyes at Nora. "You're only here because *I'm* here, ya know."

Nora rolls her eyes at him before seating herself back down on the chair. "False. Melinoë and I are friends, so I'm here because I am *wanted* here. Right?" She looks over at me, waggling her eyebrows.

I laugh. "Correct." I take a seat at an open chair while Reimus places the pizza into the oven.

He goes to grab the decanter of whiskey, pouring some into an empty glass. He moves to take a seat next to me, brushing his lips against my cheek.

As we all wait for the pizza to finish baking, we drink and talk with one another. Even after the pizza is finished and we've each helped ourselves to it, the conversation and the drinks don't stop.

"So you stay at The Sanctuary?" I ask Nora.

She nods. "I have since I was fifteen."

"And have you lived in Vulir your whole life or have you traveled from somewhere else?"

"I've always lived in Vulir. My parents became sick when I was fourteen, never seeming to get better. Doctors couldn't figure out what was wrong with them either."

I watch as the light flashes from her eyes for a moment before returning again. "They died and I had nowhere to go. So, I've been there ever since."

I narrow my gaze. "I'm sorry."

She nods. "It was before I came into my healing ability. Otherwise…"

I frown for Nora as I watch the unsaid words bounce around within the walls of her head. That if she had been able to use her healing gifts, then maybe she could've saved her parents.

I set my hand on her arm, guiding her gaze up again. "There was nothing you could've done." I say softly.

She huffs. "Maybe not, but I will always be left wondering if I could've done something or not." She goes to grab her wine glass, drinking from it.

I lower my hand back into my lap.

She lowers her glass back onto the counter. "How's your sister doing?"

I glance up at her. "She's doing better."

Nora watches me intently. "And her memory of you?"

I sigh, shaking my head. "Not there yet."

"And there's nothing that can be done to help them return?" She says as she rests her chin on her hand, her elbow propped up onto the counter. She watches me with both curiosity and sadness in her eyes.

I shrug. "Not that I'm aware of. It's been a few days since I've seen Hecate. I'll pay her a visit tomorrow to see if she found anything that can help. Otherwise, it's just been a waiting game."

Nora stares at me, nodding when she pauses. Staring off into the distance.

"What?"

She lifts her head, sitting upright in her chair. Her gaze fixates on a random spec of air until she looks at me. "What if I helped Hecate?"

Furrowing my eyebrows, I stare at her. "With what? A spell?"

"A *healing* spell. Powered both by magic *and* my gift." She raises her hands as her palms face upwards.

"I think if it were that simple, Hecate would've mentioned that as an option."

"Why not?" She asks.

"Because—" I hesitate, sighing at the complexity of my family situation. "The person who placed the compulsion spell on my sister would've made it much harder than just a simple healing spell to bring her memories back."

Nora hesitates for a moment. "Who put the spell on her?"

I sit there, turning my gaze away. "It's too complicated to explain."

"Try me."

I look at her, a ghost of a smile appearing on her lips. I watch the fierce determination in her gaze that she won't let up with her challenge. I'm beginning to understand that if Nora wants something, she will be persistent on it.

Much like how I am in some ways.

I listen to Reimus scoot his chair out, turning my gaze to him.

He gives me a faint nod as he kisses the top of my head, before patting Dimitri on the back. "Let's take this party to the living room. Unless you think the cheese from that pizza will have you preoccupied for a while."

Dimitri makes a scoffing noise as he steps out of his seat. "Can we all agree to just let that night die already? Also—I can handle a *little* fucking dairy."

Nora and I giggle to ourselves as the boys make their way out of the kitchen. Once it's just Nora and I, I settle my gaze on her. Knowing that making the decision to share this part of my life with her is a step in the right direction of forming new friendships. No matter how scary it might initially feel.

So I take a deep breath in and tell her everything.

Well—mostly everything.

I tell her about how it was growing up with Makaria, how we were lied to about our mothers death. I tell her about my journey here, who I came with, and how he died trying to protect me. I tell her about who my father really is, and the magic he had around my sister, and how I broke it.

When I finish, I realize my gaze shifted to my hands at some point. When I lift it to hers, I watch as lines from her eyes dampen her cheeks. She wipes them away, a look of deep understanding for me and all of the fucked up shit I just told her paining her gaze.

She takes a few moments to sit in silence, processing. Until she takes a drink from her wine, setting her glass down as a tilt of her head follows. "Maybe that's why she didn't think to suggest it."

I peer at her, waiting for her to explain.

Nora leans forward in her chair. "This whole time you've both been thinking of these grand fixes to bring your sister's memory back. Because Zeus would've gone to great lengths to ensure her memory of you stayed blocked. But what if he knew you'd think in that way. What if it's not some big fix at all."

I watch her, processing her words.

"My healing gift has always mainly been to heal physical and spiritual wounds, so why can't I try using that same healing energy on the *wound* of her memory loss?"

Contemplating if it could've been this simple this whole time, or if we're potentially getting our hopes up for nothing. I tap my finger against my wine glass softly. "It's possible."

Nora leans in a little further, resting her hand on mine. "Don't let him defeat it."

I look at her.

She nods towards my chest. "That small inkling of hope left inside you? Don't let him take that away."

I work on a swallow as her words glide right through me. I clear my throat. "And if it doesn't work?"

She shrugs. "Then at least we tried. Then at which point, we try the next solution. Until we get it right."

My heart lurches forward, pinning my lips together to keep them from trembling. I nod my head. "With everything that's been going on, my mother won't let her leave The Underworld."

"She might if we keep within the borders." She gestures a hand to the doorway. "We could do it right outside here."

As I contemplate her idea, I start to feel that small inkling of hope light up again. After letting that fire almost completely smolder out, accepting that my sister may never remember me again but continuing to still love her just as much anyhow. Yet now that part of me wonders what it would be like to have my sister back completely.

I smile faintly as I nod. "I'll talk to my mother and Makaria tomorrow about it."

Nora smiles as she rests a hand on top of mine. I feel the faint buzz of her energy light through me, akin to a cool sheet of silk wrapping around my skin. Energy attempting to settle the skepticism that lingers deep within me. After another moment, she lowers her hand. "Good. Now," She grabs the wine bottle before getting up from her chair. "Let's go bother the boys."

I chuckle as I grab my now empty wine glass and follow her into the living room. That ember of hope burning just a little brighter within me.

CHAPTER 47

The next day I portal to The Underworld, my hands clammy with dampness as I step out onto the palace's hardwood floor.

Wondering where my mother could be at this time, and also worried of what she will say to my plan.

I walk into the kitchen to find no one in there. I head to the living room, finding no one in there either. Not wanting to attempt to see if my mother is in her room, afraid of what I may or may not walk into, I decide to step outside into the courtyard.

Walking through the pathway, I walk all the way to the end. Approaching the edge of the cliff, I overlook The Asphodel Meadows. I begin gazing upon the souls when suddenly I see platinum long blonde hair.

I go wholly still as I watch Makaria picking fresh tomatoes with Shyla in her garden. I nearly choke on a cry of relief to see my sister feeling comfortable enough to explore The Underworld, to mingle with some of the souls.

I bring a hand to my lips, stifling the noise back down my throat. I smile genuinely for my sister, happy to see her taking that next step in getting acquainted with her new life.

"She made her first trip down there yesterday."

I turn around, wiping the tears from my eyes as I gaze at my mother.

She smiles softly at me as she approaches my side. "Something about your visit yesterday, it—she had this brightness in her face again. Some of it at least."

I look back down at Makaria as she smiles at Shyla, a tomato in her hand as Shyla talks with her. My heart swells at the sight.

"She asked if she could go back this morning. She even wanted me to do her hair for her."

I watch as a single braid falls down Makaria's back, perfectly placed down the middle. I look at my mother. "This is good news." I smile.

She nods. "Yes, it is."

I sigh as I watch Makaria with my mother for a few moments. When I look at her, I find her gazing off into the distance. Her gaze flickers amongst the cabins, shifting up deeper towards the valley.

"Are you looking for someone?" I ask her.

She trains her gaze back on me, her eyes churning brightly as she shakes her head. She forces a smile. "Not at all, dear." She nods towards The Asphodel Meadows. "Will you be visiting the souls today?"

I nod slowly. "Yes, but I also came to ask you something."

She watches me intently. "What is it?"

I exhale. "I want to try something with Makaria. To help get her memory back."

My mother doesn't break her gaze, tilting her head.

"My friend Nora is a healer, and I thought with her gift, and Hecate's magic, we could try using both to heal her memory loss."

My mother watches me, nodding slowly. "And I assume you are asking me because Makaria needs to come up by you in order to do so."

I nod.

She watches me for a long moment, worry dancing across her face before she straightens. "Okay. But I'd like to be there."

I nod. "I expected nothing else."

She sighs as she forces a smile. "Melinoë, I want Makaria to get her memory back more than anything. So we will try whatever we need to. But I just want you to be prepared—"

"I know." I softly interject. My gaze lowers to the ground briefly before lifting back to hers. "It's possible it won't work."

She nods before turning her gaze over to where Makaria is. A long exhale escapes her as she watches her. "It's taken much for her to adjust to begin with, she may not wish to leave The Underworld."

"I understand." My gaze fixates on my sister, noticing how the light has finally begun to creep back upon her face. Knowing that it will take some time to see the full extent to that bright energy my sister has always carried, but willing to wait for however long it takes. "I'll respect whatever she is comfortable doing." I watch as Makaria inspects a tomato before standing up on her two feet.

Persephone rests a hand on my shoulder, guiding my gaze back to her. "I must go see Thanatos about something, but I will find you later." She leans in to give me a kiss on the cheek.

I give her a smile. "I love you."

My mother smiles, watching me for a moment. "I love you too, my brave girl."

I turn around to the portal behind me, leading me down below to where Makaria is standing. I walk through the portal, stepping out onto the grass when Makaria turns around. She gasps, dropping her tomato.

Shyla scurries to grab it from the ground, holding the tomato in her hand like a baby bunny. "Careful! These babies are fragile." She says as she puts it into a basket. She looks up at me, smiling. "Good to see you again, Melinoë."

I nod. "Good to see you, Shyla." I turn to Makaria. "I see you've taken to exploring a bit."

Makaria nods. "I was tired of sitting in my room and—well, I want to see what else is here."

"That's good." I look at Shyla. "Would you mind if I borrowed my sister for a moment?"

She nods. "I'll be inside." She laughs as she heads inside her cabin with her basket of freshly picked tomatoes.

Makaria gazes at me. "Is everything okay?"

I step towards her. "Everything is fine. I just wanted to run something by you."

She scrunches her brows. "What is it?"

"Well," I begin as I loosen my breath. "I've been thinking about how I could help get your memory back. And I have a friend—who's a healer. And Hecate—a powerful witch in her own right. I thought with both of them, they could maybe…help heal you."

She tilts her head. "*Heal* me?"

"The memory loss." I lower my gaze, feeling awkward for no real reason.

Makaria stands there in silence, causing me to lift my gaze to hers again. "The only thing is that you would have to leave The Underworld, as we would have to do it up by me."

Makaria stands there, silent as ever and watching me.

I grow uncomfortable with the silence, wondering if I'm asking for too much too soon from my sister. Knowing she just ventured past the palace for the first time since she's been here.

I sigh. "Mother would be there. She won't let anything—*I* won't let anything happen to you."

After a few more moments of silence, Makaria nods her head. "Okay."

I whip my gaze up to hers so fast, completely taken back by her willingness. "Okay?"

She nods. "Yeah. Okay." She steps towards me. "I *hate* that I know I'm your sister, though I can't remember you.

So if there's any way I can help regain my memory, I want to do it."

I exhale a shaky breath, nodding. "Okay."

"So like—right now?" She asks.

I laugh, shaking my head. "I have to talk to Hecate first, but I'm certain she'll be willing."

"Whose Hecate?"

"When I first came to Vulir, she mentored me for a while. But somehow after that, we became friends." I smile, remembering how much she's helped me.

"Oh." She says, curiosity lighting her face.

"Melinoë!" someone shouts from down the gravel road.

I look over to see Elana, a soul who loves baking fresh bread for everyone. I smile as her unwavering enthusiasm rushes me. "Good to see you, Elana."

She approaches my sister and I, a genuine smile on her face. "Oh, I've just made the best sourdough bread I've ever baked. Please, come try some!" She exclaims.

I look over at Makaria, trying to gauge how comfortable she would be with meeting a few more souls. "Are you up for it?"

To my surprise, she smiles sweetly at the woman. "I would love to."

Makaria and I follow Elana to her cabin where she serves us the most delicious fresh, sourdough bread. And though Makaria still has no memory of me yet, I dedicate any time I do have with her by just being present, and enjoying my time with her regardless.

~

After I walked Makaria back to the palace, I portaled myself to Hecate's shop.

"Hecate, you here?" I shout into the empty shop.

I hear the shuffling of feet along the hardwood floor before she appears in the doorway. "Back here dear!"

I make my way to the back room, parting the hanging beads as I step inside. I look to find several books lying open on her table.

"What are you doing?" I ask.

She looks up from a book. "Researching. Seeing what I can find to help Makaria."

I tilt my head. "Is that all you've been doing for the past few days?"

"Well—no. I've had customers, too." She says flipping through the pages. "But otherwise, yes."

I step towards her, leaning down to try and read the book she hovers over. Having no idea what any of it means, I straighten myself up again. "Well, that's what I actually came here to talk to you about."

Hecate looks up from her book.

"What about a healing spell?"

She chuckles. "Oh, dear, Zeus wouldn't have made it that easy I fear."

"What if he knows we would think that way, and therefore wouldn't try the most obvious solution."

Hecate ponders silently to herself. She closes the book, stepping away from the table. "I'm listening."

I go ahead and tell her about Nora, and her gift to heal and how I've seen it used with my own eyes. *Felt* it myself. I tell her about already speaking to my mother, and how Makaria is okay with it all.

Hecate clasps her hands. "Okay. But I need a day to prepare. I want to give it my best work."

"The day after tomorrow then." I proclaim as this opportunity to heal my sister's memory now one of reality.

Hecate nods. "It's a date."

I nod. That inkling of hope sparking inside of my chest once more, reminding me that it's burning against the doubt that threatens to snuff it out. I hold onto it tightly, allowing my hope to fuel it. At least for right now.

"So, are you going to stay and catch up with me or just hurry off?" Hecate smirks.

I chuckle as I pull up a chair. My gaze lifts to hers as I seat myself. The other reason for my visit at the forefront of my mind. "Actually, I need to ask a favor. If you don't mind."

Hecate nods as she effortlessly exudes an energy that is up for any challenge, no matter how small or large. A bravery in her that I admire and respect greatly. "Anything, dear."

I clear my throat, her gaze alight on me as I discuss my other favor.

CHAPTER 48

"Well, I guess now we know what that vision meant."

I take a sip from my chamomile tea, the warmth soothing my usual racing mind. I set the ceramic mug down, crossing a leg over the other. I look up at Hecate's gaze, slightly wide-eyed from telling her what happened when I used my shadows on Hades. "I don't want it to get my hopes up too high for what your vision was though."

Hecate frowns slightly, setting her mug down. "But it may come to fruition."

I nod vaguely. The memory of that vision she had playing through my mind once more, the one of my sister standing behind me. Not wanting to get my hopes up if the vision was just a fluke, but hoping to The Fates that it wasn't.

"Let's wait and see what happens, dear." Hecate encourages.

I nod as I stand from my chair. "Do you have a preference for time?"

She shrugs lazily. "I'll make myself available."

A ghost of a smile appears on my lips. "Meet me at The Guardians Palace at noon." I go to push my chair in as Hecate stands up.

She smiles. "I'll be there." She brings me in for a hug.

"Thank you." I say into her shoulder, my gratitude for everything she's helped me through a solid fluidity that runs through me for her.

She pulls away, smiling. "Anything, dear." She walks with me out of the backroom.

I head for the door, opening and closing it behind me as I step out onto the sidewalk. I head over to The Sanctuary, wanting to check on how everyone is doing since the incident in the forest.

I walk through those double-doors, up the stairs until I reach the women's corridors.

Upon arrival I see Nora in the healers room. Door wide open as I walk in to find her tending to Semele's hand.

Her palm is flipped over as Nora sends white light towards the harsh burns that redden her skin.

"What happened?" I ask as I step closer.

Semele shakes her head. "I burnt myself trying to grab a pan from the kitchen." She narrows her gaze to her hand. "It was on the stove. I didn't know someone had just used it, so when I went to grab it—" She lifts her gaze back up to mine. "Yeah, I'm a dumbass."

I chuckle softly. "It gives Nora something to do."

Nora peers up at me, huffing as a smirk crawls up her lips. She lowers her gaze back down to Semele's hand, concentrating as her hands emit that bright healing light.

I look back towards Semele. "I just came to make sure everyone was doing well."

Semele nods. "We know not to leave the borders of Vulir." She hisses as Nora's healing energy heals the raised skin. She glances at me. "What happened out there?"

I know Reimus omitted to tell the women exactly what happened. Not to purposefully keep the truth from them, but more so to not cause them excessive worry. But if I were in their shoes, I think I would want to know the full extent of what happened, and not knowing would actually cause me more worry.

I sigh. "It was the Fae females that were here the other night. We found them dead in the Sephyra Forest."

Nora looks up from her work, pausing before resuming.

Semele scrunches her brows. "Dead? Isn't it some magical law that you don't hurt the Fae?"

"It is. That's why we want to find out who did this." I move to lean against the wall.

Semele lowers her voice, glancing at the open doorway. "How were they murdered?"

I rub the bridge of my nose. "Someone willed their blood to explode from the inside out. Except it wasn't blood, it was wine."

Semele stares at me, her expression motionless as her eyes widen ever so slightly. She nods slowly. "So it was the work of a god."

I nod in agreement. "I think it was Zeus. That's why we're keeping everyone inside Vulir's shield for the time being until we know for sure or not."

Semele watches me. "And what will you do when you find the culprit?"

I stare at her, calmly and steadily as my voice does not shake. "I'll make sure he pays. As will the Fae."

Because everyone knows that when a Fae brings upon punishment, it is one that is long and *slow*.

I watch Semele nod once more before forcing her gaze to her hand as Nora finishes healing it. I watch as the bright light fades away, leaving behind a patch of fresh, new skin.

"Done." Nora says, slowly twisting Semele's hand around to inspect one last time.

"Thank you." Semele says as she pulls her hand away, smiling faintly.

Nora nods as she stands up from her chair, approaching me. "Did you talk to her?"

I step away from the wall, nodding to Semele before Nora and I leave the room. We walk through the womens corridor as I lower my voice. "She said she'll do it."

Nora turns to me, surprise and relief on her face. "That's good news."

I smile faintly. "Hecate agrees to join as well. She needs a day to gather herself, though. So the day after tomorrow at noon."

Nora nods, a smile curving up her lips. "I'll be ready."

"Perfect. I'll come get you shortly before noon then." I watch as women meander about, shuffling along from room to room. Most of them look up, waving with a smile on their faces when they see me. I notice one woman heading towards the kitchen, her child in tow. The thought of that innocent child being harmed in any manner by Zeus churning a pit of worry within me that I didn't expect, being that I hardly know these people still.

"We're all fine here." Nora says, drawing my attention to her. She smiles. "We know not to leave the border."

I sigh. "I know. I just…"

"Wanted to check in anyway?"

I huff out a lazy laugh, peering at her sidelong. "Possibly."

"Well for what it's worth, we're appreciative of it. Vulir doesn't really do hierarchies, but if there was someone we'd be willing to be led from, it's you."

I look at her, shaking my head. "I—that is very kind but, I'm not meant to lead a village."

Nora shrugs. "I think you're a lot more capable than you think." She heads into a guests room. But before she enters, she turns around. "See you in two days." She smiles before she enters the room.

I stare at the doorway, stilled by her words.

Over the course of time I've been here, I have found myself growing fond of the people here. But never did I think of myself *leading* them. Claiming Vulir my home never involved leading a village of people, though the more that I get to know the people here, the more I feel drawn to protecting them.

I tuck away Nora's insightful words, cradling them to my heart as I leave The Sanctuary and head over to the cemetery.

As I walk through the countless headstones, I spruce up flowers left by their loved ones. Thankfully most people respect the cemetery and don't leave trash lying around, but every now and then I find something that doesn't belong in the deceased's resting grounds.

As I tidy up and make my rounds, I feel Keeper's energy buzzing behind me.

I turn around. "You were trying to warn me that day, weren't you?"

He nods.

"Why didn't you just say it outright?"

He steps towards me, his cloak of shadows billowing around him. "By the time I was going to, The Guardians were already flying to the site. Once you saw them, you were gone."

I nod vaguely, the image of those poor Fae females still fresh in my mind.

"Thank you for burying them." He says.

"Of course." I brush the dirt from my knees, the specs falling from the fabric of my leggings. "Are you able to know who killed them?"

He shakes his head. "I only guard the cemetery and the souls that reside within. The rest I am not privy to knowing."

"Do you know of any immortal that can make people bleed out like that? Changing their blood to wine?" I approach another headstone, smoothing out a small blanket laid on top.

"I've never heard of any god or goddess capable of doing that." Keeper says as he approaches me.

I shake my head. "It has to be Zeus." I lift my gaze to him. "As King of Gods I'm sure he can do just about anything. It's him retaliating and hurting these innocent people. Because of me."

I feel his energy pulsate briefly. "This is not your fault."

I clench my jaw. "It partly is though. He's punishing me for freeing my sister. I knew the consequences of freeing her. I knew what I was getting myself—us *all* into."

Keeper stands there, silent for a long moment. "But it was a risk you were willing to take. Because freeing Makaria was the right thing to do."

Sighing as I step away from the headstone. "I know. I just wish it didn't involve everything that will possibly come with it."

"Or is it you wish you had a normal upbringing, where the thought of your own father retaliating against you, for trying to give your sister freewill should not even be an option?"

I scoff, a small part of me splintering at his honesty. "That would have been nice." I gently kick a pebble on the ground, watching it skitter off.

"I'd say you just got dealt with a shitty card. But you're handling it better than most."

"Yeah." I look up at him. "You know, you're pretty cool for a—what actually are you?" I chuckle.

He laughs, the slits in his nose constricting. "There is no name for who we are. An entity whose sole purpose is to guard the souls that rest."

"So there's more of you out there?"

He shrugs. "Sure. Where though I cannot say."

I nod. "Interesting."

Keeper clears his throat at the sound of footsteps approaching us. "Good afternoon, Reimus."

I turn to see Reimus walking towards us, clad in dark navy jeans and a white shirt. He smiles as my gaze meets his.

He glances at him, nodding. "Keeper."

"How did you find me here?" Surprise written on my face as I look at him. I glance over to where Keeper is standing but find that he vanished.

"Did you really think I didn't know where you sneak off to sometimes at night?" Reimus says, leaning in to kiss my forehead.

I peer up at him. "You followed me?" I cross my arms, squinting at him.

He chuckles. "You can't blame me for being curious. Plus," He coils a wavy strand of my hair around his finger. "I wanted to make sure you were safe."

I uncross my arms, exhaling softly. I shrug my shoulders, glancing around. "At first I came here when I felt restless, right after I freed Makaria." I lower my gaze briefly, the memory of breaking down when I initially realized my sister didn't remember me. I train my gaze back up. "But then I found myself wanting to come here even when I wasn't anxious. It's…peaceful."

He smiles faintly as he gazes upon me. "I'm sure the deceased appreciate the company."

"Yeah." I say, wrapping my arms around his waist. Inhaling deeply as I drown myself into his scent, exhaling slowly. "It's a connection that I can't explain. I know that sounds silly considering who I am—Goddess of Ghosts and all, but I feel it when I'm here. When I'm around the deceased."

He kisses the top of my head, running his fingers through my hair before I pull away. Keeping one arm around him as we both begin making our departure from the cemetery. "Then I'd say chase that feeling, and never let it go."

We make our way through the tall stone arch, exiting the cemetery grounds. The sun glowing brightly as it begins to make its descent down in the sky.

"You know I can just portal us back, right?" I say looking up at him.

He smirks. "I know. But it's nice out, why rush the walk back?"

I smile up at him, nodding. "I couldn't agree more." I release my arm from around his waist, interlocking my fingers with his. He squeezes my hand gently as his thumb caresses my soft skin.

As we walk back to The Guardians Palace, I tell him of my talk with my mother and Makaria, and how we'll try to heal my sister's memory loss. He listens to me vent about my deep seated worries of how it may not work, and how I'm afraid to get my hopes up for nothing. I tell him I'm trying to remain positive through it all nonetheless, and how healing it would be to have my sister fully back.

As we walk back home he listens to me, giving me that safe space that I've always longed for to talk freely about my thoughts. My person, my anchor, in more ways than one.

CHAPTER 49

Shortly after Reimus and I arrived home I felt my mother's magic stir beside me.

My back rests against the lounge chair as the early evening breeze gently brushes against my cheek. I look up from my seat.

Persephone steps towards me, glancing out over the grassy terrain. She huffs a displeased noise before shifting her gaze back towards me. "Does Reimus prefer to have an ugly, open concept or does he just truly not know what to do with all of this land?"

A snort escapes me as I laugh. "I don't think he knows what to do with it." I look towards the terrain. "But I think I can convince him to make something of it."

Persephone chuckles. "At least get him to put some flowers down there. A pop of color would be a start." She goes to sit at the edge of the lounge chair.

I bring my legs up, turning to sit upright as I lower them to the floor. My shoulders nearly brush hers as I sigh softly. "The day after tomorrow. Hecate will join us."

My mother nods, her emerald eyes bright and focused. "And Makaria is in agreement?"

I nod. "She is."

She forces a smile. "Good." She trails my hair back over my shoulder, tilting her head. "I hope this works."

I narrow my gaze. "As do I."

⁓

After my mother left, I made my way down to see Alastor. I gave him lots of attention and a good grooming session before heading back inside.

After utilizing the bathroom, I made my way down to the dining room where Reimus was waiting for me. His gaze lifts to mine when he sees me enter the room, his stare both calculating and calm.

He stands from his chair, moving to pull out the one next to him. He dips his chin. "Good evening, my queen."

I dip my head as I take my seat, allowing him to push me in closer to the table. My gaze shifts to him as he seats himself next to me. "It seems I have many names now."

He chuckles as he grabs my plate, and begins serving portions of tonight's dinner onto it.

I watch as he sets my plate back down in front of me before beginning to fill his own. Aven comes around to fill my glass with wine, thanking him before he scurries away. "You've always done that."

Reimus finishes setting his plate, looking at me. "Done what?"

I nod my head to the food. "You always serve me first. Even when I thought I loathed you, you never started eating until I made it to the table."

A gentle grin curves his lips as he begins cutting up a section of steak. "Do you dislike that I do that?"

A grin of my own begins to mimic his. "Not at all."

He finishes cutting his steak, pausing to look at me. "I never really thought about why I do it. I think in an unconscious way it's just my way of showing you that I'll always put you before myself. Even in something as simple as making sure your plate is set before my own." He brings his fork to his mouth, chewing on the piece of steak. He lowers his gaze to his plate.

My fingers feel lightweight as I lay them on top of my fork, my gaze wholly onto him. My grin deepens as I pick up my fork, forcing my gaze onto my steak as I begin cutting it with a knife. "Okay." I say softly.

He takes another bite, swallowing before taking a drink from his whiskey. The brand of his stare on me like a welcomed invitation. The plea of being in service to me shining in his gaze. "Are you okay with that?"

I take a bite, the savory taste of the steak hitting my tastebuds. I swallow, looking at Reimus. Emotion clogging my throat for a moment as I nod. "Very." I smile genuinely, my heart full inside of my chest.

After we both finished our dinner, Aven came by to collect our dishes. As he carries them off to the kitchen, I turn to Reimus in my chair. I watch him sit there for a moment, his gaze aimlessly faced forward until he turns towards me.

"Where did you go?" I ask, hugging my knees up.

He chuckles. "I was just checking in with Charon. Making sure everything is well."

"And is everything well?" I ask.

He nods, a smile curving up his full lips. "He has the entrance guarded heavily. Everything is alright."

I lean my head against the back of the chair, my gaze roaming his face. "If I'm Guardian of The Dead, do you think that means I'm supposed to become Guardian of Vulir, too?"

He reaches a hand out to gently caress my cheek, lowering it once more as he shrugs. "I think it's somewhat ironic, but I don't believe it means you must do both."

I nod my head slowly. "What if I want to do both?"

He watches me, softly gazing. "If that's what you want, then I would say you should follow that feeling."

Thinking of where I started months ago, unsure of where I was going and who I was—still somewhat unsure of where I'm going. Now that I've begun to build a home here, I can't help the inclination to want to protect these people. To also want to protect those deceased.

And being Guardian of Vulir would be just that—protecting these people.

I vaguely shrug my shoulders. "It would serve to be beneficial as far as communication goes. Especially because…" Trailing off with the words of the possibility of Zeus retaliating against our people.

Reimus watches me, his gaze hardening ever so slightly. "Let's worry about one thing at a time." He smiles faintly as he pushes his chair out. He stands up, holding his hand out for me. "But first, I want to show you something."

I tilt my head, curiosity claiming me as I take his hand and stand from my seat. "Oh?" He leads me out from the chair until I'm standing before him.

He lifts his arm, gesturing for me to lock my arm with his. As I do he leads us out of the dining room and outside to the open terrain. The night sky like a limitless void, filled with shining specs of light. I watch as the stars stare back at me, illuminated like bright specks of light.

I gaze at them until I see a similar star formation high above. I chuckle as I mumble to myself. "The Phoenix."

Reimus lowers his head to mine. "Come again?"

I point up at it, the formation similar to a bird with open wings. "Nora and I named that one The Phoenix. See the wings?" I trace them with my index finger.

Reimus watches in silence for a moment before huffing. "A fitting name for it." He looks down at me smiling.

I peer up at him. "So the stars are what you wanted to show me?"

A mischievous grin curves up his lips. "Not quite."

In the next moment he's running towards the open field until he's consumed by a flash of light, vanishing entirely once he's shifted into his drago form. His wings fan out wide for a moment before laying themselves against the ground.

I take one step towards him, then another. I tilt my head. "You must be suffering from some kind of short term memory loss because I've already seen you in this form—"

A trilling noise erupts from him as he nods towards his back. He begins lowering himself onto his belly when his gaze pierces into mine.

I look at his back, not understanding—

Oh.

"You want me to ride you?" I ask, waving a hand at his back.

He slowly nods his large head, a smirk curving up his mouth as if to say *but you can ride me another way later.*

I chuckle, watching him as I stare at his enormous figure. The thought of riding him both terrifying and thrilling at the same time. I hesitate, contemplating the insanity of this. I glance once up at the starry sky, The Phoenix a reminder of what it felt like to let loose at the gathering. To be uncaring of how I looked dancing, and instead solely focused on letting myself have *fun.*

And fuck how great it felt to just let myself go like that. To let the demands of reality, and the what ifs of what tomorrow may or may not bring, fly right off my shoulders. Even if for just one night.

I turn my gaze back onto Reimus, a thrilling smirk curving my lips as I give him my silent answer.

I approach him, looking him dead in the eyes before I begin my climb onto his back. "If you drop me, I will cut your balls off."

He rolls his eyes, though his smirk doesn't fade. He nods once more to his back until I begin my climb up onto him.

The feel of his rough scales beneath my fingertips greets me as I haul myself up. I seat myself in the middle, closer to his neck. I let both legs hang on each side, lowering myself to hug him tightly. "Okay, I'm ready—"

He suddenly raises up onto all fours before shooting straight up into the night sky above us.

I scream as we plummet through the open sky, wind beating against my cheeks like a weight pushing against me. Once he levels out, he begins gliding forward. The pressure eases from my face as I look down to see our palace just a small spec of an object below now.

His wings fan out wide as he glides us over Vulir.

I look down in astonishment as I watch us fly over The Sanctuary, and then the cemetery. He continues until we reach the Sephyra Forest, and initially I tense up knowing that Zeus could be anywhere. I fear for my life for a moment. But then, something takes over me.

I look down at Reimus, and being in his presence, I know I've never been safer.

I smile as he begins to slow his speed until we're coasting high in the sky. I loosen one hand from gripping his neck, shakily spreading it out next to me. I gasp as I feel it, something I've never truly felt before.

The feeling of being *alive*.

I keep my back straight as I slowly bring my other arm out, spreading it wide beside me. I begin laughing as

Reimus glides calmly through the sky, and suddenly my whole body feels lighter than I've ever felt it before.

I find myself shedding tears of relief as the cool night air brushes against my skin. I shed tears for a life that I never thought I was able to experience. I glance down at Reimus, his head scoping out the ground below us as well as the sky ahead. I smile at the sight of someone who is a large reason for not only feeling safe, but *alive*.

I howl into the night, uncaring of how silly it may sound to anyone who could hear us. I let myself completely enjoy this moment as we soar across the open sky.

CHAPTER 50

Reimus finally lowers us to the ground on our open terrain. I crawl myself off of him, an energy buzzing through me wildly. "That was incredible." Excitement in my voice as laughter still finds me.

Reimus shifts himself back, grinning at me as he steps towards me. "I'm glad you enjoyed yourself."

Adrenaline coursing through my bones as I gaze at him. "So you just wanted me to see what it was like to ride a drago?"

He tilts his head, running his fingers through my hair as he pushes it back. "No."

I watch him, a grin forming his lips.

"I wanted you to have fun."

My grin begins to falter, my facial expression smoothing out.

His hand moves to my jaw, lifting it up. "You do so much for the people around you, you have sacrificed so much, Melinoë. And I just wanted you to be able to take a step back from it all, even if just for a moment. And *live*."

I stare at him for a long moment as if my body forgot how to function. My chest caves in as I gaze at him, a warmth spreading throughout.

I raise my hand up to his sharp jaw, my fingers meeting his warm skin. His eyes alight on mine. "Being with you is the reason why I feel alive, Rei. You give me a reason to want to choose myself. To choose love again."

His body goes taught, his gaze boring into mine.

"I feel alive because of *you*." I say.

He loosens a shaky breath, a harsh chuckle coming from him. "You called me Rei."

Understanding echoes within me. I smile as I lower my gaze to his lips. "Do you prefer I call you that?" I lift my gaze.

He lets out a rough exhale as his hands come to my jaw. "As long as I'm yours, I don't care what the fuck you call me." He kisses me deeply, devouring my every sense. He picks me up, wrapping my legs around him as he guides us back inside. "But hearing you call me Rei—" He shivers.

Shivers.

His gaze hardens on mine, a heated brand. "Portal us to the bedroom." His voice clipped and gruff.

I smirk as I do just that. An opening appears as he wastes no time stepping us through it.

Once we reach the other side I close the portal behind us as he dumps me onto the bed.

He inserts himself between my legs as he leans down to kiss me, holding my face between his calloused hands. He parts my lips with his tongue and I happily open them for him.

My hands roam from his chest downward until they reach the waist of his pants. I run a hand along his hard cock as it pushes against the denim material.

He breaks away from the kiss, a gruff chuckle escaping him. "Impatient are we?" He moves his hands to his waist, unbuttoning his jeans as he begins slipping them down his legs.

My eyes fixate on his cock as it juts out at me. I look back at him as I lean forward, my lips a mere inch from the tip. "I don't want to wait." I lean back a little, lifting my shirt over my head until my breasts are bare before him. I stare up at him as I lower my hands to my leggings, slipping them off. He hardly even blinks as he watches me, a heated hunger in his gaze.

Naked before him, I lean forward again. Keeping my gaze on him, I press a gentle kiss to the tip. I watch as he exhales raggedly, grunting. "Melinoë—"

"I just want a taste." I smile as I press another kiss, this time pressing the tip inside my lips by just a fraction.

He grunts as he moves his hand to his cock, slowly pumping himself. I watch as his chest begins to rise and fall quicker, the anticipation evident in his eyes. "You can have whatever you want. Just please put that pretty fucking mouth on me."

I watch as cum beads at the tip. I smirk as I lick it off, Reimus grunting as his body jerks forward. I watch him work himself, wetness pooling low. "I like watching you touch yourself." I smirk up at him, running my tongue along the tip once more.

He whimpers beneath my touch, his hand pumping a little faster.

After a few moments of watching him pump himself, I lower another kiss to the tip before wrapping my mouth around him completely. He stills as I slowly descend on him, his body taught as he exhales raggedly.

"Fuck—you're so fucking beautiful."

I bring my hands up to his waist, and pull him into me until he's deep in my throat. He curses under his breath as I move my mouth up and down on him, my gaze fixated on him.

"Don't look away from me." He grabs my hair, pinning it into both of his hands as he begins thrusting into my mouth. Slowly at first, then faster. "Keep those eyes on me while I fuck that pretty mouth."

I take him willingly as he pistons in and out of me, feeling his body growing even more taught as I caress a finger up his thigh.

He cums a little in my mouth and I moan as I taste him. He pulls out of my mouth entirely, his cock glistening before me.

"Get on your fucking knees." He lifts his shirt off, bared completely before me. I do as he says, getting on all fours as I face him—

"Other way." He says curtly.

I begin turning myself around and gasp when his hands come to my thighs, lifting my ass in the air as he turns me fully. I feel him lower himself to the ground, turning my head around to look at him.

He chuckles menacingly, his gaze wholly on my pussy. He leans in, running his tongue along my entrance. I gasp, arching my back as he goes back in, flicking his tongue along there.

No words, no teasing. Just straight to it.

I cry as he *devours* me. His hands stay right on my thighs, below my ass as he keeps me in place. I try to squirm out of his hold and I feel his mouth curve against me when he holds me steady.

Wetness pools out of me as I climax, Reimus demanding every drop with his lips and his tongue. I scream his name as my body shakes with release.

When I finish he doesn't let me catch a breath or wait, instead I feel him kneel onto the bed behind me as his hands come to my waist. His fingers grip into my hips as he drives himself inside of me in one deep thrust.

I gasp at the fullness of him, immediately aroused once again.

He moans as he slowly descends out of me, just before the tip. "Look at how wet I get you." He lowers a hand to my chest, driving me up until I'm against his chest. His hand comes to my neck, holding me steady as he thrusts up into me. "Such a fucking good girl."

I moan as he nips at my neck while he drives himself into me. My breasts bouncing as he fucks me hard and fast. His hand on my waist lowers to my clit as he rubs it, wringing cries from my lips.

Release finds me as I cum once again. I scream his name as I feel him tense up, pistoning in and out of me before he buries himself to the hilt. I feel him pulsate inside of me, whimpering as he does.

He lowers us both to the bed then slowly slips himself out of me. Cum drips from me as we both lay for a few long moments until he goes to grab a washcloth to clean us both up.

He lays himself back down behind me, wrapping his arms around me and pulling me close to his chest. I sigh sleepily as I nuzzle my head into his arm.

Within moments, I drift off to sleep.

CHAPTER 51

I jolt upright in bed, sweat trickling down my back as I pant heavily.

Reimus stirs awake beside me, tensing when he hears me. He sits up, his hand on my cheek. "Melinoë?"

I bring my breathing back to a normal pace as I evade the images from my head. I wipe my brow, willing my arm to cease its tremble. I look at Reimus, the worry in his face clogging my throat. I force my expression to neutralize. "Just a bad dream."

I turn towards him as he lays back down, and I with him on his chest. I lay my hand on his bare skin, my fingertips softly grazing his warm skin.

His thumb comes up to graze my shoulder, his touch and his presence a gift from The Fates themselves.

As I calm myself back to sleep, I think to myself how grateful I am to have known his love, and how greatly I will always cherish it.

~

The next morning Reimus and I take our time getting up from bed. He even has breakfast brought straight to us, serving me bites of french toast in the comfort of our sheets.

After we finally made our way to the shower—after our love making—I dressed myself to head out to the pasture. I spend some quality time with Alastor, grooming and talking with him before I head out to the village.

Quinn greets me with a wide smile as I make my way into the floral shop. "Melinoë! What a lovely surprise." He comes around the counter to give me a hug. He squeezes me gently before pulling away. "What can I do for you today?"

"A bouquet—five actually."

"Sure! What's the occasion?" He asks.

I force a smile. "Memorial."

His smile turns into a frown as he clasps his hands together. "They're for the Fae that were murdered, aren't they?"

I nod. "I'd like to go pay my respects."

He nods. "Give me ten minutes and I'll have something for ya."

I watch as he begins creating the bouquets, arranging the flowers so intricately as he pours his passion into the arrangements.

When he's finished, he lays out five bouquets. Each one filled with peach colored begonias, yellow chrysanthemums, white daisies, and green foliage pieces to fill.

My gaze widens at the bouquets. "They're beautiful, Quinn." I look up at him as I dig out the money from my pocket, handing it to him.

He takes the money, smiling. "Thank you." He puts it into his small safe, closing it before handing me the bouquets. "Does Reimus know you're venturing past the shield?" Worry creeps into his expression.

I force a smile. "I'll be fine." I assure him.

I take the bouquets, holding all five of them in my arms as I will a portal behind me. I watch Quinn's face light up, his eyes widening before I turn around and walk through it.

I step onto the small gravesite that was made a few days ago, the forest eerily quiet today.

I approach the five graves, all lined up next to one another. I lower my gaze to the flowers in my arms and begin setting each one down to its new owner.

As I set each bouquet down, I mumble a few words to each of the Fae. Apologizing that they had to get caught in the crossfire, and praying for their eternal rest.

As I finish mumbling to the fifth grave I hear a twig snap behind me. I whip my head around, tension releasing in my shoulders as I see it's Sage approaching me.

"You didn't have to do that." He says, grief stricken on his pale face.

I shrug vaguely. "I know." I look down at the ground. "But I wanted to."

"Your generosity will not go unnoticed."

I look up at him, nodding. I stand back up, wiping the soil from my leggings. "Any developments?"

He shakes his head. "On your end?"

I shake my head. "Not yet. But we'll find the one responsible."

He faintly nods his head as if the grief is too heavy for him to bear to move at all. "That we will."

I tilt my head. "Are you the only one left out here?"

He hesitates for a moment, his gaze lowering to the graves. "I am now."

I step towards him, opening my mouth when he holds up a hand.

"Save your breath, girl. I have not changed my mind about leaving the forest." His gaze raises to mine.

I close my mouth, nodding. "Understood. But should you ever change your mind." I begin to turn around, deciding to give him the privacy of grieving when he clears his throat.

"He visited me."

I turn back around, tilting my head.

He lazily chuckles. "The one who sacrificed himself for you."

My heart lurches. "Eiran." I say breathlessly as I step forward.

Sage nods. "He visited me that day after you left. He expressed his condolences and left."

A smile curves my lips at the kindness that he shares even in the afterlife, and what a gift it is for someone to know him.

Sage looks at me. "I'm sorry. I hope he at least gives you the closure of visiting you, too."

I exhale a breath, forcing a smile. "He does."

I turn back around, a portal willed before me as I walk towards it. Before stepping through it I turn around, catching Sage leaning down towards one of the bouquets. His finger brushes the bright petals, and I could've sworn a hint of a smile graced his lips.

I turn back around towards the portal and leave Sage to mourn his deceased family.

CHAPTER 52

The next day I stand before the floor length mirror, my gaze falling to my fingers as I fidget with them in front of me. Trying desperately to shake the anxiousness free I wipe my palms against my black leggings. Willing my nerves to settle.

I watch Reimus through the mirror as he appears behind me. Lowering his lips to my cheek as he presses them gently to my skin. He pulls away, watching me through the mirror. "Ready?"

I nod as I exhale. "Yes."

He brings his hands to my shoulders, slowly rubbing them to ease the anxious energy pouring from me. "Remember, I'm here with you the whole way."

A ghost of a smile appears on my lips. I turn around, facing him as I wrap my arms around his neck. "I know." I lean up to kiss him, allowing his touch to calm me wholly.

I pull away, stepping out of his reach. "I'll meet you outside. My mother and Makaria should be arriving soon. Hecate, too."

He nods his head, smiling. "I love you." He says, reminding me.

A portal opens up behind me as I force a smile back. "I love you." I turn around, stepping through it to The Sanctuary.

I step out into the women's quarters to find Semele watching me. "Well, hello again."

"Have you seen Nora?" I ask her.

She nods her head towards the healers room. "Back there."

"Thanks." I say as I start walking to the room.

I walk in and find Nora with her eyes alight on the doorway, waiting for me. She stands up from the chair, determination on her face. "Hey girl."

I smirk. "Hey. You ready?"

She nods. "Let's make this healing spell my bitch."

I chuckle as I extend my arm out, those nerves releasing a little more at her witty remark. Nora loops her arm through mine, and I feel her energy pulse ever so slightly.

A brief, gentle nudge of her healing power meant to tamper my raging nerves.

I grin at her as I will a portal open back to the palace, Nora and I wasting no time to step through it.

Stepping out onto the grass I close the portal behind me. My gaze lands on my mother and Makaria first, both of them appearing calm and steady. I look over to Hecate, her energy already palpitating the air around us. I give her a smile before I walk over to Reimus.

He watches me, assessing my every move. I give him a smile as I turn back around. "Nora, this is my mother

Persephone, my sister Makaria, and Hecate." I say as I gesture with my hand to each of them.

They all exchange pleasant greetings, and then we get right to work.

I step towards my sister, trying to gauge how she's feeling. "Do you have any questions before we start?"

Makaria watches me, pausing. She looks over to Nora, then Hecate. "Will it hurt?"

Hecate shakes her head. "It should feel quite the opposite." She smiles.

Makaria loosens a breath before turning to me. "I'm ready."

I look to Nora who turns to Hecate. She extends her hand out next to her, Hecate grabbing it with her own. "We work our magic together."

Hecate nods, and the energy around us *vibrates* as her full power comes to the surface. "I expected nothing less." She smiles.

Nora glances down at their conjoined hands and I can only imagine the sheer power she's feeling from Hecate. She turns towards Makaria, ushering her forward with her other hand.

Makaria steps up to them and takes Nora's free hand. And in a matter of seconds, a fraction of white light begins to expand from their joined hands.

I watch as it becomes brighter, and enlarges as Nora closes her eyes in concentration. She mumbles to herself as the light begins to expand up Makaria's arm, then to the rest of her body until she's submerged in it.

I look towards my mother, her eyes steady on the three of them. I notice an iridescent shield as it surrounds the perimeter of the terrain, keeping the magic from seeping past it. Knowing that if the amount of magic that is about to be performed is felt, it could attract the wrong kind of attention.

I listen to Hecate as she begins muttering words, chanting as she extends her hand to Makaria's chest. As soon as her hand rests itself there, I watch as Makaria bows her back. Her eyes widen completely as her mouth gapes open.

I step towards her but Reimus holds me back. I look up at him as he silently tells me through his body language.

Let them work. She is safe.

I turn my gaze back to them, watching them usher their magic into my sister together.

I go to bring my hands together, desperate to fidget my anxiety away when Reimus clasps his hand gently to mine. His thumb begins caressing my skin, easing that anxious energy as he comforts me.

For a long while Nora and Hecate work together. I watch as Nora's brow begins to dampen, evident that the energy work is taking a toll on her.

Hecate continuously chants the same words into my sister as her palm lays flat on her chest, my sister's eyes still wide and open.

I feel the energy pulsate wildly around us, the sensation causing my knees to wobble. I begin panting as the weight of the energy feels like I'm swallowing smoke from an extinguished fire. My hand comes up to my chest as I look at Reimus, whose breathing has begun to quicken slightly as well. "Hecate—"

She cuts me off by chanting louder. My sister shuts her eyes as she gasps deeply, tears streaming from her eyes as she trembles, threatening to fall to her knees. But Hecate's magic keeps her standing up.

I watch as the white light around Makaria flickers and brightens as Hecate continues to chant. She continues saying the same words over and over, until she opens her eyes and stops. The light vanishes at the same time as Makaria falls to her knees and collapses.

Hecate lowers her hand, and I watch it tremble as she breathes deeply. Nora doing as my sister has, and collapsing to the ground as well.

I rush to her side, running a hand over her forehead. "You're burning up, Nora." I turn around to find Reimus already behind me, leaning down next to us.

"I'm fine. I just need to stabilize my energy." She pants out breathlessly. She looks up to Reimus with a knowing look. "Get him. He knows what to do."

Reimus nods his head, sending a message down the Guardians channel for Dimitri. A few moments later, I hear wings flapping in the sky above us before Dimitri lands near us. He shifts into his human form, rushing to Nora's side.

I watch the worry in his face as he scoops Nora up, cradling her to his chest. He looks down at me, nodding curtly. "She'll be fine." He assures me. "I just need to get her inside."

I nod as he carries her inside the palace, her arms wrapping around his neck. I turn to Hecate. "Are you alright?"

She nods. "I'm fine, dear. Just a lot of power I worked up is all."

I turn to my sister, rushing to her side. The moment of truth of if it worked or not finally here. I tentatively open my mouth to speak, begging The Fates in my mind that it worked. "Makaria?"

She remains kneeling, her eyes wide as she breathes deeply. She stares wholly at the grass below her.

A choked noise escapes me. "Makaria, talk to me." I beg.

I feel our mother slowly release the shield around us as she stands behind me.

I wait anxiously as Makaria stares blankly onto the grass beneath us. Unsure if touching her shoulder would frighten her, or even possibly overwhelm her. But still wanting desperately to know if it worked.

My mother approaches me, gently placing a hand on my shoulder. "Melinoë, let's just give her a—"

Makaria slowly lifts her gaze up from the grass, her eyes still wide. She lands her gaze on me and I watch her entire upper body heave forward as it shudders. A strangled cry comes from her lips. "It worked."

The breath in my lungs suffocates itself for a split moment as I stare at her, until it frees itself entirely. The entire world around me goes mute as the familiarity etched on my sister's face, of who I am, causes me to break out into a harsh cry.

I pull my sister to me, shaking uncontrollably as we both sob into eachothers arms. I feel her wrap her arms around me tightly, her fingers burrowing themselves into my shirt. "Melinoë." She cries as she takes a shuddering breath in.

I hold onto my sister tightly as a months long anguish pours out of me. The anguish of never knowing if I'd see my sister again, to not knowing if she would ever remember me. It rushes out of me like water diving over a cliff.

She breaks away from my hold, bringing her hands to my face as her gaze roams my face wildly. A harsh laugh escapes her as she takes me in for the first time in months. "I missed you. I was so worried about you when you left. But I understood." Her lips tremble as she nods curtly. "I understood why you left."

My lips tremble as wetness dampens my eyes and cheeks. I bring my hand to wipe the loose strands of hair from her face. I shake my head. "I was going to come back for you."

She nods curtly. "I know. There was no doubt in my mind you were going to because I know there is *nothing* that you wouldn't do for me." She wipes a shaky thumb underneath my eyes, sniffling. "To have a sister that would do all of this to help me is a sister I will never, ever take for granted."

I tremble against her words. "I love you."

She brings me in for a hug. "I love you, sister."

After a long moment of holding one another, crying into eachothers arms, Makaria finally pulls away. She wipes the dampness from her eyes as I do the same.

I look up to see Reimus and our mother have made their way inside at some point, electing to give us some privacy.

I exhale slowly, feeling an incredible weight lifted from my shoulders. I force a smile. "So," I begin as I laugh.

To my surprise she laughs too, turning around to look at the palace behind us. "So you live here?" She raises an eyebrow.

I smile. "I do." I glance over towards the palace entrance, turning my gaze back to Makaria. "I'd like to introduce you to someone, if you don't mind."

I watch as the light my sister once had re-aquaints itself with her complexion. It warms my heart entirely to see that light back in her eyes.

She nods as a smile curves her lips. "I'd love that. I want to know everything about your life since I last saw you." She stands herself up, holding my hand as she guides me up with her.

My heart warms, beating steadily in my chest. Because for the past few months that is all I've wanted to do.

I loop my arm with my sisters as we head inside The Guardian's Palace—my *home*. My heart lighter than I've ever felt before.

CHAPTER 53

As I walk Makaria inside, I watch her face light up as she gazes at the interior of the palace. "This is where you live?" She gawks at me.

I chuckle. "Wait until you see the rest of the palace."

I take us through the living room before showing her upstairs to the bedroom. She immediately heads over to the clawfoot tub, pointing at it.

"Do I get to use this?" She smirks.

"I'll do you one better, if you'd like." I walk us out of the room, heading down to my old bedroom down the hall. As we enter it, I watch Makaria's face light up.

She steps towards the bed, running a hand along the silken sheets.

"This could be your room. If you'd like." I say.

She turns around. "Really?" Surprise and wonder line her eyes.

I nod, smiling. "I know mother wishes for you to stay in The Underworld, as it is safer there for you. But if you'd ever want to stay up here with me—well, you'd have a room here. As my home will always be yours."

She steps towards me, smiling widely. "I would love that." She turns towards the bathroom, noticing the similar clawfoot tub. Slightly smaller than the one Reimus and I have, but big nonetheless. "Oh, I am definitely utilizing that."

We make our way back downstairs where I know everyone is waiting in the dining room. We step through the room and my gaze locks onto Reimus immediately.

He watches me, a softness to his features unlike anything I've ever seen before. He smiles as he approaches us.

I look at my sister. "Makaria, this is Reimus."
She looks at him, watching him extend a hand.
"It's a pleasure to finally meet you, Makaria." He smiles.

She takes his hand, gawking at him as she shakes it slowly. She looks at me, leaning in to whisper. "Oh, he's cute."

I nudge her, laughing.
"Wait until she finds out what he can shift into."
I peer my gaze around my sister to Nora, sitting in a chair.

I walk over to her, leaning to give her a hug. Feeling her bodily temperature has already cooled down significantly. I pull away, holding her hands in mine. "Thank you."

She nods. "You're welcome, girl."

I smile as I look at Dimitri who stands behind her. He rests a hand loosely on the top of her chair, a casual gesture to mask the lengths he would go to in order to protect her.

I smile knowingly. "Thank you for coming."

He nods. "Of course."

I turn to Hecate standing beside the credenza cart. I approach her, hugging her tightly.

"If you're going to thank me, then the answer is you're welcome." Hecate says.

I pull away as we both chuckle. I give her a knowing look, that my gratitude runs far deeper than what words could convey. Not just for today, but for everything that she's done for me. But with her golden eyes gazing at me, I can see that silent gesture that she already knows.

I hear a loud gasp as I turn around to find Aven standing in the kitchen doorway. I watch as the excitement pours from him as a wide smile curves his lips. "Are we all joining for dinner tonight? Oh, please say yes! I know just what to make—"

"Yes, Aven." I say looking at everyone, a silent plea that they will accompany us for dinner. "They will be here for dinner."

I watch as something explodes inside of him, excitement not seeming like the right term to describe it. I giggle to myself as he hurries off to the kitchen talking to himself.

"This is the biggest party I will have cooked for! Oh, we must make it special!" The echo of his words to himself filtering into the dining room.

We all laugh in unison as we begin taking our places at the table.

My mother approaches me, bringing me in for a kiss on the top of my head. Makaria joins in, our mother wrapping her arms around us both. I feel her drink us in as she inhales deeply. The three of us safe and together again. I feel Makaria stifle a shudder against me, before pulling away entirely.

I take my seat at the table, Reimus to my right as Makaria seats herself to my left. Our mother takes up the seat to her left, as everyone else takes a seat.

Aven begins ushering out bottles of wine, offering to pour our glasses when Nora just takes a bottle from the table and begins helping herself. I laugh to myself as Reimus leans his nose into my cheek.

I smile as his warmth dances across my skin, his lips pressing softly to my cheek before whispering in my ear quiet enough that no one else can hear.

"Out of everything I've seen you wear, I love this look by far the most."

"Really?" I ask, giggling as his breath kisses my skin. I narrow my gaze down to my attire, a simple black strappy shirt paired with dark gray leggings.

He guides my chin back up, his gaze softening onto mine. "Not what you are wearing, but what is glowing on your face."

I gaze at him, those vivid eyes swallowing me whole.

He grins. "The look of pure joy."

I blink once before a smile creeps up onto my face. I lean in to kiss him, uncaring of the room full of people around us. When I pull away, he leans to press another kiss to my cheek.

"Oh, if that's how you two are going to act all dinner then I think I'll pass." Nora chimes playfully.

I laugh as I turn towards her. She looks away as I lock eyes with Dimitri, giving him a look as if to say *what are you waiting for?*

He looks away, deciding that his whiskey is far more interesting to look at. Reimus chuckles beside me as he stares at Dimitri for a short moment before breaking his gaze.

Dimitri jerks his head up, moving his hand to give Reimus the middle finger when he halts himself entirely. Forgetting that we're in front of other people who don't know about the Guardian channel. I giggle to myself, wondering what exactly Reimus said to him through the bond and making a mental note to ask him later.

We all talk amongst one another as my sister and I mainly talk to each other. Not wanting to talk about the heavy stuff until we're alone, I talk about what it's been like living in Vulir. I tell her how much I thought I loathed Reimus at first, and how he turned out to be exactly what I needed at a time I needed it most.

And as Aven brings out trays of some of his best cooking, I take a look around at the people in this room. I smile to myself as my dream of being surrounded by people who care for me becomes a reality.

At the friendship I've begun to develop with Nora.

At the relationship that I've fallen face-first into with Reimus, and how I couldn't have asked for a better person to share my life with.

At the sister next to me, who remembers me and I can begin to make new memories with.

At the mentor and also dear friend Hecate, not knowing who I would've become without her guidance and help to heal the things that were weighing me down.

My beautiful mother, who gets to be here with us today.

And Dimitri, someone I don't know too well but would like to.

As I sit here, I realize that I don't even need the fine course meal to be full.

That I am already full on the promise of how my life is turning out. And that alone, is enough to brighten the darkest crevices inside of my soul.

CHAPTER 54

I take another swig from the wine bottle, handing it to my sister as I cross my leg over the other. The hard surface supporting my ankles.

Makaria takes a swig, offering it back to me when I wave it off. "I think I've had enough for one night."

She laughs, leaning over the side of the clawfoot tub to set the bottle on the tiled floor. She turns back around, hiking her knees up to her chest.

An empty bathtub is an odd place to decide to lounge in, but hey—her choice, not mine. My sister's memories are back, and that's all that matters right now.

She sighs as she leans her head against the porcelain surface. "I'm really happy for you." She turns her head towards me, smiling. "After everything, you deserve to be happy."

I turn towards her. "Thank you. I never thought I would be happy again after Eiran." I face forward, narrowing my gaze.

I feel her continue to stare at me. "When I got your letter, my heart broke for you. I know how much he meant to you—still does."

My gaze fixates on my leggings, nodding vaguely. "He will always be my first love." I work on a swallow. "He was there for me at a time in my life when I needed him most—needed *someone* most. But he once told me that we were never meant to progress further than what we were. That I would've never realized my true feelings for him until I made the decision to break free from Zeus' control, and move to Vulir. In which case pointed me straight to who I was meant to meet."

Makaria reaches for my hand, a silent comfort that I never thought I'd feel again.

"I still hate how it had to happen, and the weight of his sacrifice will never evade itself from my bones." Emotion clogs my throat as I feel Makaria gently squeeze my hand. "But he says that this was always part of his path, and that he's at peace with it. So I have begun to make my own peace with how our story had to unfold." I turn towards her.

Makaria curves a faint, mournful smile on her lips. "Life has a horrible way of taking those closest to us at the most unexpected times. But I know he is very proud of you. How far you've come." She makes a soft huffing noise. "I know I am."

I force a smile, nodding as I lower my legs from the edge of the tub. I bring them up to my chest as I sit towards her, my head leaning against the hard surface.

Makaria lowers her gaze for a moment before slowly bringing it back up to mine. "Why do you think he treated us so differently?"

I sigh as I shrug my shoulders. "I wish I knew."

Makaria watches me, sorrow evident in her gaze. "I always knew he neglected you. I—" She pauses, starting again. "I saw the difference in how he treated me versus you. I never understood it, and felt guilty for it many times. But I never brought it up. I acted like I didn't see it, and I'll never forgive myself for not speaking up."

I watch as guilt clouds her expression, shame accompanying her gaze. I shake my head. "I never faulted you for something that was Zeus' doing. I only prayed that you got the relationship that every daughter should have. So I took the neglect for that reason alone." My gaze hardens on my sister. "But then I learned what Zeus did to you. I was enraged for you."

Makaria narrows her gaze slightly.

"Did you…ever feel the spell?" I ask cautiously.

I watch as her gaze goes someplace else, before huffing a soft noise. "Not until you told me about your gifts."

I wait patiently for my sister to continue, giving her as much time as she needs and allowing her to reveal whatever she feels comfortable revealing.

"I never felt *different*, or controlled rather. Until I found that book. I remember being angry because I was afraid for you, because that's what we were told how mother died. Obviously that wasn't the case." She scoffs at a broken sound. "And then you told me about how you had similar gifts as our mother. And I felt something flip inside of me."

She turns her gaze back to me. "I remember wanting to keep your secret, but there was this internal battle within myself that told me I *had* to tell Zeus. Even though the words from my mouth told you I would keep your secret, I felt this inner pull that *made* me tell him. It caused me such discomfort that I couldn't hold back my reaction."

My eyes widen slightly as the memory comes into my mind. Remembering when I hugged my sister, pulling away from her to find dampness under her eyes. I always thought she just felt guilty at that moment for what I said about Zeus, but now I realize…

"You weren't crying because of what I said."

She shakes her head. "I cried because I wanted so badly to keep your secret, to show you that you could count on me when I saw very clearly all our life that you couldn't count on our father. But I knew. I knew something would propel me to tell, and it broke my heart. And when I watched him hit you—" Tears begin streaming down her cheeks. She wipes the dampness away from her cheeks, looking at me. "It was like I was frozen in guilt for what I let happen. For what I caused—"

"You did not cause any of this." I insist as tears stream from my eyes. I hold my sister's gaze. "He *compelled* you to tell him. At first, I was heartbroken by that fact. But once I understood why, I forgave you. Because I knew you had no self-control over your decision to tell him."

Makaria wipes another tear from her cheek, her lips trembling slightly. "Sometimes I wish he would have treated us the same. I think it would've hurt less than to believe all my life that my father genuinely loved and respected me. But—" She ends on a choked cry, breaking my heart for her. "He never cared at all. He used me and I will never understand his motive for that."

I bring my hands up to her shoulders. "We did not deserve anything that man did to us." I squeeze her shoulders. "I am so happy I was able to free you from his control."

She nods through her tears. "Thank you for coming back for me." She begins to cry as I pull my sister into my embrace.

For a long moment we sit in silence with only the sound of us weeping to fill the room around us.

My sister pulls away, wiping underneath her eyes as she forces a smile. "Can I ask you for a favor?"

I nod, my gaze flickering over her. "Anything."

She forces a grin. "Could you teach me how to portal? I'd like to learn more about how to do it. What I'm capable of considering I'm—well, immortal." She snorts a laugh.

I can't help myself and laugh with her. "I'd be happy to teach you."

She loosens a breath, nodding as a giggled snort escapes her. "We're immortal, and your boyfriend can shift into a *drago*." She busts out laughing.

I find myself unable to resist laughing at the absurdity of everything. Having once thought we just lived simple human lives, and only read about this stuff in our fairytale books. I finally catch my breath. "I can also portal between realms."

She begins patting on her knee as she laughs hysterically. "And our mother is married to *King* of The Underworld." She hollers a laugh.

I find myself unable to catch my breath with how hard I'm laughing. We sit here cackling at the complete randomness of everything, my belly aching from how hard I'm laughing.

Tears dampen my eyes once more, but for the complete opposite reason of sadness this time.

CHAPTER 55

For the next three days I mentored my sister on portaling. As I stand before her now, I watch as she concentrates on bringing that magic to the surface. Having no idea still what her magic is capable of, I'd say it'll be a surprise to the both of us.

Makaria opens her eyes, frustrated as she huffs out a harsh exhale. "I can't do it."

"It might take you a while to even create a fraction of a portal. You're just now getting acquainted with your magic so it'll take some time." I take a step towards her. "Focus on that inner reservoir within yourself."

Makaria sighs as she closes her eyes once more. She stands with her feet shoulder width apart, her hands at her sides. I watch her steady her breathing as she travels down within. Her face begins to smooth out the further down she travels, and I watch as a tiny spec of light starts to her right.

"Good. Keep going." I encourage her, watching as that light slowly builds.

I watch as it begins to curve downward, creating a border when suddenly it vanishes.

Makaria opens her eyes, looking around frantically before landing her gaze on me again. "Did I do it?"

I chuckled. "You managed to start the formation of one. That's progress."

She smiles, clapping her hands as she jumps up. "I can't wait to make a completed one."

I smile. "It'll happen." I look up at the sun as it begins its descent downwards as we head into the evening hours of the day. I look back to Makaria. "We can practice more tomorrow. We should probably start getting ready."

Makaria nods, meeting me halfway. Her smile falters for a moment, nerves wracking her energy. "Do you think they'll like me?"

I nod my head, smiling genuinely. Her reaction entirely too similar to the one I had before my first gathering. "You'll fit right in. Just be careful with the spiked drinks. They're strong as fuck."

Makaria laughs as she extends her arms out for me. "I'll keep that in mind."

I loop my arm through hers as we head back inside to get ready for the gathering at The Sanctuary.

Having been a few weeks since the last one, when I went into the village the other day to visit the cemetery, Nora told me they'd be having another one tonight. A final festive celebration for the summer days that have begun to dwindle as fall approaches.

We both hurry inside, making our way upstairs when we enter my bedroom and spot Reimus napping on the lounge chair.

I glance at my sister, winking as I quietly walk over to him, trying to keep myself as silent as possible. My sister watches from behind.

I approach the chair, leaning down slowly as I bring my fingers to his nose. I watch as his chest rises and falls as I force a giggle down my throat. I bring two fingers to his nose, pressing the tips of my fingers on each nostril. A moment later Reimus stirs awake as Makaria bursts out laughing.

He pulls me down into his lap as he laughs. "You were trying to suffocate me?"

I laugh into his hold. "Maybe." I smirk at him.

He lifts a hand, flicking a finger at my nose. "I could think of much better ways." He winks at me.

My cheeks redden as I force a grin down.

"That's my cue to disappear into the walk-in closet now." Makaria steps inside, poking her head out as she looks at me. "I get dibs on whatever I want to wear of yours." She closes the door behind her.

I turn back around to him, leaning down to kiss him. One of his hands moves up my back, the other at my waist. He grins. "I love seeing you happy."

I lean down again, pressing kisses to his lips then to both of his cheeks. "Me too." I smile as I sit up again.

He gazes at me for a long moment, that love in his eyes so visceral I can feel it warm my skin. "What do you say tomorrow night, when you're done being hungover," He chuckles as I bat at his arm playfully. "I cook you a nice dinner." He leans up to kiss my neck. "I want to show you something."

I chuckle. "Are you going to take me on another ride?" I smirk.

He laughs. "No, but I can if you'd like."

I raise up from his lap as he rises with me. "Okay." I smile, leaning up to kiss him. "Can't wait."

He smiles, a shyness glossing over his face suddenly.

I tilt my head, chuckling. "What?"

He shakes his head as his face smooths out. "Nothing." He leans down to kiss me, this time deeply. He pulls away, his silver and blue eyes churning brightly. "I just love you is all."

I hear the closet door click open, turning around to see my sister donned herself in my white ruffled dress. The lace at the ends brushing along her calves, the straps hanging off her shoulders.

"What do you think?" She asks, gesturing to the dress.

I smile, tilting my head. "You should keep it. It looks amazing on you."

Makaria smiles, an ecstatic energy rippling off of her. "Really?"

I chuckle. "Yes. I will take you into the village to buy more clothing this week."

Makaria smiles widely. "I'm liking the sound of that." She walks towards the bedroom door, looking back. "I'll wait for you downstairs." She wiggles her eyebrows before she exits the room.

I roll my eyes, smirking as I walk to the closet.

"Just let me know how much you need, and I will make sure you have enough money to get her enough clothing." Reimus says as he enters the walk-in closet with me.

I begin shuffling through my dresses, deciding to wear one as well. Considering it will be cold out soon, and won't have the option to wear them then. "I will." I shuffle through my clothing until I land on a deep green dress. I take it off the hanger, walking out of the closet to set it on the bed.

"My favorite color." Reimus says softly as he approaches me from behind.

I begin removing my shirt over my head, tossing it onto the ground. I smirk. "I didn't know green was your favorite color."

His hands come to my hips, stilling me in place. He lowers his head to my neck, pressing a soft kiss there. "It wasn't. Not until you."

His hands slowly travel up my sides until his hands cup my breasts. I arch my back into him as his fingers lightly trace over my nipples, wringing a soft moan from me. "Rei, I'll be late."

He chuckles as he keeps one hand up, while the other lowers back down. Slowly over my belly until his hand dips beneath my leggings. "I'm confident that I can make you cum quick enough."

I gasp as he lowers a finger over my clit, slow circular motions to start. His other hand remains on my breast, his fingers so featherlight. I ache for him already.

I chuckle, a breathy moan escaping me. "What if this isn't what I want?"

He lowers his head. "What do you want?"

I take his hand, removing it from underneath my pants as I drop my pants down. I slowly bend all the way forward, my rear pressing up against him as I intentionally tease him.

I feel his hand come to my rear, smacking it and wringing a gasp from me.

I raise up, turning towards him. I reach for his pants, unbuttoning them before dropping them down his legs. "I want," I lift his shirt up as he helps lift it off his head. He picks me up, my legs wrapping around him as he guides us to the dresser.

He sets me down on it, his cock pressing against my entrance.

I lean in to kiss him, my hand moving to his cock. "*This* is what I want." I position him at my entrance.

He grunts as the tip meets my wetness. He thrusts himself in, his hands on my waist as he brings one up to my neck. "My favorite."

He grinds into me, his hand moving to the back of my head to keep my head from banging against the vanity. I moan as he fills me, pressing my heels into him to urge him in even deeper.

He chuckles, understanding the silent plea. "Anything for you, my queen." He buries himself completely, wringing a cry from my lips. He drives into me over and over, his hand on my waist moving lower as his thumb begins circling my clit.

My release finds me quickly, sending me over the edge as I clamp around him. He grunts as he pistons into me, his body trembling as he unloads himself inside of me.

My lips crash with his to stifle my moans, our tongues clashing with each other.

He chuckles as we come down from that high, pulling out of me. "Told you."

I chuckle as he kisses my nose, before using the bathroom to wash up and finish getting ready for the gathering.

As my sister and I make it to The Sanctuary, we first run into Nora. I watch as Nora brings her in for a big hug, welcoming my sister as warmly as she did to me.

We make our way out to The Garden and see everyone gathering around. Some are taking to the drinks already, some hanging back and socializing.

"Melinoë!"

I turn to see Euphrosyne rushing towards me. She opens her arms to give me a hug, and I embrace her back.

I pull away, glancing towards my sister. I gesture with my hand. "Euphrosyne, this is my sister. Makaria."

Euphrosyne turns to her, a charming smile on her face. "It's so great to meet you." Thalia and Aglaea approach her on each side. "These are my sisters. Thalia," She gestures to her left. "And Algaea." Gesturing to her right.

Makaria smiles. "Pleasure to meet you all."

Euphrosyne turns towards me, smirking. "I fully expect to see you dancing again tonight."

I laugh. "After just one of those spiked drinks, I have no doubt that I will be." I turn towards Makaria, nodding towards the buffet tables. "You hungry?"

She nods. "I could eat."

I nod towards the three sisters. "Enjoy your night. We'll catch up later."

I turn my sister and I towards the table, the spread of food similar to what was out last time. She begins taking a little of everything, as I do the same.

We head over to an open area and plop ourselves on the ground. Nora shortly after seating herself next to us.

I begin looking around, trying to find one face in particular.

"He didn't show up tonight."

I look at Nora, my smile disappearing. "I hope he's doing alright."

"Who?" My sister asks through a mouthful of cooked sliced meat.

Having not wanted to keep anything from my sister, I decided to tell her about everything that's happened before and after I freed her. She did not have much of a reaction to it. Having felt horrible for Dimitri getting hurt, and Sage losing his family, but she appreciated that I told her.

"Sage. He's usually here on gathering nights." I say, taking a bite of cheese.

Makaria nods. "Maybe he just needs a little more time to grieve. Don't give up on him though."

"I won't." I set my plate down, bringing my spiked drink to my lips. "I think I'll go visit him tomorrow just to make sure he's okay."

"It's not a good idea." My sister vocalizes. "Like you said, we should stay within the border."

"She's right." Nora chimes in, taking a sip of her spiked drink.

I sigh. "I know. But he's all alone out there. I feel bad."

My sister remains quiet for a moment, before blurting out. "I'll come with you."

I whip my head towards her. "Absolutely not."

She exhales. "Well you shouldn't be going alone."

"I'll go."

Nora, Makaria and I all look up towards Semele standing in front of us. She shrugs her shoulders. "She's right, you should have someone come with you if you want to go that badly. Why not let it be someone who's also immortal." Semele lowers herself to the ground, her gaze fixating on my sister for a moment before returning her gaze back to me.

I watch her for a moment, before nodding my head. "Okay. It'll just be to check on him though."

Semele nods her head, smiling. She turns her head to my sister. "I don't think we've met before?"

Makaria extends her hand. "I'm her sister. Makaria."

Semele's gaze remains on my sister as she takes her hand, shaking it gently. She binks. "It's a pleasure to meet you, Makaria."

Makaria forces a smile, lowering her hand before finishing off what's on her plate.

We all sit and talk amongst one another for a while, until Thalia comes over and waves her hand up for us to stand. "Get up and dance with us!"

Makaria hesitates, evident that she doesn't want to come off as rude but is also still adjusting to her new life.

I begin trying to let Thalia down gently. "Maybe later, we're still—"

"I'd love to." Makaria gets up, a grin on her face. She turns towards me and extends a hand.

I look up at her, surprised at her eagerness to be so social. I grab her hand as she helps me up.

She leans in closer to me. "I have plenty of time to grieve and be sad. But for just one night, I'd like to forget."

I tilt my head, nodding as a smile cures up my lips. I grab her hand as I pull her to the dancing area, galloping my way over. I hear my sister laughing as she begins galloping over with me.

We submerge ourselves with the other women and join the dancing. And I feel the light filter back onto not only my sister's face, but on mine as well.

CHAPTER 56

The next morning I jolt upright in bed as sweat beads at my brow. I take a sharp breath in.

Reimus stirs awake, guiding a hand to my back. "Another bad dream?"

I nod my head, lowering myself back to the bed. My eyes remain wide as I try to settle myself next to him. "Yes." I turn towards him, exhaling raggedly. "Just a bad dream."

I close my eyes and force myself to sleep it off.

When I awake again, sunlight peaks through the balcony glass doors. A dull headache accompanies me as I open my tired eyes. I rub my temple, knowing it's as an effect of the spiked drinks from last night.

I crawl out of bed, utilizing the bathroom before throwing some silk pants and a cami on before walking down the hall.

I go to my old bedroom, peeking through the cracked door when my chest bottoms out. I push the door open completely to see Makaria isn't there. I turn from the bedroom as I rush hurriedly downstairs to the dining room.

As I step through the doorway, an enormous wave of relief hits me when I see her. Sitting down with a glass of orange juice and Aven standing beside her as he talks to her.

She sees me enter the room and smiles lazily. "Morning."

I exhale, forcing a smile as I shake off my initial frenzy. "I see you've officially met Aven."

She nods towards him. "He's very kind."

Aven blushes, putting a hand to his lips before flicking his wrist. "You are a delight, Makaria." A wide smile curves his lips as he looks at me. "I will bring breakfast out now." He instantly turns on his heels and hurries off to the kitchen.

I go to take a seat next to my sister, grabbing the coffee pot and pouring myself a generous amount into my mug. I add in a splash of creamer, a dash of sugar, and take a sip.

Aven walks back out, carrying two large trays full of pancakes, fresh fruit, and breakfast sausage.

"Thank you, Aven." I say as I set my mug down.

"You're welcome, My Lady." He gently sets the trays down onto the table before walking back to the kitchen.

My hand begins reaching for my plate when I hesitate mid-air. I peer my gaze off to the side after him, wondering if I heard him right.

"My Lady?" Makaria asks with a hint of sarcasm in her tone, confirming I'm not the only one who heard him say that. She chuckles as she begins helping herself.

I furrow my brows before shaking it off entirely. Aven has always been extraordinarily polite, and this is my home now. My palace that I share with Reimus. Maybe he's just being respectable by appointing me Lady of the palace.

I chuckle to myself as I continue filling my plate.

After we both finish eating, I sit back in my chair. Thankful that my headache is already beginning to subside. I glance up at Makaria. "You don't have to go back today if you don't want to."

Makaria had told me last night that she wanted me to portal her back to The Underworld today, saying she was interested in spending a little more time with the souls. I told her it was not expected of her yet, and to do what she felt comfortable with.

I hate to admit that a large part of me is just making sure she's okay. Mentally.

Makaria looks up at me, smiling faintly. "I know. But I'd like to come back over tomorrow if that's okay."

I nod, grinning. "Absolutely. We can pick back up on portalling then."

She nods. "Cool."

I gaze at her for another moment, studying. "How are you doing?"

She narrows her gaze, pausing as a long exhale leaves her. "I'm grateful that I am no longer under the compulsion, and the memory loss is gone. I'm relieved that I get to see my sister again." She lifts her gaze back up to me. "But the why of it all has left me wounded, and the weight of it has me painfully sad."

I steady my gaze on my sister, nodding slowly. I press my lips faintly together knowing that there is absolutely nothing that I could say that would take this kind of pain away. All I can do is be by her side as she navigates through it. "I know."

She flattens her lips as she gets up from her seat. She tucks her long hair behind her ears as she forces a smile. "I'm determined to be able to form at least half of a portal tomorrow." A swift, nonchalant desperate act to change the subject.

I stand up from my seat, shrugging as I tilt my head. I walk towards her as a smirk curves up my lips. "It's possible." A portal materializes before us as I extend my hand out for Makaria.

She takes it, smiling before I guide us both through it into The Underworld.

We walk out onto the courtyard, meeting face to face with our mother and Thanatos.

I close the portal behind me as I glance at our mother. "Morning."

"Goodmorning, my sweet." She turns her head towards Makaria.

I turn my head towards Thanatos who has cemented himself in place, his gaze wholly on my sister. I furrow my brows, shifting my gaze to Makaria.

I watch as she stares at Thanatos for what feels like an eternity of a moment. Her golden eyes gaze over his golden-tanned face before I see her mentally shaking herself back to reality. She quickly turns her gaze and forces a smile as she looks at our mother. A nervousness suddenly painting her energy as her cheeks turn the faintest shade of pink. "Morning mother."

Persephone approaches her, giving her a hug and a kiss on the head. She pulls away as Makaria approaches me.

She brings me in for a big hug. When she pulls away, I give her a look, subtly raising an eyebrow. She widens her gaze at me and I smile internally at the sudden desperation that she has written on her face for me to not say a damn word.

"I'll see you tomorrow." I say, easing the silence.

She smiles. "See you then." She walks towards our mother.

"Dear, do stay for a while." Persephone says. "We can spend the day visiting the souls, or doing nothing at all." She chuckles.

I laugh. "I'd love to, but Reimus wants to surprise me with something tonight. And I kind of wanted to check on a friend of mine beforehand."

My mother raises her eyebrows, smirking. "Well, we'll be here if you change your mind." They begin walking back to the palace as Thanatos stares after my sister for a moment longer before turning his gaze back to me. He straightens his back as he notices me staring at him, observing him. He clears his throat before portaling out of there completely.

Interesting.

I portal myself back home, making my way upstairs where I know Reimus is. I entered our bedroom to find him standing out on the balcony, his back to me. I approach him from behind, wrapping my arms around him.

He brings my hands up to his lips, kissing my knuckles before I approach his side. "Did you sleep well?"

I nod. "Yes." Not entirely the truth as the bad dreams plagued me once again last night. But—well, I did sleep after. So not entirely a lie.

He looks down at me. "Do you want to talk about the dreams you've been having lately?"

I keep my gaze focused straight ahead, staring out onto the open terrain. The same dream I've had over and over again running through my mind before I will it gone. For now. "Not at this time." I look up at him as a grin curves my lips. I nod towards the open terrain below. "But I would like to talk about what we can do to spruce up this land."

He chuckles as he wraps an arm around me, kissing the top of my head. "Was there anything you had in mind?"

I make a humming noise, resting my head against his chest. "Well for starters, I think we could use *a lot* more flowers. A garden, and maybe an area for us to grow our own vegetables and herbs."

His voice vibrates the hair on my head when he speaks. "Anything else?"

"I'll let you know when I think of it." I look up at him.

He nods, grinning wide. "I will make it all happen for you."

I lean up to kiss him, his lips so soft against mine. When I pull away, my gaze smooths out. "I need to tell you something."

His expression doesn't change as he watches me, nodding.

I sigh. "I stepped out of the border the other day to visit Sage, and I plan to do so again today."

He watches me.

"Semele offered to come with me this time, so I won't be alone."

He blinks once as a ghost of a smile appears on his face. "I would feel better if I came along with you."

I exhale. "I know. I promise I won't be gone long. I just want to make sure he's doing okay."

He sighs, tucking a loose strand of hair behind my ear. He stares at me for a long moment before he nods slowly. "Okay." As he kisses my head, I feel the calm exterior in his body go tense. "Be safe."

I pull away from him, going to change into some leggings and a shirt. I slip on my black sandals as I turn towards him. "I'll be home well before your surprise." I wink

He chuckles, a nervousness in his stance now.

I turn fully towards him, watching as his body goes tighter than a bowstring. I observe the worry in his eyes as it fights against the nervous energy that hovers around him now.

I step towards him, joining his hands into mine. I steady my gaze onto him. "Hey." I say, pulling his gaze to mine.

He looks down at me, his blue and silver eyes piercing into mine. He lets out a long exhale as he brings our hands up to his lips. He kisses the backs of my knuckles before lowering them again. "I don't feel good about not going with you. In fact, I'm highly tempted to say fuck it and go with you anyway whether you like it or not." His eyes soften as the nervousness around him begins to dwindle some. "But I know how important it is for you to have free will, so I understand."

I sigh as I lean up to kiss him, my arms coming up over his shoulders. His hands caress their way up my back, the weight of them lulling me.

I pull away, locking eyes with him. "Thank you." I lower my gaze to his lips before lifting it again, a grin curving up. I release myself from his hold, the portal I've willed buzzing behind me. "I'll be back."

"Okay." He says as a gentle smile lifts his lips. Those beautiful dark strands of his hair unbound as they hang over his forehead.

I turn around as I step through the portal and out the other side to The Sanctuary.

Closing the portal behind me I walk to find Semele. As I walk down the women's corridor I see her as she walks out of her room.

"Ready?" I ask.

She nods curtly. "Ready." She meets me halfway as her eyes lock onto mine.

I nod to her as I open another portal, this one to the Sephyra Forest. I extend my hand out to her as she takes it into hers. We both step through the portal, stepping out onto the forest floor.

I close the portal behind us as we walk towards where Sage lives, but my gaze gets caught on the graves for his sisters.

I smile faintly as I approach them. I begin to lean myself down when my talisman heats up.

My hand flinches to my chest, pulling it away from my skin when the heat quickly subsides. I look down to see if a red mark was left behind, but see nothing at all.

Setting my necklace back onto my chest, I fix my gaze onto the grave before me. Noticing the flowers are perfectly intact still.

"Is that where they were buried?" Semele asks from behind me. The snap of a twig sounds as she steps towards me.

I nod as my palm lightly traces over the soil. "He wanted them buried close by."

I close my eyes to silently mutter a few words when I'm distracted by the surge of energy behind me. Potent and nothing short of palpable.

"Melinoë."

I open my eyes at that familiar voice, scrunching my brows at why she would be here. I sigh, scoffing. "I can't imagine you learned how to portal in a matter of thirty minutes." I stand up from the ground, turning around as I face my sister. I furrow my brows together, tilting my head. "Did mother portal you here?"

Her platinum hair shines brightly from the sunlight as it peeks through the trees. The gold in her eyes far more vivid than I've ever seen before. Like emanating pools of gold.

She walks towards me as she grins deeply, a grin that the wider it becomes, the less inviting it appears.

And in that moment, I realize it is not my sister who stands before me.

His name alarms itself within the walls of my mind as a chill runs down my spine.

A voice nothing like my sisters answers, dark and unkind. "Not quite."

In an instant he shifts as blinding white light surrounds him, dissipating once he stands before me.

In his true form.

The same platinum blonde hair cropped short to his head, though now as bright as spun moonlight. Those same honey-gold eyes amplified entirely more vividly, like glistening pools of gold. He hovers over me in his true form, far taller than when he masked himself as a mortal.

He chuckles a deep laugh, sending a cold sweat down my back. "We meet once again, daughter."

Immediately I whip my head around, terror in my voice. "Semele. *Run!*"

She watches me, a faint frown pulling at her lips as she remains standing. Unmoving as she glances at Zeus, before training her gaze back onto me.

My eyes widen as disbelief plagues me.

No.

"I'm sorry." She says.

It was a lie. *Everything* about her was a lie as she was *working* with him.

Her son. Running from an abusive relationship. It was all a fucking lie. I let this woman into Vulir—into my *home*, and she played me all along.

My breathing ramps up as terror no longer is the emotion that infiltrates me, but burning hot rage.

I will my shadows to the surface immediately, feeling the buzz of their energy as they form at my fingertips. But before I can even turn my body fully around, everything goes black.

CHAPTER 57

I wake up on a cold, hard floor. My head pounding as I try to bring my fingers up to my temple when I feel myself getting caught on something.

My eyes snap open, shifting to my hands.

Chains.

My breathing ramps up as the fog begins to clear away. I go to bring them up, yanking on them hard enough to hopefully break them. My gaze follows the chain, turning around to see it connects into a concrete wall.

I inhale deeply, exhaling as I try willing my shadows to the surface. Focusing in on that reservoir of power, trying, trying and trying—

Nothing.

Panic ensues as I freeze in place, jerking my head around to identify where I am. Only one tiny window far above on one of the four concrete walls around me, a fickle trace of light filtering in through it. I go to stand up, getting to my feet when I look down at the chains on my ankles.

I hurry towards the window as far as I can, making it only halfway when the chains pull on my bare skin. I hiss in pain as I hear footsteps approach the cell.

Cell. I'm in a fucking cell.

I force myself back up against the wall as I look down at my chest and notice my protective talisman is gone.

No.

No.

No.

The footsteps come closer as I try to peer through the dimly lit room. They finally approach the cell door and my heart lurches down to my feet.

"Good, you're awake." Semele says as she opens the gate, the metal grinding against the concrete floor piercing my ears. "He will see you now." She walks towards me.

I clench my fists, trying to break free of the chains. I thrash against their bindings as she continues her approach.

"They're spelled by magic. You won't break free of them." She says, her tone matter of fact.

She gets right in front of me when I spit on her. She jerks her head back, wiping her cheek away before looking back at me. I breathe heavily as I glare at her.

She chuckles. "I probably deserved that."

"I'll kill you." I seethe, rage boiling in my bones.

She goes down to unlock the chains from the ground, a latch it seems that is locked by a special key she carries. "This is not how I wanted things to go. I wish I could have you believe that." She stands up fully looking at me. "But if you attack me while I unlock the chains to your wrists, it will not go well for you."

She watches me for a moment before she kneels down to unlock them. As she inserts the key, I feel the sudden relief as the shackles free themselves from my ankles. She stands herself up as she locks eyes with me once more before approaching the wall.

I hear the clink of the chains attached to my cuffs as they disconnect from the wall. She tugs on them as she approaches my side. That's when I strike.

I wrap the chain around her, pulling the chain taught against her neck as I begin to strangle her. She fights against my hold as I pull harder, taking great pleasure in hearing her gasping for air.

She suddenly untangles herself, quicker than a viper when it attacks. Before I can make a second attempt she wails me upside the head, and her immortal strength causes me to tumble to the ground.

I loosen my jaw, clenching my fists as I glare up at her. I huff as a grin curves up my lips. "I saw the opportunity and went for it." I tilt my head, spitting blood onto her feet before I meet her gaze again. "Can't blame me."

She drags me up onto my feet by the chains. "Let's go." She starts dragging me out of the cell, down a hallway until we reach a winding staircase.

She pulls on my chains the whole way up, urging me to keep climbing the stairs. The higher that we descend, the more that faint ball of light begins to expand. And as we make it to the top, the entire room is flooded with bright glowing light. Completely illuminated versus the pitiful, dark dungeon we just emerged from.

Semele walks us down a room with golden columns on each side, with large fine tapestries hanging from them. I shift my gaze forward and halt in my steps, my stomach bottoming out as I see a dais and who sits upon it.

I try tugging my chains back from Semele but she holds them steady as she tugs me forward. I trip over my foot as I gaze frantically at the council room before me. Until my gaze lands on a wrought iron cage set next to the throne.

No.

She pulls me all the way up the dais until we reach the top. Until I'm standing before him, clad in nothing but golden robes to match the gold crown upon his head.

"Bow." He commands.

Anger ravishes within me as I glare up at him. "Over my dead fucking body." I seethe.

Zeus chuckles, a dark power rippling from him. "This could go so much easier, Melinoë. But if you insist on being difficult." His power charges, lighting the air around us. More potent than anything I've ever felt before I nearly hurl my guts up right there. I quiver against it as he raises his eyebrows at me. "Bow."

I force my knees to suddenly give out as I kneel before him, thrashing entirely against his command. "You're a pathetic king if this is the only way you can get people to bow before you." I glare up at him as I will my body to stand up again, jutting myself up onto my feet.

He glares down at me. "My people bow to me just fine." He smiles, the appearance roiling my stomach. "And it would be rude for you not to bow to your King now wouldn't it?"

A harsh laugh escapes me. "What a pitiful example you are then." I exhale a ragged breath. "What the fuck do you want?" My tone biting and short as I clench my jaw.

He watches me for a moment. "I will tell you since in a few moments, I'm going to erase your memories."

My face pales as everything in me goes numb.

"You have a power within you that does not belong to me, even though you're my flesh and blood." He rolls his eyes. "And I've decided instead of resenting you for not turning out like me, I could instead just…use your power for my own bidding." A vile chuckle eases from his lips, boiling that fury within me.

I clench my fists, feeling the sting of my fingernails dig into my palms. "You want to use me as a *weapon*?"

He shrugs his shoulders. "Precisely."

"And why would I ever agree to that?"

He waves a hand, the gesture nonchalant and lazy. As if he couldn't be more bored to be here. "Because if you don't, I will kill everyone you love. Including that dark-haired shifter boyfriend of yours."

My eyes widen, my heart cracking as a choked sound escapes me. "You wouldn't."

He peers at me. "Do you not know me by now? I don't give a fuck about anything that is insignificant to me, Melinoë. And the quicker you can understand that, the easier this transition will be for you."

My breathing begins to ramp up, the thought of Reimus being in danger killing a part of me inside. My mind blanks as I realize the last time I saw Reimus was this morning, not knowing those were going to be my last words to him. The last time I held him, or looked into those eyes of his.

Tears threaten to dampen my eyes but I force them down. I will not show weakness in front of Zeus.

I will every ounce of strength within me to regain my composure. Seeing that the dreams I'd been having lately proved to be visions. Just like I suspected they were.

Not having said anything to Reimus for fear of worrying him for no reason, but having a strong feeling that Zeus would come for me at some point.

I just didn't think it would be so soon.

I focus on willing myself not to show any relief as I want Zeus to think he won. I want him to think he has me right where he wants me.

Powerless.

But had I never asked Hecate for the favor that I did, I would be in an entirely different state of mind right now. The memory quickly flashes before my mind.

"I need you to spell my mind." I'd said.

Hecate scrunched her eyebrows as understanding smoothed out her face. "You think Zeus will do the same to you." She states.

"I don't know. But I'd like to be prepared in case he tries."

She did not pry, did not question my motive. She only nodded her head. "Okay. But I need to make sure you know what this means."

I looked her dead in the eyes, slowly nodding. Understanding the ramifications that in doing so comes with. Knowing that if the time ever came, I would have to do absolutely everything he asked of me, so as to not give him the indication that I was shielded against his compulsion. "Spell my mind. Create a permanent barrier against his compulsion, Hecate."

Hecate nodded. "Very well. Let's begin."

I glare up at Zeus before turning my gaze to Semele. She watches me, not lifting her gaze from me.

I fix my gaze back to Zeus. "I need your word that you won't go after any of them. Not even the people of Vulir."

Zeus nods lazily. "As long as you do what I tell you, I won't."

"Or the people of Elzwin." I add.

He rolls his eyes, waving a hand. "Yes, whatever. Them, too."

I exhale a heavy breath, adding to the charade of this game that we're about to begin. Though a large part of me still fears for my people, for Reimus and my family. Because in agreeing to this, I understand that I have no idea what I'm about to be agreeing myself too.

And for how long I'll have to uphold the masquerade until I have a way out.

I glare up at him, clenching my teeth. "Fine."

A wide grin curves his lips as his power charges around us. "Good." He stands up from the dais, stepping towards me. "I would lie and say that this won't hurt, but since you won't remember this after anyway, I'll just be honest."

I glare up at him, my body trembling as I beg The Fates that Hecate's spell works against Zeus without him knowing. I plead to no one in particular in my head to spare my people of any destruction that I may cause.

And I pray that Reimus still loves me after this is all said and done. That he somehow will understand that I did this to protect him. Because I love him more than the moon and the stars, and I will fight until the ends of the earth for him.

Even if I have to be the villain for a little while.

He looks down at me as sparks of light zap between his fingers. Electricity zapping the air around us like sparklers. He grins deeply. "This is going to hurt a lot."

In the next moment, my body bows back as he zaps his power onto me. My mouth gapes open as blinding pain evaporates my entire body. I scream against the fire that courses through my body, like being agonized with a smoldering brand against your skin.

Until everything goes dark once more.

CHAPTER 58

Reimus

My hands lay loose at my sides as I stand outside on the grassy terrain. My gaze trained forward on Alastor as he grazes contently. I chuckle as I watch him live such a simple life, unknowing of how easy he has it.

My fingers trace the velvet box inside of my pocket, my hands clammy the longer that I wait for her arrival back home.

I reach into my pocket, pulling out that black velvet box. I smile as I open it and see the ring I've been waiting for what feels like an eternity to give to her. Having wanted to wait until the perfect time, I finally decided that now is the time I'm going to ask her the one question I've been dying to ask for months now.

I stare at the ring as it glistens against the sunlight reflecting on it. I trace my index finger lightly around the marquise cut diamond, smiling at the incredible Victorian details the jeweler added for me.

A beautiful ring for an even more beautiful woman.

"Reimus."

I freeze as I hear Charon through the channel. I tuck the black box back into my pocket.

"Something's wrong."

Charon's tone has me shifting in an instant as I shoot up to the sky. I flap my wings as I soar to him, finding him at the entrance to Vulir.

I bank downwards and shift before I even hit the ground. I rush to him as I see Dimitri is there already. I see the grave worry in his face. "What is it?"

Dimitri's gaze shifts over me as he slowly approaches me. I watch the hesitation in his body language as he tentatively brings his hand up on my shoulder, the worry in his energy thrashing against mine.

That's when everything around me halts completely. His gaze telling me everything I need to know.

I fall to my knees as my heart sinks with me. Staring blankly ahead.

"I felt an energy stir in the forest. I picked up on her energy when I went to investigate. When I got there, she was gone." Charon says, narrowing his gaze to me. "The energy was strong. It felt familiar."

I look up at him, shaking my head. "No."

Charon watches me intently, sorrow evident in his immortal face. "It was Zeus."

My heart shatters as Charon utters those three words, the three words I've dreaded hearing.

I thought giving Melinoë ultimate freedom was the right call, as I know how much it means to her to make her own decisions without feeling like she's being hindered by others. But did I not do enough? Should I have insisted on going with her?

"She was with Semele." I look up at Dimitri.

"She is gone as well." Dimitri says, narrowing his gaze. "The girls at The Sanctuary say they haven't seen her since this morning."

My gaze hardens as it all makes sense now. Semele played us for fools.

I slowly stand up on my two feet again, rage building violently within me. I take a staggering breath in.

I will not fail you.

I will find you.

I look up at Charon. "Bring me Hades."

Charon vaguely shakes his head. "Reimus, he doesn't leave The Underworld—"

"He will this time." I seethe, fire warming my skin. My body heaves forward as I try to will myself not to shift involuntarily. I lock eyes with Charon. "Tell him what's happened, and bring him to me."

Charon seeing the intensity in my stare, understands that I won't let Melinoë suffer, and if I'm going to bring my queen home, The King of The Underworld is damn sure going to have to come out of his realm.

Charon nods his head. "Right away." He vanishes within an instant, leaving just Dimitri and I here.

Dimitri looks at me, lowering his chin. "We'll get her back." He affirms, going to grab my arm as he squeezes it.

My hand instinctively lowers to that little black box inside my pocket, tracing its round edges with my fingers.

Dimitri's gaze follows my movement, his face slackening as he understands what lies in my pocket. He shifts his gaze back up to me as it hardens with determination. The kind of determination of not only a man willing to fight for the injustice of our people, but also of the one who is the reason why I have begun to smile again. "We *will* bring her home."

I nod my head as I shift into my drago form, Dimitri following right behind me. We both take to the skies as we make our way back home to wait for The King and Queen of The Underworld to meet with us.

With nothing to occupy my mind but the rage of Zeus having succeeded in capturing Melinoë.

AUTHORS NOTE

To the reader, thank *you*! For giving this series a chance, and for coming along with me through Melinoë's journey. I can't thank you enough for reading a story that deeply moves me, and one that I hope you enjoyed reading as much as I surely enjoyed writing.

Until next time. xoxo

ABOUT THE AUTHOR

Michelle Rossa is the author of the Shadows and Fire series, and her work centers around Adult Romance and Fantasy. From writing poetry, to daydreaming fantasy worlds inside her head, Michelle has had a vast imagination since she was a child.

When she's not writing, she's most likely spending her time out in nature, snuggling with her cat Diva, or re-watching The Vampire Diaries for the millionth time. Outside of her passion for writing, she practices as a psychic medium and tarot reader. She is greatly passionate about all things astrology, the left hand path, occult studies, greek mythology, non-conformity to societal/gender standards, and advocating for women.

www.ingramcontent.com/pod-product-compliance
Lightning Source LLC
Chambersburg PA
CBHW031512010826
48973CB00013B/991